MW01114960

FATE OF THE DAE'FUIREI

Part Two of The Vanguard Legacy
Book Twelve in the Pantracia Chronicles

Written by Amanda Muratoff & Kayla Hansen

www.Pantracia.com

For Nathan.

♥

The Pantracia Chronicles:

Visit www.Pantracia.com for our pronunciation guide
and to discover more.

Chapter 1

Summer, 2632 R.T. (recorded time)

Amarie's heart warred with her head. Heat from Kin's kiss the night before still lingered on her lips.

It had ignited her soul as fiercely as it had that night in the Delphi's collection room, plaguing her sleep with dreams of what could never be. After everything that had happened, they couldn't go back.

Can we?

She swallowed, rolling her lips together and resisting the urge to glance sideways at the man riding the horse beside her.

He'd killed her the previous day.

To save her from Uriel, of course, but it'd still been a dagger to her heart. And although she understood, even forgave him for forcing the Berylian Key's power to their daughter, she struggled to let herself be vulnerable to him. The last time she'd let him in, still raw from her first resurrection, he'd left.

Restraint lost as she looked at Kin, eyes pausing only briefly on his broken arm before continuing to his face. When he turned at her attention, she averted her gaze to the man riding in front of them.

Damien. The Rahn'ka. Taking them to Veralian to meet with Helgath's king and consort.

"What is it?" Kin's soft baritone voice barely reached her over the hot afternoon air.

They'd barely spoken since the night before.

Since his mouth...

"Nothing," Amarie murmured with a shake of her head. "Just thinking."

Kin pursed his lips, but didn't question her further. He merely watched her in silence until a jostle from the horse below him caused him to grab his injured arm. Cringing, he looked away, his focus shifting to Damien. "So the king of Helgath is in on this elaborate plan? Enough so that he's willing to host the two of us who are probably Uriel's most wanted?"

Amarie played with a section of her horse's mane, braiding it as she imagined what Ahria's face might now look like. As she'd done a thousand times since remembering. Again, she tried to summon a spark of her power, but it didn't answer. It never did.

Somewhere, she's struggling with it, and I can't even help her.

"Uriel thinks you're dead, and we'll be keeping it that way." Damien glanced over his shoulder, exposing the dark blue lines of the tattoo on the side of his neck. It disappeared beneath his collar in a swirl of runes. "Besides, Jarrod Martox was a criminal long before he was a king."

"Still strange that Iedrus no longer reigns..." Amarie furrowed her brow, then lowered her voice. "Does Helgath still employ Reapers?"

"No. The hunting parties were disbanded and declared criminals within the first month Jarrod took the crown. The academies are no longer prisons but universities where Artisans *choose* to study. And new strict laws ensure the forbidden Arts are not part of the curriculum."

"And I suppose you had something to do with that? Serving as King Martox's personal advisor? You've certainly come a long way from those crumbling ruins in the Olsan mountains."

"The course of Helgath's future was already well on its way before you and I ever met."

"We should pick up the pace again." Amarie's stomach tightened, legs itching to squeeze her mount into a canter. Anything to reach Ahria sooner. "The horses have had enough of a break."

Damien turned, looking at Kin's arm. He started to speak, but Kin waved his good hand instead.

"I'll manage. But do you think you can finish healing it tonight?"

The Rahn'ka shrugged. "We'll see. If we push it enough, one of the king's personal healers can take care of you instead."

A headache bloomed in Amarie's forehead, and she touched the spot above her brow. Shortening her reins, she urged her horse into a trot, which spurred the others to join in. Glancing at Kin, she motioned with her chin to his arm. "When it gets too sore, we'll stop for the night."

As Damien remained ahead, distance grew between his horse and theirs. The rise of pounding hooves made her wince, but she rolled her shoulders.

Too tense. All her muscles were too tense. All she wanted was to find Ahria, to see her, to meet her. But they couldn't go straight to where Talon had said she was. Ziona's capital. They needed to involve politics, and it soured her tongue. Each delay, each minute spent not going after her daughter felt wrong.

Turning her head north, she gazed at the horizon line past Kin. Shimmering sweat on the back of his neck drew her eye, and her shoulders drooped. "Relax."

He looked at her. "What?"

"It will hurt your arm less if you let your mid section absorb the motion." Amarie patted her stomach. "Heels down, legs long. Sink into the saddle."

Shifting, he attempted to adopt her advice. "I've never been much for horses." He gave a weak half-smile, his eyes searching hers as if looking for something deeper beneath their words.

Amarie returned the smile. "I know. Just... try to relax. It will help, I promise."

"Never been one for that, either." He winced, rolling his shoulder as he seemed to try again. He met her eyes, those unspoken hopes and questions still hovering in the silence between them. She could sense it was all about Ahria. About the years they'd lost and would never get back.

Night engulfed the world, but Amarie couldn't sleep. She laid on her bedroll, staring at the dying embers of their fire. Her eyes burned as they always did in quiet moments. For all the loss.

Her muscles twitched, and holding still just made it worse. A sharp wound prevailed in her chest no matter how much time passed. The turmoil in her mind ceaseless and enduring. She rose quietly, slipping her boots on without buckling them. As silently as she could, she walked north, leaving the men slumbering at camp.

Damien had done more healing on Kin's arm, but it would need another session once they arrived in Veralian the following day. It took enough energy that the Rahn'ka slept soundly, not flinching even when she stepped on a twig. Kin shuffled, though, and she hurried away before he looked.

Continuing north, she entered a copse of sparse spruce trees and breathed in the comforting scent. Leaning back against one, she slid to the ground. She ran her hands over her hair, pushing it back as she looked across the terrain at the distant stars. Bending her knees, she crossed her arms over them and rested her chin on her forearm. With a slow blink, she sniffled and wiped a tear from her cheek.

Ahria.

She gazed north, willing her mind to conjure an imagined version of her daughter's face once again. What those bright ice-blue eyes would look like swirled with violet. Wet with tears like her own, for her dead father.

Amarie's chin quivered. "Oh, Talon," she whispered, burying her face in her arms as gentle sobs shook her shoulders. "Ahria."

A branch snapped beneath something to her left and Amarie's head snapped up to see the moonlight shining in Kin's eyes. He lifted his hands, the broken arm now well enough to go without the sling. "It's me, I'm sorry," he whispered as if afraid to disturb the silence of the night. "I didn't mean to startle you, I just woke up and saw you weren't on your bedroll and wanted to make sure you were all right."

Using the back of her hand, she dried her face. "I'm..." She shook her head. "I'll be fine."

"Would you rather be alone?" He started to turn back towards camp. "I can go back. I didn't mean to..." He hesitated as he studied her face, evidently spying her tears as his expression softened.

"You can stay." The words came before she could reconsider. "It's, uh... It's better when I'm not alone."

Nodding, Kin stepped closer. "I can understand that." He leaned against her tree, slowly lowering himself to sit facing away to her left. Their shoulders brushed each other on the outer edge of the trunk. He turned his head to look at her before resting it back against the bark.

"I'm going to find her." Amarie stared at the dark silhouette of the treeline north, where Ziona lay somewhere far beyond. "I will."

"*We* will." Kin looked to her again, his shoulder shifting as if he was going to reach for her, but his touch never came. He turned back out, his hand settling on the forest floor between them. "I just wonder if she'll even want to know me."

An ache sprouted in her heart. "At least you have a good reason for not being there." She gulped, chest heavy as she whispered, "I knew her and still left."

"You had a good reason, too. To protect her."

"But will she see it that way?" Amarie looked at him. "I don't know what Talon told her."

"He'd tell her the truth. He knows... knew the danger of secrets." Kin's jaw twitched. "I still can't believe he's gone. He was meant to outlive all my stupid human mistakes."

Her throat tightened and her eyes burned again, remembering his face from the Inbetween. She spoke through the hurt, her words rough and catching in her throat. "I'm grateful, you know, in a way. That you killed me, and I got to see him one more time."

And Viento.

The death of her beloved horse wasn't a surprise. Not after her being in Slumber for two decades. But Talon... Kin was right. He should have outlived them all.

"Those are words no one should ever need to say." A smile echoed in his tone, but it faded as he sighed. "It's odd that things seemed simpler when you were chasing a wyvern into Lungaz after my long-lost twin than they are now."

Amarie huffed. "It's so strange, having you with me again." Turning, she shifted along the tree trunk to angle herself more towards him. "To see your face outside my... thoughts. Dreams."

He turned to meet her gaze, his good shoulder pressed into the tree. The warmth of him permeated the space still between them. "You mentioned a dream before. I hope there were good ones."

She let her gaze drift to his hand between them. "I was pregnant, but I hadn't told Talon yet. Which was a mistake, because I lost control outside our home in Eralas and almost killed him. Kalstacia helped wake him again, but..."

"Kalstacia?" Kin shifted towards her again, his hand moving closer on the forest floor. "Talon's sister? I thought she was banished from Eralas with Talon and Alana. Why was she there?"

Amarie met his gaze. "Oh." She shook her head, briefly biting her lower lip. "We were discovered very soon after arriving in Eralas. Talon was arrested. I was too, but that's not important. They were going to execute him."

"That's exactly why I hated even suggesting Eralas. The auer are not exactly known for their mercy. How did he survive?"

She paused, considering the events that had followed. "I used my power as leverage. I made a bargain with the elders, and they revoked the rejanai title for both Talon and Kalstacia." She wondered if Talon's sister still resided there, but doubted much could convince her to leave the island.

"That must have pissed off Alana." Kin looked up to the rustling leaves above.

"I doubt Talon ever told her. He realized during that trial just how dark Alana had become. I doubt he spoke to her again." Amarie shrugged, absently touching the back of his hand with her index finger. "She probably has no idea."

Kin looked down to their hands, turning his over to expose his palm to her, and with it, the spider-webbed scar on his right forearm. The Shade tattoo still hovered beneath it in her memory.

Amarie trailed her finger tips up his wrist and over the scar, her chest rising faster. "You're still connected to him? To Uriel?"

"In a way, but Damien's buried it so deep that Uriel can't get to me anymore." He watched as her fingers trailed back down his arm. "But I can still feel it in there. The access. Like a tickle in the back of my brain. And I know that if I wanted to, I could break the barrier put in place."

Unease stirred in her belly at the thought. "Is it safe... for you to be near Ahria?" She met his gaze. "Be honest. She's your daughter. Are you a danger to her?"

Kin lifted his shoulder, taking Amarie's hand in his with a firm squeeze. "I will never put her in danger. And I will never be a Shade again."

"How can I believe you?" Amarie's voice softened. She wanted to. Wanted to welcome him back into her life with open arms, but she couldn't take any chances.

He squeezed her hand again. "Because of you. You saved me, Amarie. You made me see that I can be more than Uriel's puppet. That I *am* more. And I want to be a better man for not just you now, but for our daughter. She deserves the world we both wished for ourselves."

"It all feels too late for that," she murmured, looking at their hands. "She'll be twenty-one in a couple months. No longer a child. She's the Key, and I'm not even there to help her." Her throat squeezed again, and she sighed, dropping her head onto Kin's shoulder. "I failed her in all the ways that matter."

"Then we fight for the future she still has." He leaned into her, his head resting against her own. "As crazy as Damien sounds most of the time, maybe it is possible to imprison Uriel. Then Ahria can have whatever life she wants." He bumped her head gently with his. "And you didn't fail her. Not even a little."

Closing her eyes, she drew in a deep inhale of his scent. The scent she'd not experienced in so long. She listened to his breath, willing her muscles to relax. Her body ached to curl around him, to feel his arms embrace her. But she didn't act on the desire, the memory of all the hurt keeping her in place. "I want to trust you," she whispered. "I really do."

"It's all right that you don't." He squeezed her hand again. "I need to earn that back. And I will." He turned his head as if to kiss her hair, but stilled instead. "And until I do, I'm here for you however you need me to be. Just tell me what you need and I'll respect it."

Amarie lifted her head from his shoulder, their faces close as she examined his bright eyes. Her heart thudded in her ears, and she controlled the urge to chew her lip. "I need time. It's not that I want to be with anyone else, I don't. I just... I need time to figure that out. Can we... can we be friends? Are you..." She let her voice trail off, unsure how to word the rest of her question.

"If that is what you need, then yes." Kin met her eyes, a strength in his that eased the weight from her shoulders. "I meant what I said. And I will offer the same to Ahria. Though, I hope she accepts me as a father."

"Did you have anyone else... When you went into Slumber?" Amarie stiffened at her own question, but if he'd left someone behind, she wanted to know.

He shook his head. "Damien was the one I was closest to before Slumber."

"And what do you want?" Amarie rolled her lips to keep herself from biting one.

Kin gave her a soft smile. "I want you to be happy and free to do what *you* want. That has been the basis of everything I've done in the last year. Sorry, twenty-one years now. Though I suppose the years in Slumber hardly constitute me doing anything. Damien originally promised I'd only be out for a year." He frowned, looking towards their camp. "But I guess he had his reasons."

"Perhaps it's for the best." Amarie took a deep breath. "Otherwise we'd never have woken together."

Kin nodded, sighing softly as silence settled for a few moments. Then his brow furrowed. "You said the auer woke you to train you. When was that?"

Amarie shifted her feet, crossing her ankles. "Almost immediately after putting me into Slumber. I'd suffered many injuries in my confrontation with Uriel and I needed rehabilitation since no one could heal me. Kalstacia was there, seeing me through it. But I didn't know who she was at the time." It was strange to have all her memories back at once, including the years spent ignorant of who she was. "I knew nothing other than my name. And then they trained me."

"For how long?" When she hesitated to answer, he continued, "You seem... and don't take this the wrong way, but just... wiser. More level-headed and mature."

Touching her face, Amarie searched for signs of age, but there wouldn't be any. Her mother had never aged to the point of gaining wrinkles or grey hair, and neither would she because of the power they carried.

Until now, I suppose.

"Seven years or so," Amarie whispered.

Kin fell silent, swallowing. "How does it feel to you now, then? For me, our time together only feels like it was a year ago, but if you..."

"It's the same for me." She looked at him. "Sort of. My memories from training feel separate, somehow, and while I may have grown up a little during that time, my mind doesn't take those years into consideration. Everything from before Slumber feels just as recent."

That makes me almost thirty-one.

The thought made her huff, and she returned her head to Kin's shoulder. "Guess I'm older than you now."

Kin scoffed. "Barely."

Chapter 2

Conrad wanted to turn right around, march out the palace gates and gallop back to the northern estate he and Ahria had called home for only a few days.

Wendelin had played dirty, threatening to send Artisan messengers if Conrad didn't agree to returning to the palace for a 'short' debriefing of the events at the townhouse in New Kingston. The events that had left the queen's primary advisor dead and the city in an uproar of fear that an attack similar to Nema's Throne's destruction was coming to Ziona.

The crown prince assured himself he merely needed to meet with his mother to ensure he and Ahria could remain undisturbed, and walked quickly enough that the guards didn't have time to complete their salute before he was already past them.

Turning down the hallway towards the queen's study, he back-stepped just in time to avoid running headfirst into Chancellor Heager.

The stout older woman beamed with the fakest smile he'd seen on her yet, casting a bemused glance at the rail thin aide at her side.

"Excuse me, Chancellor." He swallowed his frustration, forcing the courtesy that'd been enforced since he'd been more or less kidnapped back into the royal family. After his respectful nod, he moved to step around her, but she blocked him.

"In such a rush." She raised a condescending eyebrow. "So eager to learn the name of your future bride, I see. I admire your dedication."

"What?" Conrad's determination to avoid her faltered. "I merely need to speak to the queen regarding a private matter."

"Things are happening, *Prince*, and your mother agrees with my suggestion. Marriage makes the strongest alliance, don't forget that."

"All due respect, Chancellor, *my* decision regarding marriage is none of your concern."

Her face darkened. "When it impacts the safety of our country, it is."

"Then perhaps you should offer your own son for such a union, seeing as the Zionan parliament remains the true ruling power." He bit back what remained of his angry retort. He knew how the chancellors saw him and his mother. Nothing but figure heads to be manipulated.

Lips tightening, she chuckled without mirth. "Princesses wed princes. Your mother will fill you in." Heager stepped to the side, allowing him to pass. "It's time to take your role more seriously, and remove unneeded complications from your life." She continued on her way before he could question her further, rounding the corner.

Bile tainted Conrad's throat as he glared after the greying chancellor. Her aide bowed respectfully to the prince before scurrying after her, his arms full of various files and dockets that had likely just been reviewed by the queen.

Mum wouldn't have agreed to a marriage without talking to me, would she?

He hustled down the elaborate hallway, his anger tangling with uncertainty. Nodding to the two guards posted outside his mother's study, he waved off the move they made to open the door for him and shoved through on his own.

A large window framed the queen, who stood staring outside.

He at least had the good sense to make sure the door was closed behind him before letting frustration take hold. "What is this bullshit Heager is going on about? Marriage? You must realize I have no intention of wedding a stranger."

Andi's head popped up from the lush bed nestled between the bookshelves and window. Her mouth opened in a happy pant, oblivious to his mood, and she looked to Talia rather than immediately charge him like she usually would.

Talia raised a hand to quiet him as she faced him, and Andi seemed to take it as a command for her, lowering her head back onto the edge of her bed. "Slow down. I know Heager wants to push Helgath for an alliance by marriage, but no one has agreed to that. Not even the Helgathian royals." Her voice sounded weary. Exhausted by the grief weighing her shoulders.

Conrad slowed as he took in his mother, her arms wrapped tightly across herself, her black tunic lined with gold embroidery. She wore all black, and Conrad swallowed as he remembered how close his mother had been to Talon before his death. A death that was only days ago and Conrad hadn't even been to see her or offer his own condolences for her loss. Urging himself to breathe and remember, he walked towards her.

"Helgath? But we haven't even formally written to them about an alliance. And isn't the princess a little young?" Not that her age mattered to him in the slightest.

"Have a seat. I need to fill you in." She motioned to one of the plush chairs.

"I can't stay long, Mum." Conrad obeyed, though, sitting where she gestured.

Andi took her opportunity and jumped up from her bed, hurrying to push her head into Conrad's lap. He began to scratch her ears idly.

"I know," she sighed, taking the seat across from him. "Helgath and Isalica are proposing an alliance between our countries. I understand King Jarrod Martox and King Matthias Rayeht will be visiting our capital in the near future to discuss the matter. We received word of their request to visit only this morning, and we must prepare. Heager believes this is a good move for Ziona and wants to solidify it with a marriage between you and King Martox's daughter, Princess Brynn.

"You can't seriously ask me to agree to such a thing?" Conrad's heart squeezed as he thought of Ahria.

Talia shook her head. "I agreed with Heager that it would be a good political move, but it is ultimately your choice. I do not expect you to do it."

Conrad snorted. "Might as well give parliament another reason to question everything I do."

"It is important you not abide by all their requests." Talia's smile seemed forced. "You are not a pawn for them to use. Our bloodline was returned to the throne to challenge parliament, to keep them honest. We cannot do that without being honest ourselves. You can marry whoever you choose and I will support that decision."

He admired the determination in her expression. In her tone. She'd never abandon those beliefs. Never force him to do anything he wasn't willing to.

Talia's voice softened. "But you will need to be here for these meetings with the foreign royals." She paused. "How is Ahria?"

"She's coping, but it will be a long road. She's lost both her fathers recently, and we have reason to believe her mother, too. I can't even begin to imagine how she feels. But it's better if she's not forced to be alone."

"I understand. It will take some time before the royals arrive, so I hope she will be in a better place when the time comes. She can accompany you, if you wish, but I understand there are limitations while she is still learning to use whatever power she now has. Parliament is pushing hard for you to get rid of her after everything that's happened, but I will keep standing my ground, for both of you. And I haven't breathed a word of what you've explained, even though I know you're still leaving things out."

"Nothing will change my mind about Ahria. If anything, this whole ordeal only makes me love her more. Despite everything, she's still fighting. And she needs to know that I'm not going anywhere."

Conrad rubbed his jaw, imagining the visit from the Helgathian and Isalican monarchs. An event he wished he'd have months, if not years, to prepare for. He could fake the formalities enough with the parliament officials and in front of his own guards, but other royals? Conrad was a ship's captain, not a prince. And the idea of being in a room with not only one king, but two, made his stomach roil like a tempest. "I'll speak with Ahria about it. I doubt she'll want to be around with royal visitors."

Especially ones known to have the Art. Any accident could look like an assassination.

"Are you certain I need to be involved in these conversations? It's obvious that parliament doesn't give a damn about my opinion, and I'm just the male child of a Zionan queen."

"I'd like you here." Talia's tone grew more serious. "I *need* you. You're my adult son who reshaped our justice system in just a few weeks. They're interested in meeting you. And while I support your decision to marry who you choose, the statement will be stronger coming directly from you. You don't need to be nervous…"

"Fairly certain I have every right to be." He pursed his lips. "But I know you probably are, too. I'll be here. But with your permission, I'd like to attend only the absolutely necessary days. So I don't have to abandon Ahria at the estate again."

Talia nodded. "I don't have an exact arrival date for them, but the message made it sound like they could be here as soon as next week once we send our acceptance. I will send a messenger to you when I know."

Chapter 3

"By the gods," Rae murmured, rising from where she sat as Damien entered their chambers' sitting room. She crossed to him, throwing her arms around his shoulders. "When you said Uriel had come for Kin and Amarie, I... Gods, I'm so glad you're all right."

Damien squeezed his wife, burying his face in her braided hair. He'd never tire of the feel of her, and hated every time they had to travel apart from each other. "We're all fine." He stepped back, brushing her smooth cheek. Her eyes shone in their normal hues, a topaz yellow and emerald green, showing off the auer heritage that also kept her looking as young as she had when they first met. He'd fought off the signs of age himself through visits to the Rahn'ka sanctums, extending his lifespan to match hers.

A glance around the front room of their chambers confirmed Rae was alone. "Sarra out with her friends again?" He'd hoped to see her so he could hold his daughter, too. Nothing like a near death encounter to make him miss his children. He'd already known he wouldn't see his son. Bellamy, already a young man, was off in the Olsan mountains training—just as he had at his age.

Hopefully Yondé is kinder to him.

Rae shook her head, touching his face. "Actually, she's apparently met a girl. She won't admit it's anything special, but they've been spending a lot of time together. Braka's daughter, if you can believe it."

Damien chuckled as he threw himself onto their old, familiar couch. "I heard he'd settled down, but I thought Jarrod was pulling my leg. Course, any person who gave Braka a tasty meal would probably hold his heart."

Laughing, his wife returned to her seat and closed the book she'd been reading before sitting next to Damien. "I hear she's a talented cook." Her expression evened as she placed her bare feet on his lap. "Matthias is already here. Brought Katrin, Liam, Dani, and Micah, too."

He lifted his head briefly before he closed his eyes and sighed. "That was fast." He urged his body to relax, Rae's comforting scent mixed with home almost lulling him into a meditative state. But the thought of Matthias already in the palace denied his body total relaxation.

Gently easing the hold on the barrier of his senses, Damien allowed the surrounding voices of the world to enter his consciousness, finding both the known and unfamiliar. "They're in Jarrod's chambers, so I have a few minutes to breathe. Did you mention Kin and Amarie to them?" He touched his wife's ankles, running his hands down to rub her feet out of habit.

Rae sighed and leaned sideways, watching him. "I did. Matthias knows they'll be joining us. We're planning on taking a portal to Ziona once we get permission from the Zionan government."

"That'll make Kin and Amarie happy. The sooner we can find their daughter, the better. Both for them and us."

"Good." She groaned as his thumb found a sore spot in her foot. "I'd be crazy if I couldn't find Sarra."

He sighed. "Certainly would have been good to know she existed *before* establishing an elaborate plan to create the *Berylian Key, divided.*"

Rae chuckled. "I had no idea. It makes a lot more sense, with the way she was when I met her. So reckless and emotional." She paused, expression growing distant. "She'd just left her baby. I can't imagine how hard that would have been, and there I was, encouraging her to... well, you know."

"And for her, that choice to leave her baby is still recent. She only just left Ahria a few months ago, though she mentioned something about the auer waking her for training. And Kin..." Damien pressed into the sore spot on Rae's foot again, working the knot. "Seeing Matthias is going to be a weird experience."

"She must hate me," Rae murmured, her throat bobbing. "I lied to her. Manipulated her. I didn't know..."

"There was no way to know. And I think she understands that. But it might just take some time." He reached up and interlaced his fingers with hers. "We're all on the same side of the fight, though."

"I should talk to her." Rae sat up, smirking at him. "Other foot later?" When he nodded, she stood. "You can stay here if you like."

"Nah, I'll come with you."

"Missed me?" Rae tugged her boots on.

"Maybe."

The intricate palace hallways were second nature now, having lived in the palace for nearly twenty years. And the distance between the royal chambers and guest wing granted him more time with his wife, for which he was grateful. Things would undoubtedly grow more chaotic from here, with the plan he and Rae had been working on for the last twenty years finally beginning to come together.

Damien walked hand in hand with Rae towards the guest chambers he'd offered to Kin and Amarie. Separate bedrooms, as she'd requested, but a shared sitting room. The tension between the two had lessened during their ride to Veralian, but there was bound to be some lingering. They'd been friendly by the last day, but he'd yet to see any affection between them.

Not that I can blame her. It's a lot to take in.

After a brief knock of warning on the living quarters' door, Damien entered past the stationed guard, intended to help keep an eye on Amarie and Kin but not to entrap them. Though the disapproving scowl from Rae suggested that perhaps Damien had overreacted on asking for an assigned soldier.

Damien only frowned back in play as he held the door open for her.

"Damien, I—" Amarie took a step from the window she'd been looking out of, but halted when she spotted Rae. "Mira," she murmured, then shook her head. "Rae. You... look the same."

Kin wasn't in the room, but Damien suspected he wasn't far.

"Auer blood." Rae shrugged, standing beside the Rahn'ka as Amarie slowly approached. His wife didn't move, and Damien could feel her guilt. "I'm so sorry, I didn't know. I never would have—"

Amarie cut her off with a hug, which Rae returned as relief washed through her ká.

"I didn't know, either," Amarie admitted. "That you were pregnant. I put you in so much danger."

Rae closed her eyes and rested her head on the woman's shoulder as their embrace continued. "I've missed you."

"And I, you." Amarie huffed a laugh, withdrawing and meeting her gaze. "Though for a little less time, I suppose."

"Where is Kin?" Damien put his hand on Rae's lower back.

"In his room. Sleeping, maybe. I'm not sure." Amarie gestured with her head to the closed bedroom door adjacent to her open one.

"We do have good news. Matthias has already arrived from Isalica, so we should be able to leave for Ziona sooner rather than later. The diplomatic invitation from Ziona should come shortly. They won't pass over an opportunity like this one."

"And Matthias is...?" Amarie tilted her head.

"King of Isalica," Rae provided, narrowing her eyes. "I thought *someone* would've filled you in." She looked sideways at Damien before rolling her eyes. "He's the abandoned host we've recruited for the imprisonment plan. King Rayeht of Isalica and King Martox of Helgath are working together to propose an alliance between their countries and Ziona. It's how we're getting an audience with the prince, who will hopefully know where your daughter is."

Amarie let out a long breath. "All right. And this won't take long?"

"Probably not." Damien smiled. "They have means of travel that are much faster than ours. We will meet with them tomorrow."

"Tomorrow?" Amarie's jaw flexed. "Why not today?"

Rae glanced out the window at the setting sun. "It wouldn't make a difference as we haven't heard back from Ziona. May as well take the time to relax a little. I don't know when we'll get another chance to."

Chapter 4

Soft grass tickled the outsides of Ahria's knees while she sat cross legged in the open front courtyard of the royal estate. Flames licked around her, not burning, not even warming, as she struggled to bend them to her will.

Shades of blue flickered through her eyelids, dancing in a frenzy despite all her focus. As her eyes fluttered open, the fire only grew, as if excited that she was finally looking at it. But she clamped her eyes shut and urged a deep breath.

Nothing changed about the blue penetrating into her vision, despite her effort.

Her heart ached, but she pushed the grief aside as much as she could whenever she practiced her Art.

Her Art.

What a ridiculous notion that would have been not too long ago. The plan had been that she'd never have to wield it. Never carry it as her burden. Her mother had taken that from her, spared her that curse with her sacrifice to remain in Slumber.

But Amarie no longer lived, and Ahria had no choice now but to learn.

She had the advantage of the loq'nali phén Talon had written for her, detailing breathing techniques and instructions on how to grasp and use the power. It wasn't ideal, but without her mother or father here to teach her, it was the next best thing.

It'd been only days since he died. Died protecting her from a Shade. Only minutes before she inherited the power, as if fate had a dark sense of humor. Perhaps she could have saved him, if her mother had shown the courtesy of dying just a little sooner.

Ahria opened her eyes and tears escaped to fall down her cheeks.

What kind of daughter am I?

Her horrible thoughts made her swallow as she watched the azure flames around her simmer lower. She willed them to diminish, but they remained.

Anger swelled in her gut, even as she tried to contain it, but it boiled with her frustration. Clenching her jaw, she stood, tears streaming faster now. Her chest heaved, and as her emotions spiked within her, she yelled.

All the hurt, the pain. The grief and despair. She screamed, as loud and as long as she could.

The blue fire leapt higher, but still didn't burn anything. It raged up the outer walls in waves, passing over the thick, flowering ivy in ebbs of every shade of azure. It crawled up the magnolia trees lining the drive to the estate gate, as if the flame would consume all. But it flickered among the flowers, like sprites.

Her voice grew raspy, her throat raw as her shout faded. Cringing, she fell back to her knees, cradling her face. "Dad, I need you." She sniffed, wiping her face with the back of her arm. "Why aren't you here?" She sobbed, flinging her hand to the side.

Heat coursed down her arm, the hairs like tiny pin pricks as lines of red and orange flowed over her skin. A pulse of flame erupted from her palm, glowing like she held it in front of a hearth. The fire spurted across the courtyard to the massive oak shadowing the eastern pool and garden.

Embers clung to the dry bark, singeing the tree unlike the blue flames still dancing through the entire courtyard.

"Shit." Ahria rose, darting through the harmless fire to put out the orange flames now clinging to life on the tree's trunk. Panting, she smothered them with her hands, wincing at the heat. "Shit," she muttered again, sighing and wiping her hands on her pants. Her palms stung from the burn, and she looked down at them. Her focus shifted from her palms to the ground, where an unnatural shape had pressed into the dirt among the oak's roots.

Tracks?

Ahria rounded the tree to get closer to the print, and knelt. She touched the edge, inspecting it closer. "This is from a boot." She looked from the print to her own boot, but the size was way off. "A man's boot." She stood, putting herself in the spot the man would have been standing.

It hid her from almost the entire courtyard, but still left her a view of the gates and front door.

Dread coiled in her gut, nerves dancing along her skin.

Conrad would have no reason to stand in that spot. To hide from her. It made no sense.

Someone has been watching me.

Ahria gulped, her pulse pounding in her ears.

Someone knows what I am.

She looked at her blue fire, now flickering low and calm through the grass. "And that I can't control it."

Closing her eyes, she took a deep breath, then exhaled slowly, pleading with her nerves to extinguish it. When she looked again, the fire was gone, but the success she expected to fill her chest only felt hollow.

Ahria walked the perimeter, watching the ground for any more signs of a trespasser. She found nothing, and the gates remained locked. Rolling her lips together, she looked at the oak tree again.

The print might be old, from another time entirely.

She wasn't experienced enough in tracking to tell. A part of her wanted to wipe it from the dirt, to see if it would return, but she would wait and show Conrad first. Perhaps he had an explanation for it.

Returning to the center of the courtyard, Ahria exhaled a shaky breath. Everything around her was perfectly in place. The sweet scent of the magnolias still tickled her nose, and bees buzzed in the ivy. None of it remembered the chaos she'd only just controlled. Barely.

She needed to keep practicing. Keep trying. Without Conrad here, the quiet ate at her. It devoured her soul with thoughts of her father. Memories of his cries of pain. His moments before death.

Shaking, she shut her eyes again, letting out a pained cry between clenched teeth.

Agony twisted inside her like thorny vines.

She needed to keep distracting herself. At least until the prince returned.

Ahria exhaled her grief and focused on her breathing the way her loq'nali phén instructed. She delved into her power, finding it buried deep within her. Channeling Talon's written words, she hovered there in her Art for minutes.

Hours.

Waiting for the pull to subside.

The massive pool of power within her always called. Begging her to dive into the center and let it rush through every part of her into the world. But she imagined the beaches instead of the water, like Talon's instructions said. The endless beaches where the water lapped towards her. She cautiously cupped a handful of a rising wave into her palm and watched it wriggle over her skin.

Gonna try this again.

She removed herself from the power, taking only the handful she'd retrieved. But as she withdrew...

The rest of the power lunged at her. It surged over her, drawn to what she had taken. It rushed to surround her, encase her in nothing but raw energy. She gasped, flooding her lungs and veins with power.

Her eyes snapped open, and her surroundings blurred with shades of purple and magenta. Fear ripped through her.

Panic.

No. No. No.

Ahria shrieked as the power tore through her limbs, throwing her head back and lifting her from the grass. It raked over her insides, swirling around her in a tornado of destruction. The world groaned as the grass pulled from the ground, rocks and debris joining the monsoon of energy.

Her mind couldn't summon Talon's advice for when she'd inevitably lose control. Only his words of warning flashed in her mind.

Widespread destruction. Massive casualties. Certain death for Artisans.

Ahria cried out, her grief raging through her and stifling any attempt to regain control. The circle of chaos widened, growing around her as she levitated from the destroyed ground. The marble benches of the central garden broke, then crumbled, joining the swirl of debris around her. Bolts of beryl and blue lightning shot like a web across the tornado's outer wall.

Images of Talon and the Shade ruptured through her head, pouring agony through her body.

What happens if I can't stop it?

She tried to remember. Tried to remember exactly what would happen to her, but perhaps it wasn't in the book. Perhaps Talon didn't know. Could she destroy New Kingston, even though it was miles away?

A voice broke through the noise, faint, but there.

Then a face appeared outside the wall of her power. Conrad, his arm lifted to shield his face as debris whipped past him.

You shouldn't be here.

She tried to speak. Tried to yell. Tell him to go. But no words formed on her lips, no sound accompanying the movement of her tongue.

Chapter 5

Conrad screamed her name again, his heart drumming in his ears.

I shouldn't have left her.

He didn't know what to do. She hovered in the middle of a chaotic sphere, at least three feet off the crater forming beneath her boots. The wall of flying debris had to be a foot or two deep, but the objects trapped in the cyclone flew at varied speeds. The debris on the outside whipped the fastest, while the pieces of marble and stone within drifted through the air like leaves in a stream.

The crater she'd made was smooth, like cut glass, regardless of whether it was dirt or stone. The ground beneath him remained intact, untouched. But it wouldn't last if Ahria didn't regain control. With each breath from her, the bubble grew slightly larger, expanding the crater as her power compacted the ground with relentless pressure.

His mind spun, and he stepped back from the sphere's edge. He couldn't leave Ahria to struggle against the power on her own, and recalled their late night conversations about Talon's lessons and what they could mean. But there wasn't time to consider all the details. The need to get to her grew with each shuddering expanse of Ahria's power.

Moving as close as he dared to the edge of the sphere, he watched Ahria within and studied the bubble's outer shell for gaps. He didn't know if Ahria even saw him. Forks of lightning shot across the upper half of the sphere as if it somehow contained its own thunderstorm, debris gathering more densely at the top.

The power was... magnificent. And utterly terrifying.

Ahria yelled again, and the sphere pulsed. She lifted her arms, muscles straining, and the flying debris rose higher. It left a short gap beneath, and he took his opportunity.

Tugging his sleeves down and collar up, Conrad backed up a few paces before he ran, timing it to miss the passage of a particularly large chunk of a marble bench. Dropping to the ground, he ignored the pain as his hip hit the stone and he slid, directly into the sphere of power.

He almost expected his boots to get ripped away in the same direction as the debris flowed, or that they'd be compressed into the ground like everything else. But he had to believe Ahria had at least a modicum of control with how she'd shifted the debris higher.

Emerging on the other side, Conrad bounded to his feet within the crater, his skin stinging from minor cuts and irritation of the tornado wall. But inside, near Ahria, the air was clear and eerily quiet. The lightning made no sound as it ran along the sphere walls, the debris like nothing but a cloud of feathers. But even without the Art, his entire being felt charged like in a thundercloud. An invisible pressure that made everything in him feel as if it might just rupture. As if some deep part of him had an innate sense of the Art, even if he couldn't access it.

"Ahria!" He reached for her hand, locked in a fist near her side.

Her head angled down, the veins in her neck pulsing. Her mouth moved as she tried to speak, but no sound came out. Those ice-blue eyes he loved shone with beryl, glowing with incandescent light.

He moved in front of her, reaching up to take both of her hands. "You can control this." He prayed she could hear him. "Breathe."

Ahria closed her eyes, her hands relaxing in his touch, then squeezing with intention. She slowed her breath, but the whirlwind continued.

Conrad tapped his thumb against hers, following the pace of her raging pulse he could feel in his fingertips, but urged it to slow with each steady tap. "You're strong, Ahria. Stronger than this power. *Breathe.*"

"I can't," she whispered, tears shining on her cheeks. Her body lowered slightly, and he took one of her hands and placed it on his chest.

"Yes, you can." Conrad covered her hand with his own, exaggerating the rise of his chest with each breath. "Feel mine and breathe with me."

Ahria whimpered, but then fell silent, brow twitching. As he slowed his breath, she did the same, and the debris started to follow suit. With a relieved glance, he noted the crater ceased expanding.

As his breath eased into a calm rhythm, along with hers, she floated back down until her boots touched the smooth bottom of the crater. Gradually, the chunks of marble, dirt, and grass whipping around them calmed and thudded to the ground. The static in the air lessened, sparks dancing across his vision until those, too, died away.

With another inhale, Ahria opened her eyes. She let the air out of her lungs in a near-sob, and collapsed against him. Her shoulders shook, and he wrapped his arms around her in a tight embrace.

"See." Conrad rubbed his cheek against the top of her head, kissing her. "I told you you were stronger than it."

"I don't want this life," Ahria cried into his neck as she shook. "I can't do this. I can't control it."

Running his hand through her hair, he kissed her again. "You can. Your father knew you could or he wouldn't have written you that book." He squeezed her harder, wishing he could carry the burden of the power for her. "And whatever it takes, I'll be here to help you figure it out. I won't leave you alone like today again."

It'd been a mistake going back to the palace anyway, to deal with stupid political games. Ahria was far more important, even if he did feel guilty for leaving his mother to handle things alone. She would understand, ultimately. And she had advisors who could help her through the process.

He kissed her hair harder. "I'm so sorry. I'm here. I'm not going anywhere."

Ahria sighed against him. "Why?" Lifting her head, she looked up at him. "You should be done with me. I have no place in a kingdom. In a palace." Pulling away, she tried to retreat, but he gripped her wrist. She tilted her head in a silent plea, eyes bloodshot and exhausted.

"Mouse, listen to me, please." Conrad loosened his grip, grateful when she didn't pull away and turned to face him fully. "I'm able to make my own choices, just as you are. And I don't know how else to say it other than I choose *you*. I don't care if that means we need to stay here at this estate forever, or even if it means we have to go live like hermits in the middle of the forest. I *choose* you." He reached for her other hand, holding them both between them. "I'll never be done with you. And there's nothing you could possibly do that will change that."

Shoulders sagging, she walked to him again, pulling her hand free to touch his face. "I hardly deserve such dedication." She kissed him, lips lingering against his before she withdrew. "I miss the days from before. The time we spent in Haven Port. The time on your ship. I wish we could go back to that."

He ran his thumb along her jaw, imagining her in front of the view from the Crow's Nest tavern wearing that infamous hat. His longing to be back at sea had never waned, and the mere mention of returning to it with her made his heart beat faster. "I miss it, too. And we'll find a way to have it again. I'm still me, and you're still you." He pressed his hand lightly to her chest above her heart. "Nothing is changing that."

Silver lined the bottom of Ahria's eyes as she gave him a half-hearted smile. "I love you. I loved you from the first time we shared fire wine in that boat tavern. Nothing will ever change that, either."

He brushed a fallen tear from her cheek. "And I love you, Ahria Xylata."

Ahria kissed him again and slid her hand from his face, but as it passed over his short stubble, she hissed. When he started, she shook her head. "It's nothing. Just a little burn when I..."

Conrad took her hand, carefully turning it over to examine the burns. "We need to get these wrapped." His eyes returned to her face, but her gaze trailed to the far side of the courtyard, where a big oak stood.

He spied a dark spot on the trunk, though the damage seemed minuscule compared to the crater they stood in. "The tree look at you funny, or something?" he teased, but her haunted expression remained.

"Do you ever stand over there?" Ahria finally met his gaze again. "Behind the tree?"

"Can't say that I have." Conrad looked back towards it, trying to think of a single occasion he'd even gone near it. Each of his times in the front courtyard over the past few days had been merely to pass through it to the front gate. "Why? What's wrong?"

Ahria hesitated, brow furrowing. "Probably nothing. There's just... There's a boot print in the dirt behind it, like someone stood there watching the courtyard. Boots too big to be a woman's."

"Could have been one of the old servants that we sent away. A gardener, maybe?"

"Yeah," Ahria murmured. "You're probably right."

Chapter 6

"How long is this all going to take?" Sleep had done little to bolster Kin's patience for the necessary games of politics. Nor had the hours of waiting for Damien to finally show up with news of a meeting rather than a departure for Ziona.

Amarie walked next to him, looking better than she had the day before. "When can we leave for Ziona?"

"I don't know, and I don't know," Damien huffed, then evened his tone. "It won't be long, and I think you'll be pleasantly surprised when you realize the journey to Ziona won't even require a boat."

Amarie looked at Kin with a raised eyebrow. "Sounds like a longer trip if we have to walk across the Dul'Idur Gate?"

"Not what I meant." Damien rounded a corner, ascending a flight of stairs towards the meeting room where they were to sit with not one king, but two. "Can either of you just be patient?"

"Would you be patient if it was your daughter?" Kin glowered. "Now responsible for unfathomable power that she likely doesn't know how to control or understand?"

Damien sighed and grumbled, "Probably not."

"Then you understand our rush." Amarie's boots tapped on the upper landing before they crossed onto another rug.

"Amarie is Ahria's best chance at not accidentally blowing a hole in the side of Pantracia. I'd think you might have a little more urgency on the matter. And Uriel…"

"Yes, yes, we don't want Uriel to find her. We're moving as fast as we can, all right? You must put a little trust in us. We're all on the same team."

Like the trust I put in you before you left me in Slumber for twenty years?

Kin hadn't had a chance to confront Damien about the lies, but felt less motivation to do so since Amarie had pointed out that it allowed them to wake together. He didn't want to give Damien the credit for crafting that situation. The fact of the matter was that Kin and Amarie had both been tools for Damien and Rae to keep in hiding until the time was right. The Rahn'ka had been playing a god, and Kin's patience for the man he'd thought a friend waned with each step through the dark oak halls of the Helgathian palace.

Though, he did save our lives, too.

Reaching a door with two sentries, Damien opened it and entered. Amarie followed next, voices already present in the room.

"He didn't eat your bacon." A deep voice chuckled. "Look at him, he's innocent."

A dog whined, drawing Kin's attention to the far side of the room where a big black dog sat next to...

Not a dog.

The wolf's ears pricked, angling towards Kin. It growled, and the man next to it stood, his dark skin contrasting his bright amber eyes. Eyes that sent a chill down Kin's spine the instant he recognized them. His heart stopped, transported back to a dirt floor arena with a raging bonfire at the center.

"You." Kin froze, eyes locked on the man. The wolf handler that'd tried to kill him all those years ago. With the same damned wolf.

How is that possible?

Every instinct in Kin wanted to back out the door, the old scars on his arm aching where the wolf had bit him. But Damien had already closed the door, and Amarie looked at him with a quizzical expression.

"I'd like to introduce King Jarrod Martox and King Consort Corin Lanoret-Martox, my brother." Damien walked around the table to sit next to his king, but remained standing.

"We've met, though you seem to have forgotten, Damien. It was very different circumstances, though." Kin couldn't take his eyes off the king. The eyes that had wanted to murder him.

Certainly wouldn't have pegged him for a king back then.

Jarrod's gaze narrowed, and he tilted his head. "We *have* met, haven't we?" He rose and stepped around the table, the wolf at his heels. "I have forgiven your actions that led to Bellamy's death. I hope you might forgive me and Neco for our unfortunately-timed encounter. I was not myself then, but I pose no threat to you now." He extended his hand to Kin, and the wolf sat on his haunches.

Amarie glanced between them, then nudged Kin in the ribs.

In formal regalia, the king looked far different than he had in the arena. Whatever aggression had fueled the attack appeared to have passed, which urged Kin to accept the offered hand. He didn't allow himself to consider that the man was a king, focusing on that Jarrod was just a man, too. A man with a wolf.

Eyeing Neco, Kin wondered how the creature was still alive and looking very much the same as he had all those years ago. Of course, whatever power that had brought Jarrod to be close friends with Damien likely played a part in it all.

"Seeing as we're supposed to be working together from what I understand, I'm glad to know you won't try killing me again. But for what it's worth, I am sorry for my role in Bellamy's death. Just as you are, I'm a different man now." Kin met the king's eyes, shaking his hand more firmly.

Just another man.

Neco let out a series of talking-barks, drawing Jarrod's attention.

"I don't think he'd like that."

The wolf yipped.

The king shook his head. "Not a good idea."

But Neco ignored him and trotted over to Kin as they released each other's hand, and the wolf licked Kin's fingers with a huff.

Kin swallowed, trying to remember the directions he'd gotten as a child in how to deal with encountering a wolf. He decided standing still was likely the best course of action. No sudden movements as Neco trotted around him to the new person entering the room.

Rae walked inside, barely glancing at them before sitting next to Corin and petting Neco. "I see introductions are going well." She leaned back, plopping her boots up on the table. "Didn't you..." She pointed at Jarrod. "Almost kill Kin once? Or am I remembering that wrong?"

Amarie followed Rae and sat on the Mira'wyld's other side. "Why would he want to kill Kin?" She playfully glanced at the former Shade, and made a face. "Not that I'd necessarily blame him."

"In Kin's defense, wrong place, wrong time is really what it comes down to." Corin picked glasses up from a tray on the table and slid one in Rae's direction. He leaned over to her, whispering something with a smile on his face.

Rae laughed, feigned thinking, and then tapped two fingers on the table before whispering back.

Jarrod returned to the head of the table and sat. "Isn't it a little early?" He looked at Corin and Rae.

"Based on the look on Kin's face, I say not." Corin turned to a table against the back wall and produced a long-necked decanter filled with an amber liquid. "Nothing better to calm the nerves, and something tells me this conversation is going to have a few of them." He popped the cork and began to pour healthy servings into each of the crystal glasses.

Jarrod coughed. "Matthias just got to the top of the stairs. Has anyone told Kin?"

"We told him." Rae nodded. "Well, we told Amarie."

"Told me what?" Amarie sat straighter.

"That Matthias is coming."

"Oh, that? Yes, you mentioned it. The king of Isalica was once..." Amarie's voice trailed off as the door opened, her face losing all color as her eyes fixated behind Kin.

Kin's head spun, trying desperately to catch up to the conversation, but all he could focus on was the look on Amarie's face. The horror within her eyes that he recognized. It made the blood freeze in his veins, and every muscle seized. He wanted desperately to turn, to see who had entered the room, but everything moved in slow motion. Damien had mentioned the name Matthias, but Kin hadn't known he was the second king for the proposed alliance.

But if he was only a king, what was Amarie so afraid of?

Amarie stood, backing away from the door and reaching for a sword that wasn't there.

The room stilled, like everyone held their breath.

"At ease, Amarie..." The bass voice came from behind Kin, calm and slow.

That voice. He'd never, *ever* forget that voice.

It sent a flurry of ice and fire through every limb, and the scars across his back felt as if they split open. Red hot memories of the torture he'd endured, never revealing Amarie and her power. The cold stone of long abandoned temples bit into his palms, his feet, his legs. The shadows in the room seemed to move in the corners of his vision.

"Kin..." Uriel's voice came again, softer than he'd ever known it. "Look at me."

He couldn't move. His tongue stuck to the top of his mouth as the room and people around them vanished.

Amarie appeared in front of him, holding his face with both hands. "It's all right. It is not him."

"You really botched this one, Dame," Corin muttered.

Kin focused on Amarie, his hands shaking as sweat beaded on the back of his neck.

"Should I jump?" Uriel's voice came again, but not directed at him.

"Give it another minute." Rae was standing, now, too. She murmured to Damien.

"Perhaps Rae's right." Jarrod rose from his seat. "Let's give them a moment of privacy."

Don't leave me.

Kin stared at Amarie, willing her to hear his unspoken request.

The others in the room quietly departed, but she remained.

"Look at him," Amarie whispered. "Turn around. Look."

Her request was insanity. Kin didn't need to look at Uriel to know he was there. Yet something in the air did feel different. It didn't hang as heavy as it always did in those temples.

Then Kin remembered where he was. A meeting chamber in Veralian. With Damien and Amarie. Uriel wouldn't find them here. And his face had changed. The auer who had attacked him and Amarie was Uriel, no longer the man owning the voice he heard now.

Memories of Lasseth Frey returned.

Of the conversation in the escaped Shade's home.

The gratitude Kin had felt while staring at his master's body. Gratitude. For the man Uriel had taken. The man who suffered and had spared Kin the same fate. The very same man who now stood behind him.

"You're safe." Amarie stroked his cheek. "Look at his eyes."

Kin sucked in a breath, forcing his lungs to work. He banished the phantom pain as he focused only on Amarie and the blue of her eyes. Beyond her, the rest of the room returned, the seats all empty.

He turned.

Before him, stood Uriel. But not.

He looked so very much the same, except the eyes like Amarie had said. He focused on the tumultuous sea-green eyes of the man who had spared him. No hint of the obsidian and gold to be seen.

Kin swallowed as he looked down at the fine clothes, not too dissimilar to what Uriel had worn, except for where the sleeves were rolled up. The man's skin was covered in ink Kin had never seen

36

before. Tattoos like sleeves depicting a shining sun and raging dragon over both his forearms.

But he looked so much like Uriel a shiver still passed down Kin's spine as he took a step back from the king of Isalica. Still urging himself to process and realize the truth. This was not Uriel. But the man who had saved him from a fate far worse than being a Shade.

Amarie touched Kin's elbow, looking at Uriel. At Matthias, before meeting Kin's gaze. "Are you all right?"

Kin's tongue felt too swollen to speak. The snakes writhing in his stomach begged for her to stay.

It's not him. I need to face this.

Touching her hand on his elbow, Kin nodded once, then she left the room, too. The door closed, leaving him alone with Uriel's former host.

The king reached for Kin, but his intention faltered, and he stepped back. "I am Matthias Rayeht. I was under Uriel's control for twenty years, as was my country. I've been free of him for fourteen now, but I remember most of those... awful events. I'm..." He looked down, a hint of shame darkening his expression. "I'm deeply sorry for what my hands have done to you."

Despite all attempts not to look at them, Kin's eyes flitted down to Uriel's hands. He ignored the searing pain that arched through his back again and swallowed. "I didn't realize Uriel was a king, but it makes sense." With Matthias's subtle shift, shadows in the room seemed to surge, but with another blink, everything remained unmoved. "Lasseth told me about Uriel's hosts, so I know... But shouldn't you be dead if Uriel was done with you? How..." He looked at Matthias's eyes again, searching for any hint of the darkness there. If Kin hadn't seen Uriel in a different body mere days before, he never would have believed.

Matthias shrugged, stepping sideways towards a window. "Probably. But to take a host, Uriel must gain permission. He broke the terms of our deal, and I was able to reclaim my body. He's tried to kill me since then, but fortunately, without my Art, he's at a disadvantage."

Kin chewed his lower lip, wishing the roiling in his gut would stop. "Lasseth mentioned something like that, too. That whatever he found in his latest host dissuaded Uriel from me..." A shiver passed down his spine. "And it was your Art?"

The king grunted. "It was. Without it, Uriel is less powerful. Still a threat, of course, but at least his energy has limits once again."

"And Damien found you, and now you're part of all of this." Kin waved his hand around the abandoned meeting room. "To imprison him."

"Precisely." He faced Kin. "I know my face doesn't instill any confidence in that, for you, but no one has greater motivation to never see him again." A haunted look tainted the man's expression, and he tilted his head. "I always, always cheered for you. I hoped you'd get away, and you did. He hated that you evaded him so much that he went after another version of you. You should know that your brother is now king of Feyor. And he's a Shade."

"I know." The numbness of everything he was learning didn't allow the emotions of anger at Jarac to creep in anymore. "He mentioned it when we..."

Before he nearly killed me.

He'd tried to forget his twin brother and the lineage Kin had technically been born into before being stolen and adopted to a winemaker's family. The only interaction they'd had proved Jarac to be the far crueler of them. His willingness to become a Shade, despite already holding the power of the crown, only furthered what type of man he was.

Kin rubbed at the scarred over tattoo on his arm. "I guess Uriel got what he wanted then. Feyor."

"He did. But he's lost a lot since you've been gone. Would you like to see how my power works?" Matthias approached him, offering his hand. The tattoos over his forearms stretched up his biceps beneath his tunic, while the rays of the sun reached onto the back of his hand.

"Why the ink?" Kin hesitated.

"So my skin felt like mine again. Helps separate the memories." Matthias motioned with his offered hand again. "Well? You want to know why Uriel kept me instead of taking you?"

Kin studied his hand for a moment, echoes of pain pulsing through his body at the thought of touching him. The one and only time Kin had shaken Uriel's hand had been during that initial meeting.

When I accepted becoming a Shade.

His eyes trailed up the black lines of the tattoos as he considered what Matthias must have gone through.

And he's still standing.

He wanted to know, and the desire to understand encouraged Kin's reach as he grasped the offered hand.

"It won't hurt." Matthias's hand heated, and then their surroundings whipped into reverse.

Kin could barely see as they returned to their previous places, and the others poured backward into the room. Events blurred until jerking to a stop.

Everyone sat in the room as before.

Amarie stood before him, touching his face. "It's all right. It is not him."

"You really botched this one, Dame," Corin muttered.

Kin blinked, his mind whirling to catch up to what had just happened. He touched Amarie's hands, sensing Matthias behind him.

"Do you understand now?" Matthias stepped around Kin while no one else spoke.

Kin met his eyes, lowering Amarie's hand from his face, but continued to hold onto it. "Not to the full extent, I'm sure. But I believe I have the gist. Though I have more questions." His gut felt calmer, but shadows still felt unstable.

"What's happening?" Amarie looked between them.

"You jumped, didn't you?" Damien eyed the Isalican king.

"You can... Uriel could travel through time?" Kin furrowed his brow. "Why not just go back to before he took you and change everything?"

Matthias shook his head. "I can only go back about a quarter hour, and only so many times. But those limits hardly affected Uriel with the way he drew energy."

"Of course..." The pieces fell together in Kin's head. "He could keep pulling power from everything around him. Drain it over and over. And that's why you're not dead. He never had to pull from you as the host."

The king nodded gravely.

Amarie's grip tightened on Kin, the gesture speaking all of her questions.

He wished he could answer them all, but he could sense everyone in the room watching him. Waiting to see if he'd crack.

Matthias rounded the table to the end opposite Jarrod and took a seat.

Letting go of his hand, Amarie reluctantly returned to her seat next to Rae. "Feels dangerous to have all of us in one room. How do we know we're safe here?"

"We don't. Not really." Jarrod tapped his fingers on the table. "Which is why we need to be brief, and get moving to Ziona soon."

Chapter 7

The nerves in Matthias's gut finally calmed, peace settling within him at finally having had the conversation with Kin that he'd waited for. At least part of it. He watched the former Shade join them all at the table, his skin still tingling from the jump. "I understand we need to approach Ziona with an alliance of our three countries, but I'm not entirely clear on *why* we must do this now."

Amarie exchanged a look with Kin, and then with Rae, before she spoke. "My daughter is in Ziona, and she's recently inherited the Key's power. I need to find her."

Matthias stiffened. "You no longer have the power?"

"Ahria received the power when Amarie died. And *we* need to find her." Damien ignored the glass Corin slid in front of him, passing it to Kin beside him. "The Berylian Key is the final missing piece of the puzzle for Uriel's imprisonment."

"She is not a piece of anything." Amarie glared at the Rahn'ka. "She is my daughter... *our* daughter, and finding her is of the utmost importance, for her own safety. Whether or not she agrees to be a part of this plan is entirely her choice."

Kin shifted his hand from the glass to rest on top of Amarie's, but withdrew quickly.

Damien's voice remained calm, but Matthias knew him well enough to hear the frustration in his tone. "Of course, but I have to hope that she will see the importance of it. That you might help in expressing that importance to her. This may be our only chance, and

Uriel knows the prison has been completed. He'll be looking for it. We don't exactly have time to waste."

Matthias spoke slowly. "No one is going to force your daughter into anything. We want her safe, first and foremost. Travel to Ziona will take minutes at most, so let's make sure we have all the information we need before we do that." He fixated his gaze on Amarie. "Does your daughter know how to hide her power?"

"No." Amarie's throat bobbed. "She doesn't. Even if Talon taught her some things before he died, this power isn't like others'. It took me years to master my hiding aura with an adequate trainer. Even with what Talon may have told her, she will still—"

"I'm sorry, who's Talon?" Corin leaned forward.

"Her father," Amarie blurted before glancing at Kin. "Her adoptive father. He helped teach me how to use my Art, so it makes sense he would have tried to prepare her."

"But he's dead?" Matthias tried to keep his tone gentle. With Amarie's nod, he let out a breath.

"A few days ago. Right before the Key's power transfer happened." Kin's expression was grim.

Chatter murmured between a few of them, and Matthias tried to follow each conversation, but they blended together.

"Is anyone with her? And has anyone seen Deylan?" Rae's voice cut through the others'.

Amarie started at the name. "How do you—"

A knock at the door brought silence back to the room before Jarrod spoke. "Enter."

A guard opened the door and held out a sealed scroll. "For your majesty."

Neco rose, loping to the door and taking it in his teeth with care before returning to Jarrod.

The door shut, and the Helgathian king opened the letter. Tension filled the space as he read, but he let it linger until he'd finished reading. "The queen of Ziona has agreed to meet. At our earliest convenience."

"I doubt she realizes how early that might be," Rae scoffed.

Amarie abandoned her question prompted by the mention of Deylan, looking desperately between the two kings. "Can we go now?"

"Not yet," Matthias murmured in a gentle tone. "We need to be prepared. Katrin and Dani are working with Micah and Maithalik to arrange our travel. We all need to get on the same page first. Assuming we find Ahria and she agrees to help us, Damien, what's next?"

Damien stiffened. "Well, we have to lure Uriel to the prison. Somehow. Preferably without the power to destroy it before we can seal him in it."

"And how do we do that?" Kin's attention shifted to the Rahn'ka, who shrugged.

"I'm still working on it."

"Where are you getting your information on how this supposed imprisonment spell works?" Amarie crossed her arms.

"The guardians. And ancient Rahn'ka texts. They're not exactly the most forthcoming with how it actually happened thousands of years ago."

"Thousands of years?" Amarie straightened. "You said it required the Berylian Key. Before the Sundering, it was a stone. With the power in a person, how will that affect the plan?"

Damien paused, scratching the back of his head in a slow, thoughtful way. Then shrugged again. "Shouldn't change anything." His tone made Matthias narrow his eyes.

"But we need it divided," Rae whispered.

"What?" Amarie looked between them. "What does that mean?"

The Mira'wyld cringed. "We don't really know."

"What *do* you know?"

Rae and Damien fell silent, staring at each other, before finally she spoke again. "Not a lot, to be honest. We know who we need, but we don't know how the pieces fit together. There are no more texts at the sanctum for us to read on it."

"So you don't even know what we're supposed to do for this to work?" Kin's fists clenched. "And you're, what? Expecting us to just wing it and figure it out? Against Uriel who presumably knows how this all went down before."

"Can't we discuss this on our way to Ziona?" Amarie fidgeted with the glass in front of her.

"It's better we wait. We're safe here for now, with no listening ears. But we don't know Ziona's alliances yet." Damien earned a glare from Amarie, but he seemed to ignore it.

"Did Uriel give any hints while you were... him?" Corin aimed the question at Matthias.

The former host shook his head. "He talked and thought about many things, many spells and threats, but without more information about the spell, I doubt I'll be much help. Do you know what the Rahn'ka call the process of sealing him?" He motioned to Damien.

"It was in old Aueric. Taeg'nok, I think."

Matthias lifted his chin. "Taeg'nok... Are you sure?" He remembered a conversation between Uriel and Alana where she'd mentioned that word. Asked Uriel about details, but...

"It's the closest thing I remember reading that could be conceived as a title of the thing." Damien looked at his wife, and she nodded in agreement.

"Then we might be in luck. I remember hearing that word before." Matthias huffed, shaking his head with a slight smile as he thought about the implications.

"I think we'll take some luck right about now." Corin settled back into his chair, sipping the whiskey he'd poured.

Neco whined on the floor, rolling onto his back between Jarrod and Corin's seats.

"He wants belly rubs," Jarrod muttered to his husband before nodding at Matthias. "Tell us."

Corin shifted in his chair to rub the wolf's belly with his foot.

Matthias shrugged. "Uriel doesn't know how it works, either. But you can bet he'll try to find out or at least prevent us from doing the same. He tried to figure it out by investigating the old prison at the center of the maelstrom in Lungaz. But the scouts he sent never returned and he couldn't go himself."

"Why couldn't he go himself?" Kin furrowed his brow.

The Isalican king hummed, wishing he could instantly fill in the gaps in everyone's knowledge. "If Uriel sets foot in Lungaz, he will be ejected from his host because of the void in the Art there."

Kin looked at Amarie, and she returned the stare as the two had a silent conversation before she cursed quietly under her breath.

"We need to focus on keeping the prison's location secret. But there's no way Uriel missed the energy wave erupting from it when it was finished. No Artisan in Pantracia did." Damien reached for the decanter, finally pouring himself a glass. "We need to determine our next steps before we go anywhere."

Amarie's chair ground on the floor as she pushed it back and stood. "I need some air." She shirked around Kin's reach and walked out of the room, shutting the door behind her.

Rae rose from her seat, not saying a word before following Amarie.

Kin stared at the door. "Rae mentioned Deylan. Do we know where he is? Has he been keeping an eye on Ahria?"

"Who is Deylan?" Matthias refocused on Kin.

"He's the man who gave me the blood I used to help free you from Uriel." Damien crossed his arms, seeming relaxed that the attention was off him. "Amarie's brother."

"He's also a member of a faction tasked with keeping an eye on the Berylian Key. They would be protecting Ahria." Kin leaned forward. "Though based on what I know about Amarie's brother and father, I doubt the faction's purpose ends with just the Berylian Key. I saw them capture a Shade without any trouble."

Matthias's gaze darted to Damien. "The man who gave you the blood is a member of the Sixth Eye?" He almost stood at the knowledge, gaping at the Rahn'ka. "And you never thought to mention that?"

"What the hells is the Sixth Eye?" Damien met his glare.

"The faction protecting the Key. It's called the Sixth Eye. They have power and influence all over Pantracia, but they almost never use it." Matthias rolled his shoulders. "Uriel often tasks Shades to find out more about them, but those Shades rarely return."

"And you never thought to mention *that*?" Damien shot back. "All I know about Deylan is he showed up out of nowhere and offered me the blood, and that was it. I wrote off whatever group he was part of because they didn't seem like a threat. I thought he'd just gotten lucky with getting the blood after the destruction of Hoult."

"I would have mentioned it if I'd known they were involved in any of this..." Matthias's heart thudded in his ears. "We need to find Ahria, and after that, we should look for Deylan. The Sixth Eye might have the information you still need on how to perform the Taeg'nok."

Chapter 8

"This is such a mess," Rae grumbled as she stalked through the hallways after Amarie. She couldn't blame the woman for wanting to go after her daughter, especially with Ahria's new power.

And she just woke up from slumber into all of this. How could we have expected anything different?

Nerves bubbled in her stomach, mostly from the plan she and Damien still didn't have. They'd hoped to have a better idea of how to accomplish the imprisonment by now, but with tome after tome revealing nothing new, admitting the truth of their ignorance felt wiser. Lies wouldn't breed trust, and trust would be paramount.

The guardians were no longer any help, nor their libraries. They had to hope someone else in the group could offer something that would lead to answers.

Rae rounded the corner to the chambers Amarie shared with Kin and nodded at the guard stationed there before entering through the ajar door.

The former Berylian Key stood at the massive windows, gazing north. The red-bricked rooftops of Veralian stretched in a jigsaw puzzle to the outer walls, where the countryside turned to rolling hills of summer grass, glowing in the morning sun. Beyond the hills and distant horizon, Rae could imagine the waves of the Dul'Idur Sea, which lay between them and Ziona. Between them and Ahria.

Amarie glanced over her shoulder before turning back to the window. "I'm sorry, I just... I want to find her."

"It's fine. I get it." Rae leaned against the desk, noting the open bedroom doors and the tossed sheets within. "We'll be in Ziona later today, I'm sure."

"How?" Amarie faced her. "Everyone keeps saying that travel won't take long, but last I checked, Ziona is weeks of travel away."

"We have access to portals. Thanks to our friends from Isalica." Rae shrugged. "We don't like to tell too many, but you obviously would have found out soon, anyway."

"Why am I even here?"

Rae furrowed her brow. "What do you mean?"

"Here. With you all." Amarie gestured with her arm. "I have no power. I'm no longer the Key. I have no part in this. I'm useless."

The Mira'wyld paused, swallowing. She had no idea what it would be like to suddenly lose the power she found within herself many years prior. Her chest weighed, and she shook her head. "You're not useless. You're still a part of this, even without the Key. We all need you, and not just for your power."

Amarie's jaw flexed, but she exhaled a long breath. "Matthias said your friends are working on our travel, which is the portal. Can I see it?"

Rae nodded. "I'll take you."

It'd been years since their infiltration of Veralian's royal palace, and she now knew each and every corridor. The old tunnels below the city still existed, but the sections beneath the palace hadn't been used since that day. They'd sealed them off. The routes beneath the city were still functional, used sparingly by the Ashen Hawks, but she didn't need them to take Amarie to the portal location.

Jarrod and Corin had set up a large room at the lowest level, hidden from the rest of the palace's staff. Down long corridors and winding stairwells that led further away from the city where an unsuspecting Artisan might have picked up on the vibrations of energy used to create the portals.

While Helgath and Isalica's alliance was not secret to the rest of the world, nor their rapid troop deployment during the battle at the

Isalican border, current situations required discretion. Especially when only two individuals could create portals—their best chance at staying ahead of Uriel.

When they arrived at what looked like a long-abandoned door, Rae knocked three times and then kicked it with her boot.

The door swung open a breath later, and Dani stood on the other side, her shoulder-length white hair wavy but neat. Her clouded gaze hovered near Amarie's face. "We aren't yet ready." Opening the door, she stepped back. "I'm Dani."

"This is Amarie." Rae entered first, steps silent on the soft dirt floor. "She was curious about the process."

Amarie followed, and Dani shut the door behind them.

Katrin stood at the edge of a mosaic circle in the middle of the room. Her dark hair coiled and braided into a refined bun at the back of her head. Not a strand out of place, despite the shimmer of sweat on her brow. She'd neatly folded up the sleeves of her simple pale yellow dress, and hiked up one side to tuck it in her belt. Even so, she looked the part of a queen, which she'd clearly grown into.

I can hardly believe it's been so long.

To keep their plans secret, interaction with their Isalican friends was limited to letters instead of face to face meetings. Even then, most correspondence went through Matthias rather than his wife. Rae couldn't even remember the last time she'd seen Katrin, despite all they'd been through together during the partial destruction of Nema's Throne.

"You have good timing for a quick preview. We're about to bring Micah and Maith back through." Katrin offered Amarie a warm smile as she smoothed the front of her skirt. "I'm Katrin."

Amarie offered a tight smile. "Amarie... Who are Micah and Maith? And where are they?"

"They are in Ziona, corresponding with the queen regarding our impending arrival. And to assure we don't scare any unfortunate guards or common folk in the vicinity of the portal when we open it." Dani strode to the other side of the room, standing opposite

Katrin with eight feet of space between them. "Micah is a crown elite, serving the Isalican royal family, like myself. And Maithalik is Jarrod's Chief Vizier."

Amarie opened her mouth to speak again, but Rae put a hand on her shoulder.

"Just watch," Rae whispered, hardening her gaze. "And don't get any ideas. Stay here. We need to follow the rules this time."

With a sheepish nod, Amarie fell silent and did as she was told.

Katrin squared her shoulders as she looked across the chamber at Dani. "Ready?" She didn't wait for her friend's response before stepping towards the center of the circle drawn on to the floor.

Dani moved at the same time, needing no cues before they met at the center, hands reaching to the other.

They both made fists, as if they grasped an invisible curtain, and pulled.

Sparks danced between them, their breathing quickening as they worked. The Art washed through the air, pressing against Rae's aura.

In a way that never failed to awe her, light erupted between the women and grew as they stepped back again. It broke into a prismatic display, rippling like the surface of a bubble.

Amarie's mouth popped open, and she stepped forward, eyes wide.

Rae touched her elbow, pulling her back to the spot without resistance, but she could see the abundance of emotion in her eyes.

Dani and Katrin pulled the portal wider, stepping apart and gritting their teeth as the energy worked. Once they reached their original starting points, the portal snapped into a circle, and two men emerged only a breath later.

Micah had once been Matthias's body double, but the years had passed for him when they hadn't for the king. Grey speckled throughout his dark beard, and laugh lines graced the corners of his eyes.

Rae smiled at Maith, who didn't look a day older than when they'd met. His auer blood was pure, unlike hers, and he'd been one of her closest friends through the years.

Micah looked at Amarie first, holding his tongue.

"It's fine. This is Amarie, Ahria's mother." Rae rubbed her palms together as the portal collapsed, the energy flowing back into the two other women.

"Well, do you want the good news or the bad news first?" Micah handed Katrin a sheet of parchment.

"Is Ahria there?" Amarie approached them.

Maith looked at her, a grim expression on his face. "She's not. Nor is the prince."

"The queen was pretty tight-lipped about where they are, too." Micah glanced at Katrin as she broke the seal on the parchment and began to open it. "But based on the way she talked about it, I'm pretty sure they're close by."

"Did they accept a location for the portal?" Dani clicked her tongue and crossed to Katrin.

"Can't say I'm surprised by the one they chose. The south barracks, where we initially checked in during that political visit ten years ago, do you remember?" Katrin folded the paper and tucked it into a pocket in her dress.

Dani nodded. "It smelled of sweat and cherry wood. I remember."

"So they put us where their army is?" Rae smirked. "You don't think they honestly thought we'd be bringing a brigade through, do you?"

"Hard to say," Micah mused. "But after recent events, I can hardly blame them for being overly cautious."

"Which recent events?" Amarie's tone weighed with tension.

"A Shade attacked one of their residences and killed several civilians, including the queen's closest advisor." Maith laced his hands together in front of him, looking at Rae. "An auer named Talon Di'Terian. Do you know of him?"

Amarie's throat bobbed, head bowing.

Rae nodded, lowering her voice. "He... He was Ahria's father."

"My apologies," Maith murmured to Amarie. "And my condolences for your loss."

"When can we arrive?" Rae touched Amarie's shoulder, squeezing.

"We're expected for dinner tonight." Micah looked to the doorway behind Rae. "I'll go get the others and we can be on our way."

Chapter 9

Conrad tore open the sealed letter as he walked back from the estate gate. At least his mother's messengers listened to his request not to come into the courtyard. Though, he would have liked to see the look of confusion on their face if they saw the destruction Ahria's power had wrought.

He skimmed the letter as he walked, but his steps faltered with the word 'tonight' and he hurriedly read back over it again, the words jumbling in his mind.

By the time he reached the front door, he'd tried to read his mother's scrawled handwriting several times, but his whirling brain wouldn't comprehend any of it. Grumbling, he lowered the paper to his side and rubbed his jaw, scratchy with the day's stubble. He abandoned the idea of reading until he had a cup of coffee, which was already prepped in their bedroom before he saw the messengers approach. He'd left Ahria sleeping, despite how late in the day it was growing.

Pushing the door open as silently as he could, Conrad looked at the elaborate four-poster bed in the main bedroom of the royal estate. The pillows had been shoved around, along with the disheveled blankets, but no Ahria.

Habit led Conrad to close the door behind him, though he didn't bother to quiet it as the latch fell into place. He glanced at the undisturbed coffee setting on the table in the corner of the room. The curtains had been drawn aside, and wind danced in through the open door to the balcony.

Ahria had to be outside, looking across the wilderness of the northern forests and mountains. He always wondered what she thought about while out there, but rarely asked. She had plenty to deal with without his questions.

Conrad dropped the letter from his mother onto the low slung table between couches and stepped on his heels to pull his untied boots off. He hadn't bothered with socks, and the wood floor was cool on the bottoms of his feet as he looked to the balcony again. Ahria was hidden from view behind the still-closed portion of curtains.

He touched his rough chin again, frowning at the pin prick of thick hair.

I need a shave.

Approaching the bathing chamber, he debated for only a moment whether he'd closed the ornate oak door the night before. Striding in, he was accosted by the sweet scents of the bathing oils his mother had sent them, and the heaviness of steam from the hot water.

He locked eyes on Ahria, who lounged in the raised tub. Windows surrounded it, overlooking the forest. Water glistened on her skin, shoulders and the tops of her breasts exposed above the rim of the porcelain tub.

She gasped and sank deeper into the water with a little splash, staring at him with wide eyes. "Conrad!"

"Oh shit, I'm sorry." He lifted his hand to shield his eyes, but the image of her was already seared into his memory. And made his throat dry. "I thought you were out on the balcony." He turned, his barefoot slipping on the steam-soaked tiles. His knee bumped into a delicate wire shelf of linens, singing in pain as he hissed and the metal clanged. "Shit."

Ahria huffed what was nearly a laugh. "I was. Until I wasn't."

Conrad grabbed the swaying shelf, steadying it. "I'll leave you be. I'm sorry."

"No, stay." Her soft voice sent a shiver down his spine. "Where did you go?"

He hesitated, already halfway out the door, debating the intent behind her invitation to stay. His blood instantly heated, despite his attempt to keep a cool head. "I saw a messenger arrive while I was making coffee. I went to get the letter from the gate." He slowly closed the door in front of him before glancing over his shoulder.

Ahria had dipped lower into the tub, and with the angle, he could only see her head now. Her hair was wrapped up in a messy bun on top of her head, but water had still found the loose strands that clung to her cheeks, rosy from the heat of the water.

The simple knowledge that she was naked within the tub riled every inch of him. Despite sharing a room for the past several weeks, modesty had always persisted between them. Their agreement to take their relationship slowly was further encouraged by both of their inexperience and recent events. Conrad had no doubts about what he wanted with Ahria, though. What he hoped to share with her. Yet, timing had been his enemy.

"You sure you don't want privacy? I can wait." He moved to the wash basin, its mirror perfectly positioned to still allow him a wonderful view of the tub and its occupant. "I was just going to shave so you don't have to look at this ragged face all day."

"I like watching you shave." Water sloshed as she draped her arms across the edge of the tub, resting her chin on her forearms. "Want me to take a look at the letter?"

"When you're done. There's no rush." Conrad met her eyes through the mirror as he blindly picked up a cloth to dip into the water basin. He lifted it to his jaw, soaking his skin.

"You sure this is a good time to shave?" Ahria sloshed in the water again. "Your hands don't look so steady."

The smirk on her face made him return it, a low chuckle reconfirming how relaxed Ahria could make him. He lifted out a hand, holding it parallel to the ground for a moment without a quiver. "I'll manage, one way or another." He retrieved the shaving kit he'd tucked behind the basin. "Besides, I'm sure you wouldn't mind playing healer for me if I do get a nick or two."

"Best I can offer is kissing it better," she murmured.

"Which is certainly the most welcome of medicines." He met her eyes again, muscle memory retrieving his blade without needing to look at it. "Can I get you anything to make your bath more enjoyable?"

Ahria hesitated, a thoughtful expression on her face. "I could help you."

"Me?" He saw his own brow furrow in the mirror, and he paused before the blade touched his cheek. "How could you help me?"

"Shave. If you want to show me how." She flicked a tiny bundle of bubbles at him. "I promise not to *fatally* wound you."

Conrad considered, watching her through the reflection. He'd never trusted anyone to shave his face other than his own hand before, but the idea of Ahria being the one oddly excited him. He imagined what her hands would feel like, and the knowledge of the trust required. He snapped the blade shut on his shaving razor, and offered it over his shoulder. "I'll show you."

To his utter shock, Ahria stood. Bubbles clung to her skin, body silhouetted against the windows behind. She stepped out of the tub, not hiding her nakedness, and crossed the bathing chamber towards him. Water dripped down her skin, falling from her fingers and pooling beneath her feet.

His heart thundered. Unable to stop, his eyes explored her through the mirror. He wanted to turn, but feared the vision would vanish if he took the time to look away.

Ahria stopped behind him, her body hidden by his in the reflection. "You might need to turn around." She touched his shoulders, dampness seeping into his shirt.

"If I turn around right now, I don't know how much shaving is actually going to take place." Conrad touched the hand on his shoulder, interlacing their fingers.

She tugged to turn him around. "Then perhaps shaving can wait."

He obeyed, tossing his razor haphazardly towards the wash basin as he did. His hands found the slickness of her waist as his eyes dared a look down at her bare body. He moved into her, seeking the strength of her against him. The water soaked through his shirt, where her chest pressed against his. And everything inside him hummed. "I am... massively overdressed for this situation."

"There's a simple fix for that," Ahria purred as she lifted her chin and kissed his neck. "I'm tired of this... distance between us. I want to be yours." Her eyes searched his, bright and clear.

His hands explored up her body, nails playing along her skin. "You are mine," he whispered, voice growing deeper. He neared her mouth, placing a gentle kiss on her lower lip before pulling back to strip off his shirt. But then he returned to her, feeling her wet bare skin against his own. He ran a hand back into her hair, gently removing the leather securing it. "Just as I am yours."

Ahria's hair cascaded down her back, sticking to her wet shoulders. Her touch trailed down his ribs, his stomach, until her fingers played with his belt. She tilted her head. "You've been waiting for me to be ready, but what about you?"

In answer, Conrad moved his hands to meet hers and unfastened his belt and the buttons of his breeches. "I want you, Ahria. And only you." With her help, he stepped from the remains of his clothing and moved into her. Her body was warm, despite the cooled water still clinging to her skin. His lips found hers, far more desperate than the brief kiss he'd given before. He sought more of her, their tongues playing as everything beyond the feel of her body blurred.

Touching either side of his face, Ahria whimpered into the kiss, nipping his lip before pulling away. Her lips glistened, and she parted enough to gaze down his body. Pink colored her cheeks as she took in every inch of him, and he couldn't help but do the same.

Her tanned skin, full breasts, and toned limbs.

His mouth dried like the sands of a desert, chest heaving for breath as his body demanded more. Reaching for her hand, he stepped backward, encouraging her to follow as they moved into the bedroom. He soaked in the sight of her body as she moved, the sway of her hips and her curious glances down at him. It felt as if he should have been self conscious, as exposed as he was. But with her, none of it mattered. He wanted to share himself with her, however she wanted him. Whatever would bring her the most satisfaction. The most pleasure.

Taking her hands, Conrad slowly turned Ahria to where she backed against the bed's edge. His hands traced up her arms then down her body, savoring every curve as he watched his finger tips explore.

"I love you," she whispered, hands on his chest. Sitting back onto the bed, she rolled her lips together as she slid backward to the center.

He pursued, crawling onto the bed between her legs. His kisses touched her knee as he moved in, caressing up the inside of her leg as he dared closer to places unknown. He felt her tense with each new wet line, and it made his body burn. He kissed onto her stomach, slowly inching further over her body as she laid back. Positioning his hips between her thighs, he nibbled on her neck.

Ahria's breath drifted over his shoulder at a fast pace, her hands gliding over his back with the drag of her nails.

It sent a chill through him that demanded he take her, but he drew away to brush a strand of hair from her jaw. "I love you, too," he whispered, feeling her breath against his lips. She arched against him, and their lips met in a flurry just as he pressed into her in a slow, euphoric joining.

A groan escaped him as she gasped, her body tensing beneath him as her mouth left his. Her breath shook, and she bit his shoulder, panting as she gripped him.

He paused, despite every instinct and desire urging him to continue after he pulled back. "Should I stop?" He knew it hurt for her, as opposed to what being within her felt like for him. He kissed her softer, shaking as he held the position just inside her.

Ahria shook her head, chest heaving. "No. Just..." She flashed him a smile before swallowing and shaking her head again. "Just go slow."

He kissed her gently as he shifted his hips, pushing deep as slowly as he could. "Tell me if you need me to stop."

She nodded, running a hand over his hair before kissing him again.

His mouth lingered with hers as he moved gently within her. With each careful motion, her body started to relax, while his only grew more needy. The sensation of her made thought nearly impossible, but the feel of her hands on his back and mouth on his brought him back to the slow rhythm she needed.

After a short time, her hips rocked with his, her heels pressing into the backs of his legs. She kissed him harder, moaning into his mouth. "More," she murmured, her tongue exploring his.

With a rough kiss, Conrad pressed harder into her, his hips moving faster. He reached back to grip her thigh.

Ahria let out a whimper, her legs tightening around him as she met each thrust. Breaking the kiss, she tilted her head back, nails digging into his back hard enough to leave marks. Her lips parted for her breath, eyes shut tight.

The combination of sensations sent lightning down Conrad's body, a moan echoing against her flesh as he kissed her neck and shoulder, teeth grazing her skin. He felt the brink of ecstasy creeping in, but fought to hold it back, forcing himself to slow.

"No, don't stop," she breathed, her voice ragged.

Gritting his jaw, he returned to the faster pace, his entire being shaking with restraint. But then her body jolted, eyes flying open as heat rippled from within. She cried out, pulling him closer, deeper, until he could hold out no longer.

Ecstasy tore through him, and his cry followed hers as he buried himself as far as he could.

They eased their pace together, slowing until she kissed him again, their bodies slick with bathwater and sweat. As she withdrew her lips, her eyes shimmered, the corners of her mouth twitching upward.

Conrad smiled down at her, tracing her jaw. His mind still felt as if it soared far above the bed, but her beauty anchored him down. "I love you, Ahria," he whispered, still unwilling to part from her entirely.

"And I, you." Ahria caressed over his back, holding him against her. "I never want to be without you."

"You never will be." He kissed her slowly, drawing out the sensual movements. "I'll always be right by your side."

She let out a breath, smiling back at him. "That was incredible."

"I'm already looking forward to the next time, so I can show you again how much I love you." He trailed a kiss over her jaw to her neck and near her ear. "However, I think we both need a bath now."

Ahria chuckled. "It can wait, can't it? I just want to lay here with you, and we have nowhere to be, anyway."

As she shifted onto her side, he withdrew from her. They moved together towards the other side of the bed, repositioning to hold each other, legs entwined.

They laid in comfortable silence for a time, until Ahria nuzzled further into his neck and murmured, "Can I ask you something?"

"Of course." There was no hesitation in his mind, which was different than he was used to. That question usually led to trouble when he was the captain of a ship, but with Ahria... He kissed the top of her head, pulling her closer. "Ask me anything, Mouse."

She sighed against him, her warm breath gliding over his skin. "You never told me much about your father. He died too, didn't he?"

His body tensed before he could control it. "A long time ago, yes. I think I was two."

"I'm sorry," she whispered, tracing idle patterns on his bare chest. "Do you know much about him?"

The question woke something deep within him. Things he hadn't thought about in a long time, even though they were so important to who he was. He hadn't really known his father, but in another way, could never forget him because of the blood they shared. Blood he didn't talk about, with anyone. He remained quiet, rubbing his thumb along her shoulder as he considered the paths that lay before him.

He'd avoided the topic of his father most of his life. Lied when he couldn't. Fortunately, at Talia's insistence, even parliament hadn't inquired for much detail. Not that there was any to find.

"You don't have to talk about him if you don't want to." Ahria pulled away slightly, looking up at him with concern in her bright eyes.

"It's not that." He chewed his lip. "I just... I've never told anyone the truth about my father, because it's admitting a truth about me."

Ahria tilted her head, propping it up on an elbow. "Now I'm even more curious."

"My mum met him on the beach in Treama when she was sixteen. He wasn't much older. She told me her fishing net had gotten caught on some rocks deep out in the strait, and she'd broken into tears in the surf when he just came walking out with it between his arms, the fish still tangled up in it. She said it was his eyes that really drew her in. I only inherited the color, though. Not the shape of his pupil or I suspect my childhood would have been far more interesting." He tried to imagine the scene as he explained it, realizing it was the first time he'd thought about the moment in years. He tried to envision what his father must have looked like, but in reality, he couldn't even begin to guess.

Blinking slowly, Ahria stared at him, lips parted in stunned silence. She swallowed. "Your father... was an alcan?"

He nodded slowly, considering how strange it felt even as she said it.

Even though I've been half alcan my entire life.

"I don't remember what he looked like at all. All I have is a strange bead that she put on a silver chain for me after he left. Mum tried to keep his face in my mind for a while, telling me stories, but over time... it just faded. And she stopped talking about it. I could see how much it hurt her when she realized he truly wasn't coming home. She said it meant he was dead. That's what I remember from when I was a child. My mum's pain." He pulled back from Ahria, studying her face to try to read what was going through her mind. He shook his head. "I've never told anyone. Even Leiura doesn't know."

Her mouth twitched in the briefest smile. "I won't say anything." Her eyes roamed over his face, searching, no doubt, for the hints of his heritage she missed. "You're half alcan." Disbelief echoed in her breathy voice, her expression unreadable.

He swallowed, touching her cheek. "I don't look it, I know. Which always made blending in easier. I got enough teasing as a child with an absent father. Then on the ships... After I stowed away I learned quickly that just because I'm half alcan doesn't mean sailors like me on their crews. So I abandoned that part of me. And now, especially, there's no room for it. I'm a Zionan prince now. My mother's son."

Ahria exhaled, and her body's tension eased with it. "Why are you telling me? It would have been easy to leave it out."

Reaching for her hand, he lifted her knuckles to his lips. "I know I can trust you with all that I am. And even if I don't accept myself, I know you will."

She gave him a soft smile, stroking his face with a slight shake of her head. "You're amazing." Her brow quirked. "Can you breathe underwater?"

He chuckled, propping his head up to mirror her. "I can... But I hope that doesn't inspire you to start testing me."

Ahria laughed for the first time since losing her father, and the sound ricocheted through Conrad in a beautiful melody. "I promise, no drowning attempts." Her expression softened, as if she, too, just realized what had happened, and she sighed. "Thank you for telling me."

"I should have told you sooner." He played with a lock of her hair. "I'm just grateful you put up with me and all my bull headedness."

Leaning into him, she brushed her lips against his as she spoke. "I think it would be mighty hypocritical of me to complain."

Heat rose in his chest and he kissed her, rolling onto his back as she followed. Conversation lost out to kisses, and time crept by in blissful ignorance.

The morning passed, filled with nothing but Ahria, pulling Conrad's thoughts far away from the demands of his life. And he hoped the distraction worked equally as well for her.

As his stomach rumbled hours later, thought gradually returned, and he remembered the letter he'd tossed on the table in their sitting room. He still wasn't sure what it said, but it mentioned that evening. Likely the royal visitors would be arriving and his mother was requesting his presence.

He grimaced at the idea. Asking Ahria to return to the New Kingston palace was out of the question, and he had no interest in leaving her alone after what had occurred before. Especially now...

"What is it?" She tilted her head, stroking his arm as she lay cuddled against him.

"The letter from my mum." He wouldn't keep secrets. "I think it said something about the royals from Helgath and Isalica arriving tonight. She'll be expecting me."

"Do you have to go?" Ahria's tone melted something in his chest, even as she tried to conceal her disappointment.

Conrad turned further onto his side, facing her. "I'm not going to go." He caressed her side. "I said it before and I still mean it. I'm not meant for this political bullshit." His mind whirled with what he would tell his mother. How he would explain his absence. All of it just led him to thinking of the sea. Of Dawn Chaser. Anything but court.

"I think we'll have a fine time entertaining ourselves this evening, anyway. Maybe you can go another day." Ahria ran her thumb over his bottom lip. "Hmm, Captain?"

He reached for her hand, touching her wrist. "Run away with me instead?" He wove his fingers with hers. "We can just leave. It'd be easy from here. I choose you over everything else. You're more important than all of it."

Ahria's brow furrowed, and she propped herself up on an elbow. "You want to leave?" She traced his jaw, inching her body closer to his.

"I've thought about it a hundred times since this whole prince nonsense started. I'm not meant to be here." He wrapped his arms around her. "All it's been doing is trying to pull me away from you, and I don't want that."

"What do you mean? Who is trying to pull you away from me?" Worry tainted her voice, and she touched her forehead to his.

"Advisors, chancellors. Everyone is so wrapped up in the politics of it all. And overly concerned about who I'm *supposed* to marry. But I don't want anyone but you." He ran his hand through her hair and over her cheek. "I'm supposed to be with you."

"You want to go back to Dawn Chaser?" Ahria laid her head back down, nuzzling close to him.

"Dawn Chaser, another ship... Middle of the woods. I don't care where it is. As long as it's not a Zionan court where I have to play diplomat and go along with what parliament thinks I should be doing."

With her lips pressed to his neck, she murmured, "I'll go wherever you want. We could pack tonight and leave tomorrow."

 Chapter 10

Travel through the portal left Kin's stomach in a tangled mess all the way through to the arranged dinner. He'd accepted that meeting Ahria would likely not happen immediately, which only worsened the turmoil.

At his side the entire time, Amarie did little to ease his nerves, on edge herself. Funneled directly from the military barracks into closed carriages bound for the palace, the group of Isalican and Helgathian royals reunited briefly in the palace foyer before being separated to change into their dinner attire. He'd loathed being forced apart from Amarie, every tension in him growing until he saw her again in the corridor outside the dining hall.

She wore clean leather pants, a red tunic, and a tan corset vest. Her hair had been done in an intricate updo, with braids similar to Zionan warriors.

Given the Zionan origin of the Berylian Key, it was no wonder she wore it so well.

Kin tried not to look too closely, too long, or admire her too deeply. She wanted to be friends, at least for now, and torturing himself felt pointless. Yet, he stared at her. The mother of his child he hadn't known of, the woman he'd never leave again.

The kiss they'd shared that night before reaching Veralian still buzzed in his memory. He wondered if it was a hint of her genuine emotions, or just a slice of nostalgia she humored him with.

"Never thought I'd be dining with kings and queens," Amarie whispered to him, stepping close. She reached for his arm, but made a fist and lowered her hand instead. "I feel so useless without…"

A small woman with long dark hair draped over her shoulders stepped up beside Amarie, her elegant ice-blue dress whispering across the polished stone floor of the hall. She looked up at Kin with a smile that spread to her dark eyes. He'd seen her briefly before and after the portal, but she'd been distracted working the Art necessary to transport them. "I don't believe we've had the pleasure of meeting formally." She held a hand out to him. "Though I have heard quite a bit about you."

Kin hid his confusion as he accepted the portal opener's hand. "I'm sorry, you have?"

"My husband has told me enough. Matthias thinks highly of you." The woman gave him a gentle smile. "I'm Katrin."

Amarie's polite smile faded. "Wait. You're the Isalican queen?"

The queen nodded as she patted Amarie's elbow. "And believe me. I never thought I'd be dining with kings and queens either, until I found myself becoming one." She looked towards the sound of the doors to the dining hall opening. "Fortunately, most of those who will be in the room come from fairly humble beginnings. Just people who are trying to do good for the world."

Neco yipped at Jarrod's side down the hall at another set of doors before promptly sitting as if receiving some unspoken message to behave. He looked plaintively up at the king, who entered the dining hall with his husband.

Matthias casually approached, offering his arm to Katrin. "Ready, Priestess?"

Amarie said nothing as the two walked inside, Rae and Damien entering behind Jarrod and Corin.

She looked up at Kin, now alone with him in the corridor. "We're surrounded by strangers." Keeping her voice low, she angled her body away from the doors they were to walk through. "I have your back. Do you have mine?"

"Of course I do, but it won't come to that. These people are still our best chance to find Ahria."

"Whatever any of this comes to. Today, tomorrow... Whatever comes, we have to stick together. No secrets between us, all right?" Her eyes bored into him, and he realized in that moment that she still trusted him. On some deeper level, she saw him as an ally, and gratitude calmed his insides.

"No secrets." He touched her arm, gently gripping her bicep. "We'll get through this."

She nodded, narrowing her eyes at him before nodding a second time. "All right." Turning from him as he let go of her, she caught his hand and gave a tug. "Let's see what they say."

Kin nodded as he gripped her hand, following into the dining hall. His memory took him back to when she'd led him into the Great Library's east tower, but before he could reminisce over their night on the beach, she let go and took her seat on the Helgathian side of the table next to Rae.

Kin looked down at his attire. The fine tunic wasn't too unlike something he'd worn before on his parents' estate, but the pale blue was still unusual. He'd grown accustomed to wearing only black for so long, that the body he looked down on hardly seemed to be his. But the attire was purposeful, to make him look like an Isalican dignitary. And reminded him of his seat at the table. He took his seat beside Dani. He'd heard Katrin say her name when first opening the portal.

The blind crown elite fixated her cloudy gaze on him. "It took me a while to get used to the Isalican colors, too." Her airy voice barely reached his ears, and she smiled.

Her accent was strange, something he hadn't heard before, but it felt rude to ask her about it. He stiffened, studying her face. "How do you know I'm having a hard time?"

Clicking her tongue, Dani found her water glass and took a sip. "You're fidgeting with your clothing more than you were before. You're anxious. I don't blame you. And you smell of discontent."

Tugging on the bottom of his tunic, Kin scolded himself for only further confirming her observations. "Anyone ever tell you that that's kind of creepy sounding?"

Dani laughed. "You have no idea."

"Careful, or she'll show you her claws." Micah leaned back from his seat on Dani's other side, grinning at Kin. "Though I'd argue the teeth are worse."

The white-haired elite broke into a grin as well. "It's been a while since you dared spar with me. Need reminding?"

Micah snickered. "It's hardly fair when you can shift into a gods' damned panther, D."

Kin's stomach flipped, the accent suddenly making sense. "If I didn't know any better, you sound like you're a Feyorian Dtrüa. But you're Isalican, now?"

Dani tilted her head, clicking her tongue again. "I am both of those things. Just as you are a Shade and yet not a Shade." She hummed. "Did you know a man by the name of Lasseth Frey?"

The name stirred a myriad of emotions within him. The combination with everything that already existed made his head ache. "I knew him." He reached for a water glass, urging himself not to down it all in one gulp. "He led me to Damien."

Talking about all of this with strangers doesn't seem right. But they already know.

He couldn't determine the true source of his anger with Damien for sharing his secrets. It only began with him telling all of these people about who he was. Did they understand the depth of his mistakes? His regrets? He looked at the Rahn'ka, who smiled in a quiet conversation with his brother. If he didn't know the truth, he might have suspected Corin to be Damien's father due to the difference in their aging.

"Lasseth helped me, a very long time ago. As did his partner." Dani touched his forearm so softly he hardly noticed. "None of us judge you for your shadows. We've all been there."

The main doors to the dining hall opened, and Kin followed suit as everyone at the table stood for the Zionan queen's entrance.

She was a small woman, not much taller than Katrin, but with her fluid steps came a grand presence. The black train of her surcoat trailed along the ground behind her, but didn't obstruct the view of the traditional flowy pants of the Zionan royal court. The corset, lined with golden embroidery, displayed wealth, and flowed up over her shoulders in a wreathed pattern of thistles. Her hair fell in tight curls to her shoulders, a gold barrette shining in the candlelight from the chandelier.

Two women followed her, advisors based on the way they were dressed, and moved to the seats directly beside the queen's at the head of the table.

"Apologies for making you wait." She looked at the two kings on either side of the table, needing to acknowledge them first. "Your sudden arrival came as a bit of a surprise."

Kin studied her all black attire, a curious choice when everyone else in the room clearly represented their countries. The two advisors both wore the traditional Zionan purple, but none of it could be seen on their queen.

Amarie mentioned Talon worked with the queen. She must be in mourning for him.

At the thought, he glanced at Amarie, who stared at the queen's black attire with bright, glassy eyes.

The Zionan queen's hand trembled as it touched the back of her chair, but before she could pull it out for herself, the two advisors on either side did it for her. She subtly jerked back, but gracefully set her hands to her side in recovery. Focused entirely on the seat she meant to take, the rigidness of her stature and squared jaw gave away just how the queen was feeling. And Kin knew the look in her eyes too well.

She's terrified.

He immediately questioned why, but as her gaze flitted to Matthias and Jarrod—and only them—he understood. She wasn't accustomed to such company, either. Katrin had said most in the room came from humble beginnings, but he hadn't realized the same applied to the queen they were visiting.

Didn't someone say she was new to this? How new?

"Not necessary." Matthias spoke in an even tone as they all sat. "Our means of arrival are far from common. Thank you for agreeing to meet with us on such short notice."

"I'll confess, the urgency alludes to something of greater concern than mere treatise conversations." The queen moved her hands to her lap beneath the table, watching Matthias carefully as if he might reveal something.

Neco groaned, somewhere near Jarrod's feet, but the Helgathian king ignored the wolf.

The hall doors opened again, and this time, serving staff brought in covered plates. Setting one in front of each guest, they removed the shiny domes at the same time, offering wine or water to fill glasses.

"Wine, please," Amarie murmured.

Kin nodded to the offer of wine as well, turning his attention back to the Zionan queen and wishing she would understand exactly why they were there. Give them the answers they needed. But she never focused beyond the kings and their partners at the table. An improvement from just the kings themselves. Kin accepted the best course of action was to listen and hope Matthias or Jarrod got to the point for him and Amarie.

"We were also hoping for an audience with your son." Jarrod sipped his red wine. "Is he here?"

"Unfortunately, your speed also prohibited my son from joining us." The tone in her voice suggested annoyance. Intonation suggested at her son rather than the question. "Conrad is not yet accustomed to the demands of his position."

"Being thrust into royalty has a way of throwing someone off their axis." Jarrod chuckled. "Believe it or not, I was once a thief. I understand." He nodded at the server who brought a plate and settled it onto the ground for Neco.

The closest to a real smile yet came to the queen's lips as she looked at Jarrod. "Thank you." She reached for the wine glass in front of her, the first movement she'd made since sitting. "If you don't mind my curiosity, why the interest in my son?"

"Because he knows someone, and we're looking for her." Amarie leaned forward, finally drawing the queen's gaze past the kings.

The queen's dark eyes widened, the wine glass freezing inches from her lips. The two advisors at her sides looked appalled, but the queen just looked perplexed. She swallowed before putting her glass down less delicately than she'd picked it up. She never looked away from Amarie. "And who are you?"

The room silenced with the question, silverware pausing mid bite.

Amarie stiffened, hesitating. "My name is Amarie."

The queen remained frozen, but her eyes spoke of a million thoughts rushing through her. Her eyes shimmered with unshed tears, confirming her knowledge of who Amarie was. She sucked in a breath, like she'd forgotten to for the moments that had passed. "You look so much like her." It came in a soft whisper.

Kin's gaze flashed back to Amarie, whose chin quivered for only a breath.

"I do?" Amarie smiled, brow twitching.

The queen returned the smile, but it faded as the water in her eyes grew. "But Talon..."

"I know," Amarie whispered, nodding through her tight voice. "I know. He died a hero."

The queen's shoulders relaxed, the tension fading before she rolled her shoulders as if trying to pull herself back together. She quickly lifted a napkin to her eyes, dabbing as she looked at Matthias. "I'm sorry."

Matthias lifted a hand, shaking his head. "Please don't apologize. We're very sorry for your loss, and for Ahria's. We only look to reunite her with family. It is why we seek your son."

Talia dabbed at her other eye, glancing at the advisor between her and Matthias, then back down to Amarie. "So there are matters beyond the treaty of a more personal matter." The queen rolled her shoulders again with a soft sniff.

"Aye," Jarrod confirmed. "We apologize for not being forthcoming from the beginning, but you must understand the sensitive nature of this knowledge."

"Seeing as this is personal, I do not see a need for you to remain and waste your evenings Sedova and Keis." The queen looked at the advisors on either side. "Please take your leave and ask the staff not to return unless we request their services."

They waited as the two advisors at the end of the table vacated their seats. They cast suspicious glances at each other, but left out the door the queen had entered, taking the one remaining staff member in the room with them. The door latched shut and an eerie quiet descended.

"I assume everyone else remaining in this room is privy to this... *sensitive* knowledge?" The queen seemed to relax now that the others had left the room, her shoulders slacking as she leaned back in her chair.

Matthias nodded. "Yes, your majesty."

"Talia, please."

"Talia," Matthias continued, glancing at Damien until the Rahn'ka nodded. "Your city has suffered an attack from a Shade. We are of the mindset to imprison the man who controls the Shades. May we see your forearm? Only to confirm that we may trust you." He pushed up his own sleeve, turning his hand palm-up so she could see his tattoos were nothing like the geometric shapes branding Uriel's minions.

She studied his arm for a moment before she lifted her own and rolled up her sleeve. Her right forearm was bare, except for a few scars that looked like burns from a stove. "And you are all working together towards this? I had believed Shades were mere legend until a week ago."

Kin hoped that they wouldn't all have to lift their sleeves to confirm their alignment, the tattoo beneath the scar burning at the mere thought of it. He didn't want to endure the queen's glares if she realized what he'd been.

Jarrod nodded, along with the others. "We wish to put an end to it."

"But to do so," Damien added. "We need Ahria."

Amarie scowled at the Rahn'ka, lips pressed into a thin line. "So that we may inform Ahria, so she can decide what to do."

Talia brushed her sleeve back down. "Is this related to the power Ahria's acquired?" She looked at Amarie again. "Conrad told me they believed you to be dead, yet here you are. Should I be asking to see your forearm as well?"

Amarie pushed her sleeve up and angled her unbranded arm toward the queen. "I did die." She pulled the material back over her arm. "A friend revived me, but not before the power I wielded transferred to my daughter."

"This all sounds like one of those epic novels I used to read to Connie when he was young." Talia lifted the wine to her lips, taking a long drink. She shook her head as she studied Amarie, as if confirming again how much she looked like her daughter. The queen then took a slow look around the room, eyeing the Helgathian side first before pausing on Kin. She stared into his eyes, and it made him want to shift in his seat. He refused to look away, praying she'd see his innocence.

"She has your eyes... But you're both so young..." Talia spoke slowly.

Amarie cleared her throat. "Kin is Ahria's father by blood. We've both been... trapped within an Aueric spell for the last two decades."

Talia drew in a steadying breath. "I think I need more wine for this."

"Will you tell us where she is?" Amarie glanced at Kin. "Or would you send word to her that we're here?"

"I will arrange a carriage in the morning to take you to her, but there will be rules governing your approach to the estate. Her power, from what I understand, is volatile." Talia finished her glass, and Jarrod retrieved the decanter from the middle of the table to top it up for her. "Conrad has been quite strict in how visits occur."

"We can respect that." Kin wasn't sure his voice still worked until he spoke. "As long as we're able to see Ahria. Amarie can teach her to control her power."

Talia paused. "What about the proposed alliance between our countries? Was that merely a ruse to garner my attention?" Her tone held nothing accusatory, but Matthias still straightened.

"Absolutely not," he countered. "Helgath and Isalica have been working together for fourteen years. Adding Ziona to our agreements would strengthen us as a whole, and we'd be honored if you'd consider aligning your country with ours."

"And these agreements pertain to this grand plan to imprison this man who controls Shades?"

"Aye, but not solely for that purpose." Jarrod scratched Neco's head as the wolf sat up. "Trade between Isalica and Helgath has never been more prosperous. Your people would benefit, as would ours."

Talia looked at Jarrod, side-eyeing the wolf. "There has not been peace between our countries in some time." She set her glass aside. "I know Helgath has changed much since your house came into power, and Ziona is changing still. You think our people are ready for us to finally not be at odds?"

Jarrod and Matthias both nodded, but Jarrod motioned for the Isalican king to reply.

"I'd like to believe so. While there may be residual tension between our people, I believe the best way to promote peace is to start with it ourselves. We wish nothing from your country but your allegiance and discretion."

Talia smirked. "Several of my chancellors have been suggesting alliance by way of marriage, but I will assure you, that is not something Conrad will agree to."

Corin barked a laugh, then promptly shut his mouth.

Jarrod chuckled. "Our daughter told us, before we left, that if we so much as thought about offering her hand in marriage, she'd take Neco and run away forever." He patted the black canine, who whined.

Katrin lifted her hand. "I can confirm she was asking me what it was like to be a priestess and devoted to only the gods this very afternoon."

"She asked me about being a soldier," Dani mused. "Perhaps she is restless."

"What else is new," Corin grumbled.

Laughter eased the room as silverware resumed and everyone allowed themselves to eat.

But Amarie stared at her plate, holding her fork without using it.

Kin wished there was a way for him to reach her across the expansive table. He leaned forward while the others around them conversed more casually. "You should eat. You'll probably need it tomorrow to keep up with our daughter."

Amarie looked up at him, a soft smile touching her lips. "Tomorrow."

Chapter 11

The sun warmed Ahria's skin in a way she hadn't felt for days. Peace settled her insides, quieting the lingering anger in her heart. The never-ending grief.

She stood in the courtyard, beside the crater she'd made a few days before, and practiced with her power yet again. Delving into her meditative state, she visited the energy, visualized it, but didn't take any.

The day before with Conrad had opened a new realm within herself. Within her soul. They'd connected in a way she'd never thought possible. And soon, everything would change. Again.

Inside the estate, Conrad packed their things. He would leave a note for his mother, and in a few hours, they'd be on the move. If he didn't want to stay in New Kingston, neither did she. She had no wish to be queen one day, and running away with Conrad made her future feel brighter. Less burdened.

The hairs on the back of her neck stood up, and her eyes snapped open. First, they fell to the large oak tree, but no one stood there. The summer breeze shook its leaves, casting shadows on the charred spot on the trunk. But there was no one in those shadows. Yet, she couldn't shake the feeling that someone was watching her.

Ever since she'd discovered the footprints, she'd remained alert. But she'd seen no trace of anyone.

Her stomach twisted, but she urged herself to remember her father's words.

Don't be afraid of it. Be certain.

Shutting her eyes again, she returned to the place of power within herself. She stood on the beach of the roiling ocean, wondering just how deep it ran. Determined not to fail again, she reached for the water and took less this time. Settling it into her palm, she followed the routine Talon had taught before she ever had power, taking the energy back to her physical body.

Somewhere in the courtyard, a branch snapped, and she opened her eyes. Her power pooled in her palm, but she didn't acknowledge it as she stared across the grass.

At Vaeler.

Her insides churned, mouth drying as her breath came faster.

Impossible. He's dead.

Vaeler barely moved, watching her from thirty yards away. He stood beside the closed gate, meant to keep anyone else out. It hadn't stopped his ghost. Which looked far too solid to not be him.

Ahria's hand burned, and she looked down. The energy in her palm had brightened into a flame, and it rushed into her veins to gather more of itself.

"Shit," she murmured, looking up to find Vaeler gone. "What's going on?" Her heart pounded in her ears, but she tried to focus on her power. Tried to put it back where it'd come from and erect walls to contain the surging waves. Her heart beat faster as whatever meager walls she built shattered, skin growing hot as beryl and blue sparks lined her vision. "No, no, no. Not again."

"You don't need to be afraid." Vaeler appeared closer this time, as if he'd merely been hiding behind the tree.

"You're a ghost. My imagination." Ahria's voice shook. "The Shade killed you." The energy coursed stronger through her, drawing more from the ocean within even as she fought it.

"Breathe," Vaeler murmured, voice calm and reassuring. "I got away. I'm alive."

She stared at him, wanting to believe what he was saying. Conrad had said someone had escaped.

They didn't find all the bodies.

Vaeler looked to the ground between them. "I'm so sorry about your father."

Grief twisted like a knife in her gut, and she could no longer contain what whipped around inside her. The hiding aura preventing the full escape of her power faltered. Invisible, save for the flicks of blue flame at her feet, the Key's energy exploded out from her, and she desperately sought to pull it back in. "You're not real."

Vaeler stepped closer, taking her hands. "I am. I am real. I'm sorry I disappeared on you, but I can explain. You're losing control, Ahria. Breathe. Breathe through the Key's desires. You're in control."

Ahria furrowed her brow, trying to do as he instructed. "How do you know what I am?"

"I can explain that later, too." Vaeler squeezed her hands. "Breathe with me."

Tension lurked in her stomach, freezing her in place. "Conrad!"

"It's all right." Vaeler didn't move, his grip unfaltering. In the reflection of his eyes, she could see her bright violet irises.

Looking down, she gasped at the flames that encircled their hands, not burning Vaeler's skin, either.

Time moved slowly as she waited to hear the front doors of the estate open behind her. The doors slammed against the outside of the building, with Conrad's boots pounding down the steps. The sheath of his sword rasped against his blade as he withdrew it.

"What the hells... Vaeler?" Conrad's steps faltered on the gravel drive.

"Breathe." Vaeler kept focused on Ahria, only glancing at the prince. "She's on the verge of losing control." He let her go, stepping back.

"I'm tired of everyone telling me to fucking breathe." Ahria still stared at her hands, breathing shaky as she tried to rein in the energy.

Conrad's sword fell to the ground near her feet as he slipped into place in front of her. He pressed his hand against her chest, the other sweeping her hair back from her face. "You got this, Mouse." His thumb tapped a slow rhythm against her sternum to set the pace of her breathing. "I'm right here."

Focusing on him and the beat of his thumb, Ahria breathed in through her nose, out her mouth, and repeated it until the power dimmed. It flowed back to her core, dissipating from the morning air.

"I'm all right." She nodded, leaning into him.

"I need you to come with me. Right now." Vaeler walked around Conrad until he could see her face.

Conrad held Ahria against him, his face pressed to her hair. She could feel the tension of his body beneath the steady beat of his heart. It was easy to imagine the glare he was likely giving Vaeler. "You can't just show up and say something like that. We thought you were dead."

"I know. I'm sorry. I can explain everything, but there isn't time right now. You need to leave here. Someone is coming, and until we can determine what his intentions are, I must keep you safe."

"What are you talking about? We? Who is *we*?" Ahria looked up at Conrad, a new fear drifting through her.

Breaking away from her, Conrad stooped to retrieve his sword, shifting to hold it between Ahria and Vaeler as he wrapped his arm protectively around her waist. "Explain." The one word, spoken in a command, took her right back to being on Dawn Chaser.

Vaeler's jaw flexed. "You can trust me. You don't need to go with me, but you need to leave here, now."

"We are. We're leaving soon, anyway." Ahria nudged Conrad. "It's all right. I'll get our packs and be right back." She waited for him to nod before jogging back to the house.

Conrad sheathed his sword as Ahria started up the front stairs, and he pointed at Vaeler. "You stay with me."

Vaeler lifted his empty hands. "Not going anywhere."

Ahria bounded up the stairs and rushed to their room. Conrad had neatly bundled their packs together, a tangle of clothes on the floor in front of the final bag. He'd probably been about to put it away when her cry for him had caused him to drop it. She hurriedly gathered it and shoved it into the pack, securing the straps with haste. Slinging both packs over her shoulder, she crossed to the tall front windows.

Breath halted in her lungs as a person raced through the trees towards the now open gate, rather than coming from the road, another stranger not far behind the first. At the distant curve of the road, she could just make out a pair of carriages. Her gaze flew to Conrad, his sword drawn again, his back pressed to the inside of the wall beside the gate, with Vaeler on the opposite side.

They already noticed.

"Shit." She turned from the sight, hurrying back down the stairs.

Someone had come for her. Learned of her power, perhaps.

Vaeler was right.

Power pulsed through her, and blue flames billowed out from under her feet as she raced for the courtyard.

Chapter 12

A few minutes earlier...

With each jostle of the carriage, Amarie's heart lurched.

This is actually happening.

She'd get to meet her daughter. Their daughter.

Glancing at Kin next to her, she wondered if he felt the same excitement. Anxiety. She'd barely slept the night before, knowing Ahria was so close. Her baby girl, who was no longer a baby at all.

Kin's jaw twitched as he stared out the window where trees bounced by, his hand pinching at the hem of his breeches. He'd been silent since that morning when he'd spoken only a quick good morning while they helped themselves to coffee and pastries laid out in a parlor shared between all the visiting royals.

Across from them now, Rae and Damien sat quietly, exchanging a glance every so often.

By the minute expressions on their faces, Amarie wondered if they could speak to each other without using their voices. She didn't understand enough about Damien's power to know for sure, but her gut suggested it was true.

Amarie closed her eyes, willing the minutes and miles to pass faster.

The carriage slowed. Stopped. The driver jumped down, and Amarie sat straighter, poking her head out the window.

The driver walked up the road.

"Why is she leaving us here?" Amarie couldn't remember what the set protocol had been for their approach, too distracted by who they were going to see.

"She needs to check in and get permission before we can proceed. Something the prince demanded of all visitors." Damien leaned to glance out the window after the driver. "The queen said something particular about Art users not being allowed to visit at all, but no one's been super clear as to why." He settled back, eyeing Amarie with lifted eyebrows.

"It's because she could kill them." Amarie only glanced at him before looking out the window again. "If her power takes control, she wouldn't be able to stop it from burning every practitioner from the inside out."

"That feels like vital information I wish I'd known earlier." Damien's hand flexed against Rae's as he looked at Kin, who only shrugged.

"I told you days ago that I could kill you in a touch, not my fault you didn't put two and two together. Besides, I don't think you can really complain about anyone else withholding information." Amarie cast a pointed look in their direction. "Seeing as both of you seem to have a penchant for keeping everyone else in the dark."

"Fair." Rae rolled her lips together. "But we tried to..." As her voice trailed off, her brow knitted. She looked at Damien, embarking in more of their silent conversation.

"What?" Kin finally spoke, staring at them.

Rae hesitated, just staring at her husband.

"This is one of those times," Amarie ground out through clenched teeth. "Care to share?"

Damien met Amarie's glare, his expression calm. "We can feel the Berylian Key... Ahria's power. We couldn't a moment ago, so something must have caused a surge." His eyes grew distant, and a faint glow erupted from beneath the collar of his shirt as the tattoos on his skin came to life. "I can't tell why." He winced before shaking his head. "But if what you say is true, we can't get any closer."

"No," Amarie growled. "*You* can't." Shoving the carriage door open, she jumped out, taking in the view of the road and forest. The trees weren't too dense, granting her the sight of a stone wall in the distance.

She hesitated for only a breath, then burst into a run towards the estate. She had no power, no Art. Her daughter's power couldn't hurt her. Keeping to the trees, she sprinted for the wall.

"Amarie, wait!" Rae's shout came before the open and close of the carriage door as Kin exited, too.

The driver still meandered down the road, but on seeing her, she balked and raced back towards the carriage.

The wall, high and smooth, offered little vantage for climbing, so Amarie ran along the outside, praying the gate would be unlocked. The gravel crunched beneath her boots, spraying bits of stone behind her with each stride. Her heart pounded, breath already ragged.

Kin ran somewhere behind her, but she hardly noticed as she rounded an elegant pillar that supported an iron-wrought gate, open towards the wilderness and her.

She glided around the gate, looking into the lush green of the courtyard when her momentum faltered.

Something caught her arm, jerking her around before her eyes could focus on anything within the estate. Her surroundings spun until her back collided with the wall. The sun flashed on metal, blinding her for a moment. Blinking, she froze when a sword and dagger pointed at her throat came into focus.

Amarie lifted her hands to the two men who stood before her.

Blades can kill me now.

She gulped, panting, but looked past them. Searching for any sign of Ahria. Her gaze landed on a crater, not unlike the one she accidentally created in Eralas when she'd temporarily lost control. A flash of Talon, sitting cross legged at the center, made her chest tighten.

The dagger disappeared, and the taller, leaner man stepped away.

The man with darker skin and ferocious eyes still pinned her, and she dared not move. "This is a private estate, and you are not welcome." The man's sword didn't waver, his hand steady.

"Conrad," the other man warned. "She's not the threat."

The front door to the estate opened, and Amarie's eyes landed on a woman about ten years younger than her. With dark chestnut hair and brilliant ice-blue eyes. Blue flames licked along the marble at the woman's feet, surging down the stairs like falling water.

Her heart would burst, she was sure of it.

"Ahria," Amarie whispered, voice cracking. Her chest heaved as she stared at her daughter.

Her daughter.

Tears burned her eyes, forming hot trails down her cheeks.

"No, not you!" The man with the dagger crossed to the gate, pulling his sword this time instead of the dagger. A runed copper sword.

Amarie twisted to the side, seeing Kin with a blade pointed straight at his chest.

The former Shade skidded to a stop in the drive, lifting his hands to the man who halted him. "I'm no threat." He kept his distance, and his grip lifted far from the sword at his right hip. "Last interaction I had with the faction, we parted on positive terms, so I'd rather not ruin that."

Amarie almost missed Kin's words.

Faction?

Ahria stared at them, unmoving. Her eyes flickered between them, azure flames still surrounding her feet and hands.

"I'm her mother," Amarie begged the man still holding her against the wall, voice hoarse.

Conrad edged his sword closer to her skin. "Amarie is dead, so don't lie."

Amarie shook her head, more tears spilling from her eyes. "I'm not lying. I did die. My friend revived me, but not before I saw Talon." She forced her gaze to harden on the man who kept her in

84

place. "He said she'd be with the Zionan prince, and that she'd be safe with him. That's you, right?"

Conrad stiffened, but his stance didn't falter. "Interesting story. Who'd you get all that information from?"

"Look at me," Amarie whispered to him. "Look at me, and look at her. It's true."

Ahria stepped onto the grass, slowly approaching through the courtyard. Her eyes bounced between her mother and Kin, the blue replaced with violet.

Her daughter.

Amarie smiled, despite the blade, and choked on a sob. "She's beautiful."

The prince glanced over his shoulder, his face softening. As he looked back at Amarie, he narrowed his eyes, hesitation in his breath. "Ahria?"

Ahria approached, the fire spreading wider. "What did you give me?"

Amarie huffed, swallowing before touching her fingers to the center of her collarbone. "A necklace. I gave you a necklace of the araleinya flower. Talon gave it to me before you were born, and I gave it to you."

Silence settled between them all for a few breaths before Ahria spoke again. "Who is that?" She pointed at Kin, held under guard by the other man.

"That's Kin," Amarie rasped. "Your father by blood."

Ahria gaped at them before shaking her head. "Let them go."

Conrad lowered his sword without delay, but the other man ignored the order. Kin remained a few feet away from him, his face pale as if he'd seen a ghost. But his eyes wouldn't leave Ahria despite the threat.

"Vaeler!" Ahria glared at the man holding the copper sword. "Stand down."

Amarie eyed Conrad as she moved around him, keeping her hands visible.

A moment later, Vaeler lowered his weapon, but muttered something quietly to Kin that kept the former Shade in place.

Stepping towards her daughter, Amarie met her eyes. She studied her, taking in every feature that she could and remembering the baby she'd held in her arms too briefly. The guilt swelled within her, doubling the growing turmoil in her stomach. But every fiber was urging her forward as she walked into the flames, meeting Ahria in the middle, and reached for her.

Ahria's fire dimmed, and she took her mother's hand.

Bright light exploded.

Light and wind and power burst from the two women, hitting the others like a shockwave and throwing them back. A rippling aura in shades of purples and blues shone against the white walls of the estate like sun off the water. The men lifted their arms to their faces, all bracing to stay within the sphere of power as it pulsed outward.

Amarie gripped her daughter's hand, power scorching through her veins and igniting her soul. Her body vibrated, knees quaking beneath her. Everything that had died within her, the dried ocean of energy, reawakened. The roar of the waves cascaded through her mind, sending a buzz down every limb and inch of skin. She fought to recall what her hiding aura felt like as the power overtook her senses. Pushed all thought and action to the bottom of its depths. Her hair whipped back, strands stinging her face before she remembered who controlled the Key.

She could feel it all. Her energy, her power, but also Ahria's. With their hands entwined, she manipulated the force pulsing through Ahria's veins. Calmed it, and put it back where it had come from, deep within her daughter..

The light around them diminished, sparks and fire dissipating through the air.

Chapter 13

Conrad stooped to retrieve his sword from where it had fallen, blood dripping from the cut across his wrist from a rock caught in the explosion of energy. The wall behind him had stopped him from being thrown too far by the Berylian Key's power, but the impact sent waves of pain through him with each pulse of his heart. The injury couldn't distract from the revelations taking place in the courtyard.

He stared at Amarie, who looked so much like her daughter. And appeared only slightly older.

How is this possible? And what the hells just happened?

Vaeler and Kin had been pushed back further from the gate, but now Kin stood again, Vaeler close, still holding his copper sword even if he no longer pointed it at Ahria's father.

Conrad searched the dark-haired man for the features that would connect him to Ahria, following the line of a scar on his right cheek down to where he could see Kin's jaw tensing. The muscle twitching like he'd seen Ahria's do. And his eyes. The same steel blue he'd gazed into just that morning. He didn't look much older than Conrad himself.

The prince slid his sword into the sheath at his hip.

Ahria spoke to Amarie too quietly for him to hear.

Kin took a step forward to walk around Vaeler. But before he could, Vaeler blocked his path, copper glinting at his side and drawing both women's attention

Ahria waved a hand. "He's fine, Vae. You can stand down."

"No, I can't." Vaeler glanced back, shaking his head. "You don't know him."

"Vaeler, he's her father. If she wants you to step aside, do it." Conrad watched the nervous twitch in Vaeler's hand as he shifted his grip.

"I'm no threat." Kin repeated, his voice even as he raised his hands. "You can ask Deylan to tell you the story about Rylorn. I'm a friend to the faction, not an enemy."

Again with this faction. What the hells is he talking about?

Vaeler's agitation only seemed to grow. "You're a Shade, Kinronsilis. And you have no right to be here."

"Shit," Amarie murmured as Conrad's hand shot back to the hilt of his sword.

"He's a what?" Ahria backed up from her mother, from them all, eyes wide. "A Shade?"

"No, no," Amarie hurried, shaking her head. "Not anymore."

"He's a Shade, my... my..." Ahria breathed hard, gaze fixated on Kin. Blue sparked at her fingertips, but didn't spread any further.

Vaeler lifted the blade, but didn't advance on Kin. "You need to leave."

"I'm not leaving." Kin reached across to his right arm, drawing back the sleeve. Beneath, he bore a grizzly scar, spiderwebbed over his flesh. "And I don't serve any longer. Listen to Amarie. You know who she is, don't you? Fine job you did protecting her."

"Not helpful, Kin," Amarie growled.

"But true. Now, let me meet my daughter, please." His glare hardened on Vaeler.

"You're not getting anywhere near her," Vaeler hissed. "Not while my orders stand."

"Who gave you your orders?" Amarie walked away from Ahria, jaw tight.

"Your brother." Vaeler glared at her.

Ahria, hands flecked with blue flames, grasped both sides of her head. She backed up, closing her eyes. The others kept arguing, but

Conrad could only focus on her. The pained expression on her face. The fire that threatened her yet again.

Conrad, forgetting his sword and Kin, moved. Rushing to her, he took her hands, carefully pulling them away from where she gripped at her own hair. "Deep breaths. I'm right here." He ignored the cold fire as it ran over his skin and around their feet.

"A Shade killed my dad," she gasped. "And yet... my... my... real father *is* one, too?" Her eyes shone with violets and pinks, hair flicking back by an invisible force.

"He doesn't have a tattoo anymore. Maybe he's telling the truth." Conrad squeezed her hand, hunching his shoulders to get close to her face. To block her view of all the madness behind him. "We can't assume anything. Just like when I go into the judiciary hall, we have to listen to all sides of the story. You told me that your mother loved Talon, right? If that's true, why would she be willing to come here with a Shade, your father or not?"

Ahria searched his eyes, chest heaving. "Maybe he forced her. Maybe..." Her eyes drifted to the others, and she paused.

Following her gaze, Conrad took in the sight of Amarie standing in front of Kin, facing Vaeler. She made no move of attack on Ahria's friend, but something in her face told Conrad that Amarie would never let any of them harm Kin.

"She loves him," Ahria whispered, throat bobbing. Her flames simmered once more, and she gripped Conrad's arms. "I need to know."

He nodded, touching her cheek. "And I'll be at your side for it all. We have the advantage right now. We'll find the truth."

Ahria strode slowly towards the others, letting go of Conrad once she stood only a few feet away. "Is it true?" she asked Kin, and the others fell silent. "That you were a Shade, once, but no longer?"

Kin eyed Vaeler, but lowered his hands. "Yes. I made a bad choice and then I did everything I could to find a way to undo it." His eyes flitted to Amarie before settling back on Ahria. "I swear to you, I will never be a Shade again."

Vaeler opened his mouth, but Ahria gave him a look.

"Were you a Shade when..." Ahria glanced at her mother. "When you met?"

Amarie put a hand on Vaeler's sword, pushing it down. "He was, and I knew. Not right away, but I did."

Ahria's jaw flexed. "My dad is dead. A Shade killed him. And my other father died of Cerquel's. Where were you? How long have you known about me?"

"I..." Kin took a step forward, but then stopped himself. Looking to the ground, his jaw twitched in that familiar way. "I had no idea you existed, Ahria. Not until a few days ago after..." He grimaced, eyes growing distant. "After Talon, your father, died. I'm so sorry."

Conrad studied the former Shade as he spoke, evaluating the grief.

He cared for Talon, too.

Anger colored Ahria's cheeks. "You never told him?" She looked at Amarie. "That he had a child?"

Amarie shook her head, eyes glassy. "He was still a Shade. I couldn't risk it."

"But you told him now?"

"He's not a danger anymore." Amarie looked at Conrad before returning her attention to Ahria. "We just wanted to find you. We learned what had happened to Talon, and I... we needed to find you before anyone else could."

Vaeler finally fully lowered his sword, but still stood sentry between Ahria and Kin without blocking their view of the other.

"How?" Conrad looked at Amarie. "How did you find out what happened to Talon? Have you been here in Ziona the whole time?"

"I was in Helgath when it happened." Amarie's eyes glistened with tears. "I only learned because of my temporary time in death. I saw him. He told me about you, where you were, who you were with..."

Conrad touched Ahria's wrist, slipping his hand into hers. "But you died, which is how Ahria inherited the power?"

"It's a very long story." Kin eyed Vaeler before looking at Ahria again. "Maybe we can take it inside and sit down? We'll explain everything."

Everyone turned to Ahria, who still stared at her parents. "All right," she breathed.

Chapter 14

Damien collapsed back into the bench of the carriage, restraining the growl in his throat. His head pounded as voices pushed through his barrier, slipping through the cracks he created to get a better sense of what was going on at the estate.

I should be immune to these by now.

"Just relax," Rae muttered, putting her feet up on the seat Amarie had sat on. "No one is dead yet, right?"

His senses buzzed in his chest. "No," he grumbled. The fact that no one had died seemed a miracle with the amount of power coursing through the air above the estate. The driver had returned after seeing Amarie and Kin making their break for the gate, taking out her frustration at the breach of protocol on Damien and Rae. They'd calmed her enough that they could remain. But the other, empty carriage, which had been for the prince and Ahria to use to return to the palace, had departed to seek further instruction from the queen.

"And there's nothing we can do, so you might as well meditate or something." Rae fiddled with the end of one of her braids. "Just stop looking like Bellamy used to when I made him put his toys away."

Damien frowned a little more for his wife's benefit before closing his eyes. "We've worked too hard for too long to have this all go wrong now." He couldn't help the lingering fear that always remained in the pit of his stomach.

Since the close encounter with Uriel at Hoult, it had refused to go away. But he tried to bury it by allowing himself to settle into the old regiment of tuning into the ká of their surroundings.

He searched the boundary of where the Berylian Key's power had spread, his power arcing out from his body like a long cord. He only received excited responses from the ká of the surrounding flora and burrow of raccoons on the boundary. They'd all sensed the surge in one way or another, but it'd energized them rather than scaring them.

Yet Damien knew that there was no chance either he or Rae could risk approaching. The air itself hummed with the remnants of the Key's energy. It might start like a refreshing boost to their own Art, but the closer he tried to get to the core of that power, everything turned white hot. Like stepping into the center of the sun.

Rae elbowed Damien in the ribs, and his barrier snapped back into place automatically as he opened his eyes.

A familiar man sat in the carriage across from him. Grey invaded his dark hair now, but Damien would never forget the face of the man who gave him Uriel's blood.

"You forgot my name, didn't you?" The man tilted his head, looking unimpressed.

"Hardly. In fact, we were just talking about you yesterday, Deylan." Damien crossed his arms. "Glad you finally decided to show up again."

"Been busy. What are you doing here?" Deylan looked between the two of them, his face weary.

"Could ask you the same thing, or is this faction of yours getting back to its roots with the Berylian Key?"

Deylan frowned. "We never strayed from our purpose. But I'm going to need you to be forthcoming this time. Why are you here?"

"Forthcoming?" Damien straightened, his voice incredulous. "That's awful rich coming from a member of a *secret* faction that literally admitted to spying on me and my wife. I see it's still the same, considering you're joining us now. Perhaps I would be a bit more inspired to share if you would do the same about this Sixth Eye."

Silence settled in the carriage for the breath, and Rae's thoughts danced around her desire for him to be civil.

"If you refuse to cooperate, I will have no choice but to detain you," Deylan warned, keeping his voice low. "You've created a very sensitive situation, and without more information, I cannot let you anywhere near the Key."

Damien gritted his teeth to hold back his retort as Rae's elbow dug into his side.

Rae removed her feet from the opposing seat. "You were supposed to meet with us after we defeated Iedrus."

"Yes." Deylan looked at her. "Unfortunately, those higher ranked than me prohibited me from giving any of you details about the faction. Since I had nothing to offer in an exchange for information, I opted not to waste your time." He refocused on the Rahn'ka. "But now you've reunited Amarie and Kin, caused the Key's death and power transfer, *and* you've brought Amarie back to life. Only to then bring her here, causing an event that could alter the course of history. It's time you involve us in your plans, should you wish them to continue."

"See, you're all caught up. What do you need me to tell you?" Damien crossed his arms tighter.

"Don't be glib, Damien." Deylan leaned forward. "You may not acknowledge my standing, but I can force you to if you leave me no other choice."

The Rahn'ka sucked in a breath. "Can we stop with the threats then? If you want me to trust you enough to tell you details of what we have been working on for twenty-one years, I hope you can understand that would be easier if you weren't being such an asshole."

Deylan chuckled, leaning back again. "Hey, I approached peacefully, did I not?"

"He did. You just weren't aware," Rae mumbled.

"Look," Deylan continued with a sigh. "You may not realize this, but you've divided the Berylian Key."

"We what?" Rae gaped.

The fear in the pit of Damien's gut shifted for a moment, turning to excitement. "What do you mean?"

Deylan narrowed his eyes. "By bringing Amarie back, you messed with the Key's existence. As soon as Amarie touched Ahria, the power split between them. I already have people researching what this means, since the last time it happened was long before the Sundering." He tapped his fingers on the hilt of his sword. "Now it's your turn. What are you planning?"

After a silent agreement from his wife, Damien finally conceded and filled Deylan in on their plan. Deylan only listened as they talked, explaining how Amarie and Kin woke, probably due to the wave of energy created by the prison's completion, and that killing the Berylian Key had been an attempt to divide it for the spell to imprison Uriel. The man didn't even react when they confessed their ignorance of how the spell worked.

"I didn't know about Ahria when I created the dagger for Kin," Damien admitted. "I only found out about her minutes before when restoring Amarie's memories. I told her she needed to tell Kin, but then Uriel..." He hated that he'd hid during the confrontation, but had seen no other choice. Uriel still didn't know he was the Rahn'ka, and it needed to remain like that as long as possible. "He must have been looking for Amarie after feeling the prison's completion. And that's why we're here, too. He's probably looking for Ahria now that he's realized the knife does nothing."

Deylan nodded. "That has been our concern, too. But now the Keys are together, which is dangerous, as I'm sure you realize."

"I don't really see how there was another way to do it, though." Damien shrugged. "Amarie was desperate to get to her daughter as soon as she realized the power had left her. And we won't be staying here much longer."

"Where will you go?" Deylan tilted his head.

"Somewhere well outside of Uriel's control. Veralian or Nema's Throne, probably. At least until we can figure out how the imprisonment spell really works and how to lure Uriel to the prison itself."

"All right..." Deylan nodded, pulling a copper device out of his pocket. It looked like a compass as he popped the lid open, but he started poking the dials within.

Rae exchanged a look with Damien. "All right? That's it?"

Deylan shrugged. "It sounds like a good plan. If you can keep Amarie and Ahria safe, then I will work on filling in those blanks that you have."

Damien blinked. He'd written off the faction as not being much help in regards to Uriel or the plan to imprison him. He hadn't heard a thing from a single member since his initial meeting with Deylan. And when Amarie's brother never reached out to meet again... He'd assumed their influence was limited, and the blood they'd recovered was a fortunate accident. "Which blanks are you referring to exactly?"

Rising, Deylan opened the carriage door. "How the spell works." He stepped outside, then looked down at his compass device as it started whirring.

"Unless you have access to texts older than those in the Rahn'ka sanctums, I doubt you'll have much luck." Damien followed him out of the carriage, Rae next to him. He glanced at the driver, who lay with her head back against the carriage, sound asleep.

Zionans don't really seem the type to sleep on the job.

He did a double take, spotting a tiny puncture wound on her neck.

"I'm sure I'll manage." Deylan absently shook his head.

"And this is information that your higher ups will be all right with you sharing? You made it sound like the faction still holding things pretty close to their chest."

"I'm higher ranking now, and if I deem information needs to be shared, then I will share it." Deylan snapped his device closed. "And we are. We always are. But trying to complete the spell without all of you is a pointless endeavor…" He paused, turning to face them. "Hypothetically, if we agree to share our knowledge with you, would you reciprocate?"

"What do you want to know?" Rae stopped next to Damien.

"All your future plans and motivations." Deylan smirked. "But I'd start with how you know the name of the Sixth Eye. I never told you that."

"Matthias told us."

"I suppose that means Uriel has been more successful than we thought at finding information," Deylan muttered to himself.

"I'm sorry, that's probably not the best news to share." Damien scratched the back of his head as he glanced towards the estate. "Regarding my future plans… Right now they're fairly focused on just taking care of Uriel and making sure as many of us as possible come out alive."

Deylan gave him a thoughtful look. "Why is imprisoning Uriel so important to you?"

"Because of what he is. The threat he is to everything." He chewed his lower lip. "Let's just say that as the Rahn'ka, I'm aware of a very large target on my back."

"On all of our backs, really," Rae added. "Including our children."

Deylan lowered his voice. "And what about you, Damien. Do you desire more power?"

Damien balked at the question, confusion blossoming into a slow understanding. "I never wanted this power." He held out his hands to Deylan before shoving up his sleeves. On his left arm, he exposed the sleeve of dark navy runes he'd crafted onto his own skin years before. They hadn't faded, and with a flex of his arm, they glowed. "I've learned to respect it for what it can accomplish, but every position of power I find myself in, I have tried to refuse."

"Why would Uriel be interested in threatening your children?" Deylan looked between them.

A familiar hesitation hovered in Damien's mind, but he quickly buried it. There wasn't a choice anymore. "How much do you know about the Rahn'ka?" Damien met Deylan's eyes as he stepped closer. Each step, he entreated the energies around him. Asking the ká to allow him to borrow more.

"They inherited your power, didn't they?" Deylan held his ground.

"We don't know for sure about Sarra, yet." Damien looked back at Rae as he stopped in front of Deylan. "You ask to learn more about me and my power. But it's not just mine." He held out his hand, the runes blazing with pale blue light. "I'll take you to meet the beings that made me, and my son, what we are. Then we can discuss who still owes who information." He gave a wry smile.

Deylan studied the offered hand, glancing at Rae before nodding. "Show me."

Chapter 15

Ahria stared at the horizon. The horizon she thought, only hours ago, that she and Conrad would be running for before the day's end. But everything changed the moment her mother sprinted through the gates. Followed by her birth father.

My Shade father.

She chewed her lip. Former Shade. He no longer served Uriel, and some deep innate trust in her mother assured her that Amarie wouldn't have led him to her if he was a threat.

The balcony railing vibrated as someone walked around inside.

Conrad had gathered them all in one of the large sitting rooms, and he hadn't moved further than six feet from her since her parents' arrival. She'd thought he'd attempt the niceties of offering drinks to everyone, but he didn't even go as far as inviting them to get comfortable in the large room. He remained quiet and stoic as he kept himself between her and them.

Ahria sucked in a deep breath, his presence behind her blocking anyone from joining her on the balcony.

She'd retreated to take time for herself after her parents had laid out the events of how they'd found her. And then they told them about Uriel. And the Key's part to play in an unknown spell to imprison him, along with other participants they didn't take the time to name. Amarie explained to her and Conrad how she'd died, spoken with Talon, and then returned.

When Amarie had explained seeing Talon in the Inbetween, pain had shone in her gaze. Grief. Possibly even regret. Like looking in a mirror. And, by the gods, they looked so alike. Save for Ahria's darker hair and lighter eyes. It was odd to consider her mother was only ten years older than her. Preserved by Slumber in Eralas.

Ahria drew in another slow breath, trying to regain her bearings. The thought of going back inside, facing all those in that room... Facing the truth of the danger they were all in...

"Could I have a moment with her, please?" Her mother's voice.

"She needs some air." Conrad sounded guarded, almost terse.

"It's all right," Ahria said over her shoulder. "Just close the door behind her?"

Amarie murmured her gratitude to the prince as she stepped onto the balcony. The door shut after her, giving them a modicum of privacy. Crossing to the railing, she leaned on it, looking out at the horizon with her daughter.

The land, dense with green summer brush, rippled in gentle hills towards the gorge of the Astarian River. If they followed it south, they'd arrive at the palace in New Kingston, but this far north, the terrain to the river was too wild and forested to give anyone access. The tops of pine and cottonwood trees, along the distant river banks, danced in an invisible breeze rushing down from the snow-crested mountains beyond.

For a time, Amarie didn't speak, and Ahria marveled at how comfortable the silence was.

"I don't know if I'll ever forgive myself for leaving you," Amarie whispered, drawing Ahria's gaze. Wetness lined her bottom lids. "It was the hardest thing I've ever done, and I still don't know if it was right."

Ahria contemplated the words, how her life had gone, and how different it could have looked had Amarie stayed. "I had a good childhood," she offered, looking over at her mother. "I had two fathers who loved me, an aunt and uncle, a big brother. Cousins. I was safe, just as you wanted me to be. I never stopped wondering about you, and as painful as I'm sure it was for him, Dad always answered all my questions. I don't know if life would have been better or worse if things had been different, but I wouldn't trade those memories for anything."

Amarie smiled at her, brow twitching. "It makes me happy to hear that. All I wanted was for you to be safe. Happy. Loved. I hoped Talon would go to you."

"He was..." Ahria choked, clearing her throat with a hard swallow as she toyed with her father's braided leather bracelet on her wrist. "He was a really good dad. The best. Him and Lorin both. Dad told me why you left, where you were. He loved you the whole time, I think. Just as I did."

"Really?" Amarie swiped at her eyes. "I hardly deserve that."

"Why did Talon never tell me about..." Ahria turned, peering through the glass door at the profile of her father. "He never told me about... *him*. I mean, I knew Talon and Lorin weren't my blood, but Dad would never talk about him, even when I asked. He'd always change the subject to be about you."

Kin sat on one of the decorated couches, distant from the others in the room. His head was bent downward, studying his hands as they twisted against each other between his knees. His eyes looked heavy. Regretful.

"He probably didn't want you to hate Kin." Amarie angled herself more towards Ahria. "He probably didn't want to risk you going to look for him, because of what he was. Talon didn't know that Kin was in Slumber next to me or that he'd severed his connection to Uriel."

Ahria nodded, understanding settling into her. "For a while, I was so angry at you both."

"Teenage years?" Amarie offered a tentative smile.

Letting out a short laugh, Ahria nodded. "Yep."

Silence settled again, lingering for a short time before Ahria spoke again. "Why are you here?"

"To help you. Protect you. I was alone when I became the Berylian Key, and I remember how terrified I was. I don't want that for you." Amarie looked down at her hands. "But I guess this goes beyond that, now."

"Because you need me for the spell."

"No, not that. Because of me and what happened out in that courtyard. Because I'm not dead." Amarie offered her hand, palm up. "I've learned to control it, and when I touched you, I could feel the power in *your* veins. I calmed it and returned it deeper within you. But it traveled through me, too, in that moment. And I wonder if I can... ease the burden of it from you."

Ahria's breath caught in her chest as she stared at her mother's hand, the blue flames of the Berylian Key's power threatening to reemerge. "Like... take it?" A sudden, unexpected possessiveness overtook her, and she struggled to understand the feeling.

"No, not take it." Amarie paused. "Well, maybe like that. But not permanently. Just until we can get somewhere safe, so I can teach you how to hide it and, eventually, how to use it."

Gulping, Ahria debated. She couldn't explain her trust in her mother beyond the blood relation, but... that wasn't true, either. Talon had loved her, trusted her with his life, and she had no reason not to feel the same. "What will you do, when it's over?"

Amarie tilted her head. "When what's over?"

"The spell. After Uriel is imprisoned. Where will you go?"

Amarie's shoulders drooped. "I never want to leave you again, Ree."

Ahria stiffened. "Dad used to call me that."

"Sorry. My mother used to call me that, too. I won't if it bothers you."

Forcing her back to relax, Ahria shook her head. "No, I, uh... I like it. It's all right." She took a deeper breath, still eyeing her mother's palm. "All right. We can try it." The idea of being able to return to the city, to not fear killing innocent people, eased the weight in her chest.

Taking Amarie's hand, she gasped as the power again responded.

It jolted between them, but not as violently as before. Her mother's eyes shifted to the vibrant pink and purple beryl tones, just as she imagined her own. Her hair stung her neck as it whipped back, and almost immediately, the strength of the power within her waned. It heated her hand as Amarie drew it from her.

Her breathing quickened. "Will it hurt, when it's gone?"

Amarie shook her head. "If anything hurts, we will stop."

Ahria closed her eyes as the energy flowed from her into her mother. Breath came easier. Smoother. And after a few more heartbeats, their hands parted. She looked down at herself, then at her hands. Delving into herself, she found no trace of the Art, and her eyes burned. "Thank you."

Her mother smiled, the color of her irises returning to dark blue. "This power isn't mine, anymore. It is ours. And when you're ready, we will take the next steps, all right?"

Ahria nodded. "All right. Until then... can I... you know, hurt anyone?"

"Only with the multitude of blades you carry." Amarie smirked. "Which I'm sure Talon taught you to use."

She laughed, and it felt so freeing that a lump formed in her throat. "He did." Her gaze drifted to the glass, landing again on the father she never expected to see. Most people had one father, if they were lucky, but now she was being offered a third.

Yet, the agony of losing Lorin swelled in her chest, which had been too quickly followed by the loss of Talon.

What if I just end up losing Kin, too?

The idea of more heartbreak sent a shudder through her, but she couldn't look away from him. He didn't look at her, but she could still see the steel blue eyes that he'd given her.

But if he dies, too, isn't it worse if I didn't give him a chance?

Amarie dipped her chin to catch her daughter's gaze. "What is it?"

After a short bout of hesitation, Ahria sighed. "Kin... I... What does he want from me?"

Her mother smiled. "Anything you're willing to give, I think. He knows you've already had two fathers, and I doubt he even knows where he fits in, either. But he wants to protect you, and I'm pretty sure he would love you if you let him. And probably even if you don't."

"He's not a danger to me? You're sure?" Ahria searched her mother's face.

"I'm sure." Amarie shook her head. "He wouldn't be here if he was, I promise." Something haunted in her expression told Ahria the heavy truth of that statement.

"Can I talk to him? Alone?"

Her mother nodded. "Of course. Want me to send him out here?"

After Ahria's confirmation, Amarie knocked on the glass door to warn Conrad she was returning inside. The prince said nothing as he opened the door, letting her in. After crossing the room, she whispered in Kin's ear, and he stiffened as he looked to the balcony. He said something, but it was too quiet for Ahria to hear, then stood.

Her heart pounded as Kin crossed the sitting room towards her.

A frown deepened on Conrad's face, but he didn't block the way as Kin walked onto the balcony. Sun brightened the scar on his face, running from his temple to his jaw, and she wondered where it'd come from.

The door shut, and Ahria swallowed. "Hi."

"Hi." He stood awkwardly away from the railing and her, his left hand at his side flexing nervously. Opening his mouth, he paused, then closed it before trying again. "I'm... not sure what to say."

"Me neither," Ahria admitted, rolling her lips together. "You knew my dad, or... sorry. You knew Talon, didn't you?"

The somber look from before returned to his gaze. "Yes. Talon and I were... very close friends for a long time. He was like a brother to me before I... made some poor choices."

Her gaze flickered down to his arm, where his shirt covered the scar. She cleared her throat. "It's... nice to meet you." Forcing a smile, she tried not to cringe at the awkwardness.

"Ahria." His tone shifted to something serious, multitudes of emotions buried within the syllables of her name. Guilt, anger, relief, joy. "I'm sorry I was never there. That I never knew..." His throat bobbed as he fought the cracking in his voice.

"That hardly feels like your fault." She lifted her chin to maintain eye contact. "And you're here now."

"And I will be. As long as you'll allow me to be." He paused before lifting a hand towards her. "You're my daughter, and I have a lot to make up to you."

"Talon was—"

"Your father, I know. And no part of me wishes to replace him."

Ahria huffed. "Actually, I was going to say that he was always reluctant to speak of you. Not of any ill-thought, I believe, but out of some desire to protect me. But I'd hope that, since you knew *him*, perhaps you'd be open to sharing..." Her throat tightened, grief cutting off her voice.

Kin's hand moved into hers, his grip firm. "I'll tell you anything you want. Even the embarrassing stories that Talon would loathe for you to hear. I do have a few, considering I knew him in his *younger* years. Young for an auer, at least."

A smile twitched her lips and before she could overthink the notion, she threw herself forward and wrapped her arms around him. Her cheek met his chest, and his earthy scent reminded her of nights in the forest.

Only a heartbeat passed before his arms tightened around her, whatever tension she'd seen in him before fading with each moment. His grip never waned, and she listened to the steady rhythm in his chest.

As Ahria withdrew from him, she looked up at his face, where tears streaked his cheeks. Her heart squeezed, and she wiped her own with the back of her hand. "I'm glad you're here, and that I have a chance to know you. You and Amarie."

"Your mom and I love you so much, I hope you know that." Kin touched her chin, lifting it lightly before he brushed a thumb over her still damp cheek. "And thank you. For this chance for us, too."

"Are you..." Ahria paused, damning her lack of ability to form words. "Together?"

Kin's tension abruptly returned, but he dismissed it with a huff and shake of the head. "No. We're..." He glanced behind him through the glass door. "Still trying to figure out what we are, exactly. Your mom needs time to mourn and adjust. I'm not going to press anything."

Ahria nodded, hiding her disappointment with a half smile. "I understand, I think." It shouldn't matter to her whether they were together, but she could see the way they gazed at each other when they thought no one was looking.

Kin finally relaxed against the balcony railing, meeting his daughter's eyes. "Do you have any questions?" He chuckled and shook his head. "I mean, you probably have millions considering everything we just told you. But I hope you know that I'll be honest. I'm done with secrets in my life."

"I have one, actually," Ahria whispered, looking down at her hands. Her now powerless hands. "I received the power only moments after Talon... was killed. Talon always told me that the Key is useless against Shades, and therefore, I have to believe that if I'd gotten it earlier, just minutes or seconds earlier, that I still wouldn't have been able to..." She choked again, gritting her teeth. "To save him. Is that true?"

He placed his hand on top of hers. "It would have been far worse if you'd tried to use the Art. Talon told you the truth. If you'd used the Berylian Key's power on that Shade, it would have exposed you directly to Uriel and given the Shade more energy."

Her shoulders slumped with relief, and she let out a breath. "Amarie has the power now." She opened a palm, but no sparks danced at her fingertips. "So at least it's under control."

His eyes widened slightly. "Is that what happened when you two touched in the courtyard?"

She shook her head. "Not exactly. It reacted to her, though. She contained it within me in the courtyard, but out here, we... we gave it all to her for now."

"So both of you have access, somehow?"

Ahria nodded. "It would seem so. She will give some back to me when I'm ready to start learning how to control it."

Kin huffed as he crossed his arms. "Damien's going to be ecstatic." He coughed at her confused look and added, "The Rahn'ka."

"Why?" Ahria narrowed her eyes, still unsure how she felt about the man. The Rahn'ka. Whatever that meant.

"He's been trying to figure out a certain part of the spell to imprison Uriel, and I think this just answered it. The Berylian Key, divided."

A knock sounded on the window, Conrad's perturbed face appearing behind the panes. He gestured behind him, where a new person stood in the room.

Ahria glanced at Kin before approaching the glass door as Conrad opened it for her. "What's..." Her gaze drifted to the newcomer, and her step faltered. "Uncle Deylan?"

"Hey, kiddo." Deylan's voice reminded her of home, and she smiled as her chest tightened. He approached her, shoulders relaxed, and drew her into a tight hug. Kissing the top of her head, he murmured, "I'm so sorry."

Ahria breathed in his warmth, the rest of the people in the room falling away as she closed her eyes. "Is that why you're here?"

He paused. "Yes and no." He hesitated, and it made her insides churn. "I came as soon as I heard of the Shade's attack and that you'd inherited your mother's gift."

"She has it again, now."

Deylan nodded. "That's good." His tone was distant, and Ahria drew away. He was asking far too few questions with everything she was telling him. It tightened the knots in her stomach to know there were secrets after all, even with all Talon had shared.

No one has explained this faction they keep talking about, yet, either.

Looking up at him, she followed his gaze to her mother and their silent conversation. Sighing, she forced her emotions to stay in check at the expected secrecy.

"Deylan." Kin walked up behind Ahria, holding a hand out to her uncle and forcing him to shift his attention. "Been a while."

"Longer for me." Deylan smirked, taking Kin's hand. "Now, perhaps you'll age like the rest of us."

Ahria looked at Amarie, but her mother's attention was on Deylan.

Conrad touched her wrist, and she jumped, but let out a breath and faced him. "You doing all right?"

She huffed, leaning into his side. "I have no idea."

"I don't want to overwhelm you more, but there are two others wishing to join us. Is there any danger to Art users?" Deylan's voice was gentle, and he tilted his head at his niece.

Ahria shook her head. "Amarie has the power," she whispered, even if the idea of meeting more people daunted her. "No danger."

Deylan patted her shoulder before returning to the door, opening it for two others to walk inside.

"Rooms getting awfully crowded." The prince moved in close behind her, taking her hand. The moment the two strangers crossed through the doorway, his grip doubled and she looked back over her shoulder at his confused expression.

She furrowed her brow. "Wha—"

Deylan gestured to the man and woman. "This is Damien and —"

"Rae?" Conrad gaped, pushing Ahria's attention back to the woman.

"You know each other?" Deylan looked between them, but for a long minute, no one spoke.

Rae took a step closer. "Con... Conrad?"

"I'm missing something." Ahria tugged on his arm.

"What are you doing here?" Conrad ignored her, focused on the two.

Rae's shoulders relaxed, and she smiled. "I'd ask you the same thing. Did Amarie and Kin not fill you in?"

"I left out your names," Amarie murmured, turning to her daughter and her prince. "Damien is the Rahn'ka, and Rae is the Mira'wyld I was telling you about."

Conrad's face paled. "What? Aren't you advisors to the king of Helgath?"

"Yes, that too." Rae blinked, still gaping. "You've grown up. And... you're a prince? Since when?"

"This is weird," Deylan muttered.

"Which part? That they know each other? Or that *you* didn't know first?" Damien raised a brow at Deylan, who only made a face at him.

"Can someone explain, please?" Kin crossed his arms. "How do you know each other?"

"Conrad worked on Andi's ship, for what? Two years?" Rae finally tore her gaze away, addressing Kin. "I haven't seen him in ages, but for a while, there, we saw each other quite frequently. He was friends with our son, too."

Amarie paused. "And Andi is..."

"*Her* mother." Conrad supplied, gesturing at Rae.

Ahria scowled, staring at the prince. "You named your dog after her."

"You named your dog after Andi?" Damien nearly choked on his own words, then let out a booming laugh. "Gods, that's perfect." He looked at his wife. "Please let me be the one to tell her."

Ahria studied the topaz hue of one of Rae's eyes, an indicator of her heritage. "You're auer? Wait... Talon told me once of a Mira'wyld who came to see him in Eralas. She was the reason he came to me, to raise me..." Her voice caught. "Was that... was that you?"

All eyes turned on Rae, and Amarie stiffened.

The Mira'wyld met her gaze and a warm smile spread over her face. "I'm so sorry about his passing. But, yes, I spoke with your father in Eralas about you. To be fair, though, at the time I was only relaying something your mother had said, and I had no idea you even existed."

"It still feels empty without him," Ahria whispered, half expecting to see Talon walk through the door next. She stared at the door handle, willing it to turn, for there to be one more surprise. One more shock. One more...

He's never coming back.

Her eyes burned, and she blinked back the tears.

Amarie smiled now, too. "Thank you," she whispered. "For delivering that message."

Rae nodded at her, unspoken emotion in her eyes.

Conrad wrapped his arm around her, kissing her hair as if he could sense every thought. "Are you doing all right? This is a lot..."

Ahria hummed with a nod, leaning harder into him as the others began a new conversation, but she couldn't focus on it. Words blurred between parties.

Her mother faced her uncle, something in her stance telling Ahria she wasn't pleased with him, and her father's name sharpened her attention.

"How did you know Kin was in Slumber?" Amarie controlled her tone, watching Deylan.

"I told him." Damien stepped forward. "I also told him that I'd helped Kin sever the bond to Uriel."

Her uncle gestured dismissively with his hands. "I still couldn't have done anything about it."

Ahria stiffened. "When did you find out?"

Everyone paused for a breath before Deylan answered. "When you were a baby."

Heat rushed through her. "You knew my..." Calling him her father felt like a slight to Talon, so she reworded. "You knew he was in Slumber, having abandoned Uriel, and you never told me?"

Deylan's expression softened as he looked at her. "I'm not always at liberty to fill you in on the details. Besides, what difference would it have made?"

Ahria gritted her teeth. It may not have made a difference to the events that followed, but it would have given her information. Some knowledge to cling to, like the stories of her mother had. "You still should have told me. I have a right to know."

"Kiddo, no one has a right to know everything. Not even me, back then, but—"

"What does that even mean?" Ahria spoke louder than she meant to, but refused to correct herself. "You speak in riddles half the time. Can you just give me a straight answer? This once?"

Deylan paused, jaw flexing, but he nodded. "I suppose it needs to come out now, anyway." His gaze flickered to Vaeler, then Conrad, before he continued. "I'm a member of a faction dedicated to the protection of the Berylian Key called the Sixth Eye. I've had someone in the city looking out for you." He glanced back at her friend and fellow Mysterium member, who looked at his boots, as if ashamed.

"Vaeler..?" Ahria backed up a step, unable to banish the sense of betrayal.

He was always meant to befriend me. So he could protect me?

"I'm sorry I wasn't enough," Vaeler whispered. "The Shade caught me by surprise, and..." As much as his tone was apologetic, his fingers twitched, and she wondered why.

"I can't talk about this right now. You've all been scheming behind my back. And you..." Ahria stared at Damien. "You just want to use me. Me and my family, and I'm just supposed to agree?"

The Rahn'ka met her gaze in surprise, shaking his head. "I don't want to use anyone. There is always a choice and that remains yours."

"Is there?" Ahria challenged. "Because so far I haven't seen many choices thrown my way."

"There is plenty of time to talk about it and answer all your questions," Rae chimed in, voice soft. "No one will force you into anything."

"All right." Amarie stood before Ahria could respond. "Let's take a break. Fighting isn't going to help anything."

"There's time to work through all of this." Conrad touched her side. "We need to focus on the next step."

"Which is to go to the Sixth Eye's headquarters." Deylan's words stunned everyone into silence again. "It's the safest place right now."

"What?" Conrad pulled Ahria closer. "Where is that?"

"That's unimportant. It's not safe here for any of you, and our library could hold necessary information about imprisoning Uriel. There is a Shade coming to investigate the incident in Nema's Throne, and I'd be surprised if today's events didn't capture someone's attention."

"What?" Kin rose to his feet as well. "You didn't think to mention that sooner?"

"When? Five minutes ago?" Deylan scowled. "I'm mentioning it now. We have some time, but not a lot. We need to prepare for the journey and get moving by tomorrow."

Damien glanced at his wife. "We need to return to New Kingston first. To Matthias and the others. If Uriel is sending Shades here, they'll be in danger, too."

"Of course. But only this group will be traveling to the Sixth Eye." Deylan motioned to the room. "The others can return to their respective countries."

"Even Conrad?" Damien eyed the prince, but aimed his inquiry at Deylan. "He doesn't need to be part of this."

"I'm not leaving Ahria's side. If she's going, I'm going." Conrad glared at Damien.

Ahria looked at Conrad, then at Damien. "And I'm not going without him."

"Believe me, it's easier not to argue," Deylan muttered. "She's a lot like her mother."

Ahria withheld a chuckle, looking at Amarie, who smirked back with a shrug.

"I agree with Deylan," Rae added, shrugging at Damien. "May be selfish, but it would be nice to catch up with him, and you never know when we might need an extra person we can trust."

Damien met his wife's gaze for a moment, and Ahria felt like there was some kind of secret conversation happening that no one else could hear. Finally, he nodded and looked back at Conrad. "All right. Hopefully your mother, Jarrod, and Matthias are having luck with the formal political meetings since we'll need to cut this all a little short."

Chapter 16

Matthias watched Jarrod have a silent conversation with his wolf, the animal barking responses. "How does that work?"

"Mostly telepathically." Jarrod glanced at the other king, then scowled at Neco. "You can wait to eat like the rest of us. Dinner isn't that far away."

Neco whined, lowering his head to the rug.

Corin leaned forward over the table adorned with inkwells and quills. "And we should be grateful it's all in their heads." He tapped his temple. "Neco is extremely persistent and annoying." He cast a playful glance at the wolf, who grumbled up at him.

They sat in a meeting room, waiting for Queen Pendaverin. Jarrod sat at one side with Corin and Neco, while Matthias sat across from them with Micah. Dani and Katrin, carting Liam along with them, had left to explore the city, chatting about finding some sort of Zionan sweet pastry Matthias had never heard of.

The door to the room opened, and the queen strode inside alone.

They all stood, including Neco, and Matthias narrowed his eyes when no one entered behind her.

Talia took her seat, and they followed suit as the meeting room door closed.

"You don't wish to have an advisor present?" Jarrod glanced at Matthias.

"Considering the subjects I expect to come up in our conversation, I felt it was probably best not to involve anyone else." She produced a leather-bound folder from under her arm, unwrapped it, then spread the mostly blank papers in front of her. "I hope you'll understand my need to take thorough notes. I'll refrain from recording anything sensitive."

"Of course." Matthias laced his fingers together on the table, his tattoos stark against the white table cloth.

Lightly touching the papers, Talia took in a slow breath.

He swore he could see her pulse pounding in the veins of her wrist.

She looked for an inkwell, her eyes flitting up to Micah, who sat the closest to it. "I'm sorry, do you mind passing that this way?"

Micah reached for the inkwell, but paused as he eyed her. "Of course, your majesty." He slowly slid it over, and Matthias furrowed his brow at his crown elite.

He's being weird.

The queen smiled, and it lit up her face as she stood just enough to take the bottle from Micah. "Talia, please. There's no need for formalities."

"Talia," Micah repeated, but when he caught Matthias's confused stare, he cleared his throat and stopped talking.

"As we previously mentioned, Isalica is—"

"And Helgath," Jarrod interrupted.

Matthias glowered at the other king, but it took all his self control not to smile. "...Isalica and Helgath would like to align with Ziona. We ask to open free trade between our countries, with the possibility of discussing immigration, military aid in the event of war, and joint research endeavors in the future."

Talia dipped her quill and began to scribble on one of the papers. "Ziona deeply appreciates the offer, and I'm certain we can come to an arrangement. Our history with Isalica and treaties between our countries runs deep." She looked at Matthias with a soft smile, and her eyes flitted to Micah, but quickly averted. "Our history with Helgath, however." She looked at Jarrod. "Is perhaps a bit more complicated. Until House Martox assumed the throne, there had been talk about another war between our countries. There are certainly far more details to be worked out for us to solidify an alliance my people will support."

Jarrod huffed a deep laugh. "I can respect that. It's taken quite some time for even the Helgathians to trust us, but we got there. I trust Ziona will get there, too, in time. But we have brought our numbers for you to look over."

Corin slid a folder over the smooth table to Talia, which, like the information Matthias brought, held the numbers of their military, practitioners, and populations. Along with trade proposals, port fees, and suggested taxes.

The master of war explained the documents as she perused them, taking it page by page while she took notes on a separate sheet.

The discussion carried out over the course of the next hour, pausing partway for refreshments brought in by the palace staff.

Matthias sipped from a glass of cider, enjoying the unusual fruity tang that accompanied the drink.

Talia lifted her hand to her mouth, failing to stifle a yawn that all of them were certainly feeling. She settled her quill across the paper, chewing her lower lip for a moment. "I will, of course, need the support of parliament before we'll be able to proceed. But this will be a strong case. I think they'd be a bunch of fools to turn down everything your kingdoms are offering."

"There is another issue we should discuss." Matthias folded his arms in front of him. "Though it is not one contained within our three countries."

"Is this related to the more sensitive topic from yesterday? About Shades?" Talia brushed her papers aside as if already knowing the coming conversation shouldn't be written down.

"More or less," Micah rolled his shoulders. "Feyor has become a problem again."

Talia made a face. "From all accounts I have heard, Feyor is in shambles due to gross mismanagement under King Lazorus. The son has certainly not lived up to the father."

Micah nodded. "Normally, we wouldn't get involved, but both our shores are seeing a massive increase in refugees fleeing the country. Disease, famine, and poverty are rampant, as they've ceased trade with even Delkest and Olsa to focus on their military. However, their military is falling apart, with desertion at an all-time high. Civilians are dying at unprecedented rates in Feyor, and we feel it would be unjust to stand by and do nothing."

Talia straightened in her chair, locking eyes with Micah. "Generally speaking, wars are wrought over land. But I hear another intention behind what you're saying. You believe the people would understand the purpose?"

"We aren't suggesting a full invasion as of yet." Micah continued first, even when Matthias had opened his mouth to answer. "But Helgath and Isalica are working to provide relief efforts for the refugees who make it to our shores. If Ziona is in support, we can discuss a joint, peaceful mission to provide aid to suffering Feyorians."

"We've already begun covert operations, sending vetted refugees back to provide aid and direction on how best to find relief." Corin nursed a half-full glass of cider near his lips. "Ziona shares a closer border than we do, however. Your support would make our efforts more effective."

"Somehow I see King Jarac Lazorus not being entirely understanding of our efforts." Talia rubbed her hands together in front of her. "I don't see how this pertains to our previous conversation, however. About the master of Shades?"

Matthias and Jarrod exchanged a look before the Isalican king took a breath. "His name is Uriel. And King Lazorus is one of his Shades."

And his brother would make a better king.

"Nymaera," Talia whispered, and sucked in a breath. "So Feyor has already been lost, and the suffering happening to its people is what that creature would do to Pantracia?"

"Or worse," Corin murmured.

"You will have Ziona's support in providing aid to the people of Feyor." Talia looked between the two kings.

"Don't you need to consult parliament first?" Micah tilted his head. "We aren't aiming to rush you into a decision."

"I will make it happen, no matter what barriers those old politicians try to put in my way. And I will do whatever is needed to aid in this effort against Uriel. He cannot be allowed to continue. For the sake of all our people."

The meeting room door swung open, and Neco leapt to his feet with a growl.

The guard tensed, drawing back into the doorway as her eyes settled on the wolf. "Your majesty, I apologize for the interruption, but Prince Conrad has asked to join you with your permission."

Jarrod calmed the wolf with a look, and the beast sat, ears still pricked to the door.

A look of relief passed over the queen's expression as she turned in her chair. "Yes, please. Allow him in."

The guard nodded, retreating back through the door to make way for the prince.

Conrad entered with a terse look on his face. His gaze passed over the others in the room before landing on his mother, who made the introductions as soon as the door closed.

"Apologies for not being here sooner, but I hope you all will understand, considering what Ahria has been going through." He remained beside his mother, standing, rather than moving to a seat. "I believe everyone in this room is aware of the situation, based on my conversations with your friends."

"Aye," Jarrod murmured, a hand on Neco's shoulders as the wolf still stared at Conrad.

Matthias narrowed his eyes. "Intimately. Is there trouble with the Key?"

Conrad's attention shifted to Matthias, his light eyes holding a deep intensity within them. "No trouble, per se. Some unexpected developments and news that require quick action. A Shade is on its way to New Kingston to investigate the events of last week."

Something dark and sharp unfurled in Matthias's stomach. "Just one? How do you know this?"

"Deylan arrived at the northern estate just after your friends did. He brought word and an offer to take Ahria to the Sixth Eye headquarters for her safety. And we're going to accept."

Matthias hummed. "That's probably a good move. Uriel doesn't know where that is, last I knew." He shifted his gaze to Talia. "We can assist with the Shade, if you're not opposed. Isalica has soldiers specifically trained to fight them, and with our unconventional means of transport, they could arrive within the next day."

"Unfortunately, we ourselves won't be able to stay. Uriel must not learn we've been here." Jarrod sat up straighter, glancing at Corin.

Talia nodded. "I suppose a united Pantracia would not be good for his agenda. I'll see to having a commander tasked with overseeing the Isalican troops. Your offer is greatly appreciated."

"Actually, it would be best to have someone familiar with them to oversee. I can stay. Uriel isn't familiar with me, and that could give us an advantage." Micah met Matthias's hard stare. "With your permission, of course, my king."

Matthias made a face at the exaggerated formality. "An advantage, hm?"

The corner of Micah's mouth twitched as his eyes flicked towards the Zionan queen. "Perhaps. Best to try, right?"

The Isalican king scoffed. "If you insist, my friend. Send word when you'd like to return home."

Matthias jolted upright, sweat beading on his skin and palms clammy as he gripped the thick blanket covering him and Katrin. He panted, looking down at his hands, his forearms, the tattoos that always served their purpose in grounding him. The rays of the sun on his skin banished the vision of shadows still lingering from his nightmare, and the dragon devoured them.

Gods, I don't miss this feeling.

He stifled a groan, lingering phantom pain burning his chest.

A gentle hand brushed along his thigh, tentative at first before growing more certain as Katrin lifted her head, blinking at him in the darkness of their bedroom. "Are you all right?"

Matthias grunted, touching her hand. Her smooth skin cooled his, and he took a deeper breath. "Mmm. It's been awhile." He looked at her. At her unending patience. "Go back to sleep. I'm fine."

His wife shifted, sitting up instead. A beam of moonlight breaking through the curtains framed her petite body. Moving into him, she pressed against his bare back and wrapped her arms around him. The thin fabric of her nightgown tickled his skin. "It's always helped you to talk about it. So tell me." She pressed her lips to his shoulder, kissing along his upper back.

"It wasn't one of the usuals," he murmured, used to sharing them with her. And she knew them all, even the worst ones about Alana. "It was of when Uriel punished Kin, killed him, over and over, to get him to confess to whatever he knew about the Berylian Key. He must still bear those scars..."

Katrin ran her fingers over the same places Matthias had watched Uriel whip, and it sent a shudder down his spine. She paused, lifting herself higher onto her knees as she firmly placed her hands on his shoulders. There, she pushed her thumbs into his muscles, rubbing at the lingering tension. "Seeing Kin probably triggered the nightmares again. It can't be easy. For either of you."

Matthias grimaced, jaw clenching despite her efforts to relax him. "He can't stand even looking at me. Not that I blame him." Still, his chest ached. He'd always wanted the best for Kin, but the former Shade only saw a monster in him.

"He just needs time. He was in Slumber all those years you've had to recover, but for him... Uriel bore your face up until only a few days ago." She pushed harder into a knot on his right shoulder, making him groan.

"I know." Yet, disappointment weighed in his gut. "I've been trying to stay away from him, give him that time, but I think... I think I need to talk to him."

"About what?"

Matthias tilted his head back, closing his eyes as his wife's masterful hands found every sore spot in his upper back. "About Feyor."

Katrin sucked in a knowing breath. "You mean about his lineage. Are you sure it's a good time to bring that up? He's got enough on his mind with this spell of Damien's, doesn't he?"

The Isalican king hummed. "He won't like it. He'll need time to consider, but I think he needs to know what shape that country is in. *His* country. He's a good man, and I don't know when I'll have another chance after we depart from here."

Katrin paused, curling herself around him. She settled naturally into his arms, her fingers running up into his beard. "So you truly believe he's been redeemed? And not just in a way that fulfills the fancy word Damien has tied onto the list of people he needs to imprison Uriel. You trust him?"

Matthias huffed, tucking her hair behind her ear. "I do trust him, and I think he needs to hear that more. It won't be easy when people keep referring to him as a Shade."

She smiled. "You're such a softie." She tugged gently on his hair, pulling his head towards her. "Exactly why I love you so much."

He chuckled, brushing his lips against hers in a warm kiss. "You know who isn't a softie?" He narrowed his eyes as a mischievous smile spread over her face. "No, that's not what I mean."

"I know." She laughed, leaning up to kiss his jaw. "Best to tell me who before I get any other ideas."

"I don't mind your other ideas." He smirked. "But I actually mean Micah. He seem weird to you today? With all that formality...

and he hardly ever says anything in *boring political meetings*, yet I had a hard time getting a word in."

She wiggled her eyebrows at him. "Would you say he seemed far more engaged? Perhaps because of a particular person present?" Her fingers played against his bare chest.

Matthias stared at her, pieces of his closest friend's demeanor falling into place. "You think he likes her. The queen of Ziona?"

"They've hardly taken their eyes off each other whenever they're in the same room. I think he's interested, and I believe the feeling is mutual." She tapped his pectoral. "I had a lovely time at tea with the queen yesterday. Did you know that she never remarried after Conrad's father died over twenty years ago?" She tilted her head. "She wouldn't talk about her husband much either."

"Whoa." Matthias tightened his grip on Katrin, lifting her from his lap in a fluid motion to twist and land her on her back with a squeak, him hovering over her. "Are you implying that *Micah* might wed? A queen, no less?"

She lifted her legs to wrap them around his hips, aggressively pulling him against her with a giggle. "It's far too early for such things. Besides..." She ran her nails over his shoulders. "Micah would never leave Isalica without your express blessing. I doubt my insistence that it's about damn time he settled down will get very far."

Matthias scoffed. "Sometimes I wonder what else you see so much sooner than I."

"I even know what's going to happen in, oh, two minutes." Her nail traced down his chest towards his abdomen.

A growl rumbled from the king's chest, and he slipped a hand beneath her nightgown. "Well, I best not disappoint you then." And before she could reply, his mouth claimed hers.

Chapter 17

Kin welcomed the fresh air as he pushed the doors to the balcony open. The sun had vanished below the rim of the canyon beyond the Zionan palace, but the sky still glowed gold. A breeze pulled on the sheer curtains behind him, brushing against the back of his legs. It sent a shiver down his spine, the sensation oddly similar to what the shadows had always felt like when he coiled them around his feet. His arm ached, and he absently rubbed at the tattoo with the thought of his old powers.

Amarie's footsteps pulled him from thought. She paced close to the shared living area's door, finally equipped with a sword and dagger she'd acquired in the city. From a place Ahria had recommended. But now their daughter was with Conrad, whom Kin still didn't have a clear opinion about. The prince's affection for Ahria had been evident, but Kin instinctively questioned the man's intentions.

But she obviously loves him, too.

Dinner within the palace had been awkward. No one spoke of Uriel or the spell or even the treaty. Small talk had reigned between silences, life only entering the conversation when they spoke of their children.

Almost everyone involved in this is a parent. Including me...

Kin had struggled to keep his eyes off Ahria, who'd sat next to Amarie across the table from him. The two looked like sisters, and his heart had swelled each time they shared a laugh or smile.

Drawing himself back towards the parlor they shared, Kin watched Amarie briefly as he leaned against the open balcony door. "You should try to relax."

Amarie kept walking. "At least she hasn't left the palace. Unless she took the necklace off." She paused, looking at him. "What if she took it off?"

"Amarie." Kin stepped forward, gesturing at the couch near the empty fireplace. "Come sit down. She's not going to leave."

"But if she took it off, I'd never know." Amarie stared at him. "Maybe I shouldn't have told her what it did..."

"She's not going to leave." He pushed more conviction into his tone as he sat, patting the seat beside him. "She wants to know you, too. You're just not seeing it."

Hesitating, Amarie groaned and finally sat next to him. "I just..."

He tapped the outside of her thigh, slipping a hand down to pull her feet onto his lap. "You're just nervous. Which is natural. You should have seen that first conversation I had with her."

She narrowed her eyes at him as he removed her boot. "I saw her hug you. It couldn't have gone too badly."

Kin shrugged as he dropped her first boot then moved to the next. "I'd say the same for you, though your hug was certainly a little more explosive." He gave her a half smile. "But she trusts you. That's already obvious."

"Or she freed herself from her power so she could run off and live a normal life with her pirate-turned-prince," she grumbled, but sighed. "What are you doing?"

"Trying to help you relax." He moved his hands to grip her left foot, pushing his thumbs into the bottom of it. "See, you already got more out of her than I did about that boy." He tried to control all the different places his mind was suddenly jumping to with the new information. "How does that work? Pirate turned prince?"

Amarie shrugged, sinking back into the seat as he worked her foot. "He was a ship's captain before Ziona reestablished the royal line. I might be exaggerating with the whole pirate part." She closed her eyes, and when his thumb pushed over her arch, she let out a soft moan.

He smiled, repeating the motion as he watched her face gradually relax. "Well, she's certainly got him wrapped around her little finger by the looks of it."

"Maybe she'll share her secret." Amarie peeked one eye open, giving him a wry look.

His stomach flipped, a familiar warmth flooding through him with it. He tried to swallow and looked at her feet as he worked his way over her toes. "Pretty sure she inherited the skill from you."

Eyes opening, Amarie gave him a contemplative expression, but said nothing. She only sighed as his hands found another good spot on her foot. Turning on the couch, she leaned back against the armrest, poking him in the ribs with her other foot. "When did you get good at giving foot rubs?"

"It's just a foot rub." Kin lifted his eyebrows to her. "I don't have much experience, but I'm pretty good at figuring out what you seem to like and repeating that." He took her other foot and rubbed both for a moment before focusing on the new one. "But I'm always open to constructive criticism, too. So you tell me. What feels best?"

Amarie's throat bobbed. "When you push into the arch," she whispered, gaze locked on his. Her mouth tightened, jaw flexing, as she again fell silent.

Every little action she made caused something within him to tremble. Even his own words sent his mind spiraling down a million different paths. He could still read her and knew how to follow her body's lead on how to please her. He cursed his own mind for rushing to recall their steamy nights in the woods while traveling to his parent's estate. To the nights in his old bed before Alana had ruined everything.

He pushed his thumb into the arch of her foot, urging his blood to cool with the slow movement. "Like this?" He met her stormy eyes, finding it impossible to look away.

She nodded, lips parting. "Are we..." Her brow twitched. "Are we friends, Kin?"

His thumbs hesitated before he could catch himself, but pressed slowly into the next movement. "I think so." He kept eye contact, despite his instincts. "I want to be."

I always looked away before, but it's different this time.

"Do you?" Amarie leaned her head against the back of the couch, using her free foot to play with the hem of his tunic.

His heart pounded, hands slowing. "Yes. But..."

"But?"

"I miss it. What we used to be."

In a motion that hardly looked deliberate, Amarie bit her lower lip. She only stared at him, expression painfully unreadable.

He swallowed the rising fear in his stomach. He'd felt fear before. During the years of service to Uriel, both fear of his master and of the acts he found himself capable of committing. Yet, all of it paled in comparison to facing Amarie now. In telling her the truth that had been burning for days.

He stopped, his hands resting against her shins. "I want it back, Amarie. What we used to have. But I know how unfair that is of me. I don't expect you to feel the same way."

Amarie sat up, crawling across the couch to him, leaning sideways against the back of the couch to face him. Inches away. Her face was inches away from his, and he could see every fleck of color in her irises. Finally, she released her lower lip. "I miss you, too," she whispered, but something else hid beneath her words. "I just..."

He blindly placed his hand on top of hers in her lap as he shook his head. "It's all right." Even if he wished there was a way for it all to go back instantly, that couldn't be done. Not with all the damage wrought. "But I've *never* stopped loving you. And I never will. Even if we can't ever go back to the way it was."

Leaning forward, Amarie touched her forehead to his. "I don't know if I'd survive you leaving a second time." Her hand came to his cheek, sliding down his neck.

Closing his eyes, Kin relished in her touch. His mouth went dry, and he wondered if he'd still be able to speak. He pressed his forehead firmer against hers, her breath teasing his skin. "I would promise that I'll never leave, but I—"

"Promise me, then." Her fingertips played with the base of his hairline, the tip of her nose touching his.

His gut twisted, and he wanted desperately to just say the words. "I don't know what's going to happen, though. I can't lie to you." He forced himself to pull from her, despite every fiber of him screaming to say whatever was necessary to kiss her. "Anything can happen with what we're about to attempt. And I might not have a choice if things don't go as planned."

Amarie stared at him with glassy eyes. "And the Key could burn my soul to shreds in the process of containing Uriel. But that's not what I mean. That's not what I'm asking you."

"What are you asking?"

Her hand slid from his hair, to the side of his neck. "If you'll *choose*... If..." Dropping her gaze, she exhaled a shaky breath through clenched teeth. "Forget it, this is foolish." She withdrew from him, but he caught her.

"No, please tell me." He reached for her jaw, fingers brushing over her face. "Let's not make the same mistakes we made before."

"That's what I'm trying to avoid," she murmured, but let him keep her there. "I'm not asking you to promise you'll always be here, alive, with me. I'm not naive. I know what we're doing comes with incredible risk. But if you're going to leave by choice, for whatever reason, I just can't..."

"I won't." Kin shook his head. "You're right, I already made that mistake. Please believe me when I *promise* I will never choose to leave you again. I swear it."

Amarie met his eyes again, gaze flicking between them. "I—"

A soft knock echoed through the room, and she took a deep breath. Her hand returned to his cheek for a moment as she stroked a thumb over his scar. "Should we..."

"Ignore it." Kin cradled her hand against his face. A smile played on his lips. "Or should I answer the door without a shirt on like I did to poor Niya?"

Amarie laughed, playing with one of his tunic's buttons. "As much as I'd like to see that..."

The knock came again, this time followed by a voice both of them knew too well. "Kin, are you in there? We need to talk."

Matthias.

Leaning forward, she placed a delicate kiss on his cheek before dragging her mouth in a feather-light touch closer to his ear. "I don't think Isalica's king would be so affected by your nakedness."

Kin groaned and leaned his head back against the couch. "He really could have better timing. Especially considering what his Art allows him to do." It took everything in him to stand, pulling away from Amarie. "Just a minute, Matthias." He shouted towards the door before he leaned over Amarie. He placed a slow, soft kiss on top of her head. "We'll finish this conversation later?" His body ached for the conversation to be finished now, behind closed doors and preferably on something soft.

Amarie nodded, the vulnerable expression on her face fading to a more controlled one. "Later." She tugged on her boots and stood. "I'll go for a walk while you talk."

"You sure?" He gave her a knowing look. "Going to check in on Ahria?"

She made a face at him. "Wouldn't you like to know. Maybe I need more blades." Quirking an eyebrow at him, she opened the door for Matthias. "Kin applauds your timing, your majesty." Exaggerating her formality, she curtsied before exiting the room.

Instantly, a knot formed upon seeing Matthias's face. Every muscle tightening involuntarily. Kin forced himself to look in the man's eyes, to see the color untainted by black.

The king furrowed his brow, watching her leave before looking at Kin. "What was that about?"

Kin waved a hand. "Don't worry about it. Just... healing old wounds." He looked behind Matthias, finding him without his friend Micah for the first time. "What is it?"

Matthias took a step into the room before pausing, focused on Kin. "Do you mind if I...?" He touched the door handle.

Another ripple of tension radiated through Kin at the suggestion, but he nodded. "Sure? I guess it's something important then?"

Shutting the door, the king crossed his arms and then leaned against it. "We need to talk about your lineage."

It took a moment for what Matthias was referring to to click in Kin's mind. He turned, walking back towards the couch, sensing he would probably need to sit if the conversation took the direction he now suspected. "So you really do remember everything from when you were *him,* then."

Matthias flinched, though it was barely noticeable. "There are a few years I'm missing most of, when I'd... lost hope. But yes, otherwise, I remember everything."

Kin grimaced as he sat in one of the chairs, wishing it was still him and Amarie on the couch together. "I don't want to imagine what that's like." He sucked in a steadying breath. "I'm sorry."

The king shook his head. "It's all right. It's taken a lot of effort, and not just my own, to help me heal to where I am now. But that's not why I'm here." He remained at the door, as if brutally aware of how uncomfortable his presence made Kin. "How much do you know about Feyor's current state?"

"Current? I'd say I know nothing. I haven't really been making time to catch up on political affairs. I didn't really know that much twenty years ago, either. But what does that have to do with my lineage? You probably know more about it than I do." Kin held out a hand to the chair across from him.

Matthias hesitated before accepting, sitting in the other chair. "If you have any questions about it, I can do my best to answer them. But the reason I'm asking is because right now, your brother is ruling the country, and you know your brother is a Shade. He's driven the economy into the ground and is taxing the people into poverty and ruin. Isalica, Helgath, and now Ziona, are working together to provide relief for refugees and those still trapped in the country. But it's not enough. Feyor can't even feed its military anymore. It needs a regime change."

All the feelings Kin's stomach had been subjected to over the past twenty-four hours finally led to nausea. He sucked in a deep breath, trying to fight off the unease at what Matthias was insinuating. Why else would he come to Kin to discuss such things? "I hope you're not proposing what I think you are..."

The king's face softened with empathy. "I know you don't want to be king... But if you... if *we* can take—"

"Stop." Kin lifted his hands. "Just stop. You're right, I don't want it. And I won't."

"You don't need to be king to fix that country, though," Matthias pressed. "Let me explain?"

Kin's head swam and took off without him to all the different implications. "I'll think it's insane, no matter what you say. That country would never accept me, anyway. A hidden twin that's now somehow twenty years younger than his brother? They'll think it's a crazy insurrection or something."

"What about what your daughter might want?" Matthias's brow twitched. "Have you thought about her?"

His chest squeezed. He couldn't begin to guess what Ahria would think of such a thing, let alone what she wanted. But based on her relationship with a prince, she had probably thought about what being royalty meant. Though, Ahria wouldn't need to marry Conrad to have access to a kingdom if it was something she wanted.

"I just want you to think about it." Matthias held up his hands, palms out. "I'm not trying to force you into anything. But a lot of people are dying, and you can help. Even if you tear the whole monarchy down and give them a government like they have here, in Ziona, at least the country would be in better hands." He sighed.

"Just think about it? Talk to Amarie, or Ahria, or Jarrod, even. Gods, he never wanted the throne, either. And he's not afraid to tell you that."

Kin nodded, swallowing the lingering nausea. "Sure. Maybe. But I'm not making any promises."

Matthias dropped his hands into his lap. "I don't expect you to. I appreciate you hearing me out." He moved to rise, but stopped when Kin spoke.

"I need to ask you something."

The king paused before sitting again. "What is it?"

The question stuck in his throat for a moment as Kin wrung his hands between his knees. "Did... I make the right decision when I left Amarie? Would Uriel have been able to find her through me?" He met Matthias's steady gaze.

Silence settled as Matthias studied him. "Are you asking about what Uriel did to Trist? How he saw through her eyes?"

"Yes. Could he have done that to me, too? I just..." His knuckles cracked as he twisted his hands harder. "How close did he get to figuring out what she was because of me?"

"Trist's rank provided a strong enough connection to allow Uriel to use her in that way. No, he couldn't have done that to you, not at the rank you were." Matthias took a breath. "But... That being said, he was very suspicious and sent Alana's ingvalds to spy on you. They didn't catch up to you until Rylorn, though. They saw you dig a grave with someone. You made the right choice"

Kin's chest ached, despite the confirmation, and he nodded. "Thank you."

"After your return, he called the ingvalds off while you captured Lasseth with Alana and didn't think he needed to keep using them. You can imagine his fury when he lost you right after. *I* am curious about one thing..."

"What?" Kin fought off the flicker of panic at the phrasing Uriel often similarly used. He met the king's eyes again.

Matthias's brows knitted. "Who did you bury?"

"Kalpheus. Amarie's father." He remembered the smell of the sea air as it rushed over the hill he and Deylan had selected for his grave. "He died during Helgath's interrogation when I didn't get there in time."

The king nodded solemnly. "The man you were with was Deylan, then." It wasn't a question. "Did you kill Trist? After she returned and Uriel demoted her, the connection died, but he never found her body."

"That is likely due to the faction's involvement, but yes. I couldn't let her live after what she did to Amarie."

"Understandable."

Kin focused on the man's face, watching it for any tells. "Do you think we can trust the faction?"

Matthias huffed a dry laugh. "They've been a thorn in Uriel's side for years, but he never took them very seriously until the events in Hoult when he battled Amarie the first time. I believe they have their own agenda, but I also believe we can trust them."

"And you'd trust them with your child's life?"

The king fell silent for a moment before shaking his head. "After everything I've seen in this world, I don't trust anyone with my children other than my family. Though... and this I'm sure is completely one-sided, Kinronsilis, I do trust you."

He tensed, surprise rippling through him. He couldn't recall the last time someone had said those words to him. It left a strange feeling in the pit of his stomach. Even though he wanted to believe Amarie trusted him, and most of her actions suggested it... hearing it was different. And he suddenly felt immensely unworthy.

A small chuckle covered the feelings. "Funny, coming from someone who should know quite well how deceitful I can be."

Matthias smirked, rising from the chair. "And from someone who knows with painful certainty that even under the most dire circumstances, you have never once given up a shred of information about those you love."

The phantom pain in the scars on his back tingled. "I'd have died to keep it."

"And you did." Matthias held his gaze. "More than once. So yes, I trust you, even if I know the feeling isn't mutual."

The information felt hollow, striking a strange chord within him. Matthias had no reason to lie, and now knowing how his Art worked... how Uriel's had. Kin knew he was telling the truth.

How many times did I die at his hands?

A shiver passed through Kin, and he didn't hide it from the king. "I hope you understand I am a little relieved that you won't be joining us." He smiled, keeping his tone light so the king would understand how he meant it. "Gives me some more time to wrap my head around accepting the new you."

A muscle in Matthias's jaw flexed, but he gave no other reaction. "I'm here if you wish to talk or if you have questions." He strode to the door, gripping the handle. He paused as if he might say more, but he only nodded to Kin one last time before leaving the room and shutting the door behind him.

Chapter 18

Rae played with a six-sided die, tossing it up and catching it. "How come no one talks about Zionan cider? Everything is all *Delkest wine, Helgathian whisky*, but no one mentioned *this* all this time?" She sipped her cold mug of the apple-flavored beverage and eyed her husband. "Can we bring some home?"

Damien lounged across the couch of Conrad's study, his shirt unbuttoned lower than normal in social settings. He usually wore high collars to keep his tattoos hidden in any company but their closest friends, but here, there were no secrets about who he was. "Don't worry, Dice. We're going to have open trade with Ziona soon and we'll get you personal shipments to the palace whenever you want."

"Have you tried Xaxos fire wine?" Ahria quirked an eyebrow. "I will trade you a case for a case."

"Deal!" Rae grinned. She very much enjoyed the fire wine from Xaxos, though hadn't indulged in it until after Jarrod had taken the throne. Too expensive for a thief's budget, but that'd changed when she started receiving regular sums of money from the crown for her service. As head thief. Though the Hawks didn't do much stealing, anymore.

Conrad chuckled, standing at a side table where he poured another glass for Ahria after she'd coaxed him into getting it for her. "I think we're getting the better side of that deal, for sure."

"Cost doesn't matter as long as Rae gets what she wants." Damien leaned back to look at the prince. "And if you don't sell it to her, she'll just steal it."

"That's true," Rae quipped. "I have sticky fingers." The slight weight in her pocket only proved her point.

"I remember. I hope you haven't put those to use here. I wouldn't want to have to arrest you." Conrad smirked.

Damien gave her a look.

Rae sighed, resisting the urge to roll her eyes at her all-knowing husband. "Fine. I'll give it back." She produced an iron key from her pocket, offering it to the prince.

Conrad's eyes widened as he reached into his pocket, revealing the six-sided die she'd left there instead. "When did you even do that?"

"A couple hours ago."

When he was busy pouring drinks for everyone, she'd happily taken the opportunity.

"She would have swapped it back some time in the next hour, too." Damien gave her another look. "Because she knows we're on a political mission and that she's supposed to refrain."

Rae pursed her lips to contain her smile, but twitched an eyebrow at him. "I can behave." But she pushed her thoughts towards Damien. *I just don't want to.*

He shook his head with a laugh as he looked back over his shoulder again. "Hopefully she doesn't make you regret inviting us to your private study for a nightcap."

"Not at all." Ahria smiled as Conrad handed her a refilled glass. "I appreciate the amusement, really."

"She can keep the key. I'm willing to pass off my duties to her, since all that will do is get her into the judiciary hall." Conrad still hadn't completely loosened up, but that didn't surprise her. He'd been reluctant to open up as a teenager, too.

Rae frowned at the key, then tossed it to him, smirking when he caught and pocketed it. "As exciting as that sounds, I already have a job."

A knock came at the door, but no guards had been stationed outside to announce who it was.

"Enter!" Ahria called out after glancing up at Conrad.

The door swung open, and Deylan strode in, shutting it behind him. He took in the room, mouth curving in a suspicious smile. "So this is where the fun is."

"We have cider." Rae shifted on the couch, sitting closer to Damien so Deylan could take the other seat.

Damien sat up straighter, wrapping an arm around his wife's shoulders. She nuzzled against him, finding the comfortable spot against his chest with the weight of his arm at her waist. He leaned in to her, placing a kiss on the side of her head.

"Something to drink, Deylan?" Conrad moved towards the side table again, ready to play the host. The tension in his shoulders doubled.

Connie really needs to learn to relax.

"You should try the cider," Rae supplied.

Deylan nodded. "Sounds good." He watched the prince with a narrowed gaze, and Rae recognized the look of a protective guardian. While Conrad went about getting a fresh mug, Ahria's uncle looked at the rest of them. "I suppose you've all heard by now that Isalica is going to head up the team that will deal with the Shade. We will be leaving in the morning, along with Kin and Amarie, for the faction headquarters."

"The crown elites will be able to capture the Shade before they have a chance to report back. It's good. Will buy more time before Uriel can put pieces together about Ahria." Damien looked across the way to her.

Conrad offered the drink to Deylan. "Are we certain that's the best action? Won't it only pique Uriel's interest in New Kingston if another Shade dies here?"

"The Shade won't die here. We are assisting Isalica and plan to capture them alive. If death does end up befalling them, it'll be far from New Kingston." Deylan accepted the mug before looking at his niece. "Vaeler volunteered to stay here and coordinate for the faction."

Ahria nodded, expression hard to read, but said nothing.

"Now that we're set to depart, any more information on where the headquarters is located?" Conrad took his place standing beside Ahria's chair again.

Deylan looked at him, then Ahria, then the prince again, a thoughtful expression on his face. "You're still intent on coming with us? Have you informed the queen of your plans?"

"My mum is supportive." Conrad narrowed his gaze. "Why? Are you not?"

The air in the room thickened.

Ahria cleared her throat and gave her uncle a pointed look.

"Things get complicated the more people there are to keep safe... And you should note that no other royals will be privy to the headquarters' location." Deylan looked at Ahria and sighed. "But since Ahria insists... I suppose I'll make an exception."

"I assure you, I won't abuse the knowledge. And I can take care of myself, too." Conrad put his hand on Ahria's shoulder.

"I'd have more confidence in that if your last encounter with a —"

"Uncle, please." Ahria said through clenched teeth. "Can you tell us now where we're going?"

Deylan grunted but nodded. "We're going to the Dul'Idur Sea. To the Gate. That should make *you* happy, kiddo."

Ahria's eyes widened. "The faction headquarters are on the gate?"

Rae stiffened, looking up at Damien.

"You're telling me the faction headquarters are in Ziona?" Conrad's stance somehow got even stiffer.

"I'd think the gate is a little high profile for how secretive the Sixth Eye is?" Damien quirked an eyebrow.

Deylan sipped his cider. "Technically, Ziona built their country on top of the faction. We were there first." His attention shifted to Damien. "And it's not *on* the gate. It's under it."

Quiet consumed the room. Rae felt herself rise with each of Damien's steady breaths from where she sat.

"There's nothing but water beneath the gate." Conrad's hard expression showed a fraction of confusion.

"Is that so?" Deylan smirked at the prince. "Have you swam down and checked?"

Conrad looked down at Ahria, frowning.

Damien sighed. "And what all is in these underwater headquarters?"

"I can't answer that." Deylan shook his head. "But I'll push the Vanguard to give you access to the library, at least."

"Books and water don't usually mix. That sounds like a bad place for a library." Rae took the final swig of her cider. "What's the Vanguard?"

"We have means of keeping the books safe." Deylan took a seat in a chair. "The Vanguard is the ruling body for the Sixth Eye. The highest rank, and the only rank above me. They won't be happy I've brought you all there, but I'll handle it."

Chapter 19

"I'll take the couch." Kin dropped his saddlebags onto the floor beside the plush furniture in one of the guest rooms of the Zionan royal estate in Dilae. They were just over halfway to the Dul'Idur Gate, and a bed felt long overdue.

Conrad's presence within the group increased their comfort in accommodations, even though the prince had initially suggested staying at a less ostentatious inn. But a local had recognized him, having attended the formal coronation event in New Kingston, and word spread quickly. Before they knew it, the old royal estate was prepared for them.

Amarie glanced at the large bed. She and Kin hadn't discussed their relationship since they'd almost kissed back in New Kingston ten days prior, but they'd resumed their agreed friendship with ease. "When I said we could share a room, I assumed we'd share the bed, too. But you're, of course, under no obligation."

Kin met her gaze, confusion in his steel eyes. "Seems a bit presumptuous of me to jump to the same conclusion. But if you're sure..."

She dropped her pack on one side. Sitting on the edge of the bed, she pulled off her boots. "You can't even stretch out on the couch. The bed is huge. I even promise to stay mostly on my side." She smiled at him, sighing and laying sideways. Propping her head up with one hand, she watched him approach. Unexpected tension sprouted in her stomach at her own suggestion, but she swallowed it.

Kin returned the smirk. "Doubtful. I remember your bed-hogging tendencies." He paused to stretch one of his legs with a wince. "How do people ride for that long?" He leaned down to rub at his thigh before making a face. "I need a bath."

"Your muscles get used to it." She gestured across the room at the internal door that led to the bathing chamber. "Go ahead. I'll take one after you."

A flutter of a thought passed across Kin's face, but he didn't speak as he turned towards the bathing chamber.

"What was that?" Amarie narrowed her eyes, having reminded herself time and time again not to hold her tongue. Not to keep the secrets and thoughts to herself. To trust him, and to ask him anything whenever she wanted.

"What was what?" Kin paused in the doorway, leaning with one arm against the frame as he turned back to her.

Why does he have to do that?

Her mouth dried as his pose took her back to earlier times. "You made a face. You thought something and then didn't say it. What was it?" It wasn't paranoia that drove her curiosity, but a genuine desire to understand him.

Kin's jaw tensed, and she swore a bit of color rose into his cheeks. "Just... a thought. Not a very appropriate one, so I figured I'd spare you."

Amarie's stomach flopped over. "Oh." She huffed, rolling her lips together and resisting the urge to bite one. "I didn't realize you... you know. It's all right, you don't have to say it. Enjoy your bath."

As soon as the door to the bathing chamber closed behind him, Amarie rolled over and face-planted into a pillow with a groan.

Gods, I can be dense.

But she'd assumed after nothing had happened before, that he didn't necessarily want it to. Sure, she had no idea what his thought had been, but... the options were limited. And they all would have involved bathing. Perhaps together. Definitely naked.

Amarie groaned into the pillow again as the sound of water flowing echoed through the walls into the chamber. She caught herself imagining what Kin was doing in there and quickly rose from the bed. "This was a dumb idea, Amarie. Why do you do this to yourself?" she muttered, yanking her boots on.

She left the room, locking the door behind her, and strode down the hallway. Something in her chest told her that if she'd stayed, she wouldn't have stayed on the bedroom side of that damned door.

Finding the dining hall with relative ease, she eyed the food spread out for evening visitors. Dinner would have been some time ago, but this would be plenty for her rumbling stomach. She collected some fruit and bread before sitting at the long, unoccupied table, and a staff member quickly came and poured her a glass of wine.

That won't help.

But she sipped it anyway, gaze lifting as another entered the room.

Ahria smiled sheepishly at her. "I guess I'm not the only one who's hungry."

Amarie chuckled. "Nope. Try the winter melon. It's actually really good."

"Winter melon that's only ripe in the summer. Makes perfect sense." Ahria took a large plate, piling enough food on it to feed a small army.

"Did you not eat today at all?" Amarie leaned back in her chair.

"Talon always said I eat a crazy amount of food." Her daughter smiled, adding two dinner rolls to the top of the pile. "Besides, Conrad's hungry too, so I was going to..." As her voice trailed off, understanding settled in.

"It's all right." Amarie waved her hand. "Go. Be with your prince. I'll be bringing something back for Kin, too."

Ahria nodded, pausing by the table. "Where is he?"

"Cleaning up."

A knowing look passed over her daughter's expression. "Ah. Is that... awkward for the two of you? You know Conrad could have gotten you each your own room."

That probably would have been smarter.

"It's... a little awkward," Amarie admitted. "But we'll manage. It's fine."

Ahria took a step closer. "I know you two aren't together, but... Do you think that will change? I know it hasn't been long since Talon..."

Amarie shook her head. "Talon and I weren't together for a while before I went into Slumber, but I still loved him. I don't think that's holding me back, now. Your fa... Sorry. Kin and I just have some things to figure out, I think."

"You don't have to do that." Ahria smiled, and it reached her eyes. "You can call him my father. He *is* my father. I know no one is trying to replace Lorin and Talon. I guess I'm used to having more than one, so having three doesn't feel like such a stretch." She continued towards the door to the hallway before pausing again. "And, for what it's worth, I want you to be happy. Both of you. So if part of you is holding back because of me... You don't have to do that, either."

Pride swelled in Amarie's heart. "Thanks, Ree. Have a good night, all right?"

Ahria nodded. "You, too." And then she disappeared into the hallway with her mountain of snacks.

Amarie huffed a laugh. "Gods, Talon, you did a damn good job raising her." Finishing the food she'd collected for herself, she downed the rest of her wine and stood.

Hopefully Kin would be finished bathing by the time she returned, but to be on the safe side, she took her time making him a plate. Meandering back to their room, she took a deep breath before unlocking the door and entering.

Please be clothed.

Kin sat on the couch, cleaning his sword and fully dressed. Looking up, he met her gaze and eyed the food. "You'll have to tell me where you got that. I'm starving."

Amarie strode to him and placed the plate on the low table in front of him. "I already ate. This is for you."

Kin smiled. "Thank you." He settled his sword on the table, plucking up a bunch of grapes. "Bath is all yours." His wet hair stuck to the back of his neck where it'd grown shaggy over the past weeks. The scruff was gone from his face, but it'd be back by the morning.

Nodding, she kicked off her boots. She wanted to offer to cut his hair, but didn't know how to word it. "Didn't feel like trimming your hair, too?"

"I'm no good at getting the back on my own. Am I getting too rugged for you?" he teased as he popped some grapes into his mouth.

Amarie laughed as she crossed towards the bathing chamber, picking up her pack along the way. "A little. But you hardly need to accommodate *my* desires."

"If not you, who else? You're the poor soul who has to look at me all day. I don't have to look at myself." He twisted in his seat to face her, blindly reaching for more food.

Pausing, Amarie stared at him. Her daughter's words echoed through her.

Why aren't we together again?

She bit her lower lip, and Kin averted his gaze as a familiar tension passed over his shoulders. Releasing it, she refrained from apologizing for the habit. "Well... If you want help cutting it, I'm here."

"I appreciate that." He looked at her again, the tension fading slowly. "Maybe after your bath?"

Amarie nodded, unbidden heat flushing through her skin. Walking into the bathing chamber, she closed the door behind her and let out a breath. The water somehow still steamed, but she didn't question the methods used by the estate.

After she'd thoroughly cleaned, scrubbed, and dried herself, she dressed in clean clothes and returned to the bedroom. Placing her pack next to the bed, she crouched to dig her comb from the depths. Finding it, she stood and scanned the room, spotting Kin through the sheer curtains out on the patio. The shared outdoor space overlooked the garden, each guest room having a door outside, but he was alone.

Not bothering with her boots, she walked out the open doorway. A rich array of flowers and ferns decorated the estate's landscape. Even if the royal family had just come back into power, their grounds had evidently been preserved and well cared for. Perhaps whatever military power had been in place in the city had lived here.

The warm buzzing of summer bees filled the air as the creatures passed from flower to flower. Leaves had grown so dense that the stone path that wound through the grounds was barely visible. The distant stone wall held it all in, containing it within the estate. The red-tiled roofs of the houses of Dilae lay beyond, but it was easy to forget the city while enjoying the lush garden.

Sitting next to Kin on the loveseat, Amarie angled towards him. Tucking her feet beneath her, she worked a comb through her long hair, starting at the ends.

Kin glanced in her direction, but his focus remained mostly on the garden. The look in his eyes seemed pensive. He let out a heavy sigh. "You never were able to see my ma's gardens in the springtime."

Sadness crept into Amarie's chest. "No. I suppose I wasn't." She hesitated. "Do you know if they're still...?"

Kin's jaw twitched as he shook his head. "I don't know about my father, but it's been twenty years. And he was never great at taking care of his own health without Ma's reminders." He looked at Amarie, his eyes glassy. "She died before I went to find Damien. Her death... it was the last straw, and it confirmed I was doing the right thing in trying to break the bond."

Amarie's heart squeezed, and she set the comb aside. "I'm sorry. Did Uriel...?"

Kin flinched. "Alana. But I'm sure it was at his behest. She'd said it was a lesson, a reminder not to get distracted from my duty. But I guess it backfired on her." He heaved a deep breath, collecting himself. "I wish Ma could have met Ahria." He gave her a side look, as if already reading her mind. "Ma was gone before she was even born."

"I'm really sorry, Kin. I wish I could have been there for you," she whispered. "But I'm grateful that I got to meet your mother. She was a warm light among the rest of it." Reaching across the space between them, she took his hand. "She'd be so proud of you."

He smiled half-heartedly as he turned his palm into hers. "I hope so. I told her everything just before Alana poisoned her. She died knowing what I had done and still loved me. She told me to focus on what I knew I wanted in my life, with you, and that it'd help me find the light." He squeezed her hand. "She was right."

Amarie stared at him. His honesty and openness struck a chord within her, cracking her heart. It tightened her throat, but she forced words out. "I don't know what's going to happen, but I want you to know that I'm in this, with you, until whatever end. We will fight this war together. For her, for Talon, for our future. Our family." The truth of her own words rang back at her.

Our future.

But she didn't try to take it back. Because she meant it, even if things between them weren't settled.

He looked at her, straight into her soul. After a moment, a genuine smile grew on his expression. Squeezing her hand harder, he nodded, and a new wetness glistened in his eyes. "You don't know what that means for me to hear. I'm grateful that we're even able to sit here, in this moment. That you're here." He bobbed their hands up and down. "And that there's even a sliver of a chance at a happier future."

Amarie let go of his hand and slid closer, tentatively curling her body against his. She leaned her knees on his thigh, finding the crook of his arm and resting her head on his chest. The settled weight of his embrace around her shoulder sent a wave of warmth through her. His rich scent, fresh from the bath, encouraged her to relax. She placed her hand on his chest, idly tracing an invisible pattern with her fingertips.

He shifted lightly beneath her without letting go, leaning into her to rest his cheek against the top of her head. His breath rustled her hair before his mouth formed a long kiss there.

They sat in silence for a time, just holding each other. They didn't need to speak.

As the sun disappeared and the air cooled, Amarie looked up at Kin. "Will you hold me tonight? While we sleep?" She craved the contact. The closeness of him, only furthered by how they currently sat. She didn't care what labels they had or didn't have. This was the man she wanted to be near, no matter what.

"Yes," he whispered against her hair. "I will anytime you want me to." His arm around her pulled her closer into his side.

Resting her chin on the side of his chest, she blinked at him and whispered, "I always want you to." The admission didn't feel as exposing as she thought it would, and her lips twitched upward. "I miss it, too."

He pulled back his head, meeting her gaze. "Then I will." His fingers brushed over her cheek, feather soft, before he cupped her jaw and ran his thumb along her skin. His hands had never been rough before, but now there were small calluses from his sword practice.

Amarie tilted her face into his touch. Letting out a soft sigh, she rested her head sideways again on his chest. "It's more than a sliver, you know."

Kin squeezed her, a smile in his voice. "Thank you for that. But we don't have to rush. I know you're still sorting through things." He rubbed his hand up and down on her arm. "But I'll be here to hold you in the meantime."

A strange sense of peace rippled through her, briefly making her eyes burn.

No rush.

He'd wait for her. He'd wait as long as she needed, and somewhere deep in her gut, she'd already known it.

She nuzzled into him, smiling. "I like the sound of that. Because this feels really good."

Ten days later...

Warmth filled Amarie's chest as she glanced at Ahria and Conrad. Her daughter and the prince rode a short distance behind her and Kin, keeping the smooth canter pace that Deylan set for them at the front.

Facing forward again, Amarie briefly thought, yet again, that she rode Viento. The black gelding had a thick build, though his bloodline wasn't purely Friesian. The Zionan horse was obedient, well-trained, but lacked her beloved horse's fiery nature.

Ahria had tried to break the news to her earlier that week that Viento had passed a few years back, but Amarie already knew. She'd seen her horse in the Inbetween before seeing Talon, though hadn't been sure if he'd been part of her imagination. Ahria shared a few stories about growing up with him, and gratitude still brightened Amarie's mood. He'd been a part of her daughter's life, and it was the best she could have asked for.

And Viento even sired a foal.

She looked forward to meeting it one day.

Beside her, Kin rode a bay, looking less awkward than he had in previous weeks. Without his Art, he evidently accepted the need to get more comfortable on a horse, despite his early teenage experiences.

The Dul'Idur Gate grew closer, a shadow on the horizon as the sun lowered behind it. The spires were still just as Amarie remembered them. Nothing had changed in the twenty years she'd slumbered, and it brought a modicum of comfort to know some things would remain the same. This gate had been the same for centuries, and if Deylan truly meant it when he said the faction had established there before Ziona's formation, then perhaps it'd been there for millennia.

A distant roar of the waves crashing against the cliff side to their left reminded Amarie of the miles of chain and gears that were still out of her vision. They ran from the massive doors down below the ocean. Whatever metal comprised the monstrosity couldn't have been iron, because it remained black and unrusted despite the age and wear of the sea.

The massive bridge of black metal spanned the distance between the land masses on either side of the strait below, easily wide enough to accommodate at least five wagons side by side. It ran in a gentle arch, though it wasn't necessary with the distance between it and the water far below. Even the largest galleon ships could sail through without coming within one hundred feet of the top of the gate.

A Zionan standard billowed in the wind at the top of the towers on either side, which looked out of place against the dark gate. The towers, built of stone, were a more recent addition to the structure, though the moss suggested they, too, were old.

The gates stood open, as they always did, and Amarie surveyed the land on either side but saw no sign of Zionan soldiers. There was hardly a reason to guard the gate in a time of peace across Pantracia. No wars raged, at least not in the open.

They rounded a chain that ran from the bottom of the arch, half-buried for the entirety of its two-hundred foot length across the ground to the side of the gate. Even with only the top half of it exposed, the links stood taller than they did on the horses, making Amarie suddenly feel small.

Deylan turned the group towards the entrance to the bridge, slowing the pace as they entered the shadow of the stone towers.

A chill blew in from the ocean below, and Amarie took a moment to look west as the sun touched the mountains beyond the strait.

The view took her breath away, and she slowed her horse to a stop. Wind whipped her ponytail around, the salty breeze bringing back so many memories. Especially as Kin's horse stopped next to hers.

Voices murmured between the others, idle chatter, but Amarie didn't bother to listen.

Now wasn't the time to think about things like beaches and sunsets, but after she'd spent most of the nights since Dilae sleeping in his arms, she couldn't help it. The only kisses shared between them were on her hair, or his cheek, but it was perfect.

Amarie looked at Kin and smiled as she nudged her horse to return to the others.

Deylan hadn't stopped, riding across the bridge with Rae and Damien. Towards...

Is that a person?

Amarie squinted, barely able to make out the shimmer of orange sunlight bouncing off someone's hair. Or helmet. She couldn't tell. But someone waited for them.

Unease curled in her gut, even though the faction members were technically allies. There was still so little she knew, other than her brother and father's involvement, and their goal of protecting the Key. The Key's power, more specifically, rather than the wielder herself.

She saw her father every time Deylan looked at her. With his greying hair and laugh lines, they looked so much alike. It made her heart ache, and she touched the ring adorning the chain around her neck. The ring Kin had given her from her father.

The painful irony that Ahria now wore her deceased father's bracelet passed through her with a pang of sorrow.

Swallowing, she urged her horse to follow her brother's, despite the stranger ahead, and the rest of their little convoy fell into pace behind her. The hooves clanged on the metal, but the sound didn't echo through the structure like she expected it to.

Reaching the man, Deylan dismounted and the stranger took his horse's reins. As she approached, Amarie spied two more people in the shadows of the gate's central tower.

She dismounted, patting the animal's neck before handing the reins off to one of the strangers, who gave her a respectful bow. The others followed suit. Once the three faction members had all the horses gathered, they walked towards the opposite side of the bridge.

The faction must have a stable on the other side.

With only the barest glance at their party, Deylan knelt where he stood and unlatched a trap door in the floor of the bridge deck, swinging it open and connecting a thick chain to a metal ring. She watched the process as he opened previously innocuous metal panels and attached more chains. Panels that were so well hidden, she couldn't see them until Deylan moved them.

Moments later, they all stared at a hole in the false floor of the gate's bridge.

Amarie inched closer, peering down into the opening, where a metal box hovered. Her stomach flopped over. "Please don't tell me we're going in that." She looked at her brother.

Damien stood farther back from it while Rae whispered in his ear.

He doesn't look like a fan of this, either.

"It's safe," Deylan assured. "It's called a lift. I will take three of you down at a time. Who wants to go first?"

"I will." Ahria glanced at Conrad.

Amarie started, but held back her protest. "I'm going with her."

Deylan nodded and looked between Conrad and Kin. "One more."

Kin gestured with his chin to Conrad, whose grip had tightened on Ahria as soon as she volunteered. "You go."

Amarie met Kin's undaunted gaze for a breath, understanding he didn't want to deny Ahria the comfort of having Conrad with her. It made her smile, and he gave the barest half smile back.

With Deylan's gesture, she crouched before hopping down into the lift, metal clanging as her boots hit.

Ahria dropped inside next, followed by Conrad.

She fought the instinct to cling to the walls as the platform below her shifted with the addition of the prince's weight. But there was nothing to hold onto.

The metal box had no windows, no holes, and her chest tightened.

She assured herself the division of their party made sense.

Amarie could protect this batch of people if anything went wrong. And Rae... Rae could manipulate the sea and keep the rest of them safe. She kept reminding herself of that as Deylan joined them, lighting the lantern hanging in a corner before closing the panels above.

Deylan pushed his hand against a panel, a lever dropping into place with a clunk. He cranked it to one side, and the whole thing lurched, leaving Amarie's stomach a few inches above where it belonged. He operated another and a dial, and then lifted the lever again and the metal box began its descent more smoothly. Chains clicked all around them outside the thick walls, but the lack of windows made it impossible to tell how fast they descended towards the water looming below.

Amarie looked up and narrowed her eyes at the slight gap in the panels above. She could just make out wide beams passing by in the dim light that escaped from the lift into the shaft above them. "Won't water get in?"

Deylan followed her gaze but shook his head. "Water won't actually touch the lift. Don't worry."

The eerie lantern light glimmered off Ahria's face and where she held Conrad's hand.

The journey down took hours, it felt like. It was probably only minutes, but by the time the lift thunked to a stop, Amarie couldn't wait to get out.

Deylan flipped another lever and then rotated metal slats she hadn't noticed before at the top and bottom of one wall. They grinded along the metal before hinges creaked and the wall parted open into two doors.

Before them laid a long hallway made of the same dark metal as the Dul'Idur Gate above them. Thin rectangular panels ran along the tops of the walls in neat lines. They stuck out ever so slightly, a glow emanating from behind them. The light shone in bright streaks along the wall directly beside the panel, but then diffused to illuminate the armored corridor with warm light. At the far end, there appeared to be two doors, but she couldn't tell where they might lead.

"Are we under water?" Ahria looked up, even though they could see nothing but a low, metal ceiling. A murky, deadened sound filled the space.

Deylan nodded again. "We are. I'll get you inside and then go back for the others."

The doors on the other end of the hall opened, and a man strode towards them. His eyes darted to Amarie first, avoiding Ahria before focusing on Deylan, and he frowned. "Why do I feel like you didn't get clearance for this?"

"Jelkin?" Ahria stepped into the hallway, focused on the stranger. "Is that you?"

"Hey, Ree," the man waved sheepishly. "Glad to see you're well."

Amarie's daughter only gaped at him, and she could imagine the pieces of a puzzle coming together, though had no context.

"I'll handle the Vanguard," Deylan muttered. "Can you get them settled? I have three more to go back for. Will need three or four guest rooms..." He quirked an eyebrow at his sister.

"Three rooms." Amarie nodded, exiting the lift behind Conrad, who'd moved to stand beside Ahria again.

Jelkin's frown deepened when his eyes landed on Conrad. "Guess you're the new guy."

Behind them, the panels to the lift closed, and a moment later, the metal box rose into the darkness and out of sight.

Conrad tensed, his face stoic. "And I guess you two know each other, but she didn't know you were part of this." He waved a hand around them.

Jelkin scrunched his face in confusion at Ahria. "What happened to Davros?"

Ahria still just stared at the man. "You're a farrier. *My* farrier."

The man shrugged. "I have many skills, sweetheart." He led them towards the doors, glancing at the prince. "You know you can't repeat any of this to anyone, right, Prince?"

"I'm aware that this is a secret faction that needs to remain so. Deylan and I already had this conversation. I'm not here as a prince. I'm here with Ahria."

Jelkin opened the doors for them before continuing down a carpeted hallway.

"You've been protecting me all this time?" Ahria trailed behind Jelkin, then paused. "Wait, was Davros...?"

"No." The farrier shook his head. "He's not one of ours."

"Oh." Ahria let out a breath. "He's fine. Living the life of a sailor as far as I know."

Amarie made a mental note to ask Ahria about Davros later, when Conrad wasn't around. "Are we going to meet with the Vanguard?"

"No one meets with the Vanguard except Locksmiths." Jelkin rounded a corner, passing by several doors before glancing between her and Ahria again. "Right ol' family reunion here. I'm sorry about your pop, Ree."

Ahria's chin dipped. "Me, too. Thanks."

"Who else is here?" Jelkin's footsteps echoed louder as they entered a rounded portion of tunnel.

Amarie watched for his reaction. "Kin, Damien, and Rae."

His steps halted, and he looked back at them. "You're telling me that Deylan brought both Berylian Keys, the Rahn'ka, a Mira'wyld, *and a Shade* to this place?" His face paled, but she wasn't sure which part bothered him the most.

But he knows exactly who everyone is.

Amarie stepped ahead of Ahria and Conrad. "*Former* Shade. Which is an important distinction. And yes, because he needed to."

Jelkin scoffed, letting out a long whistle as he kept walking. "Hope he keeps his rank after all this."

After a couple more turns, they stopped in another narrow hallway that boasted a multitude of metal doors running along both sides.

Pointing to the first, Jelkin gestured with his chin. "Room number one." He then looked at Amarie and gestured to the room across from the first. "And room number two. Go inside and wait for someone to let you know otherwise." He looked at Ahria as he spoke again, slowly. "No wandering."

Ahria nodded, exchanging a look with her mother before disappearing inside the offered room with Conrad.

Amarie entered hers, shutting the door behind her and listening to Jelkin's footsteps take him back the way they'd come.

She dropped her pack on the bed, wishing the small space had a window, but that would be impossible. Only a painting of a beach adorned the wall, and she huffed an ironic laugh. Aside from the bed, the room had a desk with a chair, and a small bedside table. The furniture took up almost all the floor space, leaving only a few feet between everything.

They hadn't seen anyone else during their trek through the underwater headquarters. Yet, based on everything Amarie had learned about the Sixth Eye, their membership seemed rather widespread. That either suggested the headquarters were large enough not to run into anyone, or most were out in the field. She guessed it was probably the latter.

Or Jelkin purposely steered us away from seeing anyone else.

The dark hallways beyond her bedroom called out to be adventured through. She wanted to know more about what lay in each of the various corridors and chambers they'd passed. All secured behind massive metal doors.

Amarie tried to sit on the bed, but nerves made her rise again a moment later. The occasional creak or groan of metal made her insides twist. Temptation had her touch the doorknob several times, eager to backtrack and make sure the others descended safely. But the hinges of the doors had been far from silent, and she didn't need Ahria joining her in breaking the rules.

After what felt like eternity, a gentle rhythm of footsteps entered the hall outside her room, the vibrations more pronounced than the actual sound.

Amarie stood by the bed, straining to hear anything else, but the walls were too thick.

A breath later, her door opened, and Kin stood there.

Letting out a sigh, she sat down again as he closed the door behind him. "Damien and Rae?"

"In the room next to us." Kin glanced around the space, placing his pack on the desk. "Little more cramped than I've gotten used to in the last few weeks."

They'd kept their interactions platonic in front of the others, though even in private it hadn't evolved beyond holding each other. She craved his embrace, the need only furthered by the growing anxiety of the walls around her, but she remained sitting on the bed. "Should I have asked for another room?" A smirk tugged at the corner of her lips.

Kin lifted his brow at her with a hint of a smile. "I think you know the answer to that." He crossed to the bed, leaning down in the narrow space between it and the wall to unlace his boots. "I don't mind the small, dark spaces. Rae, on the other hand." He chuckled. "Thought she was going to break Damien's wrist with how tight she was squeezing while we were in that lift. Paler than he was while we were up on top of that bridge."

"Yeah, she won't enjoy this." Amarie eyed him. "How long do you think we're stuck here?"

"As soon as we got to the bottom of the lift, someone was waiting for Deylan. Something about needing to report to the Vanguard immediately. I suspect we're going to be stuck here until they're done reaming him." Kin settled onto the bed behind her, laying back onto the pillows with his arms behind his head. "I'm sure it'll be awhile. Might as well get comfortable."

Amarie looked over her shoulder at him, a foreign playful feeling rising in her stomach. "At least it's a double bed, and I won't have to sleep *on* you." She bit her lip and waited for him to notice.

Kin peeked at her through half-closed eyes, and they darted down to her mouth. His chest flexed pleasantly as he tensed. "Always welcome to, anyway."

Chuckling, she laid next to him, propping herself up with an elbow. "Maybe I'll take you up on that." Before she could rethink her own inclination, she leaned over him and kissed him. Gently, lingering for a breath as his lips responded before she pulled away.

Kin looked at her, his gaze soft as he touched her jaw. "What was that for?"

She shrugged. "I don't know. I just wanted to." Placing her hand on his chest, she studied his face. "Is that all right?"

He smiled, running his thumb along her chin. "Yes. But... now I want to kiss you." His eyes flickered down to her mouth before meeting hers for a long moment. "May I?"

Butterflies danced through her, and she nodded.

Kin pushed himself up from the bed with an elbow, moving into her in a smooth motion as he wrapped his other arm around her. His lips were gentle as they moved against hers. A soft, longing kiss that threatened every inch of her.

It stole her breath. The warmth of him, the taste. Her chest rose faster as the kiss renewed, sudden heat sparking between them. She ran her hand through his hair, her leg wrapping around him.

A moment later, she broke the kiss, catching her breath. "I, uh..." Touching his face, she met his eyes. "I need to tell you something."

Kin's breath tickled her skin as he pressed his forehead to hers, running his hand up over her hair and removing the leather strap of her ponytail. His chin tilted as if to go for another kiss, but then he paused, dipping away again as he ran his fingers through her loose hair. "You can tell me anything."

The words got stuck on her tongue, and she swallowed. "I never... I never stopped loving you. I tried to, but it didn't work. No matter the circumstances, it was always you. You're being so patient with me, and—"

"Amarie." Kin pulled away just enough to solidly meet her eyes. "You don't need to explain. You don't owe me any of that."

"I know. But I want you to understand that..." Her eyes burned, and she stroked his face. "That I love you. And it's not that I love you again, but that I always have."

He watched her, the steel blue cutting through her in a spine-tingling way. Running his hand over her jaw slowly, he smiled. "I love you, too. Just as I always have." He closed the space between them, placing another gentle kiss on her mouth. It lingered, and her eyes fluttered closed.

I could kiss him forever.

Amarie bit his lower lip and gently tugged before letting it go, eliciting a heated groan against her mouth. Her insides warmed, but she rested her head on his forearm and looked up at him as she kicked her boots off. "I don't want to just be friends anymore."

"No?" Kin moved closer, his legs entwining with hers. He pressed their hips together as he nuzzled into her hair. His voice deepened. "What do you want, Amarie?"

Her stomach flopped over again as her breath quickened. "I want... us. I want you. And I want to be yours." She touched down his neck before tangling her fingers in his hair again. As he shifted his hips, her breath snagged, and she stared at him. Part of her could hardly believe this was happening, but her heart yearned for it.

They moved together as Kin rolled her on to her back, shifting between her legs. His hands ran down her sides, playing along the fabric before they danced between folds to touch her bare waist. He hovered above her for a moment before he kissed her. But it didn't last as his mouth explored down her jaw to her neck, teeth grazing the curve to her ear.

Amarie closed her eyes, focusing on the sensation as her fingers struggled to unbutton his tunic.

His breath teased as he rocked his hips into her, the pressure, despite their clothing, making her back arch. He moaned softly, tongue against her skin. "I want you, too," he whispered. "I want to make love with you."

Wrapping her arms around him, she pulled herself closer and kissed his neck and murmured, "Then take your pants off," before nipping his skin.

He chuckled, pulling back from her as his fingers made quick work of the laces on her corset. "You first." He pressed her shirt up over her abdomen before leaning down to kiss her belly. As his mouth moved over her, he unfastened her pants, peeling them away from her in a slow motion as his kisses followed the line of exposed skin.

Kin slid from the bottom of the bed to stand, taking her pants with him before he reached to unfasten his own, watching her strip away her top. He returned to her only a breath later, crawling over her until his mouth claimed hers.

Amarie's heart pounded in her ears as he pulled back again to shrug off his tunic, leaving his chest bare in the dim light of the room. Her touch wandered down him again, reaching his back, and...

She couldn't help but pause. Even unable to see his back, it only took her a moment to understand what marred his skin.

Scars. Thick, ragged scars.

Her heart squeezed, and she kissed him harder. Her hands continued to explore, undeterred by the discovery. As she wrapped her legs around him, she grasped at his shoulders, acutely aware of every shift of his body.

Their tongues danced against each other as Kin moved his body against hers. His hardness played between her legs, but slipped away as he kissed lower down her neck, her collar, her breast.

Amarie closed her eyes, the sensations swirling together. The sound of her heart beating, her breath increasing in tempo... It all drowned out their surroundings.

Kin's touch slid up her leg, caressing the sensitive skin behind her knee before venturing over the inside of her thigh. Her body tensed with anticipation, his breath cooling the damp trails left behind by his kisses.

Pleasure jolted through her when his mouth closed around the bundle of nerves at her apex, jaw clenching back a guttural moan.

He chuckled, teasing her with a feather-light lick before easing a finger inside her.

Her hips rocked, her breath uneven as he stroked her, both with his finger and with his tongue. The more she moved, the more she writhed, the harder he pressed. Her core heated, demanding more.

Everything inside her coiled tighter, until all she could hear were her own moans. Her climax ripped through her like a maelstrom, arching her back off the bed as she cried out.

Kin moved with her, riding out her euphoria until it subsided, and only then did he kiss the inside of her thigh again. Kiss her belly, her hip, a deep growl rumbling through his chest.

Amarie caught her breath as he kissed and licked his way up her body, pausing to massage her breast before nipping her neck. The tip of his thick erection touched her sex, and her hips twitched with a shudder. His mouth met hers again in a heart-breakingly gentle kiss.

His hands trailed along her hips, nails leaving goosebumps as he moaned lightly into her mouth.

Amarie wrapped her legs around him again, pulling him closer. As he obliged her unspoken request, his impressive length gradually filled her, making her gasp and break the kiss. It felt so familiar and yet completely new. The sensation of him alone threatening to send her back into absolute bliss. His mouth found the spot below her ear, and she tilted her head back, gripping him tighter as he plunged into her again, deeper. Slowly at first, but then with more urgency as he squeezed her hips.

Her legs shook as she bit his shoulder, whimpering as pleasure built within her once more at each thrust.

The room blurred, and she met each movement of his hips with her own, until they fell into a glorious rhythm.

As the pressure in her core tightened, she pulled his mouth to hers. Their kisses grew hungry and hot as he delved deeper, his body growing taut with hers.

Liquid heat scorched through her, igniting all her nerves as it exploded into another crash of ecstasy. Her grip tightened on his slick skin, her cry muffled by his mouth. His pace increased, and with each thrust, her climax spiked, making her legs shake as the pleasure tore through her in wave after wave.

She pulled him into her, her nails biting into the scars on his back.

Sucking in a deep breath, Kin shuddered and growled as he broke the kiss, burying himself inside her. His muscles quaked beneath her fingertips, damp with sweat. His mouth took hers again, more gentle than before, while he remained within her. Running a hand back through her hair, he pulled away and looked down at her. "I love you, Amarie," he whispered.

Amarie gazed up at him, tears pricking her eyes, but she did nothing to stop them from sliding down her temples. "I love you, too." Her voice came out as barely more than a breath. Fear, unbidden and unwanted, touched her stomach.

The last time she'd been with him...

He kissed her, running his fingers to catch the tears with a gentle stroke. His mouth moved slow against hers, so tender that it made the world spin.

Lacing her arms around him, she pulled him close, wanting to feel the weight of his body on hers as he withdrew from her. Her hands drifted over the scars on his back, and the fear in her gut twisted into rage, but she kept it at bay.

This isn't the time.

Kin lifted his head, touching her brow and stroking away her stray hairs. He studied her, something in his gaze telling her he already understood what she was afraid of. But he continued to just touch her, placing tender kisses on her cheeks and jaw as their breathing slowed. "I'm not going anywhere." He kissed her again. "I'm staying right here."

Amarie blinked, trying to hear his words as the truth. "You promise?" A smile twitched her lips as her heart lightened. "I just want you. I want to feel..." Pausing, she searched for the right word, and silently applauded his patience as he waited. "Safe. I just want to feel like I'm safe with you. Do you understand?"

"I think so." He shifted, moving to one side, but slid his arm under her and pulled her into his embrace as he let out a slow breath. "I could never jeopardize this again. I promise, all of you is safe with me."

Reaching beside her, Amarie pulled a blanket over them before snuggling closer into his neck. She took a deep breath, reveling in his scent that always brought her comfort. She kissed his chest, then his collar, and up under his rough chin until her mouth finally found his again.

Chapter 20

Kin sank into the kisses again with a happy groan, running his hands down her back. Amarie fit perfectly in his arms, just as she always had. In the pit of his stomach, he knew it was where she belonged. Where he'd always dreamed of having her again. Dreamed, but never fully believed would be possible.

But as they lay in each other's arms, naked and still damp with sweat, Kin floated far above his body. As the euphoria settled into a calm, he'd seen the thoughts passing over Amarie's face. Her dread, her fear. When she'd found the scars on his back, he worried she would end the moment before it could ever happen. But her hands felt like cool rain across the damaged skin.

He savored her lower lip in a slow kiss as her fingers traced the plethora of lines across his back. They would always be his own reminder of his endurance against Uriel, especially with Matthias confirming he'd never broken.

I'd never betray Amarie.

Still within her embrace, Kin slowly explored to rediscover all the parts of her body he'd come to know in their previous months together.

Tilting her chin up, Amarie met his gaze as their mouths parted. "*He* did that to you, didn't he?" Her tone held so much control, but her eyes blazed at her question.

Pressing his forehead to hers, he nodded. "Just after I helped bury your father."

Her breath shook as she whispered, "We're going to make him pay." And she kissed him again, this time with more ferocity before she broke away. Her eyes flashed with vibrant purple, but promptly faded back to blue. "Thank you, for what you did for him. I couldn't say it before, but I mean it. Thank you for burying him when I couldn't."

"I'm sorry that I could only get Deylan out when Helgath's soldiers attacked." He brushed her cheek. "It's strange to think about how much has changed since then. Now we're working with Helgath and Deylan..." Kin chuckled. "He got old. So far, that's been the most sobering evidence that we really missed so much. And Ahria, of course."

Amarie smiled, and it touched her eyes. "Deylan looks so much like Kalpheus. And Ahria..." Her voice trailed off, eyes growing distant as her mind wandered. With a blink and deep breath, she returned and whispered, "I don't want to live forever without you."

"We don't need to worry about that, yet." Kin lifted her chin slightly. "Let's just enjoy this and not worry about the future right now." Even as he said it, his mind jumped to all the things that could happen in the following weeks. They were safe for now in the faction's headquarters, but the battle with Uriel was coming. And there was still so much that could happen.

Exhaling slowly, she nodded. "You're right." Nuzzling closer into him, she looked up at him through her dark lashes. "This *is* really... nice." She licked her lower lip before biting it with a quirk of her brow.

Kin groaned, thumbing her chin to encourage her lip loose. "Don't tease. I'm not ready for more, yet."

Amarie stuck her lip out in a pout. "Maybe Deylan isn't the only one getting old." She laughed and then lowered her voice. "Perhaps I'll come up with a creative way to wake you up."

Despite the reality of staying in a hidden, underwater bunker belonging to a secret faction while researching the method they'd use to imprison Uriel forever, Kin couldn't keep the bounce from his step.

Time passed too quickly whenever he and Amarie were together, but too slowly every other moment. Damien had requested his presence in the library several times, but Kin kept finding excuses not to go. He had no interest in the books that Damien had buried himself in, especially if it was going to keep him from something more important.

The only parts of the faction headquarters they were allowed to enter without escort were the bedrooms, the nearby bathing chambers, a small dining area, and a single meeting room down their hall, making privacy difficult to come by anytime they departed their room.

Amarie and Ahria frequented the meeting room, sitting and chatting for extended periods of time, and Kin had no desire to disrupt it. Conrad didn't seem to, either, since he stayed primarily in his small shared room with Ahria, the door to the hallway wedged open with the chair during the day.

The chair ground along the floor, pushed by the heavy door as Kin tried to find the perfect position to keep his door open, too. Grumbling, he shifted it again, only for the chair to groan and grind again.

Conrad looked up from where he sat on the bed, his sword laid out in front of him to receive another polish, despite how many times he'd already done it over the past few days.

Kin waved an awkward hand in apology before he shoved the chair harder against the door. It finally held, but he stood ready to catch it while he stared.

The sound of Conrad's whetstone against his steel echoed through the hall.

"You sure that thing can get any sharper?" Kin asked from his doorway. He'd already seen to his own when trying to fill time the first day, but now it lay in its scabbard with no purpose against the desk. Beside it sat several books that Damien had brought after Kin's failure to assist in the library, waiting for him to go through for information about Shades.

Conrad shrugged. "Don't have anything better to do."

The prince's shoulders had never fully relaxed since they arrived, a tightness running through his entire body no matter what position he sat in. His stern face always looked far too serious, and Kin wondered if the man ever relaxed.

Ahria sees something in him, though.

"I could loan you some of these books Damien brought?" Kin leaned on the door frame, watching him.

Conrad frowned. "I'm good, thanks." He ran the whetstone over the steel with a satisfying ring. He paused, turning to look at Kin with a slight smirk on his lips. "Haven't seen you pick any of them up yet. Pretty sure I heard an invitation to the library for you, too."

Kin shrugged. "I've never been good at book work. Prefer to learn things first hand than read about them." He gestured back at the books Damien had brought. "I already know there won't be much in those. I think Damien is just trying to make me feel useful."

Conrad huffed. "Doubt he's worried about how people are *feeling*. Don't think I've said more than a few words to him."

"I won't make excuses for him." Kin crossed his arms. "But there's a lot at stake."

"I'm aware." Conrad looked back to his sword as if to resume work, but then laid it down on the bed, resting his hands on his crossed legs. "Maybe not quite as aware as the rest of you, but..."

"You've at least seen a Shade. It's something."

Conrad's expression darkened. "Barely. For the part of the fight I was conscious for. Talon was the one who fought the Shade."

"Don't be too hard on yourself. That Shade could have killed you with barely a thought, but you're still here. And Ahria clearly believes in you or you wouldn't be here." The words seemed odd as he spoke them.

I'm no good at reassuring people.

It wouldn't help to point out how Conrad was the most out of place of all of them. Of course, Kin didn't have the Art anymore, either. The only thing he had was what he *used* to be.

"Look," Kin stepped towards Conrad's door. "Maybe you should talk with Deylan. I know none of these people in the faction have the Art, but I've seen them take down a Shade. A high ranking one. With all things considered, and the situation we're in, maybe the faction will be generous with their equipment. Hells, I should probably ask for access. But they have a lot less history with you. I was an enemy not that long ago, so you have better odds."

Conrad straightened, his eyes wandering to the wall beside the door as he thought. "Maybe." Refocusing, he carefully sheathed his sword. "Have you seen Deylan since we arrived?"

Kin frowned and shook his head as he tried to recall if Amarie's brother had reappeared after being escorted away. "That Jelkin fellow came around again, assured us we weren't prisoners and showed Damien to the library, but no Deylan. Doesn't matter what they say, though, this place still feels like a prison."

"Sounds like you've never been imprisoned." Rae's unamused voice nearly made him jump as the Mira'wyld stepped silently down the hallway. She worked on braiding her damp hair. Her two-tone gaze leveled on him, and something stirred in the back of his memory as it had the first time he'd seen her.

Was she at the sanctum after Damien severed the connection to Uriel?

Damien had mentioned a wife at the time, but as far as he remembered, he hadn't met her until after Slumber. Yet, the veiled rage beneath her flat expression made him strain to recall why she disliked him.

Rae paused between the men, glancing at both before looking again at Kin. "Deylan will be at dinner tonight."

Kin nodded, avoiding her look as he ducked back into the room he and Amarie shared. It was better not to further antagonize Rae.

The woman kept walking, and a second set of soft footsteps emerged from where Rae had come from.

Amarie, with her hair also damp, paused between their door and Conrad's, eyeing the back of Rae's head before looking at Kin.

"I thought you were with Ahria." As Kin spoke, Conrad's attention shifted to Amarie. His expression suggested he thought the same thing.

"I was." Amarie leaned on the door frame. "But she went to the dining hall for some food, and Rae is off to get an escort to the library." She looked at Conrad. "Ahria wanted me to let you know, in case you were hungry."

Conrad chuckled. "Guess she couldn't wait for dinner." He retrieved his sword, returning it to his side before he started towards the dining hall. He evidently couldn't leave it behind, even though no threats existed around them. If the Sixth Eye wanted them all dead, it would have happened already.

All the same, Kin understood the comfort it brought. Which was exactly why he kept the set of throwing knives he'd grown attached to strapped to his thigh during the day.

Kin smirked as the prince walked away. "She didn't get that from me, you know." He gave Amarie a pointed look as he scooped up his own sword. "You and Rae run into each other in the bathing chamber?"

"Yeah. Though I don't know why they call it a bathing chamber when it's only shower stalls." Amarie's gaze roamed to his feet and back up to his face, a smile tugging on her lips. "You look good."

He'd let her cut his hair the day before, and it was more than worth the looks she'd been giving him since. Though, he wasn't sure if it was his sharper appearance or the nostalgia causing it.

Not that it matters.

"I do?" Kin gave her a lopsided smile, resisting the urge to touch her. "Wouldn't have thought that based on the way Rae looks at me."

Amarie shrugged. "Trust me, that's got nothing to do with how

167

you look. Give her time. She's probably been holding onto her anger for twenty years and it could take a bit for her to let it go."

"I never met her before Slumber, but I guess I can't blame her for hating me because I was a Shade. Or is it for what I did to you?" He knew Amarie and Rae were friends, recently rekindled despite Rae having lied to Amarie about her name while they traveled across Helgath together.

Hesitating, Amarie studied him for a moment before speaking. "I think you and me getting close again may have been the catalyst for her mood, but... It's neither of those things, really." She tilted her head. "Do you know what her son's name is?"

Kin paused, trying to recall the conversations he'd had with Damien, or those he'd overheard as the Rahn'ka mused with Matthias or Jarrod about their children. But he couldn't recall ever hearing either of Damien and Rae's children's names. From the sounds of it, they were both adults, or at least close to it. Which was still strange to consider since neither had been born when Damien had helped Kin.

He shook his head. "Why is that relevant to why she dislikes me?"

Amarie let out a soft sigh. "His name is Bellamy, Kin." She rolled her lips together. "Rae was imprisoned in Helgath and tortured, and... Bellamy, a young Shade, was her only friend in the cell next to her during that time. He meant a lot to her."

Kin winced as flashes of a conversation he'd had with Damien back in the Rahn'ka sanctum returned with the mention of the name.

Bellamy saved someone we love.

Damien had been talking for both himself and Jarrod. About Rae. He'd realized it back then, but then somehow forgot it all over again during the chaos of recent weeks.

A weight settled on Kin's chest. "Shit." Rubbing his face, he remembered exactly what Bellamy's face had looked like as Uriel suffocated him in shadow.

Pushing from the door frame, Amarie crossed to him and put a hand on his chest. "She knows it isn't really your fault. That if not you, it would have been another. Maybe just don't refer to this place as a prison?" She smiled as the metal walls groaned. The sound grew louder, making her cringe. "I don't know if I'd ever get used to—"

A boom reverberated through the hall, quickly followed by another as the ceiling crunched down, the dark metal pushing lower with a groan. The dent grew with another boom, making Kin's ears ring.

Amarie leapt back, staring at the ceiling. "What the..."

Metal crashed further down the hall, shaking the entire structure beneath their feet.

Water rushed somewhere unseen.

Heart thundering, Kin lunged for his sword where it still sat beside the desk, wishing for the first time that he could sense what power was at work. His forearm burned as he thought of his old shadows, but he gripped his left hand harder on the hilt of his sword as he drew it and looked at Amarie.

He could see in her eyes that she already jumped to the same conclusions he did.

Uriel found us.

Kin looked up as something skittered along the outside of the metal above the dorms, somewhere deep beneath the Dul'Idur Sea. Moving into the doorway, he wanted to tell Amarie to run, but she'd already turned. Her hands glowed with an iridescent violet hue as she rushed towards the dining hall.

Ahria.

Their daughter had no power. No defense. Just blades and the help of her prince, which would be useless against the raging ocean.

A louder, deafening crunch of metal came from above the nearby bathing chambers, and Kin's heart lurched as Amarie stumbled with the vibrations of the corridor. Above her, a massive dent pushed down from above before the riveted ceiling split open.

Saltwater spewed into the hallway, and Amarie's hands shot up, her power arcing from her fingertips in a vibrant display of light to restore the metal. But the ocean's strength pushed back, and her arms shook.

Something dark slipped inside with the water pooling at their ankles, landing on all fours. A fin-lined tail swayed through the water, spines continuing up its arched back.

"Kin!" Amarie breathed hard, whirling around when the metal above him broke apart.

Blinking through the salt water, he gasped when a jagged section of the ceiling lanced for his chest. It froze abruptly, inches from impaling him, a sheen of Amarie's power over its surface.

With a grunt, she threw it sideways into the prowling nightmare as it lifted its scissored jaw, lined with pin teeth. The heavy section of metal cut through the decayed-looking beast, severing its body in half. Black blood flowed into the ocean water, swirling towards Kin's boots.

"What the fuck is that?" Panic touched Amarie's voice, her wild eyes meeting his again.

His heart pounded. "Corrupted." He stepped towards the creature's head, nudging it with his soaked boot. Reaching down, he grasped the back of the head and carefully pushed the spines aside to reveal the familiar summoner mark. Two uneven scarred lines. "Alana's."

Amarie's eyes flashed with beryl. "We have to find Ahria." She groaned as something else slammed into the ceiling she supported, water still leaking in through the gaps and rising above their ankles.

Kin moved in close to her, her power buzzing on his skin even if he didn't have the Art to sense it. "You have to push a little harder. Then focus on the cracks. Can you weld it back together? Make it stronger?"

Her jaw flexing, Amarie yelled and heaved the metal back in place, reaching towards the chunk that had almost killed him. Its absence left a hole where water still spewed in, but it lifted with her effort.

Skittering claws echoed behind her, and her eyes widened. "I need time. Kin, there's—"

"I've got it." He brushed her arm with his right hand. "You just focus on the ceiling. I'll take care of the corrupted."

"Sounds good to me," she muttered, then raised her voice as he walked away. "Be careful!"

As he turned down the hall, Kin fought to remember all he could about Alana's favorite creatures.

He automatically shifted into a familiar stance as he braced for what was coming. This was a familiar enemy, but the halls of the faction bunker were narrower than the old training grounds he'd endured during his service to Uriel. The first lesson hadn't required the use of the Art he'd been gifted. He'd learned how to destroy without it, too.

A flash of black rushed at him. Ignoring the weight of his soaked clothes, Kin swung just as the creature came into range. A lizard jaw opened in a roar as his steel sliced through the flesh near its snout before it flung itself onto the wall. Scrambling, it smeared black blood along the metal while it continued to work its way around Kin towards Amarie. It could sense her Art, drawn to it like a moth to flame. But Kin rammed his blade into the creature's back, pinning the squirming creature. It screeched, viciously trying to whip back and tear at him, despite being impaled. He'd missed the thing's spine in his hurry to stop it.

Another guttural growl sounded from down the hall, and Kin took in the hulking form of another advancing corrupted.

Dammit.

Kin tore his sword from the wall, the lizard gnashing as it fell. But before it could try to get around him again, he slashed through the back of its neck, severing the spine. The corrupted stilled, and he kicked its body to the side of the hall as a wolf-like creature prowled forward, its snarl echoing against walls.

Metal groaned above him, followed by a loud crash as the entire length of the hallway's ceiling dented inward, like a giant chain had fallen on top.

Amarie cried out, but he didn't dare look at her.

The corrupted pounced, and Kin caught its open mouth with his sword as he reached for the knives secured at his thigh. Grabbing the largest one, he shouted in effort as he lifted the corrupted and plunged the throwing knife into the thing's chest, where he suspected Alana's mark to be below the fur. Tearing through its flesh, he flung the screaming corrupted into the wall.

He dared a glance at Amarie and the sweat beading on her brow. With an outstretched hand, she shoved her Art against the ceiling, and the metal flattened back into place. He couldn't imagine the pressure of the unrelenting ocean above that she fought against.

Behind her, at the other end of the hallway, a small corrupted emerged around the corner and raced up onto the wall, scurrying on six pinpoint legs straight at her.

Her head twitched to the side as she noticed it. "Kin!"

Without needing to think, he withdrew another throwing knife at his side. It left his fingers in a flash, and it struck, pinning the creature by the neck to the wall before the weight took it and his blade into the rising water at their feet.

His knees buckled as something struck, taking him down in a flurry of black teeth and sea water. Kicking, he caught the corrupted in its distended abdomen, but it clamped down on his lifted right arm. He screamed as he gripped the top of the creature's draconi-like snout with his free hand, kicking again to free himself as he sputtered for breath.

The thing fell back from him, and he struggled to stand, a shattered piece of ceiling slipping beneath his feet. Without getting a full breath, he hoisted it up as the corrupted lunged again.

The reptilian corrupted impaled its own throat on the sharp break of the heavy panel Kin wedged upward with his shoulder. He caught hold of the thick, wriggling tendrils along the corrupted's jaw, yanking it down further onto the jagged debris as it thrashed. With another yank, it stilled and Kin's damaged arm sang with pain.

"It's about to get hot in here!" Amarie yelled above the noise, and with her words, a surge of heat permeated the air. Water hissed from where she worked, and the metal raged to a glowing orange.

The heat intensified, and it scorched his skin to an uncomfortable temperature, yet he wasn't nearly as close to it as Amarie. When he looked back and forth down the hallway and no more corrupted appeared, he focused on her, but didn't interrupt.

Amarie panted, water having long soaked her clothing and hair. The red-hot metal above her stopped dripping, and with a heave of breath, she released her power, but still stared at the fused ceiling.

It wasn't pretty, by any standards, but the rejoined metal quickly cooled, and the seal held.

Blinking rapidly, Amarie looked at him, then his injured arm. "Are you all right?" Her gaze drifted behind him, where water splashed. "One of those isn't dead." She staggered as she approached him, shaking her head in an effort to refocus.

Kin heaved a breath, trying to ignore the sting of the salt water in his row of puncture wounds. He glanced to where the wolf corrupted twitched against the wall. "I cut Alana's hold on it. It's probably in shock because it's no longer receiving commands. We've got a moment. It might not even want anything to do with us when it comes to. The usual animal instincts are still in there when there isn't a summoner controlling it."

Amarie stopped beside him, breathing hard as she wiped sweat from her forehead with the back of her arm. "You didn't answer my question." Picking up his arm, she inspected the bloodied flesh.

"I'm fine. This is nothing." He hid the grimace as she twisted his arm. "We don't have time to worry about it right now. Alana's corrupted are here..."

Nodding, she released his arm and gestured down the hall with her chin. "Let's go find Ahria and Conrad. And you should still kill that thing." Touching his face, she gave him a weak smile before jogging towards the dining hall.

Kin looked at the creature, still twitching as he retrieved his sword from the thinning layer of water around it.

There must be drains in here somewhere.

He didn't hesitate before he stabbed his sword down into its skull. He recovered his largest throwing knife next, but didn't bother locating the other before jogging after Amarie towards the dining hall.

The sound of a sword being drawn echoed through the space as he passed through the doorway in time to see Amarie stab a corrupted through the back so Conrad could lop off its head.

Ahria stood on the table, sword drawn and several dead corrupted scattered around the room. Her and Conrad's work. A swell of pride grew in Kin's chest.

Black blood marred his daughter's face, which she scrubbed off with the bottom of her tunic before hopping to the floor with a splash. "The water stopped rising. What happened?"

"I sealed one of the leaks." Amarie glanced at Kin. "We need to find Rae. With her will be the safest place."

"She can control water," Ahria murmured.

"Exactly. She was heading towards the library." Amarie started, but paused to catch Ahria by the elbow. "If we're separated, just find Rae, all right?"

Their daughter nodded.

"We should head for the library, then?" Conrad wiped blood from his sword on to the edge of his pants. He was covered in dark blood, too, but hadn't bothered to wipe it off himself.

"We should go to the armory first. We're not well enough equipped to handle more corrupted. The faction must have something we can use." Kin looked at Amarie, touching her wrist. He flinched as the wet cloth of his shirt pulled over his wounds.

"We passed it the first day on our way to the dorms." Conrad pointed with his sword back down the hall they'd come from.

A gurgle of unease blossomed in Kin's gut. Corrupted were one thing, one problem, with a relatively easy fix. But… something told him they weren't the extent of this attack. If Uriel sent Shades, or…

If he's here…

They'd all be dead. No one was prepared to fight Uriel, especially not hundreds of feet beneath the ocean.

"All right. Weapons." Amarie nodded at Kin, the fear in her eyes mirroring his own thoughts. "Then the library."

Chapter 21

The ground shuddered, threatening to toss books from the shelves.

Damien looked up at the high ceiling of the library as something thudded along the outside of the underwater structure. A spine-tingling creaking accompanying it as if the entire structure prepared to give way.

What the hells...

The book he'd been studying thumped as he dropped it on the table, moving to the thick door that sealed the library shut. He'd been given strict instructions to stay within the library and wait for an escort before he left. Pausing at the door, he listened to what was happening beyond the metal, trying to piece together the sounds.

The voices that constantly assaulted his barrier had quieted, shifting into an unease that only further confirmed that something was very wrong. Touching the door handle, he banished concern about pissing off the faction and pushed it open.

Water coated the ground. Little waves formed on its surface as it rushed from the direction of the dormitories.

Something is very wrong.

Damien dove deeper into his power, tensing his arm to summon the Art into his veins as he looked down the empty hallway back towards the dorms. The ocean bubbled around the corner, lapping around the edge of his boot as he stepped into the hallway.

A shriek erupted from somewhere unseen, followed by a thud, then an eerie silence fell.

Panic spiked in his chest.

Where's Rae?

She was going to meet him in the library, but hadn't arrived yet.

Voices murmured around the corner from the junction just out of his view, moving further away as they continued.

Damien, with his back to the wall, peeked around the corner at the junction that led to the dorms, eyes landing on a body crumbled at the connector. Blood flowed from the dead man, trailing through the water in wisps of red. He recognized him as one of the faction escorts he frequently interacted with.

The solid door to the library behind him closed with a loud bang. A low ringing sounded from within. Metal ground along the door, a latch somewhere on the other side securing into place. He reached blindly behind him to the knob, and pushed with his back, but the door wouldn't budge. The low ring inside turned to a pulsing alarm.

He wondered if he'd be trapped in there if he hadn't left.

Another groan reverberated across the ceiling, a sharp clanging echoing from the halls to the doors.

A pulse of Damien's power reverberated over his skin as the tattoos on his left arm glowed. Gripping his fist, he channeled his ká into the familiar shaft of his spear. It lanced through the air from nothing, a soft ring humming in Damien's ear as he passed the weapon to his dominant hand.

The voices continued before Rae's echoed through his consciousness. *Go back to the dorms.* Even telepathically, her tone was rigid. Afraid.

The ká around him were difficult to sort through, and he wondered if it was because of some ward the faction had in place around their bunker. He no longer sensed the stray schools of fish that typically hovered in the ocean outside, or the kelp beds. With a quickly growing sickness in his stomach, he realized he didn't sense any faction members nearby either.

But if Rae could speak to him, she had to be near. And stubbornly, he sought her out instead of obeying.

The long halls circled the library in a square, and he continued to follow Rae's ká to the south, where he hadn't been allowed to travel before, but the metal all looked the same. Behind him, in the direction of the dorms, came the roar of something from nightmares, along with shouts. But he focused only on his wife and the fear that radiated from her. He could tell someone else was there, but the stranger's ká was muddled.

I'm not leaving you. He pushed his thought to her through their long-forged connection while focusing on a set of double doors ahead.

One sat slightly ajar. Beyond, he could see a large room with bench seating. But no sign of Rae and whoever was with her. He waded quietly closer, listening to the voices beyond.

"You know I won't let you have me." Rae. Her voice was steady, but... he knew that tone. That tense tone she used to cover her terror. Her bluff.

You have to. Desperation touched her voice. *Please. Don't follow us.*

"It would be a shame to kill you," a sinister voice purred. "We can make a deal. Much less blood involved."

A chill crept through Damien, his grip tightening on his spear as he leaned closer to the door. He glanced behind him at the clear hallway, more tings sounding against the ceiling as if something still sought to break inside.

"I don't make deals with you, Dae'fuirei." Rae's tone hardened, only the slightest tremor audible beneath her words. The Aueric word held so much more meaning than Common ever could for something corrupted. Something truly evil.

"But just think, my dear, with my power joined with the Rahn'ka, we'll be..." He breathed in deeply, moaning softly with a chuckle. "Unstoppable."

Fear overtook him. It made his knees suddenly weak as Damien realized who stood beyond the door with Rae. He'd had a near miss with Uriel in Helgath, where he'd remained focused on Amarie and Kin. But here...

Rae.

He'd avoided every confrontation. Hid at every opportunity. Allowed Uriel to believe falsely that Rae was the Rahn'ka for years. Something that had always threatened his wife and left him overwhelmed with guilt.

That ends now.

Damien sucked in a breath, reaching into the sea above and around them for power. He hadn't paid attention to it before, but Uriel's Art had already taken hold of so much life. It'd already consumed and destroyed much of what had naturally thrived in the water. The invisible tendrils of the creature's power were still webbed throughout. Hardening his ká within the fabric into a blade, Damien viciously hacked through the lines of energy. Sealing the channels to stop Uriel from taking more.

He closed his eyes for only a moment, centering on what remained as he erected barriers to save more energy for himself. But his power didn't steal like Uriel's.

The ká he protected seemed to sigh in relief, happily giving all they could to the Rahn'ka as he gathered power into his straining muscles.

Damien kicked the door, which slammed open against the back wall. The spear in his fist gleamed with pale blue energy, wavering around it like a wild flame.

Rae's eyes met his and widened. "No!"

The Rahn'ka stared down the tall auer standing before Rae for only a moment. There was no time for hesitation. He swung his spear, channeling his power through the runes on its shaft. Ká erupted in a dense wave, rushing through the air in a pillar of mist. It ripped Uriel from the ground, throwing him past Rae into the distant wall with a crunch.

Rae hurried to Damien, but Uriel appeared behind her faster than he could anticipate. The man gripped her by the throat, jerking her backward into him. Her hands shot up to pry off his grasp, but it held firm.

"You." Rage dripped from Uriel's voice as he stared at Damien. "Oh, I will take *everything* from you."

Damien's chest seized as shadow danced out from Uriel's feet, cascading over the floor panels in a wriggling circle around his wife. Pressure weighed on his Art as the darkness met his own ká, spread in a net around him. Their energies sparked as they met, coiling back violently into plumes of pale blue and black. It was all that moved in the room as Damien stood frozen, watching Uriel's fingers flex against Rae's skin.

Keeping her chin up, Rae held stone still, clutching the iron grip at her neck but no longer struggling against it. Her other hand slipped into her cloak, ever-needed in the chill underwater tunnels.

I need to give her more time.

Damien spread his hands out at his sides. "I'm here, so you can let her go. She's no use to you, now."

Uriel lifted a thick eyebrow, his grip shifting as coils of shadow curled up his legs. Wisps of his power danced at his fingertips, playing over Rae's exposed skin. She hissed as deep red lines trailed behind Uriel's shadows, but her hand pushed deeper into her cloak.

"Foolish to allow me to believe someone so dear to you was the Rahn'ka instead of you." Uriel forced Rae's chin a little higher as thin snakes of onyx squirmed over her. "But I don't see you using that fabled power now." He gave a wicked grin. "Not enough for you to pull from, little Rahn'ka?"

Damien met Rae's eyes as his grip on his spear tightened. *Remember that time in Privat?* She would, and he'd need her to open up to his power the same way she had when they'd gone to deal with a holdout of Iedrus supporters just after Jarrod had been crowned king.

Rae's hand tightened on something in her cloak. *Do it.*

There was no need to draw from the energy he'd quickly stock piled from the life in the surrounding sea. He tapped into the familiar strings attached to his own, following them instantly to the only other living being he was practically one with.

Rae's ká answered his request without hesitation. It swelled at his beckon, hardening into a pale cloud on her skin, turning Uriel's shadow into ash. With a pulse, it erupted against Uriel, clashing with his own corrupted ká. He growled as his hands recoiled, taking a step back.

In her moment of freedom, Rae whipped her firestarter from her cloak and squeezed. The metal scraped together, and sparks danced into the air. As she whirled to face Uriel, her Art took control of the sparks and burst them into flames. A wave of heat coursed through the room as she blasted them at Uriel's face while backing towards Damien.

Curling in on him, Uriel's shadows bubbled up over his shoulders. He spun, hands out, as lances of his power erupted from the darkness. Rushing without thought, Damien placed himself in front of Rae, lifting his left arm. The shield formed in a display of runes etched into the air, his tattoo glowing as the shadow fizzled and vanished.

With a roar, Uriel stood, his face half charred and blistered from Rae's fire.

Another attack vibrated against Damien's shield as he looked at Rae. "Get out of here." He grimaced as he pushed more energy into the shield as a third wave came. He couldn't remain on the defensive like this, not with limited power.

"Like I'd leave you," Rae muttered, still holding a flame in her palm. With her other, she made a fist, and the blue bow he'd gifted her all those years ago sprang to life. Nocking an arrow, she loosed it at Uriel's chest.

Shadow surged, catching the arrow. It snapped in half and fell into the oozing darkness. The same happened to the next she let fly.

Neither of us will be able to land a blow.

They needed to be more creative than just using their Art against his.

"Come on, little Rahn'ka. Are you just going to hide behind that shield all day?" Uriel's tone made Damien's blood boil. But it wasn't the time to fall for childish taunts.

"What are you thinking?" Rae murmured behind him. "I'm thinking some pretty wild shit right now."

"We're probably thinking the same thing." Damien looked up at the ceiling, imagining what surged just beyond it.

"Water?" Rae whispered. "I'm thinking water."

"I say you bring it in." Damien looked back to Uriel, bracing as another wave of shadow struck his shield. It shuddered, his muscles aching. "Right above him, preferably. He's limited by his host, and auer can't breathe under water."

Disintegrating her bow, Rae didn't miss a beat. She focused, silent, for a few moments before the structure above Uriel groaned. Breathing harder, she growled as a crushing force collided with the ceiling, splitting it at a seam and surging seawater onto Uriel. It crashed over him, quickly flooding the room at the same time. The door behind them slammed shut with the rush of water, eliminating an escape.

Water reached Damien's calves in a matter of seconds, but he focused on Uriel, trapped inside the deluge.

Shadow lashed through the stream, like a sea creature emerging as his auer figure faded. Panic rushed through Damien as he lost sight of him. He pressed more into his ká, pulses radiating through the water around him.

Rae stepped from behind him, hands outstretched as she controlled the liquid. She gathered what was in the room, pushing it all back at Uriel in a waterspout formation. "Drown, you piece of shit."

Water erupted as a tendril of darkness emerged behind them. It lashed at Rae, seizing her like a rag doll before either had time to react.

Another tendril came crashing down on Damien, who sucked in a breath before he was plunged into the water. The rage of the ocean rushed through his ears as he found his footing, lancing his spear back towards where the tendril had been. It connected, bruise-colored sparks mixing with the salt water as Damien emerged.

Rae let out a yelp, but the sound disappeared as Uriel tore her from the ground and thrust her up through the hole she'd created, banishing her into the merciless sea. The tendril that held her swelled, the shadow arcing out to attach to the broken metal like a spiderweb. The water slowed, then ceased, leaving Rae trapped somewhere beyond it. Somewhere in the water.

Uriel emerged from the water beneath, plucking a piece of kelp from his tunic. "That's better. Now we'll be undisturbed." He met Damien's eyes, gold and black swirling in his irises.

Damien swallowed his concern, assuring himself Rae would be fine. She would survive because of her alcan blood.

Uriel took a casual step through the knee-deep water, his shadows popping up around him like curious sea creatures. He pushed his sleeves up as if finally focusing on their fight.

Water swirled around the gaps in the closed doors behind Damien, already slowly lowering the depth in the huge chamber. And he wondered how long he'd need to stall before he'd be able to pry the doors open and run.

Run where, though?

The master of Shades kept approaching, lashing harder with his shadows. Rushing energy back into his arm, Damien reformed the shield in front of him. Uriel's blow landed with bone-shattering force and the Rahn'ka's power faltered. The glowing barrier he fought to maintain fractured.

He sought the voices around him, but already knew the answer to his plea for more energy would go unanswered. There was none. He couldn't take more without killing what remained, and the bits of energy within the exhausted life would provide little sustenance for either of them. The remaining energy within him waned, leaving hardly enough to assemble another attack against Uriel. His stomach sank as he was forced to release the barrier protecting the life outside the walls. It fell, and the master of Shades devoured the newly available resource, regardless how insignificant.

Damien's muscles shook as he funneled power back into his spear. He lunged, fighting the pressure on his shins from the deep water. He drove the spear towards Uriel's chest, ká radiating like lightning against the shadows.

Uriel caught the spear just below the point with a bare hand, a low chuckle rumbling from his throat. "Time to die, little Rahn'ka." He jerked the spear, pulling Damien's head just a bit closer as he threw out a shadow-laden fist. It collided with the Rahn'ka's jaw with excruciating force, sending him sprawling backward into the water.

The world spun as Damien fought to find his feet.

Uriel's boot impacted his side, and Damien's face briefly submerged before he surfaced, sputtering salt water.

Kneeling, Damien braced his boot against a lip of metal and brought his spear up. The butt of it contacted Uriel's gut, giving Damien enough space to jump back to his feet. He tasted blood as he whirled again, funneling what remained of his energy into the tip of his spear. Before Uriel could fully recover, he lunged again.

A tendril rushed up, catching his attack before the blade could reach Uriel's side. But he tightened his grip, and the power at the end of the spear ruptured at his command. It snaked around the tendril, rushing to make contact with Uriel's ká. The net took hold, hooks driving deep into the invisible fabric of the monster's soul.

Pushing the base of his spear into the ground, Damien yanked with every muscle in his body. A purple and black mist tangled with the ends of the net the Rahn'ka had frantically woven, and the auer grew rigid. His shadows trembled, no longer fighting as Uriel's ká struggled to remain within its host.

Damien's body screamed, but he continued to pull, crying out as he fought to hold onto his spear. The runes that ran its entire surface blazed as Uriel's being pulsed and wriggled in the net.

If he could separate the creature from its host, Uriel would have to flee.

Just a little more...

A snap lurched Damien sideways, tearing his grip from his spear and the soul connected to it. The weapon disappeared into the water, all shades of purple faded from its runes and left behind a faint pale light. It hovered for a moment before drifting away into the water, granting Damien a small burst of energy as he grappled with what had gone wrong.

The bruise-colored mist lingered near the auer's chest before he inhaled deeply, and the soul absorbed back beneath his skin.

"I always wondered what that felt like." Uriel smirked as Damien's entire body sagged in pain and exhaustion. "I should thank you for ridding me of that pesky host's soul." He tutted his tongue. "It doesn't seem he was very helpful to you, either, with how little energy he seems to have given you."

Damien dove into the water, reaching desperately for his spear, but Uriel's shadows ripped him backward. They burrowed into his arms as his back slammed into a wall, and all air rushed from his lungs.

Then Uriel was before him, a cruel grin on his face. "Would you like to make a deal?"

Damien struggled, but no reprieve came against the shadow as fire erupted down his arms. The necrotic touch tore into his already weak muscles.

Gritting his teeth against the scream, Damien refused to give Uriel the satisfaction. He clenched his jaw, blood pooling on his tongue.

He tried again to reach for more ká, but... nothing. His mind fell dangerously quiet even as he let his barrier collapse to pull anything he could from it. In a desperate act, he lashed out with what physical strength he still had, kicking at Uriel's midsection.

The room spun as Uriel's shadows lifted him from the wall and rammed him back into it again. His legs roared as burning tendrils laced up them, holding him exposed as Uriel gave him another bemused look.

"I'll take that as a no." Uriel tilted his head. "Pity." His fist flew at Damien's face again, slamming the back of his head against the wall.

And then again. And again.

Each hit brought fresh stars to his sight, warmth trickling down his neck. Blows came to his ribs, his abdomen.

Stay awake. Fight.

But even with thoughts, his limbs were leaden. He had no more tricks. No more moves to make.

Darkness muddled the edges of his vision, blurring as his knees gave out. The necrotic wounds along his limbs raged, and he didn't even know when the tendril had let go.

Cold fingers closed around his throat, and he fought to suck in a breath as the sounds of the room around them faded.

His body moved, but not by his own accord. He landed somewhere in the water, splashing into the still ankle-deep water. A sound came from somewhere, like a groan, and he coughed as water found its way into his throat.

Shaking, he struggled to rise to his hands and knees, but Uriel's boot connected with his ribs again, returning him to the water.

There was no escape, no way to stop the agony.

Blood stained the surrounding sea, drifting out from his body like mist.

I'm sorry. He tried to push the thought to Rae, but he couldn't find her ká.

A hand gripped him by the hair, shoving his face under the water.

Damien choked, fighting with what little strength he had left, but nothing worked.

Yet, air reached his lungs as Uriel hauled him up. "Give my regards to Nymaera." The ominous voice echoed through his mind as Uriel flung him like a sack of grain across the room.

His head cracked against metal, and the room darkened.

Get up. Stay awake. Stay...

Chapter 22

As much as Conrad loved the sea, he preferred it beneath the hull of a ship, rather than hidden behind ceilings and walls that seemed far too thin to hold it at bay. Every creak and groan set his nerves on edge, and that was before he passed beneath the haphazard repair Amarie had been forced to complete. Where the dark metal still stuck out in jagged edges between thick scars melted back together by her power.

The floors, still slick with water, had drained most of the way, but their boots still splashed on the drenched carpet as they all made their way towards the armory.

Nothing could calm the roiling nerves in his chest. He couldn't help but focus on the simple truth that he didn't belong here, with these powerful people, fighting such an evil creature. He'd held his own against the corrupted, armed with information Matthias had imparted to him just in case, but Conrad doubted he'd have lasted long without Ahria at his side. The beasts were unlike anything he'd ever seen, and their corpses littered the edges of the hall. What animals comprised them became impossible to discern as their masses disintegrated into the sea water.

"Has anyone seen Deylan?" Amarie glanced back at her daughter and Conrad as they stalked through the corridor. "Or anyone from the Sixth Eye?"

Ahria shook her head. "No. But if I had to venture a guess as to why, I'd assume they're having their own problems with these monsters somewhere else." She looked sideways at Conrad, a flicker of fear dancing across her eyes. She was just as average as him, in these moments, with all the power of the Berylian Key contained within her mother.

A distant boom echoed through the halls as if to confirm what Ahria said. Growls and scraping claws terrorized them as the water around their boots shifted. More flowed through from the doorway ahead of them.

Kin picked up the pace, lifting his darkly-stained sword as he drew a throwing dagger from the set tied on his thigh. "There will be more. We need to be ready."

Amarie flanked Kin, keeping a watchful eye as the two of them crossed through the junction connecting this section to the next. They paused on the other side, Amarie scanning the north hallway while Kin watched the other. Just as she opened her mouth to speak, a blaring noise erupted.

Conrad threw his hands over his ears, the sound reverberating through his fingers and making his head pound.

A bell, or something like a bell, rang in what Conrad could only assume to be warning. The noise came directly from the intersection where they stood, and a heartbeat later, a solid dark metal door crashed down between them.

Ahria lurched forward, hands pressing against the metal, which didn't budge from where it had slammed. Her mouth opened in a yell, but he couldn't hear the words over the alarm.

Conrad joined her, using all his strength as the warning sound continued to blare around them. He gave it all he had, boots slipping on the carpet, but it was unmovable.

Abruptly, the alarm stopped. But Conrad's ears still rang as they battled against the door.

"Mom!" Ahria pounded with her fist.

Banging on the metal sounded from the other side, along with muffled voices. Shouts.

"Find Rae!" Amarie screamed through the metal, panic in her voice.

More words, more voices, but he couldn't make any of it out.

Ahria looked at Conrad, at her sword, his, and then back to his face. "What do we do?" Of course she'd heard her mother's instruction, but he understood why she struggled to obey.

"We find Rae." Conrad reached with his empty hand for hers, giving a gentle tug back down the hall they'd just come.

"But..." Ahria hesitated, glancing back at the sealed junction door.

"They'll be fine. Your mom has the power of the Berylian Key and your dad used to be a Shade. They're probably the best equipped to deal with this situation. But we're not." He encouraged her again. "We need to go before anything else finds us."

She let out a breath, and the tension in her arm faded as she conceded to his request and followed. "All right. Rae was headed to the library, right? So we just need to get back through the dormitories and hope that junction hasn't also shut."

Conrad didn't want to think about what would come next if it was. He already felt trapped enough, and every instinct in him wanted to start clawing at the walls to swim himself up to the surface. But Ahria would never survive if the sea came in, and there was nothing his alcan heritage could do to help her. They had to hope that no more corrupted broke through the ceiling.

Letting go of Ahria's hand, Conrad focused on the open corridor in front of them, watching the water coating the floor for changes as well as listening for any movement ahead of them. His heart pounded as they paused at the corner of the long hall leading to the junction. Conrad leaned around the edge to peek at what would be waiting for them. There was nothing between them and the junction, and he squinted to see if it was open.

Ahria stopped behind him, pressing her back to the wall beside him. Her breath shook, hands trembling. It made his chest tighten, doubling his own fear that he fought to control.

Forcing the emotion to subside for a brief moment, he focused on the concern that flooded him next. Turning to her, Conrad reached for her hands and lifted them between them. He kept his as steady as he could, trying to urge hers to do the same. "We're going to make it through this."

Her wide eyes met his. "You don't know that," she whispered. "Why hasn't Rae come back? Where is Damien? What if..." Her eyelashes fluttered, her jaw feathering. "My..." Closing her eyes, she drew in a steadying breath. She squeezed his hand before looking at him again with a nod, dismissing whatever she had been about to say. "Is the junction closed?"

"No," Conrad murmured. "Something is on the floor, preventing it from shutting all the way."

Ahria let out a faster breath. "Corrupted?"

"I don't see any. Looks like a straight shot." He brushed his fingers over her cheek. "You're strong. You've got this."

Her throat bobbed. "I love you, all right? Whatever happens." She tightened her lips into a thin line and pushed from the wall, rounding the corner.

"I know. I love you, too." He followed her, flexing his sword hand in anticipation for what might wait beyond the junction.

Beholding what held the door open, Ahria slowed as they approached. A body. One of the men who'd often escort them to other areas of the bunker. He lay dead on his side, the sideways shield on his back bracing the door from falling. Salt water pulsed around him, washing away what blood might have drained from the wound that'd pierced his skull.

For a moment, he wondered if they should continue. More water streamed below the door, rushing from whatever chambers lay on the other side.

We could be walking into a worse situation. But... we need Rae.

Ahria must have come to the same conclusion. With unsteady movements, she crouched, getting so close to the dead man that Conrad cringed as she passed slowly under the wedged metal door. She paused part way, and he held his breath until she continued through.

The water reached his cheek as he followed Ahria under the door. Once he stood, water now soaking every inch of him, he looked south down the corridor. The sea water flowed around their ankles, coming from somewhere out of view.

Ahria slid along the wall towards the water's origin, her sword steadier than before and her steps silent despite the water.

Neither of them spoke.

The hallway ahead had only a single door with intricate carvings in the metal, but the water came from somewhere further south. Conrad stepped ahead to test the door, but nothing happened. It remained sealed and, as he pressed his ear to listen, he could make out the same alarm that'd sounded at the junction reverberating from inside.

Ahria stopped next to him, tilting her head in question.

Is this the library?

He debated banging on the door to see if Damien or Rae would answer, but even if they did, they couldn't get to them. And it would likely attract the attention of anything still around. Though it seemed eerily quiet in the halls now, as if the attack had ended.

He shook his head at Ahria's silent question.

A crash echoed from the southern corridor, and Ahria gasped. She stared down the hallway, where the water still flowed, growing deeper.

Conrad stepped around her, putting himself between her and the sound.

It could be Damien or Rae fighting.

He tried to assure himself that as far as they knew, it was only corrupted that attacked the faction headquarters. There had been no sign of a Shade, which the mere thought of made Conrad's skin crawl. They knew, through their crash course introduction to Uriel, that the corrupted were not necessarily always connected to him, but were also a go to weapon.

Conrad naively wanted to believe that all of this could be unrelated to Uriel, but something in the pit of his stomach warned him that something terrifying lay within the south room of the faction's bunker.

He moved slowly with his sword ready, keeping Ahria behind him. As they crept along, the water ebbed. Some still slowly poured from below a set of closed double doors, where the occasional thump sounded from within.

Damien and Rae are two of the most powerful Art users alive. They'll win.

As they reached the doors, the noise within the room ceased.

Conrad reached for the door handle, debating for a moment as he stood there. By the silence, all the corrupted within must already be dead. Already destroyed by the Rahn'ka and Mira'wyld, but...

As he pushed the door open, his eyes settled on a body heaped against the left wall, and his stomach sank.

Damien lay hunched against the side wall, barely recognizable beneath the visage of blood that poured from his head and face. Great smears coated the wall above him, his limbs blackened with necrosis just as Talon's had been. The only recognizable feature was the tattoo on his arm, exposed beneath his torn shirt and marred with more blackened wounds. He didn't move, and his chest didn't rise.

By the gods...

Quickly glancing around the chamber, he saw no one else. Rae wasn't there. Nor whatever had done this to him. The odd light sources that powered the entire underwater bunker were half snuffed out, leaving half the room in dim shadows. He couldn't make out the ceiling, or if there were any holes from the corrupted incursion.

Without reconsidering, Conrad hurried into the room, rushing to the Rahn'ka. If he could find a pulse... If he could stop the bleeding... If he could...

He fell to his knees before the man, scrambling to find his heartbeat.

Damien fell limply against Conrad as he pressed his bare hands to the most grievous of the Rahn'ka's wounds along his chest. The flesh beneath his fingers looked grey and melted, bringing more flashes of Talon's corpse to Conrad's memory.

You can't die, too.

Behind him, near the door, Ahria let out a squeak of surprise. "Who are you?"

Conrad turned to see her sword outstretched, pointing at a figure who hadn't been there a moment before.

"You already know my name. But I think the more important question here is..." The shadowed figure's voice grated like steel over Conrad's ears. "*Who* are *you?*"

Ahria backed up, her steel-blue eyes wide and full of terror. She didn't answer, the tip of her sword shaking.

Conrad shot to his feet, forgetting his concern for Damien or himself, and charged. His sword poised to strike, he set aside honor and struck at the man's back.

A wall of darkness rippled to life between them, and the attacker faced him. "A little out of your league, here, don't you think, Prince? Or have you come to ask me for the power you so *desperately* need?"

Shifting his weight, Conrad rushed to jump around the shadows, but they surged to intercept him again. They wriggled as if taunting him as he leaned back on his heels. He knew what would happen if the shadow touched his flesh, and the realization of what the man was offering sank in, hardening into a rock of terror.

The master of Shades pushed him back, laughing as the shadows closed in around the prince.

"Conrad!" Ahria's eyes met his, the color drained from her face. He didn't have to say the words or beg her to go. Uriel had found them, killed Damien, and now he knew of her.

She turned on her heel and did the only thing she could. She ran.

She knows Uriel would rather chase her than finish me.

He braced for the shadows to collapse on top of him anyway as Ahria vanished through the door of the large chamber. He watched Uriel as he contemplated him, tilting his head before turning after Ahria.

The master of Shades sniffed as he waved his hand and the darkness surrounding Conrad hardened. The world spun as it struck him, launching him through the air before he crashed into the water.

Chapter 23

Rae pounded on the shadow barrier preventing her from returning to the large chamber where Uriel still stood. They'd barely managed to leave a scratch on him, some burns, and that was fighting together. Weaving her power through the currents of the ocean, she lashed at the shadows, but they refused to give way. Numbness crept into her limbs, the ocean water chilling her to her bones, despite her alcan heritage.

I need help.

Abandoning the spot, she scanned the water around her. Her heart leapt into her throat at the sight of glowing orbs floating towards her. Squinting through the water, she tried to make out the shapes, and realized they weren't grotesque like corrupted, but more humanoid. They moved towards her at an alarming speed, and a breath later she realized what they were. Alcans. They were alcans swimming towards her.

Rae let out a breath of salt water, kicking to approach them. "I need help." She struggled to form the words around the water, but Andi had taught her years prior how to do it. "My husband is in there. I need to get back inside."

The alcan closest to her gave her an incredulous look, eyeing her up and down before responding in broken Common. "Way in." She motioned, webbed fingers creating mini currents of tiny sea bubbles. Her skin shone with a navy blue tint, lighter spots of blue dappled under her forearms and neck. "Come."

The alcan spun, dreadlocked hair banded together and trailing behind her as she swam with impressive speed along the outer wall of the faction headquarters.

So many other alcans—difficult to see with their complexion blending with the seascape—worked to repair the structure. Their Art-infused lanterns illuminated the extent of the damage. Great grooves and claw marks covered the majority of the structure where corrupted must have attempted to break in. The Art tingled on her skin as they manipulated the fabric with ease, emanating from little balls of light that ran along the tears, attempting to seal them.

Rae didn't linger on them, too focused on keeping up to the one who hopefully guided her to another way inside.

As they moved further along the bunker, she tried to imagine what corridors she swam above.

This is the dorms, I think. And this is the junction towards the lift...

A new wave of fear hit her stomach as she spied the glow of alcan lanterns over the northern sections of the headquarters. Entire corridors had collapsed, their metal twisted and torn apart like paper. A column of alcan lights illuminated a section of the lower gate, revealing gears bigger than houses. Between them, a rectangular column ran up the wall, but an entire section of it looked like it was missing. The lift, she realized, completely flooded with broken, jagged pieces of metal strewn across the ocean floor.

As they passed a group of alcans, she could hear their communication in trills and clicks, but understood none of it.

She focused on what lay ahead, a new desperation rising to get back to Damien as she realized the extent of the destruction. The alcan she followed stopped over an unknown portion of the structure, a seam spanning the square top. She quickly looked back the way they'd come, evaluating the route she'd need to take to get back to Damien.

A round wheel with a knob occupied one side of the seam below her, and the alcan turned it. As she worked, her irises shimmered, the roots of her dark hair glowing with a strange bioluminescence.

Metal groaned, and the seam split open.

Water rushed inside, taking her and her alcan friend with it.

They slammed down with a splash as more water poured in, the metal unforgiving against her body. The alcan recovered, hurrying to use the crank inside to close the hatch, and shortly after, the water drained.

Rae panted air again, controlling her urge to try all the levers until she found the one that would open the door. "Thank you. Please. Can you open—"

The alcan nodded, pulling a lever down and then another sideways before cranking another wheel around in circles. Looking at her, Rae almost needed to do a double take. She'd changed now that the salt water didn't touch her skin. The navy tones had faded, making her look more human except for the shimmering eyes, her crescent pupils swollen enough to almost hide all the color of her irises. The webs between her fingers faded even as they worked to crank the levers faster.

The doors started to open, grinding along the invisible gears within the wall, and Rae turned back to them, recounting her path ahead.

Shifting her weight uneasily, Rae could barely contain herself as she waited for it to be wide enough for her. The moment it was, she leapt forward and squeezed through to the hallway beyond and into chaos.

Her heart thrummed in her ears as she oriented herself, ignoring the shouts of faction members fighting corrupted around her. Dodging claws clashing with copper swords, she sprinted past strangers, praying she wouldn't be too late.

Turning a corner, she slipped on the wet floor, colliding with a wall. It kept her upright, and she barreled for the closed junction door ahead of her.

"No," she breathed, banging her fists on it before trying to pry it from the ground. But it was as immovable as the Dul'Idur Gate itself. This was the only path into the dorms, and subsequently the corridors leading to Uriel and Damien. She had to get through.

Calling her Art, she gathered the water drenching the corridor floor and that on the other side, welling it together in an attempt to raise the door. Her muscles shook, insides burning as she fought with all her strength to lift it. But the water gave way, parting to the unforgiving metal.

It didn't even give an inch.

Crying out, Rae tried again, but still nothing. Frantically, she retrieved her fire starter from her pocket, her hands shaking as she struck it over and over, seeking a spark despite its dampness.

Finally, one roared into a flame, and her Art seized it. Drawing it into her palm, she wove the fire into a sharp beam, blasting it at the surface of the door. Giving it all she had, she let it burn and burn, heating the door until the metal glowed red hot. But it didn't melt, didn't even sag, only growing brighter the more she poured into it.

Tears stung her cheeks as she screamed, letting go of her power and reaching again for the door. Her fingertips stung as she attempted to dig them beneath the metal edge.

Vaguely aware of the shouting behind her, Rae stumbled back and stared. A sob threatened her chest, and she prepared to dredge up the last of her energy.

A single high-pitched chime sounded, prompting her to cover her ears, before the door blocking her path abruptly lifted on its own, disappearing above.

Rae gulped a surprised breath and took off, feet unaware of her exhaustion as she barreled through the hallways. She passed person after person, some wounded and carried by their allies, but she hardly registered anyone until she all but collided with the doors that'd lead to her husband.

Water leaked from beneath, the pressure of the flood water on the other side preventing her from opening it.

Pressing her ear to the door, she heard nothing but the roar of the water rushing in through the hole in the ceiling, but she had no way of knowing what lay within. If Uriel was still there, waiting for her to return. But the faction had opened the junctions, which told her they considered the threat to their headquarters gone. Which meant...

Gods. Nymaera help him.

Finding her connection to the fabric once more, she pushed the water on the other side away from the doors, finally allowing her to shove them open.

Ocean poured in from the chasm in the ceiling, which she ceased with her little remaining power. The water rushed in upon itself with her gesture, reversing the waterfall until it formed a dense frothing layer to keep the rest of the ocean at bay.

Her breath shaky, she wobbled as she took in the quickly draining room, the current threatening to take her off her feet as it poured out the double doors into the hallway. It'd been up to her knees, and in a panic she searched the room for Damien. Or Uriel. But the master of Shades was nowhere to be seen. Her vision snagged on someone else first, and it took her a breath to realize it was Conrad, slowly rousing in the corner of the room.

How did he not drown?

"Damien?" She barely recognized her own voice, muffled by the fierce pounding of her heart. The wound on her neck stung, but it didn't register as her gaze landed on a heap of battered flesh on the other side of the room, partially obscured by a displaced pile of debris and furniture.

Her heart shattered like crystal on stone.

"*Damien!*" Rae plowed through the receding water, her concentration on keeping the Dul'Idur Sea from crashing back through the hole in the ceiling nearly slipping as she collapsed next to her husband. Breath choked in her throat, and she touched his neck.

The pulse of life was there, but weak. Much too weak. His face was hardly recognizable, so badly beaten that swelling overtook most of the left side. She couldn't even see his eye, just a mangled mess of skin and blood.

Lowering her ear to his mouth, she listened, waiting for the brush of breath on her skin. But it didn't come.

"Shit," she muttered, grateful the water had drained enough for her to lay him on his back.

Conrad stumbled forward, blood still welling from a slash that ran down the side of his neck and over his shoulder. He looked desperately around, but then focused on Damien. He dropped to his knees, helping Rae position her husband without speaking.

Rae pressed her hands to Damien's damaged skin, a sob catching in her throat as she pushed against the wound. Summoning more of her power, she sought the water inevitably caught in Damien's lungs, and tugged at it. It answered her call, bubbling up out of his mouth, and she waited for him to cough. To gasp for air.

Nothing.

Choking in another breath, Rae felt for a pulse, but this time, found nothing. "No, no, no." She laced her fingers together as Maith had once taught her and positioned herself beside him, pressing in rhythm against his sternum. But her arms quaked, muscles struggling to keep up with her demands.

Conrad rose to his knees. "Let me. You're exhausted." He lifted his hands, positioning near hers ready to take over without pause even as blood soaked into his sleeve.

Rae didn't want to pass it over, but she had little choice, falling back as Conrad immediately took her place.

Squeaks came from outside the doors a second before they burst open.

She spun, relief sagging her shoulders as Deylan and three other faction members raced inside, pulling a gurney on rusty wheels.

"He's not breathing," Rae sobbed, but Deylan ignored her, giving clipped commands to one of the male nurses.

The unknown man rushed to Damien's head, holding a contraption Rae had never seen before. He inserted it into Damien's mouth, and then so far down that she cringed and looked away. When she looked again, he'd replaced it with a tube that led to a large sack that he squeezed with each of his own breaths.

"Hold," Deylan instructed Conrad, and the prince paused as Deylan felt for a pulse.

The next moments were a blur as the faction hauled Damien onto the gurney and wheeled him out of the room, one of them still squeezing that thing that pushed air into the Rahn'ka's lungs.

Rae quivered on the floor, staring after them, but her legs wouldn't work, wouldn't stand. Water dripped from the ceiling as her power faltered. Her awareness waned, and someone spoke to her, but she couldn't hear it.

Heat erupted in the room, too hot, too uncomfortable, but she still didn't move.

Someone kept talking to her, and she blinked, realizing Conrad still knelt beside her. She looked at him, trying to focus on his moving mouth. "Where did they take him?" she managed, panic shooting through her again. "Where is Damien?"

"The infirmary. It's back near the dorms and all the junction doors are open now."

Rae shivered, even with the heat still coursing through the room. Her eyes focused on Amarie, who worked her Art to close the hole in the ceiling. "Is he alive?" She gazed at Conrad again, hands trembling as she tried to decide what to do with them.

"Yes, but..." Conrad chewed his lower lip and looked at the ground. "He's in rough shape, and they're not sure how long he might last." He offered a hand to Rae, a looming darkness in his gaze. "You should go to him."

Drawing in a shaky breath, Rae rose, nodding through her daze. "Damien," she whispered, heat blooming in her eyes again as she stumbled towards the doors. Towards the infirmary. Conrad never left her side, holding her elbow every time she neared collapse. As she walked through the doorway into the infirmary, she gasped at how many people worked to save her husband's life.

Men and women crowded around him as he lay on his back on a metal table. Each did something, injecting his body with an unknown fluid, or listening to his heart. She struggled to keep track of what each of them did, slowly approaching his head, where someone had attached the tube to a machine.

As she moved closer, the people working stepped aside to make space for her. She looked around, Conrad still close beside her as the nurses gathered on the other side of the room, talking quietly among each other. "They don't have healers down here, do they?" Her own voice felt far away.

"No. But Deylan said these people are better than most healers." Conrad put a hand on her shoulder.

Some of the blood had been cleared away, but the entire left side of Damien's face was disfigured by swollen bruises and cuts.

Blinking back tears, Rae touched one of the few unmarred spots on his face, bending to whisper in his ear, "Please live."

Someone dragged a stool to her, and she sat, holding onto Damien's neck as everyone worked around her. Closing her eyes, she prayed to the gods, and kept talking to her husband. "You can't leave me."

At some point, someone helped her to her feet, and Deylan murmured to her. "We need to move him. There's nothing you can do right now, and they need space to work."

Nodding numbly, Rae left the room, finding Conrad waiting outside for her. His shirt only hung on one shoulder, the other wrapped densely in a bandage that also covered his neck.

She took a deeper breath, narrowing her eyes at him. "Why are you still here?" No resentment hung in her tone, just her honest curiosity. With all the chaos, she couldn't imagine he had nothing to do. No one to... "Where is Ahria?"

Rae had seen Amarie, and glimpsed Kin at some point. But she hadn't seen their daughter.

Conrad's gaze sank to the ground again, and he shook his head. "She's not here." Anger pulsed in his jaw, vehemence in his tone. "He took her, we think. But she's not here."

Blinking, Rae's awareness came back with more force. "Uriel took her?" Disbelief radiated through her. If Uriel took Ahria, the daughter of the Berylian Key, then the likelihood of her still being alive...

This is our fault.

Guilt tore through her.

She and Damien had pushed for this, brought them all together and then under the sea to follow Deylan. And for what? For nothing. They'd learned nothing in the past few days and now Damien was hanging on by a thread and Ahria was...

Rae's eyes burned all over again. "I'm sorry," she whispered, swallowing the lump in her throat. "I'm so sorry."

Conrad shook his head, the meaning behind it too vague to understand. "Kin thinks Uriel will keep her alive, since she should be the Berylian Key right now. Hells, he might think she is it and he might..." Conrad grimaced. "She'll make it. I know Ahria. We just have to get her back." A determination burned in his unfocused eyes, fading as he looked back at Rae. "I don't blame you, or Damien. So don't..."

Rae started when movement beside her came with a touch at her elbow.

Amarie, eyes glassy but still bright violet, tilted her head.

Energy touched Rae's veins, quieting her screaming muscles as the Berylian Key passed power from herself into the Mira'wyld. Not a lot, but enough to take the edge off the soreness.

"You should get that bandaged," Amarie murmured, touching her own neck where Rae's injury still burned.

Rae touched the clotted wound that ran from under her left ear to the hollow of her collarbone. "Later."

"Come." Amarie took her hand. "I'll do it."

 Chapter 24

Ahria coughed as her back hit a stone wall, her eyes peeling open. So dry. Her eyes, her mouth, everything was... so dry. Like she hadn't had a drink in days. She gagged, tongue stuck to the roof of her mouth as her senses slowly returned.

What happened?

All she remembered was darkness. Seeing Damien beaten to a pulp, and then the blur of hallways as she ran, but...

Shadows had consumed her, snuffed out her existence. She'd thought she was dead, but this could be worse, judging by the distant screams now reaching her ears.

Where... am I?

Scarce light sources offered her little evidence, but the floor she laid on was hard, packed dirt, with stone walls on three sides. The fourth boasted thick iron bars and no door.

She'd been in enough cells in the past few months to recognize it. But this definitely wasn't Ziona.

Her breathing picked up speed, nails biting into the cold dirt as she pushed herself into a sitting position. Her cloak was gone—no, she hadn't had a cloak with her, left it in her room in the underwater bunker. The frosty dungeon air nipped her exposed skin, a stark comparison to the summer heat she imagined outside. Wherever outside was.

"Hello?" Ahria's voice came out as barely a rasp, her throat burning with the effort of speaking.

That *thing* that had killed Damien. The shadows that had come after her, it had to be *him*. Not a Shade. Not a corrupted. Their master.

Uriel.

It had to be. Who else could have destroyed the Rahn'ka like that?

Ahria's body ached, and she tried to swallow, the sound of a whip cracking somewhere far off making her stomach turn. Bile rose in her throat, but she fought to keep it down.

"Let me out," she whispered, crawling to the iron bars. The lack of a door sent a shudder through her, but she pulled on the metal with feeble strength anyway. "Conrad?" With the solid walls on either side, she couldn't see if she had company. If the other cells were occupied. If there were any other cells.

She tried listening for breath, but only the distant screams filled her ears. Her hands shook as she noticed a small opening at the bottom of those bars. A short cut-out, no taller than a few inches. Pushing her hand through, she made it to her elbow, but could touch nothing beyond more dirt and the bars above it. Not that there was a lock to try to get to, anyway.

Sighing, she pulled her arm back. No chance of escaping, there. Pushing herself to the back of her cell, she tucked her knees to her chest and wrapped her arms around them. She shivered, teeth clenched as the cold rippled through her.

Furrowing her brow, she delved into herself, seeking any kernel of power left behind. She tried to find it, to spark it to life, but... nothing. No embers. No wisp of the Art in her veins. Her disappointment curled with relief. If she had no power, then no one could take it from her.

But she'd seen the look on Uriel's face. He knew who she was. Who her parents were. And if he thought they were still dead...

Please let him still think that.

Hours passed, though it could have been days. She had no way to tell, except for the slow weighing of her eyelids and growl of her belly.

Boots sounded on the dirt in distant thuds, and she braced herself to see Uriel's face again, but it didn't come. No face did, just a gloved hand appearing through the iron bars and dropping a small waterskin inside before retreating.

"Wait!" Ahria scrambled to the barred wall, pressing her cheek to the icy iron.

A door slammed, and silence again fell, broken only by the wails that hadn't ceased for longer than a few minutes. She wondered if it was all one person, or if many endured torture that day.

Shoulders slumping, Ahria retrieved the waterskin and returned to the back wall. She opened it, sniffing for any indication of poison before daring a small sip. Just enough to wet her throat. And if nothing happened over the following hours... then she'd drink more.

Stopping the flow of water into her mouth took much of her self control, and her stomach rumbled through the dim chamber.

I'm going to die here.

The dire thought made her eyes burn, but she shook her head. She couldn't give up so easily, so fast. Hope prevailed, even if she had no idea who survived the attack at the faction headquarters. But she knew one had to be her mother. Otherwise, she would have gained the power of the Berylian Key once more. Amarie would come for her. And in the meantime, she'd try to find a way out on her own.

As her body eased towards sleep, a bang jerked her awake. She covered her ears at the harsh clang of metal on metal, the sound bouncing through the dungeon as if someone dragged a pipe along the barred cells.

Unending, it sprouted a headache at her temples.

Ahria could hardly even hear her heart over the noise, and for a time, she wondered if it would ever stop. Ever cease. Her ears rang, the noise blurring together into a constant throb. Closing her eyes, she tried to focus on her breathing, and eventually the sound stopped.

Letting out a breath, she dared open her eyes and uncover her ears. It took her some time to settle after that, her nerves on edge for any sign of the dreadful cacophony. But silence prevailed, save for the tortured screams, and she gradually slipped into a relaxed state.

Then the noise started again.

Chapter 25

"You said we were safe here!" Amarie slammed the door behind her, following her brother into his private study. Rage burned through her, barely contained while she helped Rae and Conrad. While she welded the ceilings and walls back together with the aid of alcans in the water.

Deylan faced her, his face a mask of calm. "We're still working to figure out how he found us, but it looks like we probably had a tail from New Kingston. It's the only explanation. Uriel must have sent a little minion to look into the death of his Shade and caught wind of us instead." He huffed, running both hands through his hair. His eyes were distant, already shadowed beneath.

Amarie tried to quiet her fury, tried to remind herself that Deylan loved Ahria, too. That he didn't mean for this to happen, but... "Why aren't we going after her yet? Why haven't we already left?" Her voice caught in her throat. "There must be a way out of this bunker. He has *Ahria*."

"You think I don't know that?" Deylan glared at her. "She's my niece, Sister, I know. I know! But the corrupted took out all the lifts, and we're all stuck down here until the repairs are completed."

"How long?" Amarie pressed.

"A couple weeks, maybe longer." Deylan sighed. Something else lurked under his expression, something dark and unreadable.

"What?" She held his gaze, fists clenched. "What else is wrong?"

A muscle flexed in Deylan's jaw, and he looked away. "They destroyed the viewing chambers. I can't go looking for her. We... we're blind."

Amarie swallowed, her chest rising faster. "No. *You're* blind. I can find out where she is."

His gaze snapped to her. "How?"

"Her necklace." She touched her collarbone, rubbing at the spot on her own skin. "Assuming she's wearing it, which she is if Uriel hasn't taken it, I'll be able to track her with it. But only once we get out of here. Something about these walls makes it difficult to focus on her."

Deylan gestured with a hand. "It's the wards. So no one can find us." As she opened her mouth to retort that statement, he snarled, "Yes, I realize they didn't work." He sighed as he leaned on the back of his chair, tucked against his well-organized desk.

Amarie stared hard at him, tempted to keep berating him, but in truth... This was as much her fault as anyone else's. He may have said it was safe, but she should have known better. Should have known Uriel would be investigating the death of a Shade. Should have known...

As her chest grew heavy, she dipped her chin, but kept her voice cold. "Keep me updated."

Without another word, she left the study, her power simmering beneath her skin. It made her edgy, having it so close to the surface, but she wanted to be prepared. Be ready.

If Uriel wasn't convinced they were all dead, he could easily return and finish the job.

After the attack, the regulations on their group had been lifted and escorts were no longer needed to get around the headquarters. But the maze of corridors still made Amarie feel like she was walking in circles.

Fairly certain she was heading for the dormitories, Amarie rounded a corner and nearly walked face first into Rae. A drenched Rae. Water dripped to the metal floor, pooling only slightly before running towards the edges of the hall, showing the clever construction that enabled the bunker to drain after the incursion.

"What happened to you?" Amarie's tone came out harsher than she meant it, before she remembered the Mira'wyld's husband barely clung to life in the faction's infirmary. Cringing, she shook her head. "Sorry, I—"

"It's fine," Rae murmured. "I swam to the surface."

Amarie gaped, blinking through her surprise. "I... I didn't think you could do that, even with your power."

"It's exhausting. And, fortunately, I'm part alcan." The woman heaved a breath. "I sent my hawk to an ally. An ally with a ship. Hopefully she will follow Rin back here."

Relief threatened to sag Amarie's shoulders. "Even with the ship above us, how do we get to it without the lifts?"

Rae ran a hand over her braids. "I can get a small group to the surface. My Art can keep the water pressure light enough for us to swim up, and create a current to make it easier. I'll probably only be able to make one or two trips, though, so we'll have to make them count."

Amarie nodded. "I can help with your energy levels. But, it's probably only going to be me, Kin, and Conrad. One trip should be enough." She studied the woman she'd already transferred power to once, but offered again, "I can help with the exhaustion now, if you'd like?"

The Mira'wyld shook her head. "Thank you, but this isn't the kind of exhaustion you can help with."

Silence settled between them, and when Rae went to move around Amarie, the Key side stepped to block her path, lowering her voice. "How's Damien?"

Rae's throat bobbed. "Hard to say. That thing he's hooked up to... they say it's breathing for him. That it will take a while before we know if he's still..." She sucked in a deeper breath, chin quivering. "His other injuries will heal in time, except his eye. Even if we got to a healer on the surface, he won't get that back."

Amarie put a hand on Rae's shoulder. "He's strong. He'll pull through."

The Mira'wyld nodded, but defeat weighed on her shoulders. Hope barely flickered in those two-tone eyes. "I'm going to go sit with him awhile. I'll see you later."

Squeezing the other woman's shoulder before letting go, Amarie moved to let her continue on her way to the infirmary. She watched her, imagining how she'd feel if it were Kin unable to breathe on his own.

But she and Kin weren't married. Hadn't been partners for over two decades. She could hardly imagine the pain. The fear of losing him. Kin had slept next to her for almost as long, but their actual time together had been much, much shorter. Yet, at picturing the former Shade dying on that metal table, her eyes burned.

Dread pooled in her gut, and she wondered how they'd ever make it through this. The Rahn'ka had extraordinary power, but he'd failed against Uriel just as Amarie had. How could a prison ever work? Against something as powerful as Uriel...

Amarie looked at the floor as Rae disappeared around the far corner. Her heart thudded a beat in her chest that she tried to ignore. It ached, through her muscles and into her bones. It took everything she had to remain standing as the image of Ahria with Uriel flashed before her eyes.

If her daughter even still lived.

Trapped within warded walls, Amarie wouldn't be able to tell until she left. Unless, of course, wherever Uriel kept her was also warded. But her daughter... her *daughter* was in his hands. Not just his, either, but Alana's too. And after all Alana had done to Kin, Amarie's hands shook at the horror of what the sadistic auer would do to their child. Alana hadn't stopped her own brother from death, hadn't come to his rescue, only further confirming that her heart no longer bore any semblance of love. Of family.

Amarie sucked in a breath through her teeth and continued down the hall. Aimless, mindless as she walked, barely noting the spots in the ceiling she'd welded shut. The hallways still hung with a damp scent, salty from the water that had invaded. The corrupted bodies had been removed, but their blackened blood still marred the walls and floor.

Rubbing her face, Amarie slipped inside the room she shared with Kin, mercifully empty. She shut the door, tremors rippling through her hands as she remembered the scars over Kin's back. The damage Uriel had done. Not to an enemy, but to his own Shade.

What will he do to Ahria?

Heat choked her, closing her throat until only a sob could escape. Sliding to the floor, she tried to slow her breathing, but air couldn't reach her lungs.

If Damien died...

And with Ahria...

The plan began to crumble before her eyes, fracturing like a vase striking the floor. The cracks stretched, breaking through her as more tears flowed. Each breath came as a gasp, and for the first time since waking from Slumber, azure flames licked over her fingers without her bidding. She stared at it, then closed her eyes and let the heatless inferno spread like a blanket over the room. Her power ebbed and flowed like an ocean, consuming the space in a matter of a few heartbeats.

Watching her own hands, she clenched her jaw, damning the power in her veins. It had cost her so much, cost those she loved so much. And now it was useless. She couldn't help Damien, or Ahria, or anyone else. All the energy in the world, the training from the auer, and yet...

Amarie watched the flames encircle her hands, between her fingers, and wrap around her wrists. She'd once feared it, and feared others seeing it, but now it coated her like a comforting blanket. A visage of her pain.

Uriel should have taken me.

It made no sense for him to have Ahria. She had none of the Key's power, yet she'd still suffer. If he tortured her...

The door to their room gave a protesting squeal, making Amarie jump.

Her fire shifted to spread into the hallway beyond, but she restrained it within the room. A feat she wouldn't have been able to handle before the auer training. But now it felt as natural as breathing.

The person opening the door hesitated only a moment, still obscured from view, but then the door opened the rest of the way and Kin stepped in, promptly closing it behind him.

Amarie couldn't lift her chin to look at him, staring at his boots as her chin quivered. It didn't matter if he saw her like this, and it would never matter again. She had no interest in pretending, in hiding anything from him. She just let the tears keep falling, her heart broken and vulnerable.

Without a word, Kin lowered himself to the ground beside her, ignoring the flames as they licked up around him, too. He scooted close before wrapping an arm around her, nudging her side to urge her into him.

Amarie rested her head on his shoulder, quietly sobbing as he stroked her upper arm. She sniffed, then slid her gaze to meet his. Anger spiked, red hot as she imagined those stunning ice-blue eyes in pain. The eyes that also belonged to their daughter. "Anyone who lays a hand on her..." she whispered, voice raspier than she expected.

He pressed his cheek against the top of her head harder. "I know." His lips formed a slow kiss against her hair as she wiped her tears away with the back of her forearm. "We'll find her. She'll be all right. She's too much like you to give up."

The flames simmered, but still clung to every surface.

Breathing deep, she embraced Kin's scent of cedar and sun, unease spiking like a knife through her. "It feels wrong that we get to sit here like this. When Ahria is alone. And Rae doesn't know if her husband will even live through the night."

"I know." Kin withdrew slightly, looking down at her. "But neither of them would want you to have to pull away, either. Damien will survive and we'll find Ahria so she can return to whatever life she wants. Whatever it takes. All of this suffering and fighting has always been for that. To give Ahria a world she can be happy in. None of this changes that, and we'll keep fighting because that's what you and I do." He slid his hand into hers, and she entwined their fingers.

Her fire dimmed again, diminishing until nothing remained, at least not externally. Within her, it roiled and danced and pushed against her senses. "Where do you think she is?" she murmured, resting her hand on his chest as her gaze drifted to his injured forearm, wrapped in thick gauze. He'd saved her that day as much as she'd saved him.

"Wherever Uriel has established himself. He'd keep her close. If I had to guess, she's in Feyor. He's always holed up near there for some reason, and if Jarac is a Shade it would be easy to abuse the country's resources." Kin grimaced, but didn't speak whatever thoughts she saw ripple through his expression.

"What?" Amarie tilted her head, worry pulsing through her stronger. "What is it?"

There was a time when she'd have loathed asking him such a question. A question about his thoughts, emotions, or anything sensitive. But the instinct didn't falter now, not with their new ability to be honest with each other.

"Feyor. It just made me think of something Matthias tried to talk to me about." He met her eyes as if looking for the confidence to speak about it. "Apparently my *brother*," the word was awkward from Kin's mouth, as if he still didn't believe he had a twin, "has driven the country into the ground. Which only further proves that Uriel is likely using the funds from over taxing the people. Matthias suggested that it's time for a regime change in Feyor."

Amarie gaped at him, never having considered the possibility of him sitting on a throne, even though she'd known the truth of his lineage as long as he had. "He suggested you should rule Feyor?" The question came out barely louder than a whisper. Just the idea of it would change everything. It would completely alter the course of Ahria's life, not to mention Kin's.

And mine.

But Jarac would have aged while Kin hadn't, and she wondered if the citizens would even accept his claim to the throne. Yet, a part of her doubted Kin would ever make that challenge. Not out of inability or fear, but because he'd never once shown any inclination to obtain power beyond what he'd sought from Uriel as a teenager, which he now regretted.

When Kin didn't answer for several moments, she sighed. "I guess you'd rather not."

"Obviously. Can you imagine me as a king? That sounds like the worst idea anyone could ever have. But Matthias pointed out that it's bigger than me, and he's right. I may not be used to being a father yet, but I have a family now that will also be affected by my choices." He sighed, leaning his head against Amarie's again. "I don't know what Ahria would want." He rubbed her arm. "Or you."

"I don't care." The words left her mouth before she even thought about them. "As long as Ahria is safe and happy and we're together, that's all that matters to me." She turned his hand over, studying it. "Though I'm not sure I'm suited to palace life. I think I'd rather have a small cottage by a lake." Her lips tugged upward, but the intention was quickly lost. "I just want us to have our family, whatever that looks like."

"Then it will be up to what Ahria wants." Kin shifted, encouraging her further into his lap. Wrapping his arms around her, he kissed her temple. "Though, she *is* already in a relationship with Ziona's crown prince..."

With her head against his chest, Amarie listened to his heart beat. She wanted to tell him none of it mattered yet, because Ahria wasn't with them. Wasn't safe, or guaranteed any kind of future. She wanted to tell him how terrified she felt of losing their daughter again. How she feared the whip coming for Ahria's back. But she held her tongue on her ominous thoughts.

Kin's grip tightened around her, as if his mind, too, had wandered down the darkened pathway with hers. Another kiss pressed to the top of her head, and he murmured, "Wherever she is, we'll find her."

And Amarie nodded, even if she didn't fully believe him.

Chapter 26

As Conrad stared at the open book, the words jumbled together in his mind. He glared harder, as if it would somehow cause them to form something he could understand, but it only added to the growing pain at the back of his head. Clapping the book shut, he checked the spine again to make sure it was what Rae was even looking for, then added it to the pile on the floor beside him.

The dim light of the library didn't help in his struggle to decipher the titles etched into the old leather spines. At least the room hadn't suffered any damage from the attack, which seemed a miracle. But Deylan had explained to Rae that the dark metal surrounding it was twice as thick as anywhere else, and the lockdown procedures had secured it.

Shelves filled the cylindrical space on every wall, rising up for three stories. He'd had to climb a precarious ladder to get to the second rickety metal catwalk that granted access to this level of books.

Rae sat at the single table at the center of the room, the brightest light in the space hovering close to her face for her to read by. Dark circles had formed under her eyes, and Conrad knew what kept her up at night.

For him, it was slightly different. Rae knew that Damien was fighting against near death. She could see him as he suffered. But Ahria... He didn't know where she was or what horrors she might be facing. The thoughts gnawed a hole in his stomach, making his hands shake as he reached for another book.

Conrad focused on his breath as he drew one from the shelf, running his hands over the floral etchings on the cover. Flipping through the pages, he sought the words Rae had told him to keep any eye out for. The only words he could force his mind to see. But nothing jumped out, and he slid the book back into place before checking the note Rae had written for him to where the books she wanted were located.

His shoulder twinged, the healing gash pinching as he tried to roll the muscles to make them relax. With the movement, the shadows on the metal landing to his left shifted, making his heart jump. But it was only Rae flipping a page—not Uriel.

Not Uriel.

Yet the monster's face appeared as Conrad closed his eyes. His words echoed through Conrad's thoughts. Then Ahria would be there, reaching out to him, only to be consumed by darkness.

A little out of your league, here, don't you think, Prince?

He was entirely out of his league. The guilt of that position only made every moment without Ahria in his arms worse. He hadn't had a chance at protecting her from the creature responsible for beating the Rahn'ka into near oblivion. And Damien was one of the most powerful Art users Conrad had ever met. But he'd lost, even with Rae nearby. And Amarie.

Uriel hadn't seen Conrad as enough of a threat to kill him, either. He'd batted him away like an insect.

The door to the library opened, and Rae's chair screeched across the floor as she shot to her feet at the sight of one of the nurses. She put the book down, leaving a scrap of parchment between the pages, and jogged to the doorway. They spoke in lowered tones, and Rae put her hand over her throat before nodding once. Twice.

The nurse exited, closing the door behind him, but Rae stood motionless for a few breaths. In the next moment, she spun, grabbing the trash can next to the door, and vomited into it.

Conrad grimaced, wondering what news about Damien had come today. Tucking the pair of books he had found under his arm, he carefully descended the ladder back to the main floor. "You should probably go." He looked at Rae as he set the books among the others on the desk. "These will all still be here later, but you should be with your husband."

Rae shook her head, spitting before turning and sitting on the floor with her back against the wall. "The nurse said I should stay away for another hour or so," she muttered. "They're going to be doing things I won't want to see, and I'd be in the way. But..." She closed her eyes, clenching her jaw. "They finished removing what was left of his damaged eye and the bone fragments around it." Nausea curled over her face, and her throat worked. "He will let me know when I can come back."

Nodding, Conrad crossed to her and held out a hand. "If they performed a procedure like that, there must be hope that he'll pull through, then. It's a good thing."

Taking his hand, she rose to her feet with his help. "I suppose." Her glassy eyes met his, still bloodshot, as they'd been since the attack.

He wondered briefly if she'd kept any food down in the past few days, or if she'd slept.

Rae cleared her throat, letting go of his hand, and whispered, "I can't imagine what *you're* feeling, not knowing."

Conrad shook his head, urging the returning thoughts not to take hold again. "I'm good at compartmentalizing. And I'm trying to stay optimistic."

She gave him a pained, forced smile. "I don't know Ahria very well, but if she's anything like her mother, I'd say you're right to hope." Picking the mug of coffee up from her work table, she took a sip and cringed as she swallowed it.

In the silence, Conrad sought any distraction he could in his memory, focusing on Rae and what they'd discussed over the recent days. Finding Ahria and how to get her back. "Were you able to send your hawk? To Andi?"

They'd need a ship to get anywhere, and Conrad couldn't think of a better captain to enlist in a time of crisis. Kin had already implied he knew where Uriel might take Ahria. Feyor. Which brought up an entirely new anxiety.

He didn't know if the arrest warrant still held in the country where he'd had an unfortunate run-in with the law all due to one measly, misplaced shipping tariff form. Still a fresh captain, he couldn't afford the extensive fee, and Leiura broke him out of jail so they could keep sailing, and maybe pay back the fee eventually. He'd almost forgotten about it until Kin said the name of the country.

Considering the state of the government, he doubted any officials would have wasted time figuring out that he was a crown prince now. But that might not have made a difference, though now he could afford the fee. But there wasn't time for politics, and none of it would stop him from going after Ahria.

The Mira'wyld nodded, sitting again in her plush chair. "I did. Hopefully Andi will be here soon. She'll take us wherever we need to go."

Conrad rubbed his chin. "It'll be so strange to see her. But I think I'm going to be the bigger surprise."

Rae huffed her agreement. "All I could do was send Rin to find her. I couldn't write a message in the middle of the ocean."

"You think she'll know what to do with a hawk with no note?"

Rae traced her finger over the patterns of the arm's chair. "She'll follow him. She'll know it's important."

He hummed, moving to lean against the desk, still piled high with books. "It's still crazy to think about the coincidences. From me stowing away on a random ship that happened to be your mother's... and now I'm here after Ahria stowed away on *my* ship." He looked up at the multistory bookshelves, the strange dark steel that surrounded them.

Rae gave a tight smile. "The deeper all of this goes, the more and more it feels like fate may be a real thing."

He chewed on his lower lip, eyeing the books he wished he could help her sort through more. "Have you had any luck? With this whole... Taeg'nok thing?"

Drumming her fingers along the spine of a book, she opened it to a bookmarked page. "Actually, yes. I haven't read this entire work, yet, but it seems to cover the process. In an albeit... rather confusing way. But with some time, I should be able to decipher everyone's roles." Despite the crucial nature of the information, and that she'd finally found it, her tone lacked excitement.

Because without Ahria and Damien, we're out of luck, anyway.

"Good." Conrad tried to smile, but it felt strained. Sighing, he crossed his arms lightly. "You all right in here if I go get some air? I don't think I can focus on another book right now."

The library door swung open again before Rae could answer, and she jumped, probably expecting the nurse again. But Deylan stood in the doorway, eyeing them both before settling his grim gaze on Conrad. "Are you busy?"

So much for a break.

Conrad shook his head. "Something wrong?"

"Aside from the catastrophic damage that's going to take forever to repair?" Deylan ran a hand through his hair, bags under his eyes that matched Rae's. "No, not particularly. But I've found myself short of hands in all this and I could use some help, unless Rae needs you."

"It's fine." Rae patted Conrad's shoulder, speaking to him, then. "I'll be fine. Thank you for the help."

Conrad nodded to her before facing Deylan. Another distraction would probably be best, since every time he found himself alone, he only dwelled on how inadequate he was for what they faced. But if he could help the faction, somehow, it was something. He'd already dodged working on the outside of the bunker, for which he carried some guilt. His alcan blood would have aided him in being able to work in the depths of the sea, but that secret... He wasn't willing to let go of it without absolute necessity.

Conrad gestured to the doorway behind Deylan. "Lead the way."

Ahria's uncle turned on his heel, stalking back through the corridors. Without a word, he led Conrad through the first junction, then the dormitories, and then another junction. They continued past the infirmary, into an area they hadn't been allowed to enter before. A few faction members watched as they passed yet another junction.

In this area—the damage was extensive. Several places had been haphazardly welded shut, with dents still visible along the walls and ceiling. They walked by many doors, mostly all closed, but one set in particular caught Conrad's attention.

A set of double doors, taller than the others, and carved with ornate depictions of a battle. The metal bore inlaid copper accents, but Deylan didn't stop to give him time to study it.

They reached another set of double doors, not as tall as the previous ones, but just as decorated. A giant eye covered the center, broken in the middle by where the doors parted.

"It's a little heavy handed, if you ask me," Deylan mumbled before pushing them open.

The room they entered had sustained significant damage as well. Three raised domes protruded from the floor, each with a handle, but all of them looked like they'd taken the brunt of the attack. The far wall made Conrad's chest tighten. Levers and buttons and dials covered it, unlike anything the prince had ever seen before. But some of the areas were destroyed, broken, with parts scattered over the floor.

"I know you already swore not to share these secrets with Ziona." Deylan faced him. "But I'd like to remind you of that, regardless. This room is no exception." He crossed to one of the domed lids that had fallen from its place, the hinge torn clean off. "Help me lift this."

Conrad took hold of the dome opposite of Deylan and heaved, the scent of rust and salt water rushing into his nose as he did. He wondered what the room was for, ignoring the dark shadows at the back of it. Considering the eye on the door, he pondered the faction's ability to see so many things around Pantracia. Including Ahria and all of the Berylian Keys before her.

These strange metal pods likely have something to do with how they do it.

Conrad and Deylan worked in silence, except for the occasional direction from Deylan. At the end of it, his muscles ached throughout his arms and back. "Why me for this? Why not another member of the faction?" Conrad looked towards the closed door, confirming he and Deylan were alone. "Or Kin."

"Because you need it most." Deylan wiped sweat from his brow with the bottom of his shirt. "Kin is helping with Amarie somewhere else, and Rae has embraced her distractions in the library." He met his gaze. "But I thought you might need to take your mind off things while you wait for transport."

Rubbing his sore palms together, Conrad considered Ahria's uncle. He had risked so much to bring them to the headquarters, and it all had been in vain when Uriel had found them anyway. He wondered what all Deylan had endured from the mysterious Vanguard who controlled the Sixth Eye. Not to mention his own connection with Ahria and what he had to be feeling there.

Fresh guilt rose in Conrad's chest again. "I'm sorry." He felt like a piece of his chest caved in as he thought of Ahria's face. The fear as she turned and ran.

Deylan's eyes narrowed. "What for?"

"For everything. For Ahria." Conrad wished he could claw the ache from his chest as he said her name. "For none of it being enough."

"None of that was your fault." Deylan crossed his arms. "We were caught by surprise and unprepared." His chin dipped as mirrored guilt sparked across his face. "She should have been safe here. You all should have been safe. We failed you, and that's on me more than anyone else."

"It's all just crazy. All of it." Conrad felt the hopelessness he'd been trying to bury taking hold. "I'm just a ship's captain and she was just a stowaway. And the only dire question was whether or not she would find her father. But now..." He saw Uriel's face again, his sneer as he threw him across the room like a toy. His eyes began to throb. "How am I supposed to be useful in any of this?" He looked at his hands, still raw from picking up the saltwater-worn metal. "Even this," he gestured at the pods he'd helped to rebuild, "means nothing in the grand scheme of what Damien was trying to do. What they're all trying to do. I'm only here out of stubbornness, pride, and stupidity."

Deylan remained silent for a few moments before approaching him and clamping a hand on his shoulder. "I know you're used to being in a position much different than this. Captaining your own ship, changing laws as a prince. I understand what you feel being surrounded by all this... power that other people have. I get it, I truly do, because I have no Art, either. I'm just a man, like you." He tilted his head in a similar way he'd seen Ahria do. "But that doesn't mean you aren't useful. And if you..." He paused, glancing at the doorway behind Conrad. A vague smile touched his lips. "Hmm. Come with me. I have an idea." He slapped Conrad on the back before heading for the doors.

The prince hesitated, the heaviness of his own words still weighing down his feet. Even if just a man, something about Deylan still made Conrad feel grossly outclassed. Yet, the lingering sting of the slap encouraged him forward, following Deylan out of the chamber.

Deylan led him back the way they'd come, but took the other hallway at the junction rather than towards the infirmary.

This had been where they were headed before the junction doors had slammed down, and sure enough, Deylan stopped outside the armory. Pushing the door open, he waited as Conrad strode inside before speaking. "You know how to use a sword, I assume, since you carry one?"

The faint light in the room from the sconces glowed eerily off the weapons adorning the walls and floor racks. A cabinet stood in one corner, locked with a heavy iron bar across the doors. Swords, axes, and drawers covered the rest of the area, along with the odd spear and halberd.

"Of course." Conrad eyed the cabinets on the far wall, their contents hidden, but it only made him more curious. The reflections off the copper weapons led to an odd golden glow in the room, and he wished he could understand the runes that ran up and down the blades.

Deylan eyed him, then selected a copper sword off the wall similar in size to the one Conrad carried at his hip. Twisting it, he offered the handle to the prince. "Anything I give you will be a loaner, but you'll be better equipped to face Uriel and his Shades the next time the need arises."

Conrad stared at the offered hilt before he slowly reached for it. Taking the blade, he marveled at how light it felt, giving it a careful bounce to check its balance.

"It looks like copper, I know, and while it may have once been, it is no longer just *copper*. I can't get into details of the process, but the core of the blade is xyridium, and the coating over it is imbued with an ancient Art that has the power to deflect a Shade's shadows. Nullify them, in a way." Deylan walked to a shallow drawer and slid it open, revealing a wide assortment of throwing knives, daggers, and star-shaped blades with holes in the center. "Feel free to choose a couple of these, too."

Conrad approached, studying the smaller weapons that boasted the same runes like the sword he held. Some of them had small jewels embedded in the hilts, but most looked less gaudy.

While he looked at them, Deylan opened a larger drawer in another area and chose a scabbard for the sword, along with a frog and belt. "Doesn't give you the Art, but it's something more than steel and wit."

"You sure you're allowed to *loan* me these?" Conrad picked up one of the medium-sized daggers, twisting it in the light.

"Right now, the Vanguard has more pressing worries than who I loan weapons to. But in all reality, yes, I have the authority to grant you devices should the need arise. And as far as I'm concerned, that need arose days ago." Deylan put the leather down on top of the drawers for Conrad, then crossed the room to the barred cabinet. With a key from his pocket, he unlocked the bar and slid it free.

Conrad watched him from the corner of his eye as he slid the sword into the sheath. Setting it on the drawer, he unbuckled his belt and worked to switch out the blades. The new sword felt foreign on his hip, but he touched the hilt with his palm and it oddly brought a new sense of comfort. "Does it work on all Art, or just Shades?" Conrad leaned his old sword against the wall before picking up a different dagger.

Deylan tugged the heavy cabinet doors open, revealing a multitude of shallow black drawers. "It's not quite that easy to define. They were crafted mostly to defend against Shades, but they are also effective to some degree with other forms of the Art." He reached for one of the black drawers and then paused, turning back to where Conrad stood. Approaching again, he crouched and slid out the bottom drawer. "You could use this, too." He retrieved a piece of the same copper-looking metal—two circles, barely wide enough to put a finger in each. He slid it onto his hand, then smirked at Conrad. "Throw a punch."

The prince quirked an eyebrow. "A punch?" He looked at the new device Deylan had put on as he abandoned the dagger in the drawer.

"Come on. At my face." Deylan gestured to his chin. "Try to hit me."

"Why do I have a feeling I'm going to regret it, though?"

Ahria's uncle chuckled, and the lightness felt like such a reprieve. "You won't."

Shrugging his injured shoulder first, Conrad gripped his fist and swung.

Deylan's hand bearing the double ring shot up in a fist, and coppery light burst from the metal. As Conrad's fist entered the midst of it, it slowed, like he was suddenly trying to punch through thick mud. He tried to recoil, but his fist still could only move at the sluggish pace until Deylan unclenched his fist and Conrad stumbled backward with the abrupt momentum.

Looking at his hand, he stretched his fingers to make sure nothing still clung to them, but it all felt normal. "I'll take one of those."

Deylan pulled it off his hand, offering it. "Might come in handy." Once the prince took it, he returned to the cabinet and pulled out the drawer he'd hesitated at before. "There is one more item I'll give you. But it takes a bit of practice to master."

Chapter 27

"Hope none of you are afraid of tight spaces," Rae muttered, leading the group into a small metal box that acted as the water lock for entering the Dul'Idur Sea from the faction bunker.

Amarie, Kin, Conrad, and Deylan entered behind her. Ahria's uncle had decided to join them, since repairs on the entirety of the headquarters were progressing painfully slow. She also suspected the Vanguard wanted to keep an eye on their efforts, and Deylan was the convenient choice with his existing relationship.

Deylan hid his worry better than the rest of them, but she could still see it beneath his brown eyes.

They'd journey to the surface in one trip. Rae wasn't sure how she felt about guiding not one, not two—but *four* other people through the deep water. Yet, she'd made the decision. Two trips would exhaust her even worse, if she could even make it the second time without drowning them.

Rae scrunched her toes, unaccustomed to the feel of metal beneath her bare feet. They'd all donned the least amount of clothing they dared, fearing the drag of the water and weight of boots. All valuables, weapons, and denser clothing had been placed in a water-tight wooden crate lined with an oilskin. It would float to the surface once submerged, but it contained none of Rae's belongings. She'd return to the bunker to be with her husband rather than accompany the ship.

The crate's air pockets would help get them all to the surface faster, too, allowing Rae to focus on controlling the pressure of the water rather than upward momentum. Rope wrapped around it in every direction, creating handholds for all of them.

Only an hour ago, word had come from one of the faction sentries that a ship had dropped anchor directly beneath the Dul'Idur Gate. A ship with an alcan figurehead and flying the Zionan flag.

Andi had come.

Not that Rae was surprised, but only a week had passed. Her mother must not have been too far away. The knowledge that Andi was waiting for them at the surface made her insides lurch for the waiting comfort. The embrace that would come, that would fill her chest with the warmth it'd been lacking since Damien fell against Uriel. It'd be brief, but hopefully would help restore the strength she needed.

Damien's booming laugh ruptured through her memory, followed by his voice after learning Conrad's dog's name. *Please let me be the one to tell her.*

Her chest cracked, heat burning her eyes before she clenched her teeth and looked up.

I'll be right back, Lieutenant.

Deylan sealed the chamber behind them, spinning a crank wheel while everyone else seemed to hold their breath already.

"You're sure the pressure won't outright kill... us?" Conrad, surprisingly, looked the least worried of all of them.

"It... shouldn't." Rae almost cringed at the uncertainty in her tone. "I can keep the pressure to a bearable degree. But you *can* swim, right, *Captain?*" Although she directed the question at Conrad, everyone else nodded, too.

"Of course." Something lingered behind his gaze, some unspoken emotion, and Rae narrowed her eyes.

Amarie and Kin muttered quietly to each other.

Deylan motioned to the next crank. "When I release the next latch, the ceiling will split and water will slowly fill this space. It's just the initial flow door at first, so it won't make us immediately open to the sea. The lever after that will do that part." He checked the straps securing an oil skin bag to his side, prompting the others to do the same. "It will be very dark, but Amarie will light the way. No matter what, don't let go of the crate."

Amarie nodded, breathing deeper until her skin practically glowed and a ball of bright violet light swirled in front of her chest. She nodded at Deylan, then crouched, grasping the rope-bound crate.

Rae did the same, breathing her power into her lungs as she readied herself. She needed to keep the pressure at bay, create a current for the crate's rapid rise, and make sure everyone reached the top before running out of air.

"Ready?" Deylan reached for the second lever. Once everyone nodded, he cranked it, and water spewed in from above.

The salty scent filled Rae's nostrils, water creeping over her bare feet and up her legs, where her cut-off breeches ended at her knees. She only wore a sleeveless tunic on top, her hair braided tightly back.

The crate of belongings bobbed up with the water as it rose. Each of them anxiously adjusted their grip on the ropes as it lifted higher.

As the water rose with the crate, they all stood, and Deylan watched closely. As soon as Amarie was neck-deep, he grasped the next crank.

Rae dipped her head under, breathing in the water and acclimating her lungs. The salt water burned at first, as it always did, before her body adapted and it flowed in and out with ease.

Blinking through the water, lit by the glow from Amarie and the dim light still emanating from the faction's strange Art-laden sconces, Rae watched each of her friends as the water rose above their heads.

Deylan turned the final crank, and Rae pushed her power above them.

The sea crashed down on them, but she doubted any of them felt it like she did. It made her muscles shake, and she took a moment to gain her bearings as the crate aided in their ascent.

Rae double-checked to make sure everyone held on. That everyone was with her.

Amarie. Deylan. Kin. Conrad.

Looking up, she couldn't see the surface, but she swelled her power around them and directed the water to flow as she willed it.

And swam.

Darkness closed around them, kept at bay only by Amarie's light.

Rae reminded herself to move fast, kicking as she propelled them through the sea. She could breathe, but the others couldn't, and the surface wasn't close.

With a surge of her energy, the water swirled around them, creating a stronger current.

Light sparked above, dim, but visible beyond.

Rae looked at the others, checking their faces for signs of struggle. Bubbles rose from Kin and Deylan, but they still appeared focused.

Faster.

Rae panted, drawing power from the deep well within herself to push them harder. Faster. Propel them through the water like it was a vertical river.

The light at the top grew brighter and brighter, until cool air hit her face. Coughing the water from her lungs, Rae gasped a breath, then checked those around her. Four. All four were there, and she let out a breath of relief, even if they all were gasping for air and clutching to the crate like their lives depended on it. And the air itself tasted sweet.

As they rested, floating with the crate, a shadow crept over them and Rae looked up to see such a familiar, welcome sight.

The Herald.

And perched on the banister—Andi.

"Where the *fuck* did you all just come from?"

Rae smiled despite herself, holding in the sob that threatened to escape. She swam towards the ship, dragging the crate and the others with her as shouts rang out from the deck of the Herald, Keryn's commanding tone reaching Rae. Ropes dropped from the rigging, landing in the water beside them.

Kin and Conrad worked together to secure the ropes around the crate first. Though Conrad did most of the work, moving far faster than Kin could with the knots and knew the best way to secure the crate. The way the prince maneuvered in the water, with so much ease, made her wonder who had taught him to swim.

Amarie, her light extinguished, climbed the thrown ropes with Deylan while the ship's crew hoisted the crate onto the deck.

Rae stayed in the water until the rest of them, and the crate, made it aboard. Then she grabbed the last dangling rope, breathing hard as Andi helped pull her up. Landing on her back on the deck, memories flashed before her eyes of the first time Andi had leaned over her.

"Bringing out the nostalgic side of me." Andi smirked and offered Rae a hand, which the Mira'wyld took and staggered to her feet. "Where's Lanoret?"

Rae met her gaze, but at the question, her throat tightened. Emotion coalesced in her chest, and her chin quivered.

The hardness in Andi's expression, which she always kept in front of her crew, softened abruptly. "Seems we need to speak in private." She stepped back, gesturing towards her quarters at the back of the ship. But as she turned, her gaze brushed over the others as they stood wringing sea water from themselves. "Connie?"

Conrad grimaced, but gave the first smile Rae had seen in days. "Good to see you again, Captain, but we have time to catch up. Rae first, since she's not sticking around for the adventure you're about to get dragged into."

Andi frowned, looking back to Rae. "I figured it had to be bad when you sent that hawk of yours without a message. And I suppose commandeering my ship hasn't happened in a while, so we were due for such things." She crossed her arms, hip tilting slightly where her rapier rested, as it always did. Andi hadn't changed since the day they'd first met over two decades ago. The alcan blood kept the grey hair and wrinkles away. It was doubtful her crew even realized how long Andi had been captaining.

Rae tried to smile, squeezing the water from her braids.

"Come." Andi gestured with her head towards her quarters again. "Let's have a drink and you can fill me in." The captain looked up to her first mate as Keryn descended from the upper bow deck, white shining among the cornrow braids on her head. "See to getting our guests situated. We'll remain at anchor for now."

"Aye, Captain." Keryn turned to the others as Andi's hand brushed Rae's wrist, beckoning her forward.

As voices murmured around her, Rae closed her eyes, focusing on the crash of waves against the hull as they strode towards the captain's quarters. The chatter of gulls from the distant shore, and the way stray strands of hair tickled her cheek as they dried. It eased her heart, slowed it to a rhythm that felt further from chaos, even with the struggle ensuing hundreds of feet below the water's surface.

He'll still be alive when I return.

The brief moment of sky when she'd surfaced to send Rin to Andi had offered her none of the solace she felt now. It had been night, and while the stars had twinkled, she hadn't seen them beyond her heartbreak.

Now, the sun warmed her skin, and the fresh air revived her senses—almost too much. Too much. Because Damien had none of it. Damien, hooked to a machine to make him breathe, may never see the sun again. The sky. Feel the breeze.

Her throat tightened, the calm surrounding her breaking as the dire thoughts once again rolled over her like an immovable weight. Those within the bunker with her were allies, yes. Perhaps even friends to some degree, but... They weren't *home*. They weren't family. Not like Andi, and those she sorely missed in Helgath. She yearned for Jarrod, had debated sending word to him of what had happened, but what could he do?

The windows at the back of Andi's cabin let in more of the summer breeze as it whipped through the sea cliffs around them. The sun sparkled against the stained glass, sending a kaleidoscope of color across the floor and Andi's map table. Two overstuffed chairs sat where they always had, nailed to the deck, with a small storage cabinet between them.

Rae started towards them out of habit as the door to the cabin clicked shut behind her. Stopping in front of the chair, she stared at it. At the subtle pattern of thorns within the pale green fabric.

Were they always green?

A rock hit the bottom of her stomach. A cruel, awful feeling that threatened to unravel her.

"I think I made a mistake," Rae whispered, daring to voice the nightmare that'd plagued her every moment, awake or otherwise.

Andi's calm presence approached behind her, the captain's solid grip taking her shoulder. "Sit. Tell me what's going on." She moved to the cabinet, retrieving a small tray with a pair of glasses and a decanter of amber liquid.

Rae sank into the chair, heat pricking her eyes as she gazed at the whisky. "Damien's dying." She swallowed, blinking faster to contain the tears. "He's—" She choked. "And I..."

The sound of the whisky pouring would have normally brought such joy between her and Andi, but as her mother filled the first glass and handed it to her, Rae fought to keep her hands from shaking. And failed.

Instead of taking the chair, Andi knelt in front of Rae, placing her hands near hers to help keep them from trembling. "That man is too stubborn to die. And he would never leave you. But regardless, I doubt any of this is your fault." She looked up at Rae, encouraging their eyes to meet. "Start from the beginning. What happened?"

Rae gulped a mouthful of whisky, focusing on the burn. "There's a bunker below us," she whispered, not an ounce of her worried about Andi telling a soul. "A secret headquarters belonging to some very useful allies." The rest of the story spilled out of her between sips of liquor, telling Andi of how Uriel found them and attacked. How

Damien had nearly died, stopped breathing, and how the master of Shades had stolen Amarie's daughter.

Andi didn't interrupt her story, even through the sometimes lengthy pauses when Rae just needed to cry.

"They said his chances of surviving were slim," Rae sobbed. "And that I should prepare myself, so I did. I tried. I didn't send for Bellamy, because I didn't want his father's death to rest on his shoulders. On his failure, when it was never his fault. But, now..." Her breath came faster, and she finished the glass of whisky. "I think I should have. Bell still wouldn't be here, but he'd be closer..."

"So do it now." Andi took the glass, setting it aside before squeezing both of Rae's hands. "It sounds like whatever they're doing down there is keeping Damien stable, so send for Bellamy now. I've never once pretended to understand whatever Art those two boys have, but if you think there's a chance that my grandson can help save his father, you need to send Rin right now."

Rae turned her blurry gaze to her mother. "But what if it's too late? What if I waited too long and Bell can't get here in time?"

"That wouldn't be your fault, either." Andi raised her hand, brushing back the drying strands of her hair, loose from her braids. "Bellamy might not even be able to do anything, but that doesn't matter because that wouldn't be either of your fault. All of this is on the man who hurt Damien in the first place."

Rae clenched her jaw, a spike of fury, white and hot, burning in her throat. "I need parchment."

Andi nodded, pulling away to go to her map table. She held out the writing supplies to Rae before turning back to the decanter and pouring more. This time, filling her own glass as well. "I'll go get that bird of yours ready."

Taking a deep breath, Rae dipped the quill in ink and began writing.

> *Bell,*
> *Your father's gravely injured. If anyone can save*
> *him, you have the best chance. I need you. Travel to*

the Dul'Idur Gate as fast as you can. I'll tell our
allies to watch for you.

Her quill hovered over the parchment as she debated, swiping tears from her cheeks with the back of her arm.

Please hurry. I love you.
Mom

Rae put the quill down, staring at the message. If Bellamy was still with Yondé on the border of Olsa, Aidensar, and Delkest, it would take him weeks to arrive. She tried to push aside the dread that she'd already waited a week, and rolled the parchment small enough to fit into Rin's cuff. She rose, exiting onto the deck, and balked when the sun blinded her.

I've been underwater too long.

Once her eyes adjusted, she furrowed her brow at Andi stroking her hawk's head, the bird perched on her arm.

"He likes you more than Din did," Rae managed, though the attempt at humor felt hollow as she approached. Slipping the message into the hawk's leg cuff, she scratched Rin's chest.

"Din was an asshole, and you know it." Andi gave a comforting smile as she passed the hawk off to her daughter with a light bounce of her wrist.

Rae huffed a dry laugh. "Give him a break. He was old."

Din had passed years ago, and back then, she would have loathed giving such a task to a new winged companion. But Rin had proven himself time and time again over the past five years, and she trusted him to find her son.

"Bellamy," Rae murmured to the hawk, his head quirking to the side. "Bellamy." She pushed her arm into the air, and the bird took flight, circling only once before soaring southwest. Her heart ached at how Bellamy would feel. The fear, the not knowing. The burden. But Andi was right. If there was a chance...

Rae watched Rin disappear into the cloudless sky before returning her gaze to Andi. "I know the others are eager to go."

She lifted an eyebrow. "And this is you officially roping me into whatever conflict this is with this Shade guy." She shook her head, but it was with a smile. "Good thing I tend to sail towards danger, so this won't be so different. It's been positively boring out on the seas without looking over my shoulder for Helgath, anyway."

"The others will fill you in on the details, but I think you're heading for Feyor." Rae's lips twitched in an attempted smile. "And you know you wouldn't have it any other way."

"If I wasn't certain whatever secret group below the ocean would protest to me hovering, I might fight you harder about staying here." Her gaze softened. "With you. And to see my grandson, of course." She stepped towards Rae, gripping her bicep. "Keep me updated."

"I know. And I will." Rae returned the grip on her mother's arm, resisting the urge to pull her into an embrace. "Thank you." She gazed over the side of the ship at the water, imagining the headquarters far below. Her muscles still ached, but the return would be easier than the journey to the surface.

Eyeing Andi one more time, she nodded. "Stay safe, will you? Keep my friends safe?"

Instead of speaking, the captain pulled Rae into her arms, taking her tightly in a hug, despite who might see. "I will."

Rae's eyes burned, and she squeezed before pulling away with another subtle nod. Turning, she exhaled all the air from her lungs and dove into the sea.

Chapter 28

"Conrad?" Ahria jarred upright, eyes refusing to focus on the figure standing on the other side of her barred cell. Blinking, she crawled closer, but the man didn't move. She reached between the bars for his leg, but then it was gone. His form reappeared to the right. She jerked towards him. "Conrad?" Looking up, the face—

A corrupted stared down at her, red eyes blazing, and she shrieked.

Scrambling backward, she panted as her back hit the wall, ears still ringing despite the current lack of noise. The figure vanished entirely, like so many before it.

She groaned, holding her head. She yearned to sleep, to close her eyes and drift away. But they never let her. Her eyes felt like they were coated in glue each time she blinked, her head stuffed with cotton.

"How many days?" Ahria whispered, looking at the wall she'd used a rock to scratch lines into. But the lines swirled and ebbed, forming silhouettes of strangers. Silhouettes and then mountains and trees and a broadly smiling wolf with no teeth.

Ahria huffed a laugh and touched the toothless canine, but it lurched from the stone and bit her hand. She yelped, pain lancing up her arm, but when she looked... no blood.

Squeezing her eyes closed, she moaned, gripping her head again. Nothing made sense. Deep down, she knew she was hallucinating. But it all felt so real.

How long has it been?

Even the thought ached in her head, and fear pressed in.

Why won't they let me sleep?

Not a wink in days. Weeks? She had no idea. They provided her water, but barely enough to sustain her. And no food. Not that she remembered, anyway. Her stomach ached fiercer than she ever thought possible, her mind a jumbled mess.

The hallucinations had started a while ago. Torturous visions of Conrad or Amarie or Kin, all coming to save her, and all turning into wicked amalgamations from the deepest hell.

He had come, as well. Uriel. Sometimes with her father at his side.

But he's so much older than I remember.

Kin was young, perhaps thirty, but now...

It made no sense. No sense.

Ahria yelled into the dirt, sobbing as tears streamed down the bridge of her nose to drip off the end. Her body eased, breath coming slower, and her eyes dimmed. She hovered in a semi-conscious state for minutes. Seconds. Before jerking awake again. As sleep tried to reclaim her, door hinges squealed from somewhere deep in the dungeon.

Groaning, Ahria rolled onto her side, fingernails bloody from digging at the dirt by the barred wall. But those bars ran deep. Deeper than she could ever manage with her bare hands.

"Don't you want this to be over?" Uriel's voice hung in the shadows, his hot breath tickling hairs around the back of her neck. "Just say the word, and it ends."

Ahria whimpered, her surroundings spinning into a disoriented haze of shapes and colors as she rolled onto her back. "I just... I just want to sleep," she murmured, voice echoing through her.

Sleep. Sleep. Sleep.

But Uriel wasn't there anymore. Only her father crouched at the bars, peering in at her. Wrinkles at the corners of his eyes and grey in his long dark hair.

Between blinks, youth returned to his face, and her heart swelled at the man who'd been so kind to her. So kind, when she'd struggled to even accept him. Not after Talon's death. After...

Her thoughts left her, and she furrowed her brow, trying to recall what she'd been thinking about.

Where am I?

Ahria jumped as metal groaned above her head, metal of an underwater bunker, but...

Her limbs shook, hands icy cold as she clamped them around her middle and stared up at the ceiling. It seemed to move with life, like worms wriggled in and out of the surface. Churning, constantly.

Kin's voice came from somewhere beneath the dirt floor. "Should I take you home?"

Ahria choked and nodded, "Yes."

His voice kept murmuring, kept prodding. Kept taunting her with merciful visions of peace, of home, of love.

She said yes to it all, yet... none of it happened. She begged, pleaded, and agreed. If only for a few minutes. A few hours of sleep.

Darkness crept around her, and she balked, expecting it to suffocate her. But even as it blocked the light, it embraced her like a warm night under the stars. The dirt below her vanished, and sleep overcame her.

Dreams coated her mind as her body was moved by cold, gentle hands. But she slept. Even as voices murmured around her, sounds and scents altered from screams and dirt to fresh air and wind.

Ahria spun and whirled, becoming nothingness to the world. Visions danced before her eyes, but even they couldn't stir her awake. Not fully.

But they didn't take her home.

Rousing to the smell of bread, Ahria blinked her eyes open. Bone-white stone lay beneath her, its dust caked over her damaged fingers and clothing. Nausea hit her, but as she gagged and heaved, nothing existed for her stomach to eject.

Once her insides settled, she focused on the smooth stone floor. Her confusion felt thicker than mud as she tried to piece together the events of the previous days. She hardly remembered any of it, except the raging eyes of the corrupted who had stood before her cell. Though that hadn't been real, and she wondered if Uriel had visited her or if that was her imagination, too. Not imagination, though. Hallucination.

They'd finally let her sleep. For how long, she had no idea, and her mind struggled to focus on the metal tray left on the ground a few feet away. Bread. That was *bread* occupying the tray.

Her mouth instantly watered, and she crawled over to the food and tore a piece off without bothering to check for signs of poison. Behind the small loaf of bread was half a melon, and she nearly wept with joy.

As she stuffed her face with about as much grace as a wild animal, someone cleared their throat on the other side of the barred wall.

This one was different from the cell before. The bars smoother and, she realized with a start, boasted a door. And everything seemed so much brighter. Light poured in a narrow upper window, off more ashen stone outside. It allowed Ahria a brief look around the room behind the person who stood there. Pale stonework with an unused rack at the back wall. Stairs, but she couldn't see the top of them.

Ahria hesitated, mouth full, before dragging her gaze to the woman sitting on a rickety chair fifteen feet away.

Raven black hair cascaded around her shoulders, the sides pulled back in little looping braids. It accented her bronze skin and emerald eyes.

Ahria almost choked on her bread.

I know those eyes.

They were darker around the edges than her father's had been, the tell-tale signs of age when presented within an auer. The barest sign of wrinkles graced the corners of her eyes, which seemed completely out of place. Even if she was over one hundred years old, she wasn't nearly old enough by auer standards to have them.

Rage bubbled up in Ahria's gut. Talon had told her stories of his middle sister. How she'd betrayed their family, killed her own parents, and lived a life that left a trail of death and destruction in her wake.

They'd been close once, her father and his sister. She knew that much from how sad Talon looked when he talked about Alana on the rare occasions he acknowledged her existence.

And now Talon was dead, and what had she done to stop it?

Nothing.

If she had even a fraction of the loyalty Talon had, perhaps her father would still be alive.

Ahria swallowed the bread in her mouth, though it tasted acrid as she stared as the auer woman. "I have nothing to say to *you*."

She lifted her eyebrows. "I wasn't aware we were introduced." She placed a delicate hand against her chest as if insulted, her black nails stark against her mint-colored blouse.

Brief confusion rippled through Ahria.

She doesn't know who I am?

Alana watched Ahria, her gaze boring through her as silence settled. Daylight poured through the high barred window at the back of Ahria's cell.

Even just seeing sunlight, however, eased some of the ache from her chest.

But it was eerily silent. She strained to hear the chirping of birds, or the skitter of a mouse. Anything. Normally there was so much sound. Even in her previous cell she'd heard the wails of other tortured souls. But now...

A chill swept down her spine as she looked to the hallway-like room Alana sat in, which housed several more empty cells. A set of stairs on either end went up, their top landings impossible to see.

Ahria looked down at the white stone floor, understanding creeping through her and dragging dread along behind it.

I'm in Lungaz.

Talon had warned her of the place. The place where the Art ceased to exist.

The chair beneath Alana squeaked as she shifted, crossing her arms with a bemused smile. "Putting things together?"

Ahria glared at Alana, keeping her chin angled down. "Go meet Nymaera, Dae'fuirei." She spat the insult. Looking for something to hurl through the bars, her eyes landed on the metal tray, still donning most of the melon and bread.

"You'll miss. Don't bother." Alana's expression dimmed, the wickedness turning into a frown. "I didn't think your mother was around long enough to teach you such words."

"Good thing my *father* taught me all about you," Ahria hissed. "Alana Di'Terian."

More distinct wrinkles appeared on Alana's forehead, her nails tapping thoughtfully against her sternum. "You're not talking about Kin." The statement came slowly, as if she was still considering what it meant. "Though he's the only father I'm aware of."

White-hot fury rose in Ahria's chest at the denial. The manipulation. The games.

She rose on shaky legs and gripped the bars between them. "Liar," she whispered, slowly raising her voice. "Liar! You killed your own parents, but it wasn't enough, was it?" Her whole body shook, knuckles white as she squeezed the unyielding metal. "No. You choose to serve the monster who killed your brother, too. You allowed him to be taken from me, when he was *all* I had left of my family. Don't you *dare* pretend you're innocent in my father's murder." Tears burned in her eyes, images of Talon's lifeless body flashing before her.

The auer froze, her eyes unfocusing as her lips parted. At first, Ahria thought it was to retort, but Alana's face blanched. "Talon's dead?" Her whisper was barely audible despite the silence of the Lungaz prison cells.

Ahria panted, her heart thundering in her ears, but something in Alana's tone simmered the fiery rage just a little. A tear slid down her cheek, her face scrunching as she tried to contain the rest. "Killed by a Shade," she breathed. "About a month ago." Grief welled within her, tightening her throat as her grip on the bars waned. Gritting her teeth, she glared at Alana. "And where were you? Playing lap dog?"

The chair ground along the stone as Alana stood. She avoided Ahria's angry gaze, striding towards the far stairs. Her movements rigid, she stopped at the base of the stairwell, but didn't turn back. She just stood there, a hand pressed to the wall. Her knuckles clenched, nails scraping along the stone before she formed a fist. "I didn't know."

As the auer ascended the stairs, the words settled in Ahria's mind, and she could have sworn they held sorrow and regret.

Chapter 29

A few days later...

Kin pushed the pint of stale, sour ale to the back of the bar, resisting giving Deylan another doubtful look. The crowd had thinned in the hours they'd already been sitting there, waiting. Not that there'd been many patrons in the first place.

Darian, the small, unremarkable port town not large enough for any map, was in absolute squalor. Houses along the main road from the dock had boarded up windows and empty hearths. A shepherd had led a measly herd of two sheep down the center of the filthy road, followed by his rail-thin dog.

The appearance of the grandiose Herald had caught the attention of the starving town folk, some even approaching the captain to beg for passage to Ziona. Or Isalica. Anywhere but Feyor, where their king had sent soldiers to steal their crop and herds.

Matthias's expression when he had told Kin about the refugees' plights while they met in Ziona returned to his mind.

Feyor needs a regime change.

Mud caked Kin's breeches up to the shin, the streets unable to dry, even in the warmth of summer. This far north, even the sun couldn't banish the damp muck. Despite the humidity, Kin kept his cloak around his shoulders, the dark hood in place. He didn't need anyone spotting the resemblance he bore to their king, even if it made him look like a Shade again.

Deylan slid discreet coins onto the bar top, worth more than a bottle of whisky, and caught the eye of the old man behind it. The coins disappeared, tucked into a little pocket as the keep tilted his head at Deylan.

Amarie's brother merely tapped three fingers on the rough woodgrain, and the man nodded, pouring three drinks from a bottle hidden under the counter. He pushed them closer before returning to cleaning glasses with a less-than-clean rag.

Deylan put one of the glasses in front of Kin. "Most of the ale is rancid these days," he murmured under his breath. "Because the monarchy claims anything fresh, and the general population doesn't have the coin to drink it before it sours."

"So all of Feyor is like this?" Kin eyed the new drink, wondering if the stronger liquor would be any better.

Sipping the whisky, Deylan grunted. "Most of it. Some is worse. Though the royal palaces are untouched by the poverty." He met Kin's gaze, mostly hidden beneath his hood. "Helgath and Isalica have been sending aid, trying to keep it subtle, but it's not enough. Most provisions get confiscated by officials before the population ever benefits from them." Sadness lurked beneath his stoic tone, a sense of helplessness.

Kin huffed, lifting his drink. He downed it quickly enough to avoid it lingering on his tongue. The back of his throat burned as he swallowed, and he hoped the alcohol would aid in the guilt growing in his chest. "*King* Lazorus has certainly done a number on the country."

Deylan eyed him, though his voice held no pressure as he whispered, "Your brother is a shit king."

Kin shot him a glance, stiffening before he rolled his shoulders. "Shit, of course you know. What doesn't your damn faction know about?"

With a shrug, Deylan tossed a casual glance over at where Amarie sat with Conrad, idly talking in a shadowed corner of the dingy tavern.

The prince kept a hood up, angled away from the door.

"There are things." Deylan sipped his drink again, a thoughtful expression passing over his face. "It's good to see you and my sister working things out. And to see less shadows around you. Dad was right, after all, I suppose."

When Kalpheus died, all those years ago, he'd made some bold statements and requests of Kin, which he'd shared with Deylan while they dug the grave.

"Your sister will always be worth it. Whatever it takes." Kin thumbed his empty glass, thinking back to what all he'd felt in that moment on a hill outside Rylorn with Deylan. He'd helped put Kalpheus to rest, ignoring the call of Uriel that burned in his tattoo. He'd known he'd suffer when he finally returned, and he had.

The scars on his back ached as he looked back at Amarie. He saw their daughter in her face, reigniting the guilt for sitting in a tavern in Darian rather than continuing to sail in the direction Amarie had last sensed Ahria.

The Art she'd laced in Ahria's necklace pointed directly at the heart of Feyor. West towards Jaspa, the country's capital, until it altered further north and then vanished. For a time, no one seemed willing to acknowledge what land lay north of Jaspa and where she had been taken.

If the necklace had merely been taken off, Amarie would still sense it. But it'd vanished. Sucked into a void.

Kin frowned. "How long are we going to wait for this spy of yours? We need to keep moving."

"She'll be here soon," Deylan muttered, finishing his whisky and eyeing the third, untouched glass he'd likely ordered for his friend. "Don't worry, I want to get Ahria back just as badly as you do."

Kin sighed, forcing the growing anxiety back down. He knew Deylan cared about Ahria, having been there when Kin couldn't. Deylan had been the one to save Amarie when the pregnancy had grown difficult. And the one to ultimately protect his daughter from a life of running and hiding. Until Kin had thrown her head first into it by killing her mother.

Chewing his lower lip, Kin nodded curtly. "Maybe I should go back to the ship. Do you need me here?"

The tavern door swung open, a man entering at a hurried pace. He slowed as soon as Deylan shot him a warning look and sauntered over to the bar. He took the stool next to Deylan, keeping his hood drawn. "Veli got caught up," he muttered, and something about that voice tickled the back of Kin's memory.

Deylan stiffened, but slid the unclaimed glass of whisky to the newcomer. "Is she all right?" His tone, usually rigid, held tangible fear.

"She's fine," the man said quickly, downing the drink. "But I had to come here, myself, instead. I apologize for the delay."

"Where is she?" Deylan pressed.

"In questioning."

"Is it bad?"

"No. She can handle it."

Why do I recognize that voice?

Deylan let out a breath, making a fist to stop his hands from— shaking. They were actually *shaking* as he crossed his arms over his chest. "Are you sure?"

The man turned and finally looked at Deylan. "Veliandra can *handle* it." With his hood slightly back from his forehead, dim tavern light illuminated his features. The deep brown eyes, deeply tanned skin, and handsome features now two decades older. Grey dappled the stubble along his jaw, and his eyes narrowed at Kin's inspection. "Do I know you?" He tilted his head, as if trying to peer under the former Shade's hood.

By the gods, I didn't think I'd ever see him again.

"Maybe." Kin lifted his chin slightly, wanting to trust that this man's membership with the faction meant it wasn't dangerous for him to know of Kin's presence. "I know you, though it's been a long while since I visited the Delphi estate. Longer for you than me." He couldn't help the half smile, despite the circumstances.

And the expression on Coltin Delphi's face dimmed as his back straightened. He glanced between Kin and Deylan, but kept his voice low. "Why is *he* here?"

"Because he's the Scion's father, and he's here to help." Deylan overpaid for a refill of all three glasses before opening his mouth to continue. But he stopped, seeing the look on Coltin's face as the Delphi bachelor's eyes locked on someone else in the tavern.

Kin looked at Amarie, and found her staring back at Coltin, utter shock on her face. She made to stand, but Conrad said something to change her mind.

A spark of jealousy ignited before Kin buried it with the memories of Amarie and him at the Delphi estate. The heat that had risen between them so quickly in the collection room, partially fueled by his distaste for Coltin. But now Coltin was older than both he and Amarie, and they had a daughter.

But a burning question rose within Kin. Why had Coltin joined the faction after their encounter? He wondered if perhaps the events of that evening had been what led to the Sixth Eye approaching him in the first place. He made a mental note to ask Deylan about it later.

Amarie still looked at Coltin, and mouthed, *I'm sorry.*

Coltin gave her subtle, single nod before returning his gaze to Deylan. His brown skin had gone wan, like he'd seen a ghost. "Gods, she looks almost exactly the same."

"It threw me off, too." Deylan gestured with his head to Kin. "This one and his... *almost* youth, too."

"I'm sitting right here." Kin grumbled, picking up his whisky. "At least I'm not going bald like you."

"We'll see about that when you age normally for the next twenty years," Deylan shot back, a wry grin on his face.

Coltin chuckled. "Veli doesn't seem to mind, either."

Kin quirked an eyebrow, but Amarie's brother ignored him, giving Coltin an incredulous look.

"Give it a rest, will you?" Deylan cleared his throat, sighing. "Did you bring the documents Veli acquired?"

The Delphi paused, narrowing his eyes as if debating pressing the matter of the woman further before deciding against it. "I did." He pulled an envelope from his cloak, passing it to Deylan, who slipped it into a pocket within his cloak. "Prisoner transfer orders are in there, too. It looks like they took the Scion to Jaspa originally, kept her there for almost a week, and have now relocated her to an outpost in Lungaz."

"Do you know which one?"

"No. But that isn't all." Coltin eyed Kin again before continuing with a lowered voice. "The king left Feyor just over a week ago, out of Jaspa. The envelope has his departure paperwork in it from the royal port."

Kin didn't care about Jarac, but the fact that he'd left could be good for them. It meant one less Shade between them and Ahria. But tasking one of his few Shades to go elsewhere meant something of greater importance had caught Uriel's attention.

A shudder rippled down Kin's spine.

"Where's he heading?" Deylan whispered.

"The documents say Nothend, but Isalica closed the Nothend port two months ago to upgrade its infrastructure." A grave heaviness weighed in Coltin's voice. "I think he's headed to Orvalinon."

Deylan straightened, a muscle in his jaw feathering. "How sure are you?"

"He took a host of royal guards and changed out his flag to bear Delkest colors. He wouldn't even give *me* details on the journey. I'm ninety-percent sure he's going after Seph." Coltin downed the second glass of whisky.

Deylan groaned, rubbing a hand over his jaw, and swore.

"Who's Seph and why would he be after them?" Kin's heart thudded with the mention of Orvalinon, too. While he had never been to the far east city in Isalica, he'd heard its name plenty of times in the meetings with Matthias and Damien. He knew quite well what had just finished being built in the Rahn'ka ruins near the city.

"It doesn't matter," Deylan breathed. "What matters is what he'll find once he reaches those ruins."

The prison.

"And Seph will lead him to the ruins?"

"Seph is *in* the ruins," Deylan ground out. "Under them, to be more precise."

Coltin stood, slapping a hand on Deylan's shoulder. "I should go. I've been gone long enough."

Deylan nodded. "Tell Veli—"

"Yeah, yeah. I'll tell her." Coltin chuckled and gave Kin a single nod before striding away. He paused by Amarie and Conrad's table, dragging a chair out to talk to them. To her.

Downing the whisky, Deylan winced and slid the glass away. He cursed under his breath again, oblivious or uncaring that Coltin hadn't immediately exited the tavern. "This is bad."

Kin tilted his glass, watching the whisky inside slosh near the edge. "Someday, I'm going to want to hear the story of how and when you recruited the Delphi heir to your faction, but it sounds like you better tell me about Seph first."

Deylan grunted, eyes darting to the tavern's door as it opened with Coltin's exit, Amarie walking out with him. "Not here. I'll tell you everything, but even this place has too many ears. What matters is we need to stop *him* from finding it in those ruins near Orvalinon. I can write to our northern friend, but he won't be able to control the situation. I need to be there." Regret shone through his eyes as he stared at the bar top.

Kin grimaced. "If he left over a week ago, he's got a good head start. Don't you have faction members over there already who could help?"

"This is a particularly delicate situation," Deylan murmured. "We've recalled many of our numbers to help rebuild the headquarters until we can consider relocating them. And those still in Isalica aren't enough. They don't understand Seph." The man ran a hand through his hair. "We don't have time to sail to Jaspa. We need to change course to Orvalinon."

"Because Jarac may find the prison as well as Seph." Kin eyed the whisky before finally downing it. "Amarie won't accept this change of plans, you know."

Deylan nodded through his agonized expression. "I know. And I don't blame her, but..." He looked at Kin with something the former Shade had never seen before. Something that looked a lot like a desire for forgiveness. "I love Ahria, but I have to prioritize the greatest threat."

"We won't be able to discuss this here. We should go back to the ship and fill the others in." Kin looked back to Conrad, who now sat alone, doubting he would agree with the course change either.

And as much as his insides warred, as much as he hated the idea of traveling farther from his daughter... Kin understood. Because if Uriel found the prison, Ahria's life would end, anyway. And not just hers.

As they exited the tavern, Deylan didn't even glance at Amarie, who now stood alone outside. She waited until Conrad left and then walked with him several yards behind Deylan and Kin.

"You want to *what?*" Back in the safety of the captain's quarters of the Herald, Amarie gaped at her brother. "We can't just leave her. I *won't* leave her." She looked at Kin, at Conrad, for an ally.

Andi stood back near the windows, silent as the other four hovered near her map table. Conrad had tucked himself into a corner behind the table, his arms crossed. He hadn't spoken a word yet, but the look on his face was easy to read.

He hates the idea, too.

"If Jarac finds the prison," Deylan warned. "Everything everyone has worked towards for the last two decades will be for nothing. And who knows what Uriel will do next."

"Uriel has a grander plan." Saying his name aloud still caused goosebumps to rise on Kin's arms. "And he's inevitably feeling the pressure to accomplish it faster because he knows what we're trying to do. If he's allowing Jarac to impoverish Feyor as much as he has, then Uriel is no longer satisfied with political power. Something bigger is coming."

Clenching her jaw, Amarie glared at Kin with disbelief. "You... you agree? You want to abandon our search for Ahria? For your *daughter*?"

"Hold on." Deylan lifted a hand. "It's not like that."

Amarie huffed. "If you need to go to Orvalinon, then you go. But I won't. I can ride to Lungaz on my own and find Ahria."

"You won't be alone." Conrad spoke for the first time, stepping from where he leaned. "I'm not leaving Ahria either."

A glimmer of approval passed over Amarie's face, and she nodded, facing Kin and Deylan. "We can start on foot until we find horses to purchase." She met Kin's gaze. "Are you coming with us, or staying on this ship?" Her tone held enough bite that he flinched.

"I can't believe you're asking me that." Kin met her angry eyes, saw the hurt buried beneath. The disbelief that he could leave her again. "She's my daughter. Of course I'm coming with you." Despite his understanding of Deylan's plight, it didn't change that Ahria needed to be found.

"It might be better if you don't, actually." Deylan offered an apologetic glance as he sighed. "I hate to point it out, but you'll attract attention. Traveling by ship you wouldn't have caught strangers' eyes, but across land... Anyone who's seen the king, twenty years older or not, will see the resemblance." He pursed his lips. "You'll slow them down and create additional risk."

"I'm sorry, did you say *resemblance*?" Conrad uncrossed his arms.

Everyone else stilled for a breath, even Andi. And they all looked to Kin.

Now everyone knows.

Kin bit the side of his tongue, resisting the urge to punch Deylan for revealing it to the other two, but he was right. "King Jarac is my twin brother." He met Conrad's surprised expression, watching all the implications of the statement rush through his eyes. "Not that Feyor is particularly aware I was even born, but when people are desperate, they cling to desperate notions. I suppose they'd presume I was Jarac's illegitimate child or something."

Amarie let out a breath, the anger ebbing from her posture in resignation. "So you'll go with Deylan, then," she murmured, chin dipping.

"No, that isn't what—"

"I'm going to pack my things," Amarie interrupted him with utter calmness before facing Andi. "Is it all right if I bother your cook for some travel rations?"

At the captain's nod, Amarie left the room, boots tapping over the wooden deck.

"It's not a good idea," Deylan said to Kin. "I know you want to go, I get it. But you could jeopardize her and Conrad if you're seen with them."

"I know." Anger bubbled up in Kin's tone, frustration guiding his glare at the door Amarie had left through. She wasn't even willing to have the conversation. Grumbling, he ran a hand up through his hair, tugging at the roots. "I'm destined to be useless either way."

Deylan scoffed. "I doubt that's true. You could be very useful in Orvalinon. I won't have the faction support I'd normally have, so an extra sword could make all the difference."

"Does Ahria know?" Conrad tensed, his tone dark as it drew Kin's attention back to him. "About your claim to the Feyor throne?"

"No." Kin rubbed a growing sore spot on his temple. "It's not important right now, anyway. I have no intention of taking it."

"That doesn't particularly matter when your heirless brother is already wrapped up in all of this. He dies and Feyor will need a leader." Conrad crossed his arms, his stare making Kin grimace.

Deylan stepped between them, breaking the growing tension. He looked at Conrad. "You should prepare your pack, as well. We won't be staying here for the night, if our captain is amenable to a speedy departure." His gaze drifted to Andi, and he tilted his head.

The captain shrugged. "Makes no difference to me. What's a quick sail across the entirety of Pantracia?" She smirked at Deylan as she walked towards her cabin's doors. "Shall I be billing Helgath, Ziona, or Isalica for this little adventure? Or this elusive faction I keep hearing more things about. Oh, or maybe even Feyor." She gave a pointed look at Kin and he frowned.

Conrad had locked his eyes on Kin again. Unspoken words seemed to only echo everything Matthias had tried to say to him. And the molten knot that hadn't left Kin's stomach since his initial conversation about becoming a king grew hotter.

Deylan chuckled. "Let's say Isalica." He smirked, shrugging. "Matthias can afford it."

"I may grow used to being personal transport for all these dignitaries." She gave Kin a glance that heated the fire inside him. The door banged shut behind her, shouts ringing out across the deck. They grew in volume as Conrad slipped out the door as well.

Kin rubbed his face, frowning at Deylan. "I need to talk to her."

Amarie's brother nodded, waving him off. "Go. I can give you details later."

The sun had lowered behind Feyor's mountains, and great fields of orange and red spread across the sky. Looking to the land he'd avoided most of his life, Kin wondered what all Feyor could hold for him. Uriel had forbidden him from even visiting while he was a Shade, the purpose clear when he discovered his twin.

Looking north, beyond the mountains, he imagined the ashen rocks of Lungaz, his daughter in the same outpost he'd been imprisoned in by his twin.

Everything in him ached as he imagined her. Alone. It'd already been weeks. And suddenly he wished he could tell her everything. He wanted nothing more than to tell her she could be a princess if she wanted. But now he wondered if he'd get the chance.

His eyes burned at the thought, and he swallowed the growing lump in his throat as he tore his eyes from the scenery and focused on the door at the bow of the ship. It led to a simple hallway with two doors, one storage, and one the room he and Amarie had shared.

The door wasn't latched when he gently pushed his way in.

Amarie had finished stuffing her belongings into her pack, fastening the buckle on top as she looked up at him. The anger was gone from her eyes, but she said nothing.

He carefully closed the door behind him, and they just stood there for a moment. "That wasn't fair." He schooled his tone as best he could.

She hefted her bag up and dropped it on the bed. "I know." She took a step towards him, but stopped just out of arm's reach. "I'm sorry. I just... didn't want to have that conversation in front of everyone else."

"Then say so. I didn't necessarily know to come talk to you."

"I'm saying so now." Amarie kept her tone level. "And if you hadn't come to talk, I would have found you before I left." She sighed and lowered her gaze. "But I *was* right, wasn't I? You're staying on the ship?" Her voice softened, the question holding no accusation.

"I was going to ask you that." Kin eyed her bag, which they had shared upon leaving the faction headquarters. But none of his clothes had been pulled from the drawers Amarie had stored them in. "Am I staying on the ship? You know I want to go to find Ahria."

Amarie looked at him again, then, and her shoulders slumped. "I know, but my brother has a point." She hesitated before approaching him, touching the front of his tunic. "I know you want to come with us, but if someone recognizes you..." Silver glittered along her lower lids. "You should help Deylan deal with Jarac. I will find Ahria, I promise."

He placed his hands over hers. "I know you will." A piece of him broke, knowing he had to leave. Shattering apart like the broken stained-glass windows of the Capul's Great Library. "And you know I'll find you both as soon as possible."

She nodded, but hesitated, debating. Debating sharing something else with him.

Kin didn't push, only angling his head as he watched her.

Amarie's throat bobbed. "I think I need to go to Jaspa before Lungaz."

"Jaspa?" Kin thought of the dirty streets he'd flown over as a raven while pursuing her. He couldn't imagine what they'd look like now with the country's decline. "What's in Jaspa?"

"Coltin told me that Jarac still has the shard I traded him all those years ago in Lungaz." Amarie's gaze darted between his eyes. "If I have to go back into Lungaz, having access to my power could change everything."

He nodded. "Uriel won't be in Lungaz, according to what Matthias said, but he might still be in Jaspa."

"I know." She sighed. "Coltin told me how to find him in the city. He said if I need help, he'll do what he can. He's apparently a spy inside the palace, and knows it pretty well, so..." Her eyes pleaded with him, and a spark of appreciation danced through him that she'd decided to share this plan with him. Perhaps even sought his approval.

Running his thumb along her jaw, he nodded again. "It's a good plan. You'll need whatever advantage you can get if Ahria is in Lungaz."

Her shoulders seemed to relax, if only slightly. "If I see Uriel in Jaspa..."

According to Rae's recount and Conrad's description, Uriel had been within the same auer host they'd seen outside Hoult when he'd attacked the underwater bunker. So at least she'd recognize him, unless he'd exerted too much breaching the headquarters. Then he might have needed to change hosts.

"If he's there, you run. All the way to Lungaz." Lifting her chin, Kin kissed her softly. "Don't try to fight him." He huffed. "If only we'd known to step within the crater in Hoult, things would have gone much differently." Regret hung heavy behind his light tone, and he shook his head.

Easing the knot in his gut, Amarie let out a mirthless laugh. "If only. I won't fight him." She paused, her gaze boring right through him in a moment of lingering silence. "Stay alive, will you?" she breathed the question. The plea. "Don't do anything stupid. We need you."

"I could say the same." He cupped her face in his hands. "So let's both promise." Leaning into her, he placed a gentle kiss on her lips.

Amarie's hands moved to either side of his face, and as the tender affection came to a close, she kissed him harder. Kissed him like it would be her last chance. Just in case... in case it was.

Kin lost himself in that moment, trying to memorize the way her lips felt against his. How she tasted, her scent. Sensations he once believed he'd never experience again. And now, with them parting ways and entering dangerous situations yet again...

As she pulled away, breathing faster, she pressed her forehead to his. "I promise," she whispered, but the truth shone in her eyes. The truth that neither of them had any business making such a promise at all.

Chapter 30

Autumn, 2032 R.T.

While Darian didn't boast any stables with horses available for sale, Conrad and Amarie were pointed in the direction of a farmer further inland who might be persuaded by the coin they carried.

Traveling with Amarie had been quiet. They didn't share in many conversations, but that could be attributed to the unsavory environment of the rugged streets of Darian, which took half of the first day to navigate through.

Conrad didn't mind the quiet, leaving him to his thoughts as he considered their route. Jaspa first, then Lungaz. He'd never been to either, but had sailed around the peninsula that housed the barren lands and its maelstrom. He didn't like the idea of the detour to the capital, even if the king wouldn't be there, but at least he'd yet to see one of his own wanted posters. Amarie seemed convinced that the Berylian Key shard inside the palace would be helpful in rescuing Ahria.

Despite the faction blade on his hip, Conrad was still far outclassed. Deferring to Amarie would be best, considering what he'd seen of her power during the repair of the underwater bunker.

Late on the second day of trudging through slowly drying mud and then fields of sunburnt grass, hints of life started returning to the land. As they wandered northwest, praying it was the correct direction, the grass greened and trees donned the orange and yellow tones of autumn.

As the sun dipped low, its rays caught on the roof of a farmstead in the distance. As they grew closer, occasional lowing filled the evening air from cattle sheltered in a barn.

Conrad's legs ached, blisters forming on the sides of his feet from the endless walking. He looked sideways at Ahria's mother, and those black leather boots so similar to the ones her daughter usually wore. Her feet wouldn't be any better off than his. But she hadn't complained, so neither would he.

It was odd, traveling with her. He often spied her out of the corner of his eye and thought she was Ahria. They looked so alike, and were close in age, but he tried not to let the constant disappointment show. But the more time they walked, and the more time he saw her, the more the differences stood out between their faces. Differences beyond their eyes. Ahria's face was slightly more angular, the tip of her nose vaguely upturned, and her eyebrows fuller. Amarie was paler, her hair auburn instead of Ahria's deep chestnut.

"Gods, I hope they sell us horses," Amarie breathed, the first hint she'd given at her discomfort in walking.

"I'll take a cow at this point, if that's all that's available." Conrad turned off the main road onto the driveway for the farmstead. A man rose from a chair on the front porch, a lantern near him casting a dim shadow. A puff of smoke billowed around his head as he watched them

Conrad kept his hands clear of his weapons, though jumped at the yip from a scrawny dog as it bounded from the porch.

Gods, why am I so jumpy?

In the back of his mind, he knew it was the shadows. The wind caught in the drapes of the open windows, spinning the dark shapes they cast across the porch.

Amarie paused as the animal raced towards them, not reaching for a weapon either. It stopped a few yards away, barking, its coat a mess of gray and white, spots of tan near its feet. "Hey, pup," she cooed, keeping her tone light. "What's your name?"

"We don't got nuthin' worth stealin'," the man shouted as he descended from the porch, side stepping towards a stump with a wood axe sticking up from it.

She and Conrad had discussed who might do the talking, and decided that Amarie was less threatening.

Ironic.

Amarie held her palms up, glancing at Conrad before continuing her approach alone. She walked right past the dog, who only sniffed at her knees. "We mean you no harm, and have no desire to steal. We were hoping to purchase horses."

The farmer spat to the side, lifting his pipe back to his lips. He didn't move away from the axe. "Horses make my job a lot easier, so ain't going to be cheap." He eyed Conrad as the captain crouched, holding his hand out to the dog.

The creature stopped barking, edging closer to sniff Conrad's fingers before he succumbed to a pet. Then scratches lured him to lean against Conrad's thigh, his wagging tail shaking his body.

Slowly lowering her hands, Amarie shook her head at him and the dog with a smirk before returning her attention to the farmer. She patted the coin purse tied to her hip. "We'll pay a good price. Can you spare two?"

"Ten florins." The farmer frowned at his dog, but then refocused on Amarie. "Each. And another three if you want the tack, too."

Conrad flinched, knowing the farmer saw the opportunity to mark up the prices. But he and Amarie didn't have another choice.

Amarie ceased her approach, untying the pouch from her belt and looking inside. They'd discussed how much someone may ask for two mounts, and had stashed the rest of their coin in their packs to appear less well-off. Bandits targeting them as easy marks wasn't something they needed. She dumped the coins into her palm, then looked at Conrad with a feigned sense of worry. "Do you have six more florins? I only have seventeen."

Conrad gave his own look of pretend distress, but nodded and stood, touching his coin pouch tied opposite his sword. Fishing out the coins for Amarie, he stepped forward to pass them off, but kept his distance as the farmer tensed.

Taking one more step towards the farmer, Amarie slid the twenty-three silver florins back into the pouch and held it up. "We will pay your price." When the farmer advanced a step towards her, she backed up. "Horses first, if you don't mind."

He nodded curtly before turning back towards the house. "Percy!" After a moment, the head of a young boy, maybe twelve, popped up in the window.

"What!"

"Go tack Fyfer and Jinx. Then bring them out here."

The boy whined, but his father, presumably, answered with a quick. "Now."

Conrad resumed scratching the dog, debating pulling out a bit of jerky from the pack on his back.

With a pointed look, Amarie seemed to read his mind. "Do not give that dog our food." But she smiled beneath her disapproval.

The prince frowned. "Poor thing is skin and bones," he whispered back to her. "Wish there was more to be done."

Amarie's smile faded. "I know." And he knew she agreed. He'd seen her long stares at the poverty stricken townsfolk in Darian. The begging children. She'd given away so much of Deylan's money already, but her brother had given her plenty. "Twenty three florins will buy him some food," she murmured.

As if sensing they discussed him, the farmer gave a sharp whistle. The dog tensed before yipping and running to his master. He panted happily as the man scratched behind his ears, bringing some comfort to Conrad.

He must be getting fed enough to stay loyal.

Amarie and Conrad didn't dare speak more as they waited, and eventually, the boy led two horses from somewhere behind the homestead. Not prize beasts, by any means, but they were muscled and made no effort to fight their small handler.

"I'd like to look them over," Amarie said to the farmer, gesturing like she'd toss him the pouch of coins. "You hold this while I do that?"

The farmer nodded, catching the pouch with her easy toss.

Crossing the rest of the distance, Amarie left Conrad behind and stroked the blue roan gelding.

"His name is Jinx," the boy piped up, then patted the other horse's neck. "And this is Fyfer."

"Percy, come stand with me." The farmer's instruction held no fear, but Conrad understood the tone.

What have these poor citizens been living through?

Amarie smiled her thanks to the boy before inspecting the horses. She checked the tack, their feet, joints. She moved from the roan to the buckskin, performing the same inspection. They must have passed, because she nodded to the farmer. "Thank you." With his dipped chin in response, she led the two horses back to Conrad.

"Jinx doesn't like water!" the boy shouted, earning a quiet reprimand from his father.

Amarie chuckled, then buckled her pack to the saddle. "I'll keep that in mind."

Conrad took Fyfer's reins from Amarie, patting his neck as he stripped his pack from his back. Looping it on to the buckles of the saddle, he watched as the farmer led his son and dog into their home, followed by another puff of smoke from his pipe.

She ran her hands over Jinx again, moving to stand in front of him as she stroked the sides of his face. Her expression seemed more at peace than he'd seen it in a long time as she whispered softly to the animal in Aueric, but didn't hear any words he recognized.

"What were you checking for?" He was certain there were telltale signs of things that might have lowered the horses' value, but he certainly didn't know them.

"Lameness, mostly." Amarie shrugged. "The state of their hooves, shoes, and if they've been fed enough. How fast their hearts were beating, and how stiff their joints are. I checked their eyes for signs of internal problems, but they seem healthy. Sound. A bit old, but that can be good, anyway."

"Good." Conrad checked the buckles on his pack before mounting. It took a moment for him to find a comfortable position, but riding had never been something he was used to. Rather, it had been forced upon him after becoming a prince. A ship was simpler, but his sore feet were grateful for the ride now.

Amarie settled into her saddle a breath later, putting her feet in the stirrups before promptly removing them and dismounting to adjust the length. Once done, she looked over at his, assessing, before returning atop her horse. Her posture relaxed as she took up the reins. "Much better." Nudging her horse, they moved off at a walk, and she looked over at him. "I suppose spending most of your life on a ship doesn't leave much room for travel on horseback."

"No, and I honestly never thought I'd leave a ship long enough to learn." In some ways, being back on Andi's ship had been its own form of torture. It reminded him of what he had been forced to abandon. But it was different now, even standing on the deck felt like such a distant past. And it was one he was still willing to leave behind for Ahria.

Conrad hardened his expression, hoping he hadn't given Amarie too much to read.

Amarie tilted her head at him, eyes flickering narrower. "Why do you do that?" Her voice lowered. "We're not in court, and I'm not your enemy." Something lingered beneath her tone. Something akin to disappointment.

It took a moment for him to understand what she was talking about. He frowned, looking to the muddy road their horses trekked. "I know you're not my enemy. It's just the way I've always been. I'm not good with... opening up." Saying the words felt awkward, even though they were true. It still felt silly telling her, Ahria's mother or not.

Returning her gaze to their path, Amarie let out a light breath of a laugh. "I understand that better than you know." Her mouth twitched upward as she met his gaze once more. "You have no obligation to be open with me. I don't expect it. But I appreciate the truths you do give. They grant a bit of a window, you could say, into seeing the man my daughter has fallen in love with." Her expression darkened, attention averting as she murmured, "I always wanted the best for her."

Conrad had tried since meeting Kin and Amarie to understand their perspectives, considering the time that had never passed for them. It was still bizarre to consider in many ways. It wasn't too different from if he suddenly had a twenty-year old child. There had to be so much regret. But Ahria didn't want that for them, so he didn't either.

He nudged his horse closer to hers. "From what she's told me, her life was good. You did give her the best, and considering everything... I highly doubt anything different could have been done. But she had a happy childhood. And she's happy now, too. Yes, there has been suffering and loss, but those things will always happen. No one can be fully protected from that."

Amarie's smile touched her eyes then. "Will you tell me? How you two met? I mean, she told me she stowed away on your ship— thank you for not throwing her overboard, by the way—but I never got the story's details."

"She'd have found a way back on, even if I *had* thrown her overboard." Conrad chuckled, then welcomed the distraction of memory as he told Amarie how he'd fallen head over heels for her daughter.

Jaspa's tunnel district was just as Conrad imagined.

Dark. Damp. Cold.

What he hadn't predicted was the number of civilians' homes and businesses within the tunnels themselves. The eastern entrance to the city, which had started out as purely that when the city had first been constructed, had evolved into a thriving community. Well, as thriving as anyone could be while their king stole every iron mark he could.

And judging by the looks on people's faces, the state of their clothing, and sparse goods for sale, even the capital city wasn't exempt from Jarac's taxes.

Dim lights spaced every thirty feet hardly illuminated the tunnels, more coming from the windows of the shops and homes. Though some of those remained dark, too. The center of the road was clear, except for the occasional unattended cart they had to weave around.

Thanks to travel, his and Amarie's clothes appeared worn enough that none of the people pegged them as worth begging from. And their cloaks, now necessary with the northern country's autumn chill, hid their weapons. So they passed through unseen, unremarkable, and forgettable.

Perfect.

"Where did Coltin say we could find him?" Conrad didn't look at Amarie as they made their way on foot, having left their mounts outside the city to lessen the chance of losing them to thieves. His legs ached from the days of riding, but Amarie had coached him to better form, lessening the strain on his back.

The faction communication device Deylan had given him weighed inside his inner chest pocket. He, in theory, understood how to use it, but the man had given him strict instructions that it was for emergencies only. And on top of that, Conrad wasn't sure he'd be able to keep up with the device's whirring to record all the letters fast enough. Not with how his mind jumbled even those on paper, already arranged and unchanging. With another way to contact Coltin, he wouldn't need to fiddle with the delicate copper dials.

Amarie didn't dare look at him, either, scanning their surroundings to keep a watchful eye out for trouble. Threats. Any sign of Uriel or a Shade. "There's a tavern in the trade district called Fenrick's Keg. I'm supposed to ask the barkeep for Keleb and book room twenty-three to wait for him."

Conrad nodded, falling silent to contemplate the specific instructions.

It didn't take them long to find Fenrick's Keg. The trade district, slightly better off than the tunnel district, still boasted a fair share of activity. Though, it appeared most of the patrons were either guards, soldiers, or nobles. The streets turned to dry paved stone, cracked and in need of repair, but it kept their hems from accumulating further muck.

Amarie strode up to the tavern, past a weather-worn mini keg in the front scrawled with the tavern's name in red lettering. The door swung open on rusty hinges, and Conrad trailed after her.

Not one of the seven people dining or drinking in the tavern bothered to look up as Amarie approached the bar. The barkeep nodded her greeting, her tired hazel eyes focusing on her new customers. "What can I get ya?" A twang of an accent colored her tone. One Conrad couldn't pinpoint the origin of.

"I'm looking for Keleb," Amarie said as she slid a ten-iron mark onto the counter. "And two ales."

"Sorry, m'dear." The woman took the coin. "No one by that name 'ere."

Amarie glanced at Conrad before trying again as the woman filled two steins. "I was told I could find Keleb here, and that room twenty-three would be available to us."

To her credit, the woman didn't miss a beat. "Aye. O' course. I'll let ya know when ya room is ready."

Following Amarie into the dining room, ale in hand, Conrad kept a close eye on the other patrons, trying to discern their roles in the city.

Three guards, sitting together playing a quiet game of cards. A couple sitting near the hearth with drawn faces. And two individuals, taking up separate spots in the corners far away from anyone else. Those two looked at Conrad and Amarie as they sat at an empty table by the stairs, not balking when the gaze was returned. Perhaps thieves, working together, trying to blend in separately. But they didn't even glance at each other before resuming their meals.

Amarie, the picture of ease, settled into a chair. "The one in the north corner gives me the creeps," she whispered.

He nodded, positioning himself so he could keep the entire room in his peripheral vision. He hadn't bothered to remove his pack from his shoulder, keeping it close to his side and his sword within reach. "Not many friendly faces in Feyor, that's for certain." He lifted his ale. "Not that I can blame them, all things considered."

Taking a long swig of her ale, Amarie huffed her agreement. As she lowered her mug, he caught the vaguest hint of a tremor in her hand. "I never told you how I know Coltin." Her gaze settled on him, but he could tell her awareness was heightened for the entire room.

He'd asked her about it earlier that day, but timing had been against them and his question had gone unanswered. When he quirked an eyebrow, she continued.

"When Kin and I first met, he wasn't fond of the alias I'd used. He actually came up with the name Ahria, and we agreed, since he'd invented the name, that I'd only use it as either an alias for myself, or could give it to my child, one day." Her eyes became distant as she spoke, but he didn't interrupt.

"When I met the friend we're meeting today, I used the alias of Ahria. I was a thief, hells-bent on stealing his family's Berylian Key shard. Kin showed up and ruined all my plans for the second time. We staged this fake-hostage situation..." She laughed, shaking her head. "Everything was simpler back then. But we took the shard, and we ran. I ended up surrendering the shard to Kin's twin, but... I had no idea Cole joined my brother."

"Sounds like history is just catching up." Conrad tested the ale, pleased to find it not nearly as pungent as the one in Darian. He took a longer swig, still watching the two potential criminals in the corners. "We're lucky this friend is willing to help. Considering you ran a con on him from the sounds of it?"

Amarie shrugged with a sheepish smile. "That... sounds like exactly what I did. For a few months, too. He probably thought we were going to get married." She sighed. "It was a shit thing to do, but back then, I had no allies." Her eyes guttered. "No friends, no family. It's easy to stop caring when you've got little left to lose. I'm grateful he's forgiven me."

"Family, blood or not, does tend to change things." Conrad gave her a knowing smirk. "Do you regret how things changed?"

Shaking her head again, Amarie smiled through a wince. "I have regrets like everyone else, but meeting Kin... Having Ahria... I could never regret that. Especially now." Darkness still loomed behind her deep blue eyes, so unlike her daughter's, but he couldn't tell from where it stemmed.

He watched her for a time, trying to decipher whatever hid inside her head. But he could only guess at what it all might be. It all came back to Uriel, though, and what he'd taken. The suffering and time he'd caused them to lose. The people. He shivered as he recalled the cold ocean water pouring around him, the new jagged scar on his shoulder burning with the salt. Uriel's shadows dancing along the metal walls of the faction headquarters. Then the darkness that had swallowed Talon and mangled his skin.

His knuckles ached as his grip tightened on the handle of his stein.

"We'll find her." Conrad focused on the grain of the table before meeting Amarie's dark gaze. "Then we'll end all of this."

Amarie slowly nodded, then spoke, barely loud enough for him to hear. "Do you know who Alana is?" When he shook his head, she hummed. "Alana is Talon's wicked sister. She is the *master's* right hand." She paused, but something in her tone urged Conrad to remain silent. "If she's here... Or if she's in Lungaz..."

For a moment, Conrad wondered if she'd complete the thought, but the barkeep approached a breath later. "Yer room is ready for ya. Up the stairs, to the left, at the very end. Just past room twenty-two."

She placed a key on the table, not waiting for a response before bustling away.

Letting out a deep breath, Amarie finished her stein and eyed his, also nearly empty. She gestured with her head and a raised eyebrow towards the stairs.

Nodding, he downed the rest of his ale before standing and moving to the stairs. He waited for her to climb first, then followed. One last glance promised no shadows behind them.

Their boots echoed through the hallway as they walked past room doors.

Nineteen. Twenty. Twenty-one. Twenty-two...

The door at the end of the hall, past room twenty-two, had no number.

Amarie eyed it, then looked at Conrad.

On the other side of the hall, the numbers started over at *ten*, since all single digit rooms were on the bottom floor.

He rested a hand on the hilt of his borrowed sword as Amarie inserted the key into the lock. The knob turned, and she cautiously inched it open.

Conrad followed her inside, shutting the door behind them.

The room had the barest of furniture, a tiny, curtained window letting in only subtle light. A chair and small desk occupied the far corner, with three more chairs gathered near the center. The once-patterned upholstery, torn in places, leaked stuffing from the armrests. Whatever color it had been lost beneath years of wear.

"Charming," Amarie muttered, stepping around the space without touching anything.

Conrad glanced back at the handle of the door, barely hesitating before turning the lock.

Coltin will have a key if he's meant to meet us here.

Looking across the room at the small window, its curtains mostly drawn, he considered the sliver of Jaspa he could see beyond it. The Feyorian palace perched up against the mountain side. Dark stone towers blended into the rockface behind it, hard to distinguish. He already suspected it's where they would need to go to find the shard Amarie needed. If it belonged to the king, it was the most likely place. If they were caught, he'd have to face the political ramifications should Feyor discovered not just who he was, but also the warrant... Yet, considering everything at stake, he didn't care.

Evidently satisfied that the room bore no traps or threats, Amarie settled into a chair, propping up her feet on another's seat. "This could be a long wait. We should rest in shifts."

Fair enough.

Obtaining the shard may not be possible during daylight, and they'd already endured a long morning and afternoon of travel. Going into a heist exhausted only brewed disaster. Not that he knew particularly how heists should go.

Conrad eyed one of the chairs as he stripped his pack and set it on the ground. "I'll take first shift." There was no way he'd be able to fall asleep with how tense everything felt after the walk through Jaspa. Pulling his sword from its sheath, he carefully leaned it against the arm of the chair within easy reach.

Amarie pulled up her hood, wrapping her cloak tighter around her. "Just don't take Coltin's head off. We need him." A lilt of humor touched her tone, so different from whatever she'd been about to say about Alana downstairs.

He opened his mouth to ask her about it, but on seeing the peace on her face, he smiled. "I'll keep to just his arm, then."

A light chuckle came from her before silence settled, her eyes shutting.

Chapter 31

Ahria stared at the long, empty hallway outside her cell. Days had passed since she'd lost her temper at Alana, and the auer hadn't returned. Only the same guard, who never spoke to her, only bringing her food and water twice a day.

Two days prior, she'd requested a blanket from him. Autumn's chill seeped through the pale stone with the wind, preventing her from ever warming. Like her previous requests—for more food, or coffee, or a pillow—she expected it to go unanswered.

But to her surprise, that evening, he'd brought her a thick blanket and shoved it through the bars without so much as a word.

Sitting at the back of the cell, blanket wrapped beneath and around her, Ahria wondered about the purpose of keeping her here. Compared to her previous cell, the conditions had considerably improved. No more torture or sleep deprivation. No more endless noise or distant screams. But in a way, this was worse. She had no idea what was coming, what to expect. When the blanket would be stolen and replaced with a bucket of ice water.

Even as her mind and memories returned to her, she couldn't recall most of those days, or weeks, or however long Uriel had kept her locked in the prior dungeon. His face and her father's had blurred together so fiercely that she wondered if she'd imagined the whole thing. Logic told her that Kin hadn't aged so much, so perhaps the manipulation had been flawed. Her blood father wouldn't have done those things, either. She didn't know him well, but she'd gleaned enough in those weeks together to know he'd never hurt her.

Ahria eyed the half-eaten plate of food beside her. She hadn't had the appetite to eat it all. Unusual for her, but she decided not to force it down. The portions were far from her norm, and even amid her lack of hunger, she'd lost weight. Her pants were looser in the thigh, where muscle had once been, and her tunic flowed more easily around her ribs.

Tracing her thumb over the necklace pendant, she tried not to let despair take over. The Art within the jewelry wouldn't work, not here, if everything Talon had told her about this place was true. Her mother wouldn't know where to find her within the vast wasteland of Lungaz.

Gentle footsteps sounded on the stairs, different from the usual guard. And the sun hadn't progressed far enough for it to be dinner time, either. The flowing hem of a burgundy skirt kicked up around Alana's feet as she descended.

Ahria stiffened, warning bells ricocheting through her mind. Her heart picked up speed, but she dared not show the fear on her face as she hugged the blanket tighter. Clamping her lips together, she promised herself she wouldn't be the first to speak. Or perhaps speak at all. Alana would get nothing from her, no matter what she did.

Her steps were slow, casual, as she made her way through the hallway. Clasping her hands in front of her hips, she studied Ahria in silence, her emerald eyes unreadable. She took in a slow breath after a few minutes, finally speaking. "I'm not going to take the blanket from you."

Huffing, Ahria frowned. Not what she'd expected Alana to say. But it didn't matter, and she kept her mouth shut.

The auer pursed her lips. "I know you won't believe me, but I loved my brother." A muscle twitched in her jaw, and Ahria narrowed her eyes. "He was the only one I ever cared about. Even after we parted ways. And now I understand why he was so adamant all those years ago. The secrets he kept. And why he pushed me away." She lowered her gaze. "And I'm angry. Furious. About what's transpired. I had hoped we would be brother and sister again, someday, somehow."

Ahria only blinked at her, confused at the angle the woman was taking in her questioning. If it even *was* an angle. The emotion, the grief, looked so genuine that she wanted to believe it. Wanted to believe this auer wasn't the skilled deceiver and manipulator Talon had described her as. So she kept quiet, listening, daring only one simple question. "And had you known the Shade would kill Talon?"

"I would have warned him. Hidden him, kept him away from it. I had no idea Gredis would be anywhere near Talon. His task was..." A hint of desperation entered her tone as she turned, pacing away from the cell as her hands slackened at her sides, and she grew quiet for a moment. "Talon was never supposed to get tangled in all of this."

Sitting up, Ahria studied her. A weight settled in her gut, familiar and retched. "The Shade came for me," she whispered. "Not because of my parents, but because of my proximity to the Zionan throne."

Why am I talking?

Ahria scowled at herself and closed her mouth again, sighing at her inability to be silent. Not that the information she offered would mean anything. It wouldn't give Alana anything Uriel didn't already know. But why hadn't he told his right hand the truth about who'd been caught in the crossfire if she was so close to him?

Alana is acting.

Keep her back to Ahria, Alana tensed but gave little indication to her emotions. "Talon was a father to you. While Kin and Amarie were gone." Statements, not questions. Like she was only just coming to terms with them. She turned her head only for a moment. "He protected you, just as a parent is supposed to."

Ahria loosened her hold on the blanket, her heart squeezing. Her next words spilled from her mouth before she could stop them, her eyes burning at this unique form of torture. "I miss him so much."

Alana's attention jerked back to her, a shine in her eyes before she looked away again, walking towards the back wall. Her body shook as she took in a deep breath, arms wrapping around her middle. Silence swelled around them.

Ahria closed her eyes, sniffing as she tried to regulate her breathing. Calm her heart. Since Talon's death, her grief came in waves. Sometimes that ocean of agony settled, but sometimes... it thrashed like a storm, bringing her right back to that basement all over again.

Seeing him laying there and being unable to help him. Heal him. Do anything other than hold him as life slipped from his body.

Her hands shook, throat too tight to speak, even if she'd wanted to. She felt grateful Alana had her back turned, and wouldn't see the tears she couldn't stop.

Whatever form of interrogation this was—whatever form of torture... Cruel. It was nothing but cruel. But she shouldn't be surprised. This auer had killed her own parents, had...

Alana's shoulders shook, a hand moving as if to grasp at her face. After a moment, she straightened, rolling her shoulders as she turned and strode for the stairs again.

Anger rose in Ahria's gut. "He protected me," she choked out, her voice cracking. "But where were *you* to protect him?"

"Lost," Alana muttered without stopping. As she stepped onto the landing at the base of the stairs, her hair blended into the darkness of whatever room lay on the other side of them. She hesitated for only a breath before she stormed up the steps.

Ahria let go of her blanket, rushing to the bars and shaking them, regardless how pointless. "If you truly cared about him, you wouldn't be keeping his daughter prisoner!" she shouted, knuckles white. "That makes me your niece, you know!" Huffing, she let go, her words disappearing in the air without a response. "Damn it."

Hours passed, and Ahria returned to her blanket. She said nothing as the usual guard arrived with her dinner, sliding it into the cell and leaving without a word. The plate of autumn berries and grainy bread did nothing to whet her appetite. So she left it, curling up on her side with an arm under her head.

Closing her eyes, she thought about Talon and Lorin. She'd always been closer to the former, but both had been kind and generous to her. Her brother, Lorin's blood son, had been a rockier relationship, and a small voice at the back of her head whispered that she'd never see him again. He'd ventured to Delkest's academies years ago, returning only briefly while his father died. Taking a shaky breath, she imagined Talon's arms around her, his scent, and his voice murmuring stories to her. Stories of his life, of her mother, of the beauty of his homeland.

Ahria's heart splintered, tears free-falling over the bridge of her nose and soaking the blanket beneath her temple. She made no effort to control the sobs, not now. A wave of warmth settled over her, seeping through the blanket and easing her sore muscles, and a breath later, sleep claimed her.

Dawn found her, and she woke, touching her puffy eyes and cringing. After relieving herself in the bucket at the far side of her cell, she returned to her blanket and picked at her bread, now dry and crusty after being neglected all night.

The guard brought her breakfast, and as usual, took her bucket to clean and return.

Ahria eyed the food with a narrowed gaze.

Eggs. Scrambled.

No one had cooked her anything for weeks, giving her only fruits and breads and sometimes the occasional piece of dried meat. Her body yearned for protein, and as her stomach grumbled, she gave in and devoured the eggs.

By midday, Ahria's bleary eyes had finally cleared, but the weight in her chest remained. Her mind drifted to Conrad, and her lips twitched in a smile as she recalled the chase through the streets of Haven Port with the captain.

The captain.

She longed for those days, again. At sea, with him. With her captain, her prince. She ached to feel him against her, hear his voice, and have him beside her when she woke.

Get your head straight.

Centering her breathing, she rolled her lips together. She wouldn't get anywhere, wouldn't get out of her cell, by just laying down and taking it. Regardless of whatever game Alana was playing —if it even *was* a game—she could use that. She could play along, perhaps even get the auer to tell her things. Maybe even let her go, if she played her cards right. The fact that she didn't know about her brother's death meant that Uriel had kept it from her.

Exploit that.

Sometime in the afternoon, a pair of guards came down the stairs, carrying something between them. But they stepped off the opposite side of the landing into the other room, leaving Ahria to peer curiously through the cell bars at them. They moved up and down the stairs several times, the racket causing her to bury her head beneath her blanket, dreading whatever was coming.

They finally stopped when the sunlight dimmed, Ahria's stomach growling for the meal that hadn't come yet. The sound of her approaching dinner was different on the stairs that night, softer footsteps revealing it was Alana, and without a tray in her hands. She crossed the room casually, moving to Ahria's cell door as her hands delicately plucked a ring of keys from her pocket.

Ahria started, retreating until her back hit the stone wall, eyes locked on the auer.

The door clicked as the key turned. Pulling the door open, Alana took a step back. "I'd advise against trying to run. There are guards at every doorway of the outpost. You'd never make it out."

"Sounds like a challenge," Ahria murmured.

A wry smile touched Alana's lips before she turned, walking towards the landing of the stairs that led to the other room on the opposite side. Ahria hadn't noticed, having hidden beneath the blanket, but lantern light now filled what had been dark before. Though it was still impossible to see what lay beyond it.

"Come."

Ahria stared after her, still unsure what the guards had been doing in there the last few hours. "What is this?" she called after Alana, eyeing the open cell door and the stairs on the side of the room opposite where Alana led her. It would take her moments to cross the room, to leap up those stairs...

Her heart thundered in her ears as she stepped silently out of her cell, facing Alana's back. She eased towards the opposite set of stairs. Listening.

She could be bluffing about the guards.

Alana paused at the bottom of the stairs, looking back at Ahria. "Please don't squander this moment of trust. I'd rather not regret the decision to invite you to a more refined dining environment."

Dining?

Ahria hesitated, wondering just how fast Alana could move if she made a run for it. But her chances of escaping, even if she evaded the guards, were dire. She had no idea where she was, and Lungaz wasn't exactly known as a hospitable landscape with abundant foraging.

Swallowing, Ahria forced her feet to move towards the mysterious other room. Towards Alana, even though her hands shook. As she approached, the auer crossed into the other room, letting her step onto the landing alone and observe what awaited her.

The room beyond was sparse, with white stone walls carved out of the terrain of Lungaz like where the cells were. However, there were no bars here. Instead, just an open room with piles of furniture in the far corner. There were iron rings in the wall, their nefarious purposes something Ahria could guess at, but the table at the center of the room somehow made it seem a little less imposing. The oval table donned two place settings, opposite each other on the narrower portion. Between the settings and on the edges sat plates of various foods that made Ahria's mouth water. Some kind of roasted fowl dominated the right side, the dressings around it like something she expected to see at a feast in the palace in Ziona. Baskets of various breads and cheeses, roasted vegetables, and a bottle of—wine. That was *wine* next to the two empty glasses.

Warning bells rang in her head.

"Why?" Ahria looked at Alana, resisting the urge to fall face first into the spread of food.

"You're my niece." Alana said it simply, as if there was nothing strange about the idea. "But I am not the one who wants you here, only the one here with you, tasked with keeping an eye. He did not specify as to how." She gestured to the chairs.

Ahria approached the table, keeping Alana in her line of sight. "Uriel, you mean," she whispered, watching for a reaction to the name so few dared speak.

The hint of a flinch crossed Alana's expression, though it seemed to harden her further. "Yes." She waited for Ahria to choose the seat closer to the stairs, then took the one around the table.

"And you think he'd approve of this?"

"Doubtful." Alana settled into her chair, reaching for the bottle of wine. She popped the cork before pouring her own glass full. "But he's not here."

Ahria remained hyper aware of each movement the auer made. "Why not just let me go?"

"That... he would be aware of. And that would be an end. For both of us." Alana held out the bottle towards her glass but paused before pouring, raising an eyebrow.

Lifting the glass, Ahria sniffed it before setting it down and nodding. "So instead, you're going to feed me and heat my cell?" The warmth from the night before had prevailed into the morning, and with the encroaching winter, she realized someone had intentionally kept the space warmed. "Does this mean I get a pillow, too? Perhaps a nicer *bucket*?" She didn't bother keeping the bite from her words, still unsure what to make of the entire affair.

"You have every right to question all of this." Alana poured her glass and set aside the bottle, beginning to fill her plate. "I would if I were in your position. And I would be angry, too. If you want to take out that frustration on me, I won't blame you. But I'm a prisoner, too. Just in a different way. Lighting the hearth felt like the least I could do."

Ahria studied her for a long moment in silence before finally succumbing to her hunger. She piled food onto her plate—seasoned duck, spiced rice, and a variety of the other side dishes. It all smelled glorious, and she, perhaps foolishly, didn't even wait before digging in. Her ribs, too prominent on her sides, begged for the hearty meal.

She even sipped the wine, though not until she'd watched Alana do the same. "Why am I here? Are you supposed to interrogate me?"

"The direction I received was remarkably vague. He didn't give any particular instruction, which implies he might have already achieved what he hoped back in Jaspa." Alana savored a long sip of her wine, a strange look in her eyes before she closed them briefly. "Do you recall what he may have been asking you?"

Ahria blinked, but shook her head. "Not really. I remember he had a man with him who claimed to be my father. My blood father." Careful. She had to tread so very carefully, in case Alana didn't know that Kin lived. "But I don't know if that was real. If any of it was. They didn't let me sleep or eat, and..." She shook her head. "He asked me a lot of questions. I don't know what they were."

Alana didn't seem to react, hiding it with more bites of food. "I don't know what all you are aware of, exactly. But it wasn't your father. Kin is dead." Sadness clouded her eyes as she focused somewhere beyond Ahria.

Ahria furrowed her brow, eating a slice of roasted carrot. "Then who was he?"

What is happening?

Confusion reigned within her. Ahria hadn't even had an opportunity to be deceptive, to use Alana's ruse against her. The auer was just... offering her information without ever asking for something in return. And it couldn't all be lies. The demeanor, the food, the trust. Talon had warned her once that Alana was a convincing actress, but this didn't feel like acting. Not if she started divulging Uriel's secrets.

Unless she's going to kill me. Then these secrets mean nothing.

"Jarac." Alana spat the name in disgust. "Your father's brother. His twin." She rolled her lips together. "Uriel's new little toy."

Ahria's gaze shot up at the use of her master's name, narrowing her eyes at the bitter undertone. Yet, the explanation made sense. The man had appeared so much older than Kin, but he hadn't been in Slumber for twenty years. "Is he a Shade?"

"Yes." Alana didn't hesitate, and Ahria sipped more wine. "Uriel had intended to use Kin to gain the throne, not realizing it would be so easy to sway Jarac even though he was already powerful as the crown prince of Feyor. Now king."

Ahria at least had the good sense to turn her head before the wine sprayed from her mouth. She coughed, blinking at Alana. "*What?*" She set her glass down. "But if Jarac is the king of Feyor and he's my..."

Uncle. She couldn't say it. That made her...

Nausea rose in her throat, but she swallowed it.

Alana quirked an eyebrow. "I suppose it's possible Talon didn't know. I believe he and Kin had already drifted apart when Kin learned the truth so many years ago. I can tell you about your blood father, if you would like." She pierced a roasted potato, lifting it to her mouth. The sadness had returned to her eyes, burying whatever amusement they had held at her reaction.

Ahria shook her head, dabbing her mouth with a napkin. She wanted to say it, she realized, even as she held her tongue. She wanted to tell Alana that Kin lived. That Amarie lived. But that was dangerous information to share, and Alana's sadness wasn't her problem. "If Dad... If Talon had known about Kin, I think he would have told me. He told me everything else."

"I'll confess, your entire existence is a bit of an enigma." Alana smiled slightly. "No one knew you existed, which means my brother was effective at hiding you. A prudent decision, considering who your mother was." Alana paused, her lips turning into a slight frown. "I am not asking, so don't feel you need to answer, but... Uriel felt the power of the Key in that place before snatching you. He'd assumed you held the power after your mother's death, but in Jaspa there was nothing." She eyed Ahria only a moment before shrugging and putting another bite on her fork. "It does lead to the question of where the power has gone. Which is likely the information Uriel was attempting to extract from you. Though he seems satisfied to leave me in the dark."

She's either the best actress ever, or...

"What if I told you the Rahn'ka removed the power from me and hid it somewhere? Would you tell your master?" Ahria took a bite of duck, unable to ignore the perfection of the glaze.

Alana shrugged again. "Perhaps believable enough. It would explain your presence near him. Though, you realize, the way you say it makes it sound like a lie." She smirked, but shook her head as if dismissing the idea. "It doesn't matter. Uriel can come to his own conclusions."

Ahria furrowed her brow again. "Are you not relaying any of this to him? Will you not report back with what you've learned?"

"If he asks, I may answer, but Uriel doesn't take much interest in me these days." Something unspoken showed in her eyes, a secret she still kept. "Despite what he may believe, I am still my own woman." She finished her glass of wine, lifting the bottle to refill it.

"But if you deem it important, you'll tell him?" Ahria pressed. "If he asks, you'll tell him whatever I tell you?"

She paused, watching the wine filling her glass before topping up Ahria's. She twisted the bottle, examining the engraving on the glass. "This bottle of wine is from Kin's family's estate." Something in her tone made it sound like she was surprised she even spoke. "I... I made a mistake many years ago. I followed an order and caused your grandmother's death." She let out a deep breath, not meeting Ahria's gaze. "I hurt your blood father beyond measure, and if I could take that back, I would. After Kin disappeared, his family no longer mattered to Uriel, and he told me to stay away. But I heard about the estate failing, drowning in debt with a grieving widower. I returned and worked with Hartlen whenever I could until he passed. He left me the estate, but I didn't want it. Didn't deserve it. So I passed it on, and again, it thrives." Alana finally met Ahria's stare. "I have made *so many* mistakes that have hurt people I care about. I realize there is no true atonement for some of my crimes, but if my brother is to be believed, it is never too late to try to earn forgiveness."

Ahria nodded, letting the words sink in. She sipped the wine, feeling the faint buzz at the back of her mind as she huffed, offering Alana a faint smile. "Does that mean I get a pillow?"

Alana smiled back. "I'll arrange it. In exchange for more meals like this. With my niece."

The way she said the word struck something in Ahria's chest. Something real and yet untouchable. She wasn't sure how far to press, painfully aware of how gross her skin felt after weeks without a bath. How her hair was knotted, her back sore from the hard ground. And that bucket... But not yet. If Alana wanted more time together, that meant there'd be more opportunities.

"I can do that," Ahria agreed. "You know, Talon told me a lot of things. Some about you." When Alana looked ready to interrupt, she held up a hand. "There was this one night, after my eighteenth birthday party, and he'd let me have more than a few sips of wine. He did, too. I don't think I'd ever seen him so... at ease. It was after my brother left for the academies in Delkest, and although Talon wasn't *exactly* a father figure to him, they were still family. But I was sad that Byron left, and Talon admitted that he missed you. He visited your sister Kalstacia every few years, but he said it wasn't the same. That he regretted the path you'd taken, and despised some of your actions, but at the end of it all... He still loved you. He missed you, *all the Uriel bullshit aside*." She said the last words like Talon had, waving her hand with the phrase as she mimicked him. It eased the grief to talk about him, yet her eyes still burned. "Anyway... I thought you might want to know."

Silver lined Alana's eyes as she lowered her glass to the table. She dipped her chin, looking ready to turn away before she chewed the inside of her cheek, like Talon used to. With a steadying breath, she lifted her head again. "Thank you."

Chapter 32

Two weeks later...

Kin squinted at the northeast horizon, barely able to make out the speck Andi assured him was the rear guard of Jarac's fleet. She'd given the command to lift the sails to half mast, widening the gap between them as was customary between ships of different countries, as set forth by the accords after the Great Wars.

"Do you think they saw us?" Kin looked at Andi as she lowered the spyglass.

"Possibly. But we're already acting as they'd expect so we shouldn't get any trouble. Far as they know, we're just a trade vessel on our way to Icedale." Andi jerked her chin towards the mast where an Isalican flag now flew. Despite the tenuous relationship between Isalica and Feyor, war treatises would protect them.

They're pretending to be Delks, anyway.

"And after we pass Icedale?"

Andi gave him a smirk. "Then we make sure we're not seen." Her smile faded as she turned towards the distant land mass to the south. Above the tip of the Yandarin Mountain range, dark clouds roiled. They'd already coated the top of the rocky crags with a dusting of snow and looked to be barreling out to the sea. "It's that storm I'm not too keen on."

Deylan snapped his faction communication device shut as he approached them from the other side of the bow. "King Rayeht is aware of the threat we're pursuing." He kept his voice low for the three of them. "And I've sent word to Rae, too, but based on the message I just got, Damien isn't doing any better."

Kin cringed. "Anything from Coltin?"

Deylan shook his head, expression grim. "Nothing."

"Will our Isalicans send aid?" Andi faced Deylan.

Amarie's brother shrugged. "If they're planning to, they haven't told my informant."

Kin looked back to the horizon, wishing he could see more of the supposed Feyorian fleet. They didn't even know exactly how many ships were there. "They'll help. With what is in danger, Matthias will probably come himself." He crossed his arms, turning to lean against the banister. Hopefully Deylan had warned the king with plenty of time.

Kin had thought long and hard about what Matthias had endured, and his respect for the man had flourished. He'd always wondered about him after learning from Lasseth that there was someone trapped behind Uriel's infection. It was still strange to imagine Matthias's face, the same face that had inflicted so much cruelty, and truly accept he was a different person. But knowing his master's new face, the auer, aided in that delineation within Kin's mind.

A flash of lightning lit the white tops of the mountains, the clouds growing darker.

Andi collapsed her spyglass with a snap. She glanced over her shoulder to where her first mate, Keryn, had already started shouting commands to prepare the ship for the coming storm. "You best stay in your quarters if we hit rough seas." She looked between Kin and Deylan. "Both of you."

Kin gave an absent nod, despite his desire to remain rooted to the spot. He didn't want to take his eyes off of that tiny speck on the horizon that was his brother.

After seeing the condition of the people in Feyor, the guilt in him had mounted. With Slumber stealing so many years, the conversation with Alana and his parents remained so fresh in his mind. Her confession of who his blood parents truly were. The story of Uriel saving him was a perversion of the truth, considering the danger might not have existed without the whispers he put in the king's ear. The country had feared civil war, led by opposing twin brothers, both greedy for the throne. But the fall of Feyor that the king feared had happened anyway without the war.

Deylan, still next to him at the banister even after Andi's departure, eyed him. "What is it?"

Kin sucked in a breath, contemplating how to answer. "Jarac should have wanted for nothing, but Uriel still convinced him to become a Shade. And now the people he was supposed to protect are suffering."

"Not everyone is fit to rule," Deylan murmured, leaning against the banister.

"Maybe it's just in his blood to make selfish decisions." He glanced at the exposed edge of the scar beneath his right sleeve, imagining the tattoo beneath it. "The Lazorus monarchy should fall. Feyor will be better off without a king."

"Maybe." Amarie's brother shrugged. "But that's not what history suggests." Kin thought the man would continue, but he fell silent again, gaze drifting to the horizon.

Deylan was luring him into a trap, and he stifled a groan. "You don't think the country would find a way to right itself if Jarac just died without an heir?"

"Is that a question you really want the answer to?" Deylan quirked a brow at him, but Kin's slight nod was enough for him to elaborate. "If Jarac dies and there is no one to take his place, the country's current state would look peaceful and thriving by comparison to what'd happen next. A kingless monarchy would open the door for anyone to challenge for the throne. It would be bloody and potentially deadly for the remaining civilians. Did you know that Olsa was once a monarchy until it collapsed in eighteen-fifty-three?"

"I've never been one for history." Kin shrugged. "I thought it was always a republic. Like Delkest."

Deylan hummed, glancing at the approaching storm. "It happened during the Second Great War when Olsa's heirless king perished in battle. The country was already struggling. The war was only just beginning, and with the death of their king, things got much worse. There are many books that detail the events and the hardship that followed. It took the country fourteen years, and thousands of deaths, to reform into a republic with an elected senate and prime minister. Delkest, hundreds of years later, formed their government based on Olsa's."

Angling towards Kin, Deylan tilted his head. "What you do is your choice, but part of that choice is whether you take a potential upcoming opportunity to kill your brother. It could very well happen, with what we're aiming to do. And if you *choose* to kill him... you need to understand what you're forcing Feyor to endure if you aren't willing to step in." No judgment laced his tone. No pressure or disapproval. Only facts, history.

Yet, it still weighed on Kin like an anvil on his shoulders. "The kingdom doesn't even know I exist. I can't imagine they'll blindly accept me." The idea of actually donning the mantle sent a chill down his spine. "There are so many factors."

Deylan nodded. "I'm not saying it would be easy. Isalica was just about ready to overthrow King Rayeht after the destruction of Nema's Throne when he regained control of his own body. But he recovered. King Martox started a civil war and kicked Iedrus off the throne. He had a rough time in the beginning, earning the people's trust, but he did. If they can overcome those odds, so can you, if you decide that's what you want."

Kin frowned. "I don't know what I want." He leaned heavily on the banister, his mind jumping to Amarie and Ahria as he imagined them beside him as he took the throne. They were what mattered most to him. But considering his own family made him realize just how many other families in Feyor were suffering. He'd seen the children, mostly skin and bone, playing in the streets of Darian. The weary mothers, thinner than their children, watching over them.

"Then start by thinking about what you want for the people of Feyor." Deylan's mouth twitched in a pained smile. "Because you have the power to help them, and sometimes what *you* want comes secondary."

Kin's breath stilled in his chest as he considered Deylan's words. He'd only recently started to think in such a way. Of more than just himself. Amarie had been his inspiration. Convincing him he was worth more. He *was* more than just Uriel's pawn. He nodded slowly, wondering what he would choose if he came face to face with his brother.

He's a Shade. A threat. There won't be an option.

"Who is Veli?" The name had lingered in his mind, and the way Deylan had reacted to her potentially being in danger. "Your lover?"

Deylan rolled his shoulders, but his face relaxed. "Something like that."

"Have you heard any news about her?"

"They released her from interrogations." Deylan looked at Kin. "She's returning to the faction to aid in relocation."

The former Shade smiled. "So you'll get to see her soon." When Amarie's brother only nodded with a peaceful expression, Kin continued, "Tell me about Seph. If Jarac is after it for Uriel, it's probably best if I know."

Patters of rain hit the deck with another flash of lightning, drawing their gazes to the darkening horizon.

"Inside. We should get out of their way." Deylan motioned for Kin to follow and headed for the stairs to descend to the main deck, making the sharp turn towards the door that led beneath where they'd just stood.

Less ears, too, I suppose.

Entering his quarters, the ones he'd shared with Amarie before they'd parted ways, Kin closed the door behind them. Her scent still lingered in the sheets, and he tried not to stare at her side of the bed as he took a seat at the foot of it while Deylan took the desk chair.

Silence settled for a breath before Amarie's brother spoke. "Its name is Sephysis. It's a dagger, though to simply call it such would be a gross understatement."

Kin lifted his brow. "I wondered if it was a person the way you spoke about it. But it's a weapon... and it's in the Rahn'ka ruins where the prison is located?"

"Mhmm," Deylan murmured.

"Does Damien or Matthias know about it being down there? You'd think that'd be important information considering it's where they built the thing needed to complete Taeg'nok."

"I doubt they know, or they likely would have chosen a different spot. By the time I learned about their plans, it was too late for me to warn them." Deylan leaned back. "Which means you're the first granted this knowledge, and I expect you to keep it to yourself, save for our closest allies."

"I might need you to be a little clearer about who qualifies for that. We have a lot of them these days, and I'm not exactly clear on how secretive your Sixth Eye is trying to remain."

"Those who came to the Sixth Eye headquarters and those who traveled to Ziona." Deylan paused. "Sephysis's full name is Sephysis the bloodstone blade of Fylinth, destroyer of Mentithe, and protector of the light. I helped my father imprison it a long time ago."

"That's a lot of titles for a hunk of metal." Kin smirked, already knowing Deylan would correct him. "So why does Uriel want it?"

Deylan sighed. "Aside from its Art related abilities, I don't know. Not a lot is known about the dagger, but I doubt he'd have success claiming it. I'm more worried about Jarac unleashing it on the world again."

"So it's imprisoned for a reason." The words sounded strange for something that should be inanimate. "The way you talk about it, it sounds like this dagger has a consciousness of its own. And judging by the various names, it probably likes destroying things. Which means we want to make sure it doesn't get released?"

"Precisely." Deylan made a face. "But there is the small chance Jarac could claim it, and that would be even worse." Before Kin could question, he continued, "There are rumors in various historical books that Seph will occasionally choose someone. Willingly accept a master, more or less. The details aren't clear. But if Jarac successfully claims the dagger, we'll have a bigger problem alongside the possibility of him discovering the prison.

"This dagger isn't something you hold, you need to understand. It moves on its own accord, flying through the air like an arrow, but without need for a bow. And it's fast. Really fucking fast." Deylan's eyes unfocused, as he briefly went somewhere else before coming back. "It would be beyond bad."

"I'll take your word for it." Kin crossed his arms, considering what a Shade with such a weapon would be like. Especially one as cold-blooded as Jarac. "On top of keeping Jarac from the dagger, we need to make sure he doesn't discover the prison and get word back to Uriel about it. *And* hope that Uriel assumes the reason we're stopping him is because of the dagger and not something else."

"It's a lot," Deylan agreed, and for a moment, he looked just like Kalpheus, carrying the weight of the world. "But we must succeed. Any other option is catastrophic."

Thunder shook the core of the ship, jolting Kin awake as the whole room pitched. He'd managed to fall asleep, but as his stomach lurched, he doubted he'd be so lucky again.

At least it seems to have calmed a little.

The commotion up on the deck had grown eerily quiet, launching him into a new discomfort. He expected to hear the crew shouting as they wrestled with the sails, but something had changed. The entire energy on the ship felt different as Kin stepped out of bed. The wood floor of his quarters had been soaked by the storm, water rushing in through the cracks beneath the doors leading to the main deck. It sent a shock through his body as he approached the door, his steps splashing the cold water above the top of his boots.

The horror of him being alone on the ship spurred him to unlock the door, the silence outside leading to visions of the entire crew being washed off the ship by a rogue wave.

But as he stepped out onto the deck, he saw the dark shadows of the crew still rushing between their posts. The lantern on the main sail had been extinguished, but his eyes adjusted enough to make out the now familiar shapes of the Herald. A flash of lightning illuminated the scene for a second, and he spied Andi back by the helm, her eyes locked on the sea in front of them with Deylan next to her.

Kin turned, gripping the wet banister of the stairs. The rain had slowed, but the dark clouds still loomed in the night sky, blocking out the stars and moon.

Reaching the side of the ship, he peered out into the dark sea. The waves churned, the flash of lightning casting dark shadows beneath the waves. As if great sea monsters swam below.

But his eyes flickered to where the light illuminated the mast of another ship. Another not far beyond it. And at least four more.

That was... That was Jarac's fleet.

A rock plummeted in his stomach.

They were close—far too close.

That's why everyone is silent.

The sails on Jarac's fleet were raised as they rode out the storm in place rather than continue through it. And now the Herald was the same, sitting in absolute silence and hoping they wouldn't be spotted.

As lightning flashed again, a call echoed over the air before the thunder. A guttural howl Kin recognized from days he wished he could forget. While he couldn't see the wyvern, nothing else could have made that sound.

Deylan descended the stairs behind him, approaching the banister. His dark hair dripped, sticking to his skin just as his clothes did. He pushed his hair back from his face, skin wan. "We don't think they've seen us," he murmured, keeping his voice low even though the chances of it carrying over the stormy water to Jarac's fleet were slim. "But it sounds like they have a wyvern, maybe two." His casual tone didn't match the statement.

Kin nodded. "One of the few things Feyor is good at, I suppose. Training those things." He looked at Deylan. "You think Matthias will bring troops that can handle them?"

Deylan looked at him, eyes slightly widening before he smiled. "Troops? No. If all I know about him is correct, Matthias will bring the dragons."

"Dragons?" Kin nearly jumped when thunder cracked above them. "Matthias has *dragons*?"

Gods, I missed a lot in the last twenty years.

"Technically, Isalica has a treaty with them." Deylan smirked. "They came out of hiding years ago, though they stick to the northern regions and away from Feyor. They can handle a wyvern or two, no problem."

Chapter 33

Amarie tried not to squirm with Coltin's arm around her. When she'd pretended to let him court her, kiss her, all those years ago, she'd had no one else to consider. But Kin would understand, and an arm around her waist was hardly something to be jealous over.

Get over it.

She leaned into him as they approached the palace entrance, heart beating wildly in her ears. They had to be convincing, regardless of how she felt.

Coltin looked down at her, warmth in his brown eyes as he smiled. "Don't worry," he murmured. "You're safe with me."

Words that could have meant any number of things, but she understood.

They were walking to Jarac's palace, Uriel's lair. And *he* was home, which Coltin had confirmed when they met at that inn. The Delphi heir had helped them devise a plan to get in, steal the shard, and get back out.

If only it were so simple.

He must have felt her nerves, because his grip around her tightened. "It's much different when I'm in on the ruse."

Amusement rolled through his tone, and her eyes shot to his as she prepared to explain. Apologize—again.

But he only smiled at her and shook his head. "Relax. I haven't been upset with you for a good ten, fifteen years."

Amarie huffed, grateful he remained the kind, honorable man he'd been when they'd first met. "You deserved better," she muttered.

"I know." His eyes glittered. "And I've had better. And worse, for that matter. Life goes on."

Guards opened the front doors to the palace without inquiring about her presence, and she wondered how many times he'd escorted random women inside without it being a ruse.

Even though they chose a side entrance, it was still grand. In distinct contrast with the dirty, decrepit city around them. Though the outside walls were dark beyond the open double doors, the warm pine interior of the palace shone pristine. The vaulted hallway ceiling boasted polished beams of pale wood, gleaming silver chandeliers between them. Traditional, real flame lit the corridors, not Art-laden like the faction headquarters or even the palace in Ziona. Intricately woven rugs covered the floor, hiding the stone and painting the interior of the palace in a rich array of dark blue and green.

She could make out a door on the left side of the hallway ahead, the right side housing a series of glass doors that must have led to a courtyard. A second hallway to the far right seemed darker, but only because it lacked windows and disappeared quickly into a turn that led somewhere deeper into the palace.

Coltin had picked the entrance because of the sharp corner that would hide them from the guards quicker. And more importantly, hide Conrad... once he slipped past them from where he waited outside in the shadows.

"Master Delphi," a tall man clad in formal attire greeted them with a surprised tone, pausing mid-stride to approach from the right. He glanced at Amarie, but his face bore no hint of his thoughts as he shifted his gaze to Coltin. "Will you be joining us for the acquisitions meeting this afternoon? Word is the Heffman breeders have new stock to show us."

Coltin's grip on her withdrew. "Master Linthre, I have prior commitments this afternoon, but I look forward to hearing your report." He'd said he'd come up with a distraction for the guards in the moment rather than an elaborate plan, and she sensed his perceived opportunity. "Thank you for your support at the hearing, by the way. Couldn't have done it without you." He extended a hand, and the other man accepted it to shake.

Amarie did her best to look bored, scanning the area with disinterest.

As Coltin shook the man's hand, he clasped his other around it, too. The other, where he wore a copper ring donning a tiny pinpoint. What he'd laced the metal with, he hadn't told her.

But Linthre twitched at the grip, letting go and looking at his hand. "What...?" A spot of red marred the back of his hand.

Coltin looked at his own fingers. "My apologies, my ring must have a sharp edge."

Amarie returned her gaze to Linthre, furrowing her brow as the man wavered.

"I, uh... I don't feel well." He put a hand to his chest, face paling.

Coltin wasted no time, turning back to the doors that were still open to outside. "Guards! We need some help!"

The two guards raced inside, just in time to see Linthre stagger backwards. They caught him by the elbows, looking at Coltin.

"I don't think he enjoys the sight of blood," Coltin mused, patting the man's shoulder. "Perhaps a lay down, and he'll feel better." He removed the ring, pocketing it. "I'm very sorry, I'll get this old thing smoothed out right away."

Linthre muttered some kind of attempt to save face, that it wasn't the speck of blood that caused him to swoon. But Coltin waved his hand in dismissal, as if trying to ease the man's embarrassment.

"You go." One guard pushed the man's weight over to his comrade, forcing them both to turn their backs to the doorway.

Amarie didn't look behind her as a shadow darted past, disappearing into the hallway to their right with barely a sound.

The guard with poor Linthre started down the hallway ahead, practically carrying the man while the other gave Coltin a nod. "Have a good day, sir." He then excused himself back to the door, picking up the decorative spear he'd leaned against the doorframe. It seemed a miracle that Conrad hadn't tripped over the pair of them when he slipped in.

Coltin placed his hand on the small of Amarie's back as they started down the longer hallway. They'd have to take the long way around to the tower where Jarac kept his prized possessions, so as not to arouse suspicion.

"What was that stuff?" Amarie whispered as she took Coltin's arm.

I'm sure he's also enjoying being the one with secrets this time.

He led them through a corridor, barely glancing down at her. "A mild poison. Just speeds his heart a little. Should wear off in a few hours."

Amarie nodded, falling silent as she walked, though her eyes lingered on his face.

Gods, how is this the same man?

He'd changed so much. No longer the boy who'd swooned over her, who'd professed his feelings lakeside and asked her to attend the party Kin had infiltrated. Grey dappled his hair, vague lines around the corners of his eyes. Handsome. She'd be a fool to deny it. She hoped, somewhere, beneath it all, that he'd found happiness. That he'd found love.

Yet, with her on his arm as his feigned lover to gain entrance into the palace, she doubted it. Would be a poorly thought out ruse if someone glimpsed them and told his wife. No wedding band decorated his hands, and a darker thought slipped through her like wicked silk.

Unless I ruined the idea of love for him.

As if reading her thoughts, Coltin squeezed her arm. "You're making me feel like I have something on my face."

Amarie huffed a light laugh, tearing her gaze forward. "It's just weird. It's been so long for you, but for me..."

His brow twitched. "How long has it been for you?"

"Almost two years." Amarie rolled her shoulders, but the invisible weight didn't budge. "Well, sort of. Seven more, if you count the time I was awake without my memories with the auer. But those years don't feel connected to my life, as strange as that sounds..." She swallowed. "Did you hate me? In the beginning?"

They turned and ascended a curved stairwell lined with tall windows displaying the city. Smoke drifted into the sky from chimneys, blending into the clouds blotting out the blue sky.

Coltin took time to answer, but she waited, keeping her cloak tight around herself. "I never *hated* you. I was hurt, but something had felt off about it from the start. Shortly after I got your letter, your brother recruited me. Then it all made sense, and I understood why you found me. Why you stayed when you seemed uninterested in *me*." He paused, smiling and nodding at someone they passed. "I met my wife three years later."

Hope blossomed in Amarie's chest, and she smiled. "What's her name?"

A shadow passed over his face. "Her name was Laicia."

Was.

Amarie swallowed. "How long were you married?"

"Almost fifteen years." Coltin gave her a grim smile. "Most people never experience love like that. I was fortunate to have as long as I did with her."

Amarie nodded, not daring to intrude by asking more. "I'm glad. That you found her."

"Me, too." Coltin squeezed her again as they entered a spacious atrium, heading casually for the open doors at the other side. The aesthetic remained the same as the rest of the palace, but along the sides of the room stood statues of dark marble. The old kings of the country forever left to survey the mingling people.

Aristocrats mulled about in the space, talking while drinking coffee or eating pastries. Like nothing terrible transpired in their country. Like no one starved. It made Amarie's blood heat, but she kept her power locked down. With Uriel so close, she couldn't risk even a hint of it escaping. He might even be in the room, if he'd changed bodies without any of them realizing, but Coltin led them confidently forward.

Tilting her head away from the people as they passed, she hoped it would seem she was just being shy. With her head turned towards the inner wall, her breath caught at the marble statue that stared at her. She couldn't even blink from those eyes—*Kin's eyes*. Her chest ached as she still failed to look away from the face she missed so much. It had been done of Jarac, of course, but something deep in her gut responded. Kin sailed that very moment in pursuit of his twin, with the possibility of killing him. If Feyor's king fell...

He doesn't want to rule.

Their conversation flowed back to her, when he'd asked her what she wanted.

I don't care, she'd said. *I'm not sure I'm suited to palace life. I just want us to have our family, whatever that looks like.*

And those words were still true, but heat pricked her eyes.

As long as we both survive the next few weeks.

Amarie forced her gaze away, forced her thoughts to focus on their task.

Mercifully, no one stopped to talk to Coltin, and they exited the huge chamber on the other side. He glanced both ways before side-stepping into a narrower corridor, leading her up another level.

"Are we getting close?" Amarie could only wonder where Conrad was, if he'd run into any trouble. It would be next to impossible to explain the Zionan prince's presence sneaking around the Feyorian palace.

Coltin's boots were nearly silent on the carved stone steps, and he paused as they reached a landing. At the end, the hallway split perpendicular, with another entrance near where they'd exited the stairs. Three windows adorned the right side, latched closed against the cool autumn air.

Coltin hurried their steps, and they reached the end of the hall. A single click sounded from within his coat, and he withdrew the communication device akin to the one Deylan had loaned Conrad. He popped it open, eyes widening before he shut it and dropped it back into his coat. "We—"

The knob on the door ahead twisted before he could finish his thought, and her heart leapt.

Coltin pushed her away, and she stumbled around the corner back into the windowed hallway as the door clicked open. Pressing her back to the wall, she listened, holding her breath.

"Lord Delphi."

That voice.

Amarie would never forget that voice. Images of their battle in the fields of Helgath flashed before her eyes. Pain sparked in her back from the dagger that'd killed her before Uriel could take her.

"Lord Bryllon," Coltin greeted, and Amarie imagined his chin dipping. "I was just looking for you."

Gods, it was Uriel. Right there, on the other side of that wall. And she had nowhere to hide, nowhere to run, that he wouldn't see her. Find her.

"Will you be attending the council tomorrow?" Coltin sounded remarkably calm considering the situation.

"Yes. With our king absent..."

Amarie lost track of their conversation as her mind whirled. As long as they were talking, she had time, but the annoyance in Uriel's tone at being held up with pleasantries suggested she didn't have long. He'd be turning down the hallway she stood. She had seconds, at best.

Amarie pressed herself against the glass as she looked out the window, then up.

Her chest heaved as she bit her lip, unlatching the glass pane. She prayed to whatever god would listen as she pushed it open, nearly collapsing in relief when the hinges didn't squeak. Climbing onto the sill, she kept her focus up as the wind whipped her hair.

Don't look down.

But her eyes betrayed her and surveyed the long, deadly fall waiting beneath her. Gritting her teeth, she reached up, finding purchase on a brick, and climbed out onto the outside of the stone wall. Using her boot, she pushed the window closed.

Get out of sight.

Even then, if Uriel rounded the corner, he'd see her clutching to the side of his palace like a bat.

Centering with a breath, she climbed. Another window was ten feet above her, and she aimed for it. Her bare fingers stung against the rough stone, wind threatening to yank her from the wall and fling her to her death.

As her hand found the glass on the higher level, she pushed. Nothing. She lurched a step higher, bracing her boots on jutting stones. No latch. Not on the outside.

Shit. Amarie's heart sank. *Shit, shit, shit.*

Daring a peek inside, she glimpsed a figure that immediately focused in her direction. She gasped, lowering her head and losing her footing.

Amarie barely contained her yelp as her legs swung beneath her, hands desperately clinging to the stone.

A breath later, a hand clamped down on her wrist, and she looked up.

"Conrad," she breathed, relief tearing through her.

The prince grabbed her with his other hand, too. "Hold on."

Amarie clenched her jaw as he hoisted her up, pulling on the windowsill with her free hand before tumbling into the room. She panted, hands shaking as she remained on her hands and knees on the floor of the small room. "Thank you," she whispered, still catching her breath. "Uriel..."

"I know. I'm sorry. I tried to warn Coltin..."

She nodded. "He saw it just in time, otherwise we would have walked right into him." Accepting Conrad's hand, she stood, knees wobbling. "Should we go find Coltin?"

It wasn't the plan, in the event they were separated. Amarie and Conrad were supposed to continue without him, as he had other objectives to help them succeed. But it felt wrong to abandon him with Uriel.

Conrad shook his head. "Too dangerous." He pulled out the faction device, bobbing it in his hand. She spied the slightest tremor within his fingers, but he fidgeted with the device, probably to hide whatever fear he felt. "He'll contact us if something happens." As if in response, the device clicked, and he popped it open.

Amarie stood beside him, eyeing the dials as they spun around to different letters.

A-L-L… C-L-E-A-R…

And then nothing.

She loosed a breath, damning her hands for still trembling, too. "We're in the tower, now, right?"

"I followed the directions Coltin gave me, so yes… as far as I can tell." Conrad gestured with his chin towards a spiral staircase behind him partially hidden by bookshelves. "One more level up and we should reach the beginning of the collection rooms. But we should hurry."

Amarie nodded, following him to the stairs.

Around and around, they climbed. They passed no windows, their path only lit by small candles encased within sconces every few steps. By the time they reached the first landing, her thighs burned from the foot-tall steps, but at least they'd stopped wavering.

"Do you feel it?" Conrad stepped into the first chamber, but looked only at her as she took in the display cases and shelves.

Amarie closed her eyes, keeping her hiding aura intact while using a trickle of energy to test if anything answered it. Nothing. She shook her head, and they continued up.

They repeated the process at each level, finding nothing each time, and Amarie started to wonder if she'd feel the shard at all. If they were going about this in a hopeless way. Perhaps it wouldn't answer her. Perhaps even if it did, she wouldn't feel it. See it.

They passed level six. Level seven.

But on level eight... something finally tickled the back of her senses and her eyes darted to Conrad. "It's here."

Amarie hurried into the room, but between the shelves and crates and displays, it was impossible to see anything clearly. To find something as small as the shard. She dared to send her power again, and felt the call return from the back of the room. "This way."

Conrad followed behind her, keeping watch of the entrance as she searched.

A massive apothecary-style cabinet occupied the back wall, boasting at least a hundred tiny drawers.

"What kind of torturous organization is this," Amarie muttered, yanking drawers open two at a time.

Conrad maintained his position behind her, facing the stairs with his hand on the hilt of his sword. He glanced over his shoulder after she'd tried at least half of the drawers with no luck. "You sure it's here? We've been in this place a long time..." She could hear the growing tension in his tone.

He twitched when the device in his pocket clicked, quickly digging it out. The dials whirled wildly after he opened it. He'd told Amarie how it might be difficult for him to decipher a message on the fly.

"Say the letters out loud," Amarie instructed, flinging the drawers to the floor once they proved fruitless.

"G-E-T..." Conrad's free hand grew tighter on his sword hilt. "Out. He's... C-O-M..." He snapped the device shut before finishing, but he didn't need to. "Fuck. Time's up."

Amarie ripped open two more drawers, her heart thundering in her ears. "It's—I found it." She snatched the Berylian Key shard necklace and pulled it over her head.

Conrad drew his sword, the copper surface shimmering in the dim candlelight.

Coltin had to be ready for the next step of the plan.

"Send the signal." Amarie braced herself at the soft footsteps ascending the stairs. Distant and without rush. There was only one way into the tower, and *he* didn't need to rush. "Now! Send it."

"We were supposed to wait until we were out." Conrad gaped at her.

"We don't have time. I'll get us out. Send it." Amarie stared at the doorway to the stairs, not bothering to reach for her hidden weapons. They'd be useless against Uriel. "Send it!"

Conrad flipped the device open again, forced to abandon his sword on top of one of the nearby shelves so he could manipulate the dials. He squeezed the buttons on either side of the device in his palm before throwing it back into his pocket. "Now what?" He stood his ground by the stairs as he took his sword back up, sliding something copper over his fingers.

Amarie looked around the room. No windows. This high up, a fall would kill them both. But once Coltin did his part, they might stand a chance. But only if...

"Well, well, well..." Uriel's voice made every tiny hair on the back of her neck stand straight. "She lives."

Uriel climbed the final steps, and Conrad backed away. Ice ran down Amarie's spine as she met Uriel's gaze. The darkness and gold flecked within those bright auer eyes. Her power surged beneath her skin, but she contained it, not daring to look away.

"And you," Uriel purred at Conrad. "I thought you'd drown. I guess you're full of surprises like the rest of them. Ready to die like the rest of them?"

Before Conrad could respond to the mocking words, the floor beneath their feet began to rumble and the room swayed.

Black blurred at Uriel's feet, tendrils vibrating with whatever force caused the rest of the tower to move. As his attack swelled forward, Conrad stepped between Amarie and the shadows, his sword sweeping from the ground in an arc. A high-pitched whine joined the rumble of stone as shadow split, collapsing into wisps of obsidian ash.

Something far beneath them ruptured, and the tower jolted sideways. The floor cracked with another massive shudder, and Amarie grabbed onto a shelf to keep from falling. The entire structure dropped at least ten feet in a terrible heave, then again, as the foundation failed. She rallied her power, unleashing it in a blast at the stone above Uriel's head.

Shadow suddenly engulfed him, boiling around his body like a shell, bits of stone sticking to the tar-like surface as everything jerked sideways with another crack of stone.

As more debris caked Uriel's shield, she wheeled around and sent another surge of her Art at the outer wall.

The room tilted, like a slowly sinking boat. She reached for Conrad. "We need to jump!" She pulled him towards the opening she'd created, where cold wind rushed inside. The view of the city skyline angled as the tower leaned more and more to the side, making Amarie dizzy.

To his credit, the prince didn't hesitate at her order. Gripping her hand, he kept pace behind her and they launched themselves into open air.

In the rush of air around her, stomach still somewhere in the collapsing tower, Amarie lost track of Uriel. If he emerged from the rubble, if he leapt after them. She didn't know, and she didn't care as she and Conrad plummeted. The direction they'd jumped overlooked the back of the city near the cliff side of the mountain. A sudden stony landing grew closer as they plummeted towards the dank street and buildings. Over the sound of the wind rushing by them, she couldn't hear the commotion of the people, but saw them fleeing the open streets for shelter.

Breathing deep, Amarie held tight to Conrad's hand, and channeled her energy beneath them. The surrounding air sparked with violet and pink, hardening until the wind barely touched their skin. "This will still hurt," she warned, vision tinted with the color of her power. She stretched it out, thrusting it at the ground to slow their fall.

Her energy hit the ground first, power seeping into the cracks between the stones and pushing outward in a web, but it didn't slow them enough. Not nearly enough, and Amarie braced for the impact.

Conrad's fist shot out, the copper bands on his fingers shining, and the encroaching ground slowed. It actually *slowed* as Amarie gasped. With their bodies practically suspended in the air, they moved so slowly that she had time to feel the pressure of the device's Art against her skin.

The cobblestone fractured, caving inward like a great invisible boulder had landed there. The combination of her power and whatever he'd done. They struck the incline a split second later, and all the breath rushed out of Amarie as she curled to roll, letting go of Conrad.

She came to a stop a few yards away, gasping and quickly inspecting her limbs to feel if anything had broken. But while she'd surely have some colorful bruises, nothing screamed as she staggered to her feet and looked at Conrad lying on his back. "Are you all right?"

Conrad groaned before staggering to his feet. "I think so." He rubbed his shoulder as he looked back towards the tower. "Remind me never to jump out of a crumbling building again."

"What is that thing?" Amarie motioned to the double copper ring on his hand.

"A gift from your brother." Conrad turned his hand over, huffing as he looked at them, too. "Didn't think *this* is what I'd use it for, though."

Amarie wiped her hand on her pants, turning her attention to the giant cloud of dust hanging in the air from the tower's collapse. "Well, it saved our legs from breaking, so I'd say you used it well. We should get out of here." She wondered if Coltin had gotten out, gotten away. If Uriel would suspect him, or if his cover would still be intact.

The device in Conrad's pocket clicked.

Coltin's alive.

She waited as the prince opened the device, reading the letters over his shoulder.

A-R-E... Y-O-U... A-L-I-V-E...

Conrad responded slowly, but deliberately, with the affirmation. The conversation was short, concise. Coltin was fine, but couldn't leave. No word on Uriel.

But they needed to get out of Jaspa. And now that she had the shard, it was time to go to Lungaz. Making their way back to the tunnels as quickly as they could without drawing too much attention, they retrieved their satchels from where they had stashed them that morning, then hurried to the horses while the city still reeled from the collapse of part of the palace. The chaos made it easy to blend in.

Uriel knew she was alive now. The danger of the knowledge meant that perhaps he would have no purpose for Ahria anymore. Her heart ached as she thought about the situation her daughter had to be in, and it only spurred her to hurry. She'd funnel her power into the horses, making them faster. She could tell Conrad's mind was thinking similar thoughts as he returned to his usual pensive silence.

We're coming, Ahria.

Chapter 34

Ahria leaned against the wall, the mattress of her cot soft under her. Pillows lay scattered around her cell, and the door wasn't locked. Not anymore. Alana had spared her the need to keep using the bucket, granting her open access to the lower floor and its amenities. Which, thankfully, included a privy.

Over the past two weeks since their dinner together, her aunt had offered more and more chances to earn trust, tastes of freedom. Her skin no longer reeked of filth, having been allowed to take baths, as well. She'd stayed in that water as long as she could the first time, enjoying it well after the heat had vanished. Alana even let her venture above ground one day, just to see the sky for a few minutes.

There was no telling what she may have offered the guards to look the other way.

Or threatened.

Ahria gratefully listened to her stories of Talon, never feeling like the woman was lying to her. Yet, she'd continued to be careful not to share any sensitive information in return, and Alana didn't press for it. If this was still an interrogation, it was the longest deception she could have imagined.

In a quiet moment alone that afternoon, restlessness ached through Ahria's body. She tried to stifle it, delving deep into her memories to sustain her from the madness of boredom. Her mind took her back to New Kingston, to when she'd been searching for Conrad.

Before she knew it, the words of the song she'd written and performed with Mysterium came from her lips, drifting over the heavy, stale air in a melodic tune. She kept her eyes closed as she sang the song that had been meant to find Conrad. To find her father. It pressed a mixture of peace and grief into her soul, burning her eyes, though no tears fell.

As she finished, she opened her eyes and nearly leapt out of her skin.

Alana stood calmly beyond the open door of her cell, her hands clasped in front of her. She had a vague smile on her lips, which were painted a vibrant red that complimented her dark complexion. "I thought I might invite you to tea. Disrupt the tedium?"

Ahria let out a breath and nodded. "Where were you?" She hadn't seen the auer since breakfast the day before, and it was unlike her to stay away for so long. Standing, Ahria crossed to the barred door and swung it open. "When you didn't show up for dinner last night..."

"Just temporarily disposed. I needed to return to Jaspa for the evening." The tone in her voice suggested she wasn't pleased with the fact.

"Why?" Ahria followed her towards their dining room.

"Expectation. I'm still required to check in from time to time with him. But there's nothing to worry about." She approached the table where she'd already brought down a tea setting. She poured the cups for them, placing one beside a pair of sweet cakes on a plate for Ahria. "And no, I did not inform him of the liberties I've taken with your imprisonment here. He doesn't need to know."

Ahria sat, a curl of dread licking through her. "Why is he still keeping me here? To what end?" As much as she now enjoyed getting to know her aunt, it didn't make sense. Why keep her here if not to question her? To get something from her? "Has he truly given you no direction for what to do with me?"

Alana sat, pouring her own cup of tea. "Nothing clear. Only that you are to remain here. I suspect it has more to do with keeping you away from those who may threaten him."

Ahria's shoulders slumped. "So I'm supposed to stay trapped here while he kills my friends?" She sighed, studying Alana. "Will you ever consider letting me leave?" To keep her question light, she reached for a sweet cake and took a bite.

"Imprisonment is better than death, isn't it?" The look in Alana's eye suggested she already knew the answer, but she sighed. "I can't let you go. But I will continue to try to make your stay more comfortable."

"What if I escaped while you weren't looking?" Ahria tilted her head with a broad, innocent smile that faded faster than she'd wanted it to. "I can't just stay here. They need me."

They.

Her blood parents. Conrad. Even if Damien had died, the plan couldn't just fade to nothing.

"If you escaped, then death would be a mercy compared to what Uriel would do to me." Alana set her cup down without ever taking a drink.

"What if they come for me?" Ahria whispered. "Will you hurt them?"

Alana quieted, focused on Ahria, but with an expression impossible to read. "I will defend myself." She lifted her tea again, taking a slow sip. "But isn't the whole scheme impossible to accomplish without the Rahn'ka?"

Sickness curled in her stomach at the memory of Damien's broken body. She swallowed, banishing her uncertainty. "He might have lived." She rolled her lips together, opening her mouth to say more before closing it.

She had to believe that there was still hope. That Damien would recover, and everything would continue. Imagining a world with Shades, like the one who'd killed her father, was not something Ahria wanted.

She set down her sweet cake, her pulse quickening with the words desperate to escape her. "Nothing will be over until Uriel is gone from this world." Meeting Alana's gaze, she added, "You'll have to choose a side, you know."

"In the eyes of your companions, I've already chosen a side. The luxury of choice no longer exists." A darkness hovered in her eyes, despite the casual tone in her voice. "I have always been perceived as a villain, rightfully so, and am content to continue to play the role even if my... desires no longer align with it."

"It doesn't have to be that way," Ahria whispered. "It's not too late."

"It's far too late." She leaned back, resting her cup in her palm in front of her chest. "You can't save me from the past, Ahria. I've gone too far... far too many times. Blood coats my hands. Including your father's."

Ahria's shoulders drooped. "You said you didn't know about Talon's death, so how could you have prevented it?"

Alana looked confused for a breath before she lightly shook her head. "I speak of Kin. I could have made different choices to protect him. To keep him from ever becoming a Shade. But instead, I blindly obeyed because I believed a monster could love."

Air stilled in Ahria's lungs, daring her to speak.

If I can sway Alana...

She chewed her lip, her heart picking up speed. "You loved Uriel?"

Alana's fingers twitched against the porcelain of her cup. Her gaze lowered to the liquid inside, but saw something far beyond the tea. "And believed he loved me, too. But I was wrong. And he proved it soon after he lost control of the Isalican king. After I..." The rims of her emerald eyes grew even darker. "After he took control of me for a time."

"I'm sorry," Ahria murmured, resisting the urge to ask what it was like to be possessed by such an evil. She'd heard Kin talk about Matthias, though hadn't met the king herself. "Isn't that enough? To consider changing sides? Help us. Help us lock him away so he can never torment the world again. Never do *that* to anyone else."

Alana's lips curled in a dry smile. "You speak as if it's that easy, but you've lost so many pieces of your puzzle already. I know enough about Taeg'nok to realize the truth. So does Uriel."

Ahria clenched her teeth, hand shaking as she thumbed the handle of her tea cup. "And what if you're wrong?" she whispered. "What if Uriel is mistaken?" She lifted her gaze from the tea to Alana's piercing emerald eyes. "What if we haven't lost anything?"

Trust. It stretched so thin between them, but Ahria couldn't help it. Couldn't help but throw the rope—the tether. To see if her aunt would grasp it and change her mind. Telling Alana the truth could condemn them all to a horrible fate, but if it didn't, if they gained an ally... Alana would be invaluable. Especially if she remained in Uriel's good graces.

The room hung in daunting silence for a moment as Alana stared at her niece. Absolute stillness reigned over her body for at least a minute before she leaned forward and gently placed her cup back on the table, its clink deafening.

"I'd say you're quite daring to say such things to me." Her eyes flickered to the stairwell behind Ahria, but her shoulders eased as their eyes met again. "And I'd question how you know."

Ahria lifted her chin. It was too late to hesitate now. "Because a few corrupted aren't enough to kill my blood parents, underwater or not." She swallowed hard, but held the auer's stare. "And I don't believe Damien is dead. My uncle and his friends would be able to save him."

A vein in Alana's temple pulsed. "Those are bold statements." She folded her hands into her lap beneath the edge of the table. Another wry smile crossed her painted lips, but she rolled them as if to conceal it. "Your parents survived Hoult, then?"

Gods, I hope this doesn't come back to bite me.

"If they hadn't, I never would have met them." Ahria's mouth twitched in a faint smile. "But they came for me. And they will again." She almost touched the necklace at her collarbone, but ran the hand through her hair instead. "No matter if I'm kept in Lungaz or at the bottom of the sea."

"With what I know of your mother, that is certainly not in doubt." Alana eyed her cup of tea, considering it again, but leaned back without it. "It won't be a quiet rescue, either. Which is good. More of a possible show for Uriel to witness."

Ahria furrowed her brow. "Uriel can't enter Lungaz to witness anything."

Alana's eyes guttered. "I suppose it's my turn to share sensitive information."

Chapter 35

Two weeks later...

Frozen air whipped through Matthias's hair, ruffling the fur around his shoulders as he stared down at the ruins occupying the small island off the coast of Orvalinon. This high up, Jarac's soldiers were specks on the decks of their small fleet. A few wyverns circled in the sky, not noticing the two dragons with riders perched on the mountain side.

Zelbrali shifted beneath him, anticipation rippling his golden scales.

To their right, Zedren held perfectly still, bearing Liam and Dani on his back.

The islands jutted up out of the ocean like teeth, their grey crags too steep to support snow. Though it didn't stop the flakes of the first autumn storm from trying at the highest points. But where they waited, the dragons' claws dug into the rocky face, forcing them to stand precariously like mountain goats on the shadowed south side. Looking down on the ruins, it seemed as if the ancient Rahn'ka had scooped out a section of the mountain between crags to build their sanctum. The monoliths had crumbled like fallen children's blocks from their vantage point.

Jarac's fleet had angled themselves near an arch in the jagged stone, the only narrow entry point into the ruins from the sea. They maneuvered the lead ship as close as they could without skewering it on the stone, and the tiny ant-like crew worked to lower longboats into the turbulent sea.

So far, their hovering presence so close had gone unnoticed by all except one wyvern and rider, whose bodies now lay in pieces higher on the mountain.

The weight of their deaths still burdened Matthias's shoulders, despite the necessity. Despite more imminent bloodshed. Every life took a toll. Especially when piled on top of the deaths he'd witnessed, even if they weren't his hands.

The Dtrüa angled her head, eyes, like the falling snowflakes, unfocused on the horizon. "Jaxx and Zaniken should be here soon. Any sign of the Herald?"

Matthias studied the ocean below, but saw no indication that Kin and Deylan were close. Their infrequent messages indicated they were only half a day behind the Feyorian fleet. Soon. They should arrive soon, and chaos would erupt. "Not yet."

Uriel couldn't discover the prison, and the king's hands itched for his axe. He hadn't seen Jarac in years, not since the Shade had fled the battlefield over a decade ago.

Matthias tracked another wyvern and rider, and with each dull glint of the sun off the rider's helmet, his heart sank. The creature's webbed wings looked different from the typical wyvern. Spiked scales ran along its length and the thicker membrane of its wings blotted out the sun. Its maw, more wolf than dragon, sent chills down his spine. And when it banked towards them, and their secret perch, he gritted his teeth. "That's not a human rider," he warned. "Looks like Uriel sent the Hollow Ones."

Only two wyverns flew above the small fleet, including the one angling towards them, growing dangerously closer with each breath. They were bound to notice the one missing, and if another suffered the same fate...

If this weapon is important, you'd think he'd have sent more...

The king's mind raced, looking for what they'd missed. Something didn't sit right, didn't *feel* right. Warning bells rang through his soul, and his tension must have radiated into his mount, since Zelbrali shifted beneath him.

Though, it could also have been the corrupted wyvern now flying practically straight at them.

"Move. We need to take this one out." Matthias dismissed the feeling in his gut that something was off, if only to take care of the current, more pressing threat. But he kept the thought in the back of his mind.

We're missing something.

Yet, even another scan of the sky revealed no hidden ranks of Hollow Ones. No disguised corrupted wyverns.

"Watch for more," the king added towards Dani, Liam, and their dragon mount. "It doesn't make sense for there to be only three wyverns with the fleet."

Before either could answer, Zelbrali dropped off the rock face, a steep dive tactic they'd used countless times in battles and skirmishes. But it still made Matthias's stomach flip over.

Diving lower and lower, he watched the Hollow One soar for Dani and Liam's position.

A warning screech split the air, vibrating in Matthias's ears as he looked up at the wyvern, then at the second one still closer to the ships. Beating its wings, it gained altitude, head turning in their direction. He swore under his breath and gripped the dragon's scales tighter. "Let's go get 'em."

Zelbrali banked hard, Matthias's saddle straps digging into his thighs as the dragon shot up towards the sky. And not just the sky, but the underbelly of the corrupted wyvern now distracted by Zedren.

But the answering call of the other wyvern rattled through Matthias's bones.

Zelbrali struck without slowing, without faltering. His giant jaws clamped around the wyvern, far smaller than him, propelling it and its rider higher into the sky. Blood leaked from Zelbrali's jaws, speckling across Matthias's thick riding leathers. Black blood. Only confirming his suspicion.

Howling, the corrupted wyvern lashed in Zelbrali's grip as the pair of them leveled out before plummeting, a tangle of claws and scales and teeth. The dragon beneath Matthias jerked, narrowly avoiding each strike intended for him.

Somewhere above, rock scraped against claws, and he imagined Zedren taking to the sky to handle the other incoming wyvern.

As Zelbrali free fell through the air, he threw his head sideways, crashing the corrupted wyvern into the side of the mountain and dragging it along the rocks. Letting go of it, Zelbrali corrected while Matthias watched the Hollow One and its mount splatter over the stones below.

"Matthias," the dragon's rough voice, like two stones grinding together, drew the king's gaze back up.

And his whole body stilled, frozen.

Not one wyvern flew towards them, as it should have been. Not one, but... three.

And in the second it took him to count them, something burst from beneath the churning ocean waters, shooting straight into the sky. Water dripped from its form, wings beating to throw the salt water from its black scales. Its wide tail curved at the end like a shark's, but altered into a wyvern's body until its head. Squat and wide, its mouth bared hundreds of rowed teeth, like a sea monster of old.

"Nymaera's breath," Matthias whispered.

Another sea wyvern erupted. And another.

And another.

They kept coming, rupturing from the ocean, as if they'd been waiting beneath the ships the entire time. As if they'd *traveled* beneath the ships.

Kin and Deylan needed to turn around. Needed to go back. Get out before they could be spotted.

Matthias scanned the horizon, hoping for no sign of the—

The Herald.

There she was, approaching from the west. White sails billowed in the strong winds from the Isalican coast.

Jarac hadn't unleashed his hidden ranks of Hollow Ones for Matthias. He'd unleashed them for his brother, knowingly or not.

Zelbrali and Zedren launched for the open sky above the fleet, answering the threatening cries of the corrupted with their own.

Chapter 36

Keryn's commanding tone somehow overpowered the crew's shouting. "Get those sails up! Hard to port!"

But Kin could only stare at the scene ahead of them.

The grey craggy shape of the island looked fearsome on its own, but the horizon peppered with all the monsters now bursting from the ocean...

Kin knew fear. But the sight of the corrupted rising from the surf elicited something different in him. More primal. He wanted to get away. Needed to. Dive off the side of the Herald and swim away as quickly as he could, since these insane sailors seemed to be preparing to stay.

"Clear the fore-deck!"

Movement sped in the corner of Kin's vision, but he didn't look away from the island. He forced himself to focus on Jarac's lead ship, the one that surely carried his brother. The others remained anchored further from the shore, though one loosed their sails and turned towards the Herald. Ignoring it, he narrowed his eyes at the hull of Jarac's ship.

Is that a longboat?

Kin focused on the movement as men climbed into a smaller vessel on the side. The corrupted were their distraction. They'd be rowing towards land soon, and if Jarac got inside, there was no telling what would happen. Especially if he found what he was after.

A bellow echoed through the sky, tearing Kin's attention back up.

A corrupted wyvern dove towards the bow of the Herald, at him, and he swore he could see malice in those depthless eyes as it bared rows of jagged teeth. He didn't know how it'd gotten so close without him seeing it sooner.

A snarl ripped from its throat as it neared.

The former Shade tried to back up, tried to move, tried to *breathe*, but his body refused to work. Refused to respond as that inky black beast opened its maw, wide enough to wrap around his torso. For every one of those tiny teeth to sink into his flesh.

He jerked for his sword, already knowing it would be futile.

The wyvern's hot, rank breath reached Kin's nose, and he braced himself for pain. For death.

But the wyvern stopped short as something scaled and massive and *gold* crashed into it from the side.

Kin's lungs filled with a startled breath and then stilled.

A dragon.

A gods' damned dragon had just saved his life, and the wyvern's bones crunched between those jaws before the great draconi hurtled the body and its rider back to the sea.

Golden scales glimmered in the sunlight as the dragon banked, a rider positioned near the back of its head. It circled, approaching the Herald again as the rider maneuvered from his seat. Kin lost sight of him as the dragon slowed, flying past at a more careful pace so its rider could drop from its neck and land on the fore-deck.

Kin gaped as King Matthias Rayeht stood from a crouch, panting, his gaze scanning over the former Shade. "You were going to let it eat you?"

He glowered at the king, trying to get the tension in his muscles to relax as he looked Matthias up and down. Thick fur lined the shoulders of his riding leathers, a gilded sword secured to his back rather than his side, where an axe hung on buttoned straps. His windblown hair looked far messier than Kin had grown used to seeing, and it somehow helped remind him that he was not Uriel.

He ignored the question. "We need to get to the ruins. Before Jarac makes it in."

"What's the rush?" Matthias stalked closer, glancing at the dragon he'd ridden as the creature returned to the fray. "We can kill Jarac before he leaves with the knowledge."

Steps echoed on the stairs behind him, but he didn't turn as Deylan arrived beside him, the man glancing around the fore-deck. "How did you get here?"

"Dragon," Matthias murmured, as if it was all the explanation needed. He still looked at Kin. Waiting. "We have wards around this area. Even if Jarac tries to communicate with Uriel, or have Uriel see through him, it won't work."

"There's a bigger problem than him finding the prison." Kin looked back to the island, and the motion of the long boat now heading to its shore.

The king stiffened. "What could possibly be a bigger problem than him finding the prison?"

Kin looked to Deylan, still trying to control the instinct to run rather than convince Matthias to get them to the center of it all.

"There's a dagger beneath the ruins. An enchanted one, that... *theoretically* can choose a master. It's contained right now, by the faction, but if Jarac frees it... Even if it doesn't respond to him, it will reek unimaginable damage." Deylan's throat bobbed. "It's a bloodlust dagger, so even without a master..."

"Sounds lovely." Matthias's humor didn't reach his dry tone. "Why didn't you mention this before?"

Deylan lifted his hands. "Is that what you want to talk about right now?"

The king grunted. "Fair enough. Do you know where it is? The underground tunnels aren't exactly small."

Amarie's brother nodded. "I was part of the team that trapped it."

"Then let's make sure it stays that way." Matthias spun, lifting his finger and thumb to his mouth, and let out a sharp blast of a whistle. He eyed Kin. "You coming with us?"

Kin's mind buzzed as he considered how Matthias intended to get them to land. He started to turn to see if Andi would just take the ship towards land, but then spied the Feyorian ship that'd broken off from the rest of the fleet. It grew closer, and the Herald's crew was working to turn their own ship to face off with it.

They're going to be busy with their own battle.

Returning his hand to his sword, Kin worked quickly to wrap an extra strap of leather around the hilt to lock it in place. "Jarac's my blood. And I want to see his face when he realizes I'm still alive. I owe him for the last time we met." The scar on the side of his face tingled at the thought.

Matthias smirked, something beneath his gaze that wasn't there before. But his attention left Kin, as the drum beats of giant wings grew close. The golden dragon slowed above the Herald, lowering enough that the beast's head was within Matthias's reach.

The king grabbed the dangling straps of the saddle in a flurry of motion, pulling himself up without hesitation. Climbing to where he'd sat before, he shouted, "We're taking these two with us to shore, if you don't mind, my friend."

The dragon's throat rumbled as it flew a little higher, clawed hands reaching for Deylan and Kin. Claws that were coated in black blood like its maw. "I will try not to squish you." Another deep rumble came from its chest, but Kin couldn't tell if it was laughter or something more sinister. He tried to control his surprise at hearing it speak... Matthias had mentioned that the dragons allied with Isalica, but to witness their sapience first hand was something wholly different.

Kin could hardly breathe as the dragon's talons wrapped around him with such gentleness. Such care, that even the sharp tips of its claws didn't graze his skin. It distracted him so thoroughly that he didn't notice when they'd risen higher, leaving the ship behind and soaring for land.

"Nymaera's tits!" Deylan shouted from the dragon's other hand. The man had an arm wrapped around one of the dragon's fingers, his face blanched. His eyes closed a breath later, but Kin took in the view.

Below, Jarac's longboat sat beached on the rocky shore, void of its previous occupants.

He's already inside.

Kin tried not to dwell on it. They'd get there in time. Deylan had the advantage of knowing its exact location. They'd stop him from touching that dagger. They had to.

The feel of the wind rushing past him was far different from all the times he'd flown before. Without feathers and wings, he missed the ability to control how he hit the wind currents. He'd considered many times the things he actually missed about his power, and flying was the most prominent of them. Even though he'd avoided transforming into a raven when he first received the ability, now he longed for it again.

Knots tangled in his stomach at the sudden desire to accept the power again, just so he could soar among the clouds. Looking up at the sun glinting off of the dragon's scales, he marveled. Matthias had found another way to gain access to the sky, and he could only hope he might find an alternative way, too.

If I take the Feyor throne, I suppose I'll have access to their wyverns.

A strange thought. And perhaps the first one that *actually* made him consider accepting the role.

Banking to avoid the jaws of a corrupted, Kin clutched harder to the dragon's talons as his stomach lurched. But the golden dragon stayed the course towards the rocky beach as an emerald dragon swooped around them. Flesh and bone crunched as the other dragon's jaws tore apart their attacker. Kin glimpsed the two riders, recognizing Dani's white hair.

The golden draconi reached the shore a moment later, gracefully swooping down to deposit Deylan and Kin at the base of carved steps. They led up towards a pair of monoliths, runes like Damien's tattoos carved into their surface. Despite the joy he'd felt in the air, Kin's knees wobbled as he gained his footing.

Matthias slid from its neck, landing beside them as his dragon-friend returned to the sky. He smiled at Kin before eyeing Deylan and frowning. "Not your favorite means of travel, then?"

Deylan held up one finger before turning away, a hand against his gut.

The king cringed at Kin. "Should we get a head start?"

"No," Deylan ground out, his voice unsteady. "No. I'm good. I'm good. Just..." He sucked in a deep breath before blowing it out slowly. "I'm good. Let's go." Composing himself, Amarie's brother hurried up the steps.

As they entered the ruins, no structure was clearly discernible. Kin recognized the general layout, since it matched the sanctum he had spent months at when Damien had first severed the bond. But this one was in far worse condition. He'd wondered where in the hells they'd have fit the prison when he was first told about this place, but Matthias had said something about tunnels.

All the secrets must lay beneath the ground.

As they passed under a rough archway, the stone smoothed into carved walkways. They passed another pile of stone, all sense of direction lost as they rounded more broken structures. He could just make out the runes of the Rahn'ka upon the surface of a looming archway, and he knew with certainty he'd never seen this section of the sanctum in Olsa.

Descending steps, they entered the darkness of the underground tunnels. Deylan led them through the pathways, the glow from outside fading as they walked deeper. A single light source shone further within, flickering and casting shadows along the wall directly ahead.

A strange curved lantern hung on the wall beside another doorway, the shadows beyond it hidden deep from the sunlight. Within the shining silver lantern house, a faint blue flame burned, reminding Kin of Damien's power. It cast flickering light on the wall beside it, adorned with iron hooks hosting torches. Kin counted ten hangers, but only seven still held torches. Deylan took one, lighting it with the Rahn'ka-powered lantern

Matthias paused by the next hallway, listening, before he, too, took and lit a torch. "How far is it?"

Kin looked into the darkness ahead, contemplating taking a torch for himself. But he felt the need to have his hands free far more than a need for his own light. Darkness had never frightened him.

Deylan started forward, looking back at Matthias as he passed through the doorway. "Seven levels down."

"Seven?" Matthias followed, glancing at Kin. "We built the prison on the deepest level, but that was level five. There's nothing below that."

"I can see why you'd think that," Deylan muttered, keeping his voice lower now. "But you're wrong."

"That means Jarac will find the prison before the dagger." Kin looked between the other two men. "Do we know he'll keep looking instead of just turning around to report to Uriel?"

"He may not realize what the prison is. It doesn't exactly look like iron bars." Matthias shook his head. "Uriel would recognize it, but I doubt anyone else would. I'd bet he'll keep going."

Deylan hummed. "What *does* it look like?"

"You'll see, I suppose."

Their footsteps echoed softly against the stone walls and Kin watched the carved symbols as they passed them. Some were familiar, but others made this place entirely different from the sanctum in Olsa with Damien. He winced as he thought of the Rahn'ka, wondering at the progress with his recovery. Leaving had felt wrong, though Damien would ultimately understand because they were pursuing Ahria. And even if Damien had been responsible for so much manipulation, he'd done a lot for Kin at the same time.

Traveling between the two men, Kin looked back at Matthias and considered all he'd done, too. All that had been sacrificed to get to this point.

We may not be able to complete the spell to imprison him if even the smallest thing goes wrong.

"Did you hear about Damien?" Kin focused on the king, unsure what messages Deylan had sent. And despite all they rushed for now, it seemed imperative to tell him. They were friends, too, weren't they?

Matthias's expression turned grave as he nodded. "Not the details, but I know his life is hanging in a precarious balance." His shoulders drooped, if only minutely. "Has there been an update?"

"Not recently," Deylan murmured. "Last I heard, he was still holding on, but things weren't looking good."

The king's shoulders fell another inch, and he ran a hand through his hair.

Something in Deylan's pockets clicked, and he halted. Flipping open the strange communication device, Amarie's brother stared at the whirring dials.

Matthias looked at Kin but said nothing.

Kin tried to guess at what Matthias was saying to him in that silent moment. Considering Damien and everything they were working towards. It felt insane that he was standing where a prison for his old master had been built. That they were so close. Yet... so terribly far away now with Damien dying and Ahria captured.

And if Jarac figures out what this place is and sends word back to Uriel...

But that would be impossible. Kin trusted the wards Matthias said were in place. Jarac just couldn't escape from the ruins.

One pending disaster at a time, Kin.

Deylan blew out a breath, the sudden tension that had strained his body at the start of the message having faded. He closed the device and kept walking, only giving the other two a nod.

Matthias furrowed his brow, not following. "That's it? A nod? What was that message?"

Amarie's brother paused, turning to look back at them. His gaze lingered on Kin before meeting Matthias's. "Now isn't a great time. We need to be focused."

He means that I need to be focused.

"Is it about Ahria?" Kin took only a single step after Deylan, pausing at the edge of light from Matthias's torch. "Amarie?"

Deylan hesitated. "It was a more detailed report from Coltin about the events that transpired a couple weeks ago, and an update on Uriel's movements. I have no new information on either Amarie or Ahria, just that she'll be in Lungaz by now, and that Uriel survived the tower collapse. It looks like he is heading to Lungaz, himself, now, too."

It'd taken Kin days to shake the paranoia created by the knowledge that Amarie and Conrad had been so close to being caught by Uriel. And Deylan had needed to repeat the vague details provided by Coltin several times before Kin felt satisfied that Amarie was actually safe. Kin wished he could believe that the collapsed tower might have killed the master of Shades, but Uriel would survive it. Even if his body didn't.

It was the final detail Deylan gave that made Kin's body tense. Uriel pursued Amarie. But it didn't make sense...

"Uriel can't enter Lungaz," Matthias whispered, though the statement sounded more like a plea.

Deylan shrugged. "Conrad hasn't reported any updates, so we have to assume they're all right." He stared at Kin. "All you can do is help stop Jarac. Then we can worry about catching up to them."

Kin already planned on requesting Matthias's help for their return to Feyor. After weeks on a ship, he had no interest in taking another long trek by sea. Flying would be far faster.

One pending disaster at a time...

He focused on his own repeated thoughts as he nodded. If the plan to imprison Uriel failed for any reason, removing Jarac from the equation remained necessary. If they could wrestle Feyor back from Uriel, it would be a blow no matter what. Even if he had to rule to make it so.

Deylan continued his stride, and Matthias watched Kin for another moment before following.

Why does he keep looking at me like that?

They continued on in silence for a time, letting Deylan lead them through caverns and down stairs, the air growing thicker and more humid with each step. The dankness reminded Kin of the ruins where Trist had murdered Amarie, and he blinked away the image of her sightless eyes.

As they stepped down to the fifth level, Deylan lifted a hand and motioned for them to remain silent as they crept through the narrow tunnel.

How could they build a prison down here? We can barely fit through these halls.

Kin studied the dusty floor, marking each boot print left behind from Jarac's soldiers. They were denser on this level, as if they'd walked back and forth many times instead of just passing through like the other levels.

But no voices echoed through the stones as they approached an archway.

What lay within stole Kin's breath right out of his lungs.

The room—so much larger than he would have guessed this far beneath the ground—boasted a giant cube at the center, spanning at least twenty feet on all sides. The domed ceiling above boasted ten ancient stone buttresses that met at the center. The surface of the cube cast back fractals of their torches, dimly lighting the room around them. Peering at the dark surface, Kin saw himself in a pristine reflection, and a shiver passed down his spine.

Pure black obsidian, just like the dagger he'd used to kill Amarie. Smooth as a lake's surface, it gleamed, seeming to absorb all the sound in the room. Endless black, with no markings on any surface. No hint to its purpose.

Kin had never seen anything like it. And judging from the look on Deylan's face, neither had he.

Matthias gave them time to absorb the sight before quietly clearing his throat. "We should keep moving."

"Yeah..." Deylan struggled to follow the advice. "This is..."

"I know." The king placed a hand on Deylan's shoulder. "Show us how to get to the lower levels."

Amarie's brother snapped out of it, eyes clearing as he looked at the king and nodded. He continued down the hall, but Kin couldn't follow right away. He stared at the smooth surface of the prison, understanding its purpose as a strange, unfamiliar sensation passed through him. Trying to reconcile the feeling, he glanced behind him at Matthias. The king faced the direction Deylan had gone but was watching him. A brief nod confirmed he understood Kin's thoughts, even if he didn't himself.

This is where it will all end.

He wanted to touch the obsidian surface, despite the twisting of his stomach. But the sound of Deylan's steps halting tore Kin from his trance, encouraging him to turn to where Deylan's torch glowed inside a half-collapsed stairwell. Forcing himself away, Kin walked past Matthias in time to see Deylan wipe a hand over the wall beside the rubble, though the dust had already been cleared.

By Jarac.

How his twin brother knew, he could only guess.

Deylan touched five barely distinguishable divots in the stone, and spread his hand so his fingers and thumb each occupied one of the inset spots. Twisting his wrist, the spots moved with it, glowing with an orange hue.

The rubble before them vanished in a flicker like a mirage, exposing the stairwell clear of debris.

Matthias sighed. "How did Jarac know about this?"

"No idea." Deylan started the descent, shaking his head. "The illusion is tangible. We constructed it that way. Someone must have told him."

They fell silent again, tension rippling between them the further down they walked. Close, now. They passed the sixth level, which also bore a caved-in door, and Kin wondered if that one was false as well.

Deylan slowed once they reached the seventh level, though the stairs continued lower. The entrance archway to the seventh level boasted an iron door, already swung open. Amarie's brother drew his sword, quieting the rasp with a hand on his sheath.

They were distant, but voices echoed inside.

The three of them eased around the door, where light glimmered within. Bright—too bright for them to enter unnoticed. With their backs pressed to the wall, they inched closer, and Kin took in the room.

They entered at the top of what seemed to be a grand amphitheater. Ten feet ahead, the platform they stood on dropped five feet to the next level, then the next after another ten feet. Then the next. It went, like an inverse crescent-tiered cake, down at least seventy feet. At the bottom of the seating rows was a large, flat circle of packed dirt. And every seat in the half-wrapped arena would have a perfect view of whatever action took place upon it.

Around the top level, fire burned in a narrow trough running along the outer wall. It slanted down at the far wall where the tiered seating ended, dropping to then encircle the space at the bottom. The orange and yellow glared off a large, pale-blue mound positioned halfway up the side of the amphitheater, opposite where they stood. Gathered around the icy lump were ten men, armored and muttering to each other.

Behind them stood Jarac, his arms crossed and a deep enough frown on his face that Kin could make it out despite the distance.

Deylan inched forward, his chest rising faster as the men started mucking with the copper cylinders protruding from the ground surrounding the frozen chunk. "I have to stop them," he whispered, panic lacing his tone. "I have to warn them."

Kin considered the group of soldiers who severely outnumbered them. Nevermind that Jarac was also a Shade. "Maybe the dagger will kill them and then we can just retrap it?" He already knew the answer before Deylan started shaking his head.

"If they break those devices, there will be no retrapping it. Sephysis will kill us before we can even reach the stairs." Deylan opened his mouth again—to say what, Kin would never know, because before he could speak or shout, a crack reverberated through the room.

The men below bellowed, several diving to the stone ground as ice exploded. A small shape, impossible to make out the details of, gleamed fiery red as it rushed through the air, circling the debris of what had been its prison.

A loud click sounded somewhere in the room. And another.

Click.

Click.

The dagger surged towards Jarac's guard.

Deylan spun towards Kin and Matthias, eyes wide as he kept his voice low. "*Run.*"

Chapter 37

Click. Click. Click.

Rae leapt from her seat, staring at the machine keeping Damien alive. It whirred and clicked in a way it hadn't before, and panic scorched through her. "I need help in here!"

Two nurses rushed into the isolation room, wearing masks over their mouths and noses as they hurried to Damien's side. Another nurse entered and pulled Rae away from her husband.

He laid on the same device he had for weeks. Something like a table, supported by a single curved arch of metal that merged with the floor. A brace on one side clamped down over his wrist, keeping his right arm always in the same position. Another device curved up over his head, partially shielding him from her sight, with a tube flowing down his throat.

"What's happening?" Rae stared as they moved dials, levers, and injected something into the tube running into the cuff at Damien's wrist. They spoke in words she didn't understand, numbers and measurements. When no one answered her, she spoke louder. "Please! What's happening to him?"

The nurse who'd moved her out of the way glanced at her, his eyes solemn. "His heart is too weak. He isn't getting enough oxygen in his body."

Rae lifted her hand over her mouth, tears pricking at her eyes as she watched. Watched—because it was all she could do. Bellamy wasn't here yet, and she couldn't heal. She'd never damned her power more than she had the past weeks, unable to save him. To help him. To be anything other than useless.

She fell silent, trying to let them work. Let them keep him alive.

Just a little longer.

Wetness trailed down her face as she resisted the urge to reach for him. Touch him. "Stay with me," she whispered. "Please."

His face had healed from the bruising, but a bandage still wrapped around half of his head, obscuring the eye he'd never get back. Otherwise, he looked like he should have been alive. Should have sat up and kissed and held her. But his remaining eye stayed closed, and the tube in his throat still made his chest rise with breath.

Rae's back hit the wall as she stepped away, struggling to contain her sobs as they tried to stabilize him. Her hands shook over her mouth, and she closed her eyes.

Faster, Bellamy.

Chapter 38

Amarie's eyes hadn't returned to blue in days, mixed with the colors of the Berylian Key, despite the barren wasteland they'd entered a day ago. The shard they'd stolen never left her clenched fist.

The grey stone rolled like hills, the surface smoothed by the wind. The traveled paths through the terrain wore down into the rock, creating an easy crevice for them to follow.

Without the Art, he thought he wouldn't notice the shift of energy when they crossed Feyor's northern border, but his blood still stirred just enough to make him nauseous. The horses had reacted far worse. It'd taken them almost an hour to convince the animals to continue. And even after that, Amarie had to lead on foot for a while to put them at ease.

Or as close to at ease as possible.

As they cantered north, he glanced at Amarie. She held the reins with one hand, while the other held a fist. The shard glowed, subtly shining through her flesh.

Collecting my power, she'd said. *Using the shard to store it.*

She rode as though she'd traveled this route a hundred times, when the barren rocks had disoriented him five minutes in. But she had gone this way once before. To save Kin. She'd told him the story nights earlier by their campfire.

He wondered how many bad memories this journey dug up for her.

How many more it would create.

Conrad's chest squeezed as his mind drifted to Ahria. What state they may find her in. He did his best not to think too long or too deeply about her, for every time he did, his sanity slowly unwound.

Yet the images of Ahria, bruised and beaten, in front of him for trial kept coming in flashes.

Rubbing sweat from his forehead, he focused on the foreign terrain, spying a flicker of color above the crest of the ashen stone ahead. A bit of dark grey canvas billowed atop a flag post.

Amarie had either not seen it, or didn't care, because she kept the pace even as they neared the outpost. Their horses' hooves clattered on the stone, and Conrad's heart jumped into his stomach as he realized guards might have already heard them.

"Wait." Conrad didn't shout, hoping Amarie might still hear. Or at least notice when he urged his horse to stop. "We need to be strategic."

Amarie wheeled her horse around, slowing to a trot to circle back around behind him. "You're right," she panted. "If Alana is here, she's mine."

Conrad frowned. "That's not exactly a strategy. We're going to be outnumbered."

With a growl, she brought her horse to a halt next to him. "I've cleared this outpost before. I can do it again. I'll be the distraction. You just watch my back and if taking soldiers out makes you uncomfortable, don't worry. I'll do it." Her horse pawed the ground, mirroring her anxiousness to go.

"This is different from last time. If this is even the right outpost, they'll know we're coming. We can't help Ahria if we get killed just charging in."

They might even kill Ahria before we can get to her.

He sighed when Amarie just continued to glare. "Is there a second entrance into the outpost?"

"No." Amarie's horse shuffled beneath her, and finally, she sighed. "I don't know. Maybe. Jarac had his wyvern here last time, and I didn't see them near the front. There's probably a back entrance."

"Then we should split up. Divide their attention to give us both better odds—"

"No." She held his gaze. "We stick together where we can watch each others' backs. I'm not getting her back just to tell her you didn't make it."

He narrowed his eyes, swallowing the frustration.

Does she think I'm completely incompetent?

His face must have said it, because she shook her head. "It's not an insult. I'm sure you're adept with a blade, but separating puts us both at risk, and I'm—"

"It's fine." He waved a hand, trying to steady his tone. Looking ahead to the outcropping of stone that curved down, he gritted his teeth. "We should at least leave the horses here and try to maintain some stealth. If we go down into that area, any sentries will see us in seconds."

Amarie considered, following his gaze briefly before yielding a nod. "Fine." Dismounting, she held the reins. "These horses aren't going to stick around, though, and there's nothing to tie them to."

"At least they won't be collateral damage to the sentries' arrows." Conrad swung down from the saddle, plucking his bag from the ties. He tossed it to the side of the path as Amarie did the same. "Humor me with at least attempting to enter from the side rather than dead on?"

She stared at him instead of immediately arguing like he expected her to, and eventually nodded again. "All right. But I'll go first." Unbuckling her horse's bridle, she removed it and laid it next to her pack. Once released, the horse immediately turned and trotted south. "I hope they have horses to steal if this is the wrong outpost."

Conrad's horse lingered, casting a baleful glance as the other headed for Lungaz's border. He nosed Conrad in the chest as he removed his bridle. "Might get lucky with Fyfer." He watched as Amarie drew her sword. He stroked the horse's nose a final time before he did the same, the sun catching on the copper. The hilt of the new sword already felt natural in his hand, as if he had been meant to wield it. Looking ahead to the curve in the stone again, he waited to see the direction Amarie turned. It wasn't worth trying to argue with her further.

Reminds me of her daughter, so I shouldn't be surprised.

Amarie looked at him once more before angling around the outcropping to approach the outpost from the side. She kept to the hills of stone, following an invisible path as he trailed behind her.

He caught glimpses of the structure as they worked their way around the outer edge. The entire outpost seemed to be sunken into the ground, deep grooves carved in the stone to lead to doorways. The front entrance was the lowest, which would have given them some cover, but it was impossible to see if any guards stood there.

Amarie led them towards what looked to be a drop off, a deep incision in the landscape that served as a walkway between the main structure and some kind of outbuilding. Amarie angled towards a sunken walkway with a sharp curve in it, casting a wary glance at the south watchtower before she slid along the ashen ground and dropped down.

Conrad held his breath as he followed, knees barking as he landed roughly beside Amarie. Immediately pressing his back against the corner's wall, he waited as she positioned herself near the corner.

Subtle movement scuffled within, visible through the narrow cut windows just above the ground, but no voices.

Peeking around for only a second before straightening again, Amarie whispered to Conrad, "Two guards stationary. One patrolling away. He should be out of view in about ten seconds. Take the one on the right?"

She still breathed hard. He'd thought her breathlessness had been from the ride, but... Her eyes flared bright. Her power. It was the energy within her making her chest heave.

One hand still clenched that shard.

He nodded, counting down in his head. There wasn't time for him to question if she was all right. If it was safe for her to continue trying to channel her energy while they were in Lungaz.

She'd keep doing it, anyway.

A breath later, they moved in tandem.

Amarie bolted for the one on the left, and he centered his gaze on the other.

The guards' eyes widened in unison, mouths opening to shout a warning, but too slow.

Conrad spun his sword as he charged the guard on the right, bringing the pommel of it down hard on the soft spot between the armored pauldrons on the guard's neck. Before he could cry out, the prince whirled behind him, his arm catching the guard around the throat and he squeezed.

The man squirmed, and Conrad winced as his armored elbow caught him in the stomach. His grip loosened against his will, but his left hand flashed to his side as the guard turned. He shoved the faction dagger beneath the layers of armor, the metal plating pinching Conrad's wrist as he buried it at an angle into the guard's ribcage.

Wet heat trailed on to his fingers, and he doubted it would be the last blood on his hands that day, but he wished it hadn't been necessary.

"Move them." Amarie looped her arms under her limp target to drag him out of sight around the outpost entrance.

Conrad followed suit, dropping the guard where they'd been hiding before. When Amarie moved to return, he grabbed her arm. "Wait. The patrol." They both stilled, and in the quiet, sure enough, the soft footsteps of the third guard returned.

And then paused.

Amarie looked at him, and he read the question.

Attack right away and risk him getting away, or hope he approaches to inspect the scene and ambush him then.

Conrad lifted his hand to her. *Wait.*

The shuffle of the guard's footsteps resumed, but his gait seemed slower. More cautious. "Rendell?" His voice sounded young, making Conrad cringe for what would likely be coming.

Even when neither Amarie nor him offered a response, the footsteps continued to grow closer.

Amarie looked up, her jaw clenching as her throat bobbed. "Fuck," she whispered, so quiet he barely heard her. She waited another moment before leaping from behind the wall, Conrad surging with her.

With a surprised gasp, the guard lashed out with a halberd at Amarie, but Conrad had been ready. He caught the beak with his blade, twisting it downward. Kicking quickly, his foot contacted the shaft, and the weapon clattered to the ground.

Looking back to the guard, he stared at the wide eyed shock locked on Amarie rather than him.

The young soldier began to back away, but Amarie stepped around Conrad. Her fist hit the boy square in the chest, and a small ripple of violet light burst from her skin as the guard crumpled to the floor.

Amarie stood over him, then looked at Conrad and narrowed her eyes at the self-loathing for attacking a kid that must have been all over his face. "He's just unconscious."

He paused while she stalked ahead, crouching to confirm the soldier's breath fogged against his silver pauldron.

Amarie peeked around the next corner before motioning with her hand. "Bring him over here."

Obeying, Conrad sheathed his sword so he could scoop under the boy's armpits, dragging him to where Amarie directed as quietly as possible. Straining to listen down the hall as he deposited the unconscious soldier in a shallow supply room, Conrad marveled that they hadn't been detected yet. He could hardly believe how few guards were stationed.

Maybe this isn't the right outpost. There'd be more guards if Ahria were here.

There was no way Uriel would let her go easily.

Amarie closed the door to the supply room, and when she let go, the handle glowed for a second before fading. "This feels wrong," she whispered, eyeing the empty corridor ahead of them.

Ash colored boot prints dappled the ground, but no sign of the guards remained.

Conrad knelt, touching the disturbed dust. "It's like they left." His heart sank.

If Ahria was here, she might not be anymore.

Amarie walked ahead, jogging to the end of the walkway where it split in two directions. She looked both ways before facing Conrad with a shake of her head.

The quiet only further encouraged him to draw his sword again. Natural sunlight poured into the hall from narrow slits near the ceiling, eliminating the need for the unlit torches along the wall. If there hadn't been the three guards at the front, he might have thought the outpost abandoned.

Conrad looked both ways down the long hall. "Which way?" He looked to Amarie, reading the same thoughts he was having on her face.

Ahria's mother gestured with her chin. "This way."

With her leading, they maneuvered through the outpost with strange ease. Even with all the boot prints, they came across no other guards. No soldiers. No defenses.

They reached the top of a long staircase, carved into the stone and leading deeper beneath the ground.

Amarie's eyes were distant as they halted, listening. Her hands were steady, and she sheathed her sword, her other hand still gripping the shard. With her head angled towards the stairs, he couldn't see her face when a voice reached his ears.

Female. But not Ahria.

Alana?

His blood ran cold as he looked at Amarie, but only in part due to who must be at the bottom of those stairs. But the sight of Ahria's mother sent a shiver through his body.

Her power had... spread. Her eyes still glowed with energy, but it cracked and split through her eyelids, across her temples and the bridge of her nose. Like lava beneath parched desert ground in a strange, otherworldly mask.

His gaze shot to her hand, where shimmering light escaped between her fingers, the skin there also cracked and glowing.

Gods.

"I'll be back before dinner," the female's voice came again, and the simmering rage over Amarie's face told him all he needed to know. "Remember what we talked about."

Definitely Alana.

A wave of excited worry made his hand on his sword go numb. If Alana was present, it meant Ahria likely was as well. Somehow, they'd gotten lucky. She was imprisoned at the same outpost her father had been so many years ago, and with so few guards...

But that luck twisted in his stomach, daring him to think it might not be luck at all.

Amarie slowly straightened and descended the stairs. Both of her hands readied with power.

"How could I forget?" Ahria's voice nearly brought Conrad to his knees. "I'm your prisoner, remember?" The words said one thing, but her tone... It made Conrad's brow furrow. That tone didn't fit. It seemed almost—playful... But she was there. She was right there, at the bottom of those stairs, and the details no longer mattered.

Amarie strode down the last stairs as if she owned the outpost, slowing at the bottom and turning to face the voices as she stepped onto the landing that split into two different rooms.

Conrad started down the stairs behind her, crouching as he went to see beneath the ceiling of the room containing Ahria. The woman standing in the middle of the space looked so familiar, with those bright green eyes and midnight hair. Talon's sister, without a doubt. Her eyes were wide, dark stained lips parted in surprise as she stared at

Amarie. She didn't even seem to notice him, her shoe scuffing as she stepped back.

His gaze flicked to the middle cell as he moved to jump off the side of the steps to avoid Amarie all together.

Ahria's expression matched Alana's, and she stood from her bed, approaching the bars. But unlike her warden, she noticed him, and her brow upturned in the center. Her mouth moved in a silent plea. *Conrad.*

Amarie snarled and sparks danced at her fingers as she stared at the auer. Deadly calm radiated from her as she stepped off the landing towards Alana.

Chapter 39

Matthias turned to obey Deylan's order to run, but when Amarie's brother didn't follow, he hesitated. "What are you doing?"

Screams and shouts echoed from lower in the amphitheater, but he tried to block out the sounds.

"I need to contain it." Deylan shook his head. "This is my job. The failsafe will kick in any second now to slow it down. But you should go, both of you." He gestured between him and Kin.

Click.

The king still hesitated. Containing powers like this may be the faction's duty, more or less, but it still occupied Isalica's land. His land. And as much as the dagger was Deylan's responsibility, he had an obligation to his country to see that the weapon didn't escape to wreak havoc on his people.

Shadows lashed into existence lower in the amphitheater, but the Shade's Art did nothing to stop the dagger from killing the soldiers. The onyx power only protected its wielder, wrapping around Jarac like thick layers of a cloak. They twisted, hardening into a carapace as the dagger lunged. It pinged as it struck the surface bubbling up over the king of Feyor. But Sephysis, undeterred, spun back upon the soldiers. Crimson splattered through the air with the glimmer of steel, another soldier collapsing with a cry of pain.

Click.

Matthias's heart skipped a beat at that sound, breath catching in his throat as it came again. The blackness formed a smooth cocoon around the Shade, and he gritted his teeth.

Click.

"I could jump," the king offered with a strained voice, making Deylan pause partway down the stairs.

Deylan held up a hand, eyes narrowing on him. "Not yet. We wouldn't have made it in time to stop them anyway. Save it for if I really need you to."

He heard those unspoken words and nodded, even though his head screamed.

Click.

Matthias groaned, images flashing across his mind of his knee pressed to Amarie's chest. Hurting her, bloodlust in his veins from killing all those faction members in Hoult.

Click.

A pressure closed on his shoulder, and Matthias whirled, catching himself before slamming a surprised fist into Kin's concerned face.

"You all right?" Kin pulled back, examining him up and down. "What's wrong?"

Click. Click.

Memories cascaded through him of the Art-laden devices that trapped him... Trapped Uriel within a bubble temporarily. Sounds below faded to murmurs, like he'd descended beneath the surface of a lake. His heart pounded in his ears, and he reached for something, finding rough rock to brace himself against as that sound, that energy, pressed over his skin.

Kin stepped closer, holding his hands out as if he expected Matthias to attack him. "Take deep breaths. You look like you want to kill something."

"Amarie," Matthias whispered, his voice raspier than usual as he found Kin's face and then his own arms. The ink. The ink that *he'd* put there, not Uriel. "I... *He* tried to kill her. That sound..."

Click. Click. Click.

The king closed his eyes, feeling the rock under his palm, the handle of his axe in his other.

The Art energy that had been building within the chamber snapped, and he breathed a sigh of relief. The damn clicking finally stopped.

Kin threw a look behind him, and Matthias forced his body to turn.

Reaching the level where shattered ice still coated the steps, Deylan lifted his sword to catch an attacking Feyorian, and the sound of metal clashing rang through the room. They both were forced to duck as the dagger, now moving slower through the air, rushed over them. It turned sharply, pivoting back to where Jarac had been covered in shadow.

The Shade's power had fallen away, wriggling at his feet. He stepped out of the weapon's path, and it began a lazy loop up and around like a circling hawk.

Another soldier moved in towards Deylan, sword raised.

"We have to help him," Matthias breathed, straightening as he caught his breath. His bearings. He freed his axe from his belt, descending the stairs towards the chaos. Shaking his head, he tried to clear it of the visions. The past that clung to him, still haunting him whenever it could gain purchase. It'd been years since he'd experienced one of those flashbacks, but he couldn't let it win.

But as he raced to help Deylan, boot steps thudded from above. He turned, eyes widening at the dark steel armored soldiers at the top of the stairs, swords drawn.

More Feyorians.

Matthias swore. He counted the soldiers still standing around the Shade, and then the ones up top. Too many. They wouldn't stand a chance against almost two dozen.

If he could go back, stop the dagger from being unleashed somehow...

Kin pushed ahead of him, swinging his blade up just in time to catch that of the second Feyorian attacking Deylan. But Matthias blocked out the sound of clashing steel as he focused on the power in his chest.

The Art scorched into him, and he pulled on the threads of time. But, something felt different. Wrong. Something was... wrong. But he couldn't stop it. Time blurred. Forward. Faster.

Instead of watching himself and Kin ascend the stairs backwards, they continued forward. Kin caught the blade of a soldier, pushing him back and kicking him in the gut. But his actions were fast. Far faster than they should have been as if time swelled forward at double its usual speed.

The Art-propelled blade darted through the air, traveling the outer wall of the amphitheater in seconds before circling back at them on its own accord. It spun as it flew, light flickering off its onyx handle and blood-red blade. It soared along the curve of the amphitheater back towards him and Kin, glinting.

Yet, the weapon slowed, considering the former Shade. It left Kin, banking towards those still near where it'd been trapped.

Deylan jumped sideways, shouting as Sephysis grazed his shoulder, which was lucky considering it'd been aimed at the back of his neck.

The blade twitched through the air before arcing towards Matthias faster than he could comprehend.

Kin whirled towards them, exposing his back to the soldiers as he yelled, "No!"

As time staggered to a stop, Matthias gasped, unable to breathe as the tip of the dagger halted an inch from his chest. It hovered, obeying.

Obeying.

Time yanked backward.

The events reversed, crashing to a halt at the original moment he'd tried to jump.

What the hells...

Matthias looked at Kin, hardly able to believe what he'd just seen. The former Shade had pushed back a soldier, kicking him hard in the gut, just as Matthias had seen in fast motion a moment before.

"Command the dagger," he said to the former Shade. "It will listen to you."

"What?" Kin paused before he lunged, and the soldier attempted a wide slash, but Deylan caught it this time, the soldier he'd been fighting now bleeding out across the stone.

"No time to explain." Matthias faced their opponents at the top of the stairs, axe ready. "Command it!"

The dagger had finished its loop, rushing past Jarac, who started up the stairs and waved his sword in command to the new group of soldiers. The red blade gleamed with blood as it angled towards Kin, intent somehow palpable.

Kin furrowed his brow, but turned towards the dagger, straightening his spine. He looked ready to dive to the ground as he lifted his free hand. "Stop!" The word rang through the hall but didn't seem to deter the blade's intention.

Sephysis flew at Kin's chest, ignoring the command.

Matthias stared, breathing hard as he replayed the previous time in his mind. What he'd seen.

But Kin held his ground, obviously trusting whatever Matthias had seen even as he began to question it. The king prepared to jump again, praying it would work this time.

He braced to watch Kin's death before the blood-coated dagger jerked to a halt. It tilted up, as if examining the former Shade.

Command it.

Matthias gulped, eyeing the advancing soldiers from above but kept his attention on Kin and Sephysis.

Kin stared, the look on his face the same Matthias remembered from when he'd been forced to train in combat when first made a

Shade. A quiet determination that came before his stubborn refusal of defeat. Something like a shiver seemed to pass through the weapon and it floated closer to Kin's face, gleaming tip almost touching his eye.

But Kin held still, his empty hand flexing as he lifted it. His finger grazed the black hilt, and Sephysis gave another shiver, dipping down.

It twirled before darting away.

Amarie's brother jumped sideways as the blade grazed his shoulder, his attention remaining on the soldiers he fought.

"Command it," Matthias murmured, finally facing the descending soldiers. He spun his axe, and gave them a wicked grin.

The first soldier faltered at that, just a moment of hesitation that gave Matthias the opening to lunge. His axe sank into the man's chest, ripping a bellow from him before the king moved to the next.

An impossible fight, against so many, and without confidence in his ability to jump...

The firelight around the edge of the room flickered against the dagger as it whizzed past Matthias's head, close enough to cast a breeze through his hair. The red dart dove into the neck of a soldier as he lifted his sword, ready to slam it down into Matthias. The man choked, a bleeding mess of torn flesh all that remained beneath the edge of his armor. Flashes continued through the line of soldiers like they were panes of glass. Blood coated the stairs as the men still standing leapt to the side to get out of Sephysis's path.

As they fell, Jarac scrambled towards the doorway they'd entered from.

Matthias hadn't noticed them before, but on either side of the door were runed copper cylinders. The air above them shimmered, as if they were casting a web across the doorway. It created the same gold shimmer like the bubble Uriel had become trapped in at Hoult, and the surface of it extended up along the domed ceiling of the amphitheater, coating the entire space in the protective shield of the faction.

The failsafe.

The faction device must be affecting his Art, too. He's going to destroy it.

Matthias's blood surged as he angled towards Deylan to shout a warning.

But Amarie's brother was already on it, charging for the Shade without a second of hesitation. Copper sword raised, he deflected a soldier's attack as he took the stairs two at a time.

Jarac slammed into a copper cylinder a breath later with his entire body, crashing it to the floor.

The golden hue surrounding them all flickered and disappeared.

Deylan reached Jarac, but the Shade's power erupted from the stone, from the crevices, and launched at him, colliding with the copper blade. He held strong, maneuvering the runed weapon to cut through the shadow, slicing his way closer. White hot cracks appeared in the viper-like shadows. Lines carved into them by the Art-laden sword.

But a tendril behind him whipped along the stone, knocking his feet out from under him. His sword skittered across the floor as he landed on his back with a grunt.

Matthias took the stairs two at a time, trying to reach Deylan. He didn't want to attempt a jump, just in case the power didn't work as expected again.

Twenty more stairs. Eighteen. Sixteen.

Deylan rolled out of the way as Jarac lashed with onyx tendrils from above, but one struck his back and he shouted.

Matthias glanced behind him to where Kin stood.

Sephysis's blur whizzed along the lower levels faster than before, clearing the space with gruesome efficiency.

Efficiency that should be used on the king of Feyor.

"Kin!" Matthias's shout drew Jarac's attention. As if the Shade, Feyor's king, finally realized who stood in the room.

Chapter 40

Chaos roared in Kin's ears, a strange new hum pulsing through every inch of his body. Sephysis's touch had been like a thunderstorm. The moment his finger had grazed the hilt, something buried blazed to life. The familiar tingle of the Art within him awoke, but this time it didn't burn in his arm. Instead, the Shade mark numbed, and something in his core sizzled to life with each movement of the dagger.

It's so hungry.

He could sense it within the metal. Its desperation to plunge into each new victim. And he felt it. Felt the blood roiling within him as if he was the one pushing the metal into flesh. He knew death. But this was different. It came with a strange calm. A certainty that it was meant to be this way.

It conjured images of Trist's blood on his hands. The sound his sword made as it pierced her chest. He'd been calm, then. Not anxious and wild like some of the other times he'd killed. And Sephysis felt just that as it tore through the line of soldiers, clearing the entire midsection and lower level. And with each kill, a growing elation.

An almost giddy energy passed up Kin's arm as something in the room changed. The gold sheen surrounding the amphitheater like a curtain subsided. And Sephysis cheered.

Matthias shouted his name.

Blinking from the foreign reverie in his mind, Kin tried to focus on the king. He ran, faster than Kin thought possible, up the stairs.

At the top, Deylan was on the ground, darkness engulfing him.

And Jarac. His face was cruel as he stood near the doorway, the copper cylinder that'd held the barrier together broken at his feet. He outstretched his hand to Deylan, sleeve pushed up to expose the tattoo on his right forearm. The twist of geometric shapes on his skin made Kin's stomach churn, and Sephysis responded.

The dagger swung wide, spinning in the air like a discus as it looped to the upper level towards Jarac as Kin hopped up to the next level, avoiding the blood-coated stairs. The blade sailed past Matthias, narrowly avoiding him as it angled for the Shade.

It sliced through the long tendrils as if they were nothing more than grass, red cracks of power radiating up through the blackness that had pinned Deylan. A bestial whine radiated through the shadows as Sephysis turned and passed through them again, forcing Jarac further down the curve of the upper level.

Matthias rushed for Deylan, who pulled himself across the floor on his stomach towards his sword. The wound on the man's shoulder soaked his sleeve, and the back of his shirt bore burns that undoubtedly reached his skin. The king looped an arm under him, hoisting him up.

Kin cleared the final rise to the top level of the amphitheater, the heat of the fire still lighting the giant chamber warming his face. He tugged on the current of energy inside him again, not unlike what he used to do when controlling the shadows. And Sephysis responded. Though a bit more reluctantly than his Art ever had.

The cold hilt of the blade pressed into his hand. He looked down at the blood dripping down the red steel, filling the carved runes. The color grew richer, even as he looked at it. The wetness faded, as if the runes consumed just as the blade begged. With each lick of the steel, something pulsed up Kin's left arm from where he held it. Radiating the same desires into him.

Bracing himself, Kin tackled the sensation. The greed and hunger. He recognized the desire, but told it no. Told it to wait.

The time will come.

The dagger sighed in his mind, but obeyed. It quivered in his palm, but allowed him to hold it as he met the glare of his brother.

Shadow wriggled around Jarac's shoulders like a demented cape.

"Give me the blade." Jarac stepped forward, a web of darkness washing out from his feet. It passed along the stone towards Kin, and he resisted the instinct to step back from it. He knew the burn of a Shade's Art. But with Sephysis in hand, he refused.

"You'll have to take it from my corpse if you want it." Kin advanced, daring his brother. And Jarac took the dare.

Shadow swelled up from the ground, corporeal as it moved in a wave directly at Kin.

With a whisper of a thought into the blade, Kin swung Sephysis in an arc in front of him, releasing his grip at his side. The blade continued, curving around him like a personal cyclone as it tore through the Shade's power. The tendrils ruptured, like shattering blown glass. Red sparks ebbed along the edges, radiating lines coursing down into those still remaining on the ground.

The gleam of Sephysis's blade flashed past Kin's vision again and again as it spun, continuing around him in a whirlwind.

Each new tendril that lanced at Kin was met by Sephysis, steadily increasing in speed.

"I suppose I shouldn't be surprised to see you alive," Jarac ground out, face contorted with the effort of controlling his shadows to fend off the bloodstone blade. "Damn cockroach for a brother."

Kin walked calmly closer, unfazed by the war of shadows wreathed around him. The dagger kept them from touching him, moving with such speed that no inky blackness even brushed his shoulders. "Everyone is a cockroach to you. Your kingdom, your people. You step on them like they're nothing at all."

Jarac lifted his chin. "A king doesn't need insects." He waved a hand, summoning a new wave of darkness from the ground.

Sephysis dropped like a stone, slamming into the ground with rays of crimson lightning breaking through the onyx. It flaked into the air in puffs of ash.

"You *had* a kingdom, yet you still choose to give in to Uriel. You're a fool, Brother. You've only grown more idiotic since you interrogated me in Lungaz. And now you've destroyed the one thing you should have protected."

Jarac sneered. "Uriel was just a means to further greatness. He doesn't control me."

Doubt in his brother's eyes hinted that he didn't believe his own words. That he already knew they were lies. And the look turned into a cringe as Kin laughed.

"See... a fool." Kin gestured to the shadows, now stilled around them. Waiting as if they expected the dagger to do something more as it remained motionless, blade partially embedded into the ground. "You know I won't let you leave here, Brother. This is the end for you. You'll never get to see what I do to save *my* kingdom."

The words lit a raging fire in Jarac's face, his sneer turning into a scream. A sword materialized from the shadows at his side, snakes of darkness shooting for Kin.

The former Shade pivoted, catching his brother's sword on his own as Sephysis ripped from the ground. It whipped up and around Kin's shoulder, tearing through the shadow that dared lance towards its master's back.

Jarac bore down on him, forcing Kin back several steps, and each time, red cracks banished the Shade's power, like a miniature storm followed Sephysis.

Kin's boot connected with Jarac's knee, and he fell, hitting the ground hard. A flash of red light lanced through the air around the dagger as it dropped, landing in Kin's hand as he forced it to wait just a little longer. Sephysis wanted more blood. And looking at Jarac's throat, even he craved to see it spilled.

A kernel of guilt nestled in his chest.

He's still my brother. Even with everything he has done.

"The dagger never would have chosen you." Kin squeezed the hilt tighter, the metal pinching into his skin. "Uriel sent you on a fool's errand."

"It doesn't matter. You'll all die. The end is coming." Jarac fell back onto his hands, crawling backwards from his twin. He looked so much older, deep creases around his eyes and forehead. He kicked at Kin's feet as the former Shade approached, grasping the fire-filled stone trough to get to his feet.

As he spun, spikes of shadow ruptured from his fingers. Like a thousand arrows, they coated the air.

Sephysis twitched in his hand, even before he could beckon it. It moved his arm for him, and his fingers fell away as the bloodstone dagger swung in a wild circle in front of him. Black worms fell to the ground, and the blade would wait no longer.

It twisted in the air and shot forward, so fast that Kin could barely see it.

Lightning tore through the armored shadows Jarac threw up in desperation, but they fell apart like paper in water. Crimson metal found its mark with a satisfying squelch.

Jarac's eyes widened as he looked down at the black hilt protruding from his chest. He reached for it, but it ripped free before his fingers could even graze its surface. Gliding lazily, Sephysis, satiated and finally content, returned to Kin's hand as the king of Feyor fell.

Silence settled through the chamber, broken only by rapid breathing.

Soft footsteps at Kin's side barely registered before a hand gently closed on his shoulder. "Kin…"

He caught himself before he spun, a jolting excitement for more pulsing briefly in Sephysis but quickly fading as Kin took in his friend's face. The face that had haunted so many of his nightmares, but now felt so welcome.

"Are you all right?" Matthias tilted his head, studying him.

"Fine," Kin lied, lifting the dagger to stare at it. It now appeared far more innocent than the wicked power that'd flown around the room. Killed every last Feyorian soldier without regard.

The Isalican king gave the dagger a wary look. "Can you control it?"

Kin read the underlying question in his gaze.

Do we need to lock it up again?

Sephysis quivered in disapproval.

"Yes." He hadn't fully believed it until it came out so certainly. Something in the webs of power further confirmed it. The dagger *wanted* him to control it. It wanted to have a master rather than roam free. But not just a master. A partner. Someone it would obey, but also influence and negotiate with.

"You're a lucky son of a bitch, you know that?" Deylan rasped, cringing.

Matthias glanced towards Amarie's brother before whispering to Kin, "He needs a healer."

Dark rotted skin poked out near Deylan's collar, where it had crept up his neck. But he supported himself on a stone bench, face pained.

Kin followed Deylan's gaze to the blade in his hand. "Lucky is one way of putting it. Though I think those old texts you mentioned were a little off."

Deylan groaned and bowed his head, breathing ragged.

"We can discuss this later," Matthias gave Kin a half-hearted smile, patting his shoulder. "We need to return to the Herald. See if they need any help out there."

Kin surveyed the amphitheater and the thick layer of carnage that now coated it. His chest tightened and Sephysis purred. "We got all of them, right? None made it out?" Just because Jarac lay dead didn't mean none of the soldiers would report to Uriel. Explain what they saw. Even if they didn't know *what* they saw, Uriel could recognize the prison if described.

"There were no tracks leading out when we entered, and no one escaped while we fought." Matthias shook his head. "The second group that arrived may have sent someone back to report. We will be able to tell as we leave, if there are tracks."

"Good." Kin moved towards Deylan, pausing to eye Sephysis before tucking the dagger into the back of his belt. It seemed less pleased about the position, but quickly quieted so Kin could focus on hoisting Deylan to his feet. "Hang in there. We'll get you to Lygen." And hopefully the half-auer Artisan on the Herald would be able to heal the necrotic wounds.

Matthias retrieved Deylan's copper sword before surveying the carnage, eyes landing lastly on Jarac before he offered Kin a grim smile. "We have a lot to figure out. We can talk on the way to Feyor."

Chapter 41

Ahria gaped at her mother, hardly able to believe the sight.

She'd somehow accessed her power in Lungaz. She'd managed what Talon had always said was impossible. Yet, here she was, eyes glittering with shades of beryl and purple. Conrad at her side, copper faction sword in hand.

Violet cracks spread from Amarie's eyes, creating a mask of energy glowing from within... from *under* her skin. It mirrored the power sparking at her hands, barely contained, though her left fist glowed the brightest.

And her deadly gaze was focused on Alana.

Fear leapt into Ahria's throat.

She's going to kill her.

Her mother wouldn't waste time with speeches. With last words. She would strike and strike hard, especially with her daughter seemingly locked in a cell. And Conrad looked poised to go around the confrontation to reach her.

Ahria jolted for the cell door, shoving it open as power sizzled in the air. It crawled across her skin like lightning ants, standing every hair on end as she rushed forward.

Amarie pulled her hand back, preparing the strike, while Alana merely lowered her chin. Ready to take it. To accept her fate, despite Ahria begging her not to earlier that day. They'd theorized during their breakfast together what might occur in this exact situation, and now it was happening.

Alana had confessed to her that Amarie had been spotted in Jaspa, which confirmed what Ahria had believed. That her mother would come for her. But Amarie's presence, paired with the orders Uriel had sent to the outpost, didn't bode well for Alana.

The soldiers had been called away for a training exercise, and their replacements delayed... It all raised flags. Flags that suggested Uriel's intention to take advantage of Amarie's predictable desire to kill Alana, and the auer would be defenseless in the wasteland outpost without her Art.

Sliding to a stop on the ash-stone ground, Ahria turned her back to her aunt and faced her mother with her hands extended. "No, don't!"

A single breath had Amarie's power dimming, but not disappearing as she only stared at Alana. "Get out of the way." Her voice was breathless, intent, as if she hadn't even noticed her daughter no longer stood within the cell.

Conrad approached, hand outstretched to her. "Ahria." She read fear in his expression, his eyes flicking back to Amarie and then Alana. "What are you doing?"

Behind her, Alana held still.

Ahria shook her head. "Look at me," she murmured to Conrad, and then louder towards Amarie. "Look at me!" She waited until her mother's fiery gaze finally landed on her and motioned to herself. "I'm not hurt. I'm not starved." She gestured to her cell. "Look at all my pillows! The door wasn't even locked."

Amarie, at first, didn't blink. But when stillness prevailed for another minute, she tore her gaze away and eyed the cell. Eyed the length of her daughter's body. Her throat bobbed. "She's manipulating you. This whole thing. She *killed* your *father*."

"She didn't know about Talon," Ahria pleaded, stepping forward. "This whole thing is a setup. Uriel knew you'd come, why do you think he cleared out the guards?"

Amarie straightened, glancing at Conrad. Her hands lowered, but that fist remained white-knuckled.

Conrad shrugged without relaxing his sword arm. "It's possible. He knew we were heading this way." He looked back to the stairs, a thought seeming to hang on his pursed lips. Then he looked back at Amarie. "It was too easy to get in here. It could be true."

"It *is* true," Ahria pressed.

"Even if it is," Amarie hissed. "She still deserves to die." Her hands shook, though whether it was from power or nerves, Ahria couldn't tell.

Ahria took another step closer to her mother, casting a pleading look to Conrad. "Please, just listen. Please."

Amarie's shoulders relaxed minutely, power diminishing from her hands as she blinked at Ahria. She breathed hard, then advanced and pulled Ahria into a tight embrace.

Ahria sighed, closing her eyes and hugging her mother back. "I knew you'd come for me," she whispered.

Conrad moved in behind them, taking a position between Ahria and Alana, and the auer's shoes whispered against the floor as she stepped back. His hand grazed Ahria's waist, applying a gentle pressure as she let go of her mother. "We need to go. Uriel was behind us all the way to the border of Lungaz. He'll send troops in, even if he can't come himself."

"You don't have all the information." Alana spoke softly, and Amarie tensed as she stepped around her daughter. "Ahria may have convinced you not to kill me as Uriel may have intended, but he won't just let you all go. Especially if he has all pieces of the Key in one place."

Ahria touched Conrad's chest, heat burning the back of her eyes as she leaned into him, savoring his warmth and scent as his arms looped around her. "Uriel can enter Lungaz."

Amarie's gaze darted to her, then back to Alana. Nothing but air occupied the space between them now. "How?"

"Much the same way you've learned to use your power here." Alana motioned to Amarie's hand. "Uriel forged his own shard out of one of yours."

Looking at Conrad again, Amarie's face paled. "We need to go."

"She's coming with us." Ahria stared at her mother. "Alana is my aunt and she's coming with us."

"Ahria..." Amarie warned.

"She's our best chance against him. I trust her." Ahria hardened her tone. "And that needs to be enough."

Conrad, with his arm still around her, looked at Amarie. "She didn't need to warn us." He looked at Alana, who stood perfectly still, her hands folded together in front of her hips. "Better to just go."

"Fine," Amarie said between clenched teeth, looking at Alana. "Don't make us regret this." She turned her back to the auer, and they all started for the stairs.

Ahria blinked against the bright, overcast sky, but welcomed the fresh breeze on her face. She'd spent plenty of time in the upper levels of the outpost, but this felt like a new kind of freedom. She looked behind her at Alana, who gave her a slight, grateful smile.

Amarie and Conrad checked every passage before they rounded corners, but each time, the corridors were empty.

"Where is Kin?" Ahria told herself she used his given name for clarity's sake, but the truth... This wasn't the time she wanted to remember as the first time she'd called him her dad. For that, she wanted him to hear it.

Amarie whipped around, wide-eyed, looking between her and Alana.

"It's all right. She knows he's alive." Ahria grimaced, but then forced a sheepish smile. "She was relieved to hear it."

"Lovely for her," Amarie breathed. "He's... detained with your Uncle Deylan. They're looking for..." She eyed the auer, then sighed. "For Kin's brother. But it's very important, and it was a difficult decision. He wanted to be here."

"Does he know what Jarac was pursuing?" Slight concern colored Alana's tone.

Amarie's face still simmered with power, the cracks in her skin still glowing, though it didn't lash out at the auer. "Yes. But we don't know why. Do you?"

Conrad cleared the next corner for them, and they entered the last corridor before the main entryway to the outpost.

"This is hardly the time." Alana paused before clearing her throat as if apologizing. "I'll tell you, but we should get away from here first."

Nothing showed on Amarie's face as she turned away, nearing the entrance arch, and then halted as she rounded the final corner.

Ahria's steps slowed as she, too, came into view of their exit.

Or what should have been.

But instead of open stone hills beyond the doorway, an entire troop of Feyorian soldiers stood waiting for them, weapons drawn. There were so many, at least fifty men. Their dark armor stood out against the pale stone, their front line curved to prohibit any of them from attempting to slip through. More lined up behind. It should have been far too many for only four of them, but Uriel seemed to be taking no chances.

Ahria's heart picked up speed.

Is Uriel already here?

But she didn't see him within the ranks, didn't see that wicked face that had haunted her dreams since those sleepless days and nights in her previous cell.

Ahria gaped as Amarie resumed her stride, approaching the waiting army. She wanted to call to her, tell her to run. They could find another exit, couldn't they? But her mother still gripped that shard in her fist, her power still blazing through her. She must have summoned more of it, because the cracks that marred her face spread from her hands, then up her forearms.

Conrad stepped back, closer to Ahria, as they all watched the Berylian Key advance on the soldiers.

"You have one chance to alter your fate," Amarie murmured, stopping ten feet from the closest soldier. "Leave now if you wish to live."

No one moved.

Not a single soldier took a step away, and Ahria's heart sank. She couldn't decide if they were brave or foolish.

Six soldiers in the front—three on either side—raised crossbows, bolts loaded and aimed at her mother. The six in the middle kept their swords raised as a soldier with a more decorative helmet stepped forward.

"Loose!" The commander shouted the order, and the bolts flew.

Ahria's stomach lurched into her throat, but the bolts disintegrated to ash with a gesture from Amarie. The air hovered with a thick dust, sparks of purple and blue dancing between them before the Lungaz breeze swept it all away.

Yet, the soldiers didn't balk.

Foolish, then.

"Charge!" The commander's voice boomed through the air, and the unit moved as one. Sights set on Amarie, they lunged at her.

She waited one second. Two. And then unleashed herself.

Blinding violet light erupted from her as the closest soldier lifted his sword to bring it crashing down on Amarie's head. But everything froze as power blasted over the soldiers like a wave of lightning. It tore through them, their bones visible through exposed flesh for a brief moment before Ahria shielded her face from the brightness.

Her mother shouted, but she couldn't look, hair whipped back from her face as the air itself exploded.

Conrad yanked her behind him, holding her tight as the power unfurled with incredible ferocity.

The silence that followed thrummed in her ears, only her heart beat breaking through the quiet.

Ahria opened her eyes, hand covering her mouth as she took in the remnants of the army.

Nothing.

There was nothing left of them beyond a mist of blood in the air. On the ground.

Amarie bent over at the center, gripping her left wrist as she fell to a knee and let out another cry.

Ahria drew a shaky breath and rushed to her, gasping at the carnage of her left hand.

The hand that had held the shard. The crystal had... shattered. Ruptured. And every piece of it embedded into Amarie's hand, some protruding all the way through to the other side. Blood ran down her forearm, dripped from her fingers, and pooled in her palm.

Amarie only stared at it, her face finally devoid of the Key's power.

Conrad dropped to the ground beside Ahria, reaching for Amarie's hand without hesitation. He moved fast, ignoring her cries as he tore shards of blackened crystal from her wounds. Slivers remained, and after several attempts to grab at them, he resigned to wiping his bloody fingers on his pants. "We'll need the packs to get the rest." He looked out across the ashen terrain, now tinted red for twenty yards.

Still shaking, Amarie stood. "I... I can't access my power anymore."

Ahria watched the horizon, noting flickers of movement. "Conrad."

"We need something to wrap this." Conrad looked at Alana as she joined them, the auer offering the gossamer scarf that'd wrapped lightly around her throat.

She deposited the soft blue material into Conrad's hands.

"Conrad," Ahria whispered again.

Conrad nodded. "This should staunch the bleeding." He made quick work, wrapping it around Amarie's hand as her mother hissed.

More movement. Widespread, across too much of the horizon.

"Conrad!" Ahria barked. "Look!"

They all lifted their chins and obeyed, gazing southwest over the low slung ridge ahead.

Hundreds. There had to be hundreds of soldiers approaching. And a man on a horse led them, black cloak billowing behind him. His pale grey hair blended into the stone behind him, but even at the distance, the gold flecks in his eyes seemed to gleam.

Uriel.

Amarie swore, tucking her makeshift bandage in tighter and standing with Conrad.

They were defenseless. Beyond defenseless, with Uriel having access to his Art. He could wipe them off the face of Pantracia with little more than a thought.

"We need to get to the coast," Amarie breathed. "I need access."

Conrad moved first, turning sharply to survey a possible escape. He looked back to Ahria, the fear she'd seen before far more prominent. "We have to pray we can lose them in the terrain."

"Go north first." Alana looked oddly calm, lifting her hands to pull the dark strands of her hair back behind her head. "Then cut east when you reach the spires. It'll be easier to stay hidden among the canyons."

"You're coming with us." Ahria stared at her aunt. "You need to come with us."

Alana gave her a gentle smile, twisting knots into her raven locks. "No. I will do what I can to slow him from following." She gracefully snatched a short knife from inside her boot, slicing along her skirt with a smooth motion. It freed her legs of the fabric, revealing fitted leggings beneath.

"He'll kill you." Ahria reached for her.

"Yes." Alana took her hand and squeezed. She looked at Amarie. "The dagger, Sephysis, is for Melyza, in Kiek. She has information he seeks."

Amarie only nodded. "Thank you."

Ahria threw herself forward, wrapping her arms around Alana. She had no words, nothing that would ease the tightness in her throat.

"Don't mourn for me." Alana touched lightly under Ahria's chin, lifting it to meet her eyes. "This is my penance. All I need is your forgiveness."

Ahria's chin quivered. "I forgive you. All of it. And Talon will, too."

Alana's smile deepened. "I will tell him about the woman you've become." She gently pushed Ahria back, nodding. "It's time for you to go. All of you. Run, and don't look back."

Chapter 42

Fire lanced along Amarie's hand, but not the flames she commanded. No, these were shards of agony ripping through her, radiating with each tiny bit of the shattered crystal still embedded within her hand. Conrad had removed the larger pieces, but the small ones screamed with each movement as they ground against bone and flesh.

She watched Alana walk away from the outpost, her stride smooth and certain. She moved towards Uriel. Towards death. Her dark figure stood out against the ashen terrain, and with a growing twist in her gut, Amarie realized the auer didn't have any weapons on her beyond that little knife.

She could be lying to us.

Doubt churned in her as she followed Ahria and Conrad around the outer wall of the outpost to head north, as per Alana's directions.

This could be a trap.

They had few options, left here on foot without the Art. And Alana had given them some pertinent information, but how much could they trust it? Alana could be telling Uriel every bit of sensitive information Ahria had divulged *right* then.

The other side of the coin weighed on her, though she tried to ignore it. Whether or not she liked it, Alana was Ahria's aunt. And something had happened between them during these weeks that led her daughter to trust her. Believe her. Even care about her. And they were leaving her to die.

"Fyfer!" Conrad's surprised voice broke through Amarie's thoughts as they rounded a jutted corner of the outpost wall.

Amarie slowed, blinking at the buckskin horse standing before them. It shook its neck, striking a hoof against the stone. It looked as relieved to see Conrad as they were to see it.

A way out.

Conrad took the reins, looking between Ahria and Amarie. "We can move faster, now, at least."

Amarie eyed Conrad. "Get on. Both of you." Her heart beat wildly as she watched Ahria mount.

"We can all fit," Ahria started, but her mother shook her head.

"Three people on one horse, and we may as well walk." Amarie nodded at Conrad, wondering if he could see her choice written all over her face as she lied, "We can take turns running."

Conrad nodded once, a solemn look on his face as he mounted the horse behind Ahria. He wrapped his arms around her waist, muscles already tense as he anticipated her next action.

Amarie swallowed. "Ride north, then east, just as Alana said, but keep your eyes open."

Ahria's gaze shot to her. "What—"

"I need to make sure she's telling the truth." Amarie backed up, feeling like she waded through mud as she looked at Conrad. "Keep her safe. And don't come back for anything."

"Mom, no—"

Amarie cringed at the title, jaw working. "I love you, Ree." She touched the hilt at her belt. "Go now." When Conrad hesitated, she raised her voice. "*Go!*"

The prince needed no further push, even as Ahria kept protesting, and spurred the horse into an immediate canter north.

Amarie watched them, relief cascading through her in waves. Taking a deeper breath, she gathered herself and ran back towards the outpost entrance where she could watch Alana face Uriel and remain undetected.

With her back to the pale stone wall, she slid to the nearest corner and peeked around it.

Alana was only twenty feet from Uriel and his army, but she'd stopped closer to the outpost than Amarie expected, letting the soldiers close the distance. Uriel's mount walked with them, but his men slowly maneuvered to circle the auer on three sides, leaving the outcropping of stone Amarie and Conrad had rounded on Alana's left side. The steep, sharp rock hardly looked like a possible escape route, but Amarie imagined Alana could scale it if necessary. The armored guards on the other hand...

Bodes well if Alana is keeping to a defensive position.

Amarie kept silent, watching.

Uriel's silky voice sent a shudder down her spine. "Don't they know the border is to the south?"

Alana didn't even glance at the troops surrounding her, a bland expression on her face. "The army is a little much."

And truly, the forces behind Uriel *were* an army. Three hundred soldiers, at least. Whatever reserve Feyor still had.

Uriel stroked a black shard that hung at the curve of his throat. "One can never be too careful with the Berylian Key involved."

"And yet, it's *me* you've chosen to..." She gestured with a lazy hand in a circle. "Intimidate." The dryness of the word made the monster's upper lip twitch.

Uriel smirked through his annoyance, lifting his leg in a smooth motion to dismount from his massive horse. "You have betrayed me." He took a casual step forward. "*Allowed* my enemy to escape. Unless you are here to offer me information. Beg for forgiveness."

Alana stiffened, but only for a breath. "I offer nothing to you. Not anymore. You never intended for me to leave this place."

Amarie's breath caught. She dipped her chin, swallowing the lump in her throat.

I hope you're seeing this, Talon.

Uriel let out a loud, exaggerated sigh. "So disappointing. You really were my favorite."

Ahria had been right. Yet Amarie could do nothing to help the auer. She looked down at her hand, her blood soaking the scarf wrapped around it. One sword would do little against that army. Against that monster.

"Pretty sure your only favorite is yourself," Alana crooned. "Which is ironic, since you are so, so *weak* without anyone else."

Uriel's mouth curled into a sneer. He stepped back, nearing the front line of the ranks behind him. The troop filled the space, putting twenty soldiers between him and Alana. "Such a waste."

Amarie's breath came faster, daring her to move. Daring her to charge them, but the futility of it weighed her boots in place.

Dying with her would be a pointless endeavor.

But the logic charred her heart, even if she'd spent years hating the woman who now stood between her and death. Where was this woman decades ago? If she'd met Ahria as a babe, would the outcome have been different?

None of that matters now.

"Kill her."

The soldiers rushed forward, and for a moment, it looked as if Alana were simply going to stand there and let their swords skewer her.

But in a serpentine motion, she moved.

Alana curled to the side of the closest soldier, his sword cutting through the loose fabric of her skirt as she spun. Her empty hand caught his arm at his elbow, and she twisted. The snap of bone echoed, then steel on steel as she used the first soldier as a shield against another. She spun low to the ground, moving beneath their blades in a blur. Soldiers fell, their feet knocked out beneath them and clashing into each other. In a smooth motion, Alana curled her body around another, throwing him to the ground and taking his sword.

Uriel's laugh rang over the stoney hills. "Always one to entertain me, weren't you? I preferred you on your hands and knees."

Alana scoffed, breathing slightly faster. Her newly acquired blade found its mark in the next three who charged her, slicing through the openings of their armor with preternatural swiftness. "With all your years of life," she huffed, angling the sword into another's ribs. "You still have no skills of your own. Fight me yourself." She managed a moment to point her sword at him in challenge before being forced to break off and down another two. Bodies piled up around her feet, and the four still alive from the original twenty gave pause at the edge of the carnage.

"You wouldn't stand a chance against me." Uriel bared his teeth in a menacing smile.

"Then fight me. Or are you a coward beneath this face, too?"

Uriel snarled. He stepped forward, reaching a hand to one of the four soldiers that hesitated. He grabbed the man by the side of his neck.

The soldier paled, his eyes rolling back as his skin shriveled beneath his armor. When he collapsed, a thin puff of ashen dust rose around the soldier's body and black veins crawled along Uriel's hand. A swirl of shadow bubbled in his palm as he outstretched it, wrapping upon itself to form a blade. The wicked scimitar absorbed all light that touched it as Uriel exposed his chest to Alana in a taunt.

"Come then, *sae'quonei*." He grinned, a deeper black hovering at his feet and the curve of his neck beneath the shard. "I'll teach you the lesson you didn't learn while I inhabited that body of yours."

Alana threw herself over the bodies at him, moving faster than Amarie thought possible. Their blades met in a hollow ring. Darkness erupted from the blade, tendrils wrapping around hers. Alana cried out as they danced down to her fingertips, and the sword vanished into the shadow. More shadow reached up from the ground, tangling around her ankles as Uriel's hand shot to her throat.

Amarie urged her feet to move, to run. To follow Conrad and Ahria and get away, get as much space between her and Uriel as possible.

But her body wouldn't react. Wouldn't turn. Wouldn't even look away. She needed to see this, be here, so someone may one day tell the story of how Alana saved them.

Assuming I live to tell it.

Alana gasped as Uriel squeezed. She raked at his wrist with her nails, but flecks of his power chewed at her fingers, leaving them raw. "You just can't help but cheat, can you?" she choked out.

"I *win,*" Uriel hissed. "No matter the cost. Not my fault you never learned."

"Didn't I?" Alana let go of his wrist, and snatched the shard dangling at his throat. "This time, you *lose.*"

Power surged through the air, tingling against Amarie's skin as Alana's threat registered on Uriel's face.

Amarie held her breath as darkness exploded.

Great waves of shadow snaked upward through the sky and straight at her. She ducked back behind the corner of the outpost wall as screams scorched the air. The stone vibrated against her back, but then the air grew deathly quiet. Breathing hard, she dared look again, mouth falling open at the sight. A black star stained the ground, char marks that'd broken the stone itself. Deep grooves painted the normally pale terrain, like trails of lightning. At the center lay Alana and Uriel's desiccated bodies, surrounded by at least fifty soldiers and Uriel's horse. As if the power of Shades had ripped everything from them all at once.

Dead. Their bodies shriveled and decayed.

She shattered the shard.

Amarie gasped in a breath, her chest seizing.

Alana didn't move, lifeless eyes staring blankly at the sky.

Unexpected pain murmured within her, and she looked at the recovering army, now without their leader. Only those in the crescent shape outside the blast remained. And with a shudder, Amarie realized she'd barely been outside its range.

Her eyes moved to Uriel's body again. The grey-haired auer no longer a threat.

Uriel's not dead, just... without a host.

Shouts rang up over the destruction, a soldier with a more decorated helmet stepping out from the back of the confused formation. The army reacted, regathering to the side of their fallen comrades.

She couldn't make out the words, her mind still hazy from what she'd narrowly escaped, but the new commander pointed north.

She needed to move.

Now.

Amarie turned and sprinted back the way she'd come, racing north.

The clatter of boots and armor followed a few moments later.

Gripping her left hand into a fist to keep the scarf in place, she gritted against the pain and ran. She followed the hoof prints north, her wrapped hand steadying the sword at her side.

The soldiers charged after her, coming into sight as Amarie crested a northern hill. Their shouts echoed over the land once more, confirming they'd spotted her.

Fuck.

She slid down the other side, the stone biting her palm until she found her footing at the bottom and saw the hoof prints again.

No time. She had no time to cover any tracks, for a chance at hiding.

And there were far too many soldiers remaining for her to fight without her power. Still loyal to Uriel even in his absence.

With no other options—Amarie ran.

Chapter 43

The water never rose high enough to fully submerge him.

He wasn't entirely sure why it didn't, why he'd been able to escape it so many times. It rose and subsided with no apparent pattern, frequently chasing him to the highest points he could reach in his Inbetween. It was low again, now, and he walked through the constant puddles at his ankles. He'd visited the Inbetween enough times, read about it enough in Sindré's texts, that he knew what should have been happening.

Hang in there.

Come back to me.

Rae's voice, perhaps, stopped the water from fully claiming him. Stopped them from rising to surge over the sanctum ruins. Even though every stone looked the same as the sanctum where he'd been granted the power of the Rahn'ka, none of it was real. All conceived by his ká to ease the final passage into death.

Death. He was dead. Yet he wasn't.

Sometimes he wouldn't hear his wife's words, only quiet sobs that broke his heart over and over. A pressure around his hand, or on his chest, as if she were there, right then, touching him. Mourning him. And it ate at him, every moment, knowing her torment.

The invisible thread between his ká and body had eroded. Sometimes, with his wife's words, he could almost see it. Almost grasp it. But every time he tried, it fell through his fingers like the water that pooled at his ankles.

Pulling himself up onto the altar at the center of the familiar monolith circle, Damien closed his eyes and brushed water droplets from his feet. The closest he ever felt to finding the line back to his body was when he could get away from the cold. The hanging darkness within the water.

He needed to get back.

Uriel's auer face flashed inside his eyelids, pain rumbling through his body as it remembered all the ways it'd broken.

Grimacing, Damien tried to swallow. Tried to reach again into the star-flecked air above him. A distant beating, like a metal drum, echoed through his head. It vibrated against the shadow of a rope, dangling down. Again he reached for it, and again it shattered into more stars to coat the abyss.

Sighing, Damien opened his burning eyes and slouched forward, hands on his knees. Blinking through the despair, he murmured, "I'm sorry, Dice. I don't know how to get back to you."

I need you, Rae's voice echoed through his soul. *Please.*

Sindré's phantom passed among the stones near the sanctum center. Damien had tried to plead with them, but they weren't truly there. It was his own creation. His memory formed the stag with intricate antlers.

As their hoofs trailed through the constant sheen of water along the sanctum's ground, his heart thudded.

Higher. The water was higher than it'd been a moment before.

"Shit." Damien hopped back off the altar, landing in the now knee-deep cold. It sent a chill up his spine, accompanied by the now familiar feeling of wanting to stay. It wanted to envelope him and begged him to just accept it. Submerge and breathe it in.

His skin tingled as he waded towards the sanctum ruins, the metal drum in the distance beating faster. The water lapped at his skin, but he ignored its begging in favor of remembering his wife's words.

Come back to me.
You need to live.

Turning to the same path he'd used to escape the water before, Damien grabbed a branch of a tree growing to overtake the ruins. Hauling himself up, he swung his legs to catch the second level of the sanctum.

Water surged below, white froth forming on peaks as it swirled higher and higher.

Desperation touched Rae's voice. *Damien!*

His hand burned, skin tight as if she didn't dare let go of him.

"I can hear you," he whispered, eyes closing for a breath.

But the water kept crashing, kept rising, and the lower level of the sanctum disappeared beneath its surface.

As it lapped over the edge of the second story's floor, Damien rushed to a crumbling set of stairs.

Higher. He needed even higher ground to outrun Nymaera's waves.

To what end, he didn't let himself consider.

He needed to live. For his family. Uriel be damned, he just wanted to see his wife again. His daughter. His son.

His wife's timbre altered, as if she spoke to someone else, but the emotion within it remained. *I believe in you.*

Damien huffed as he scaled the steep incline of the arena's roof. The water still rose behind him, now a roar that covered all other sounds. He reached the open hole in the arena roof, the same they had watched Jarrod through as he struggled against the wolf. Looking down into the arena, all he saw was black water. Rising still.

"Da."

Damien whirled around at the sound of his son's voice, and his eyes widened as he saw the young Rahn'ka standing twenty feet away on the arena's roof.

Bellamy let out a breath, shoulders easing. "We don't have much time."

Chapter 44

Amarie's legs screamed with every stride. Every step. Every pound of her heart. Her thighs burned.

But she couldn't stop.

Not when Uriel's army charged after her, maybe a hundred feet behind. Three men were gaining, though, running faster and harder than their comrades, hells-bent on the prize surely on her head. She could hear their breath not far behind, but to stop and fight them...

Amarie drew her sword, sliding down another steep slope. But as her boots connected with the bottom, she whirled and struck the closest soldier.

He howled, but she couldn't pause for longer, and ran once more.

She stumbled when her knees tried to give out, gasping as she nearly landed on her face, caught only by her knee hitting the ground first. Swearing, she rose, daring a glance behind her.

Some of the soldiers slid down the slope as she had, while others raced around it. They wouldn't end this pursuit. Not until she'd fallen. Until they had her. Until her blood stained the bone-colored ground red.

Sucking in an iron-laden breath, Amarie spurred herself on again.

No horse dotted the horizon. Ahria and Conrad had escaped, and that joy was almost enough. Almost enough for her to ease her stride. But she wanted to live.

A bolt whizzed past her head, and she yelped, ducking and zigzagging to the side.

The Lungaz border, where her Art waited for her, would be impossible to reach. It was days away on horseback, and she was a speck of dust on a map. Her legs would give out, sooner than later, and the army would be upon her in moments. There was no escape. No hope for reaching her power.

Another soldier neared, huffing like a bull behind her, and she gritted her teeth.

Slamming to a stop, she swung her blade with the momentum, and gutted the man with relative ease.

Agony scorched through her sword arm's shoulder, and she dropped the blade with a scream.

Gasping, Amarie gaped at the bolt protruding from her right shoulder. "Fuck," she groaned, whimpering as she eyed the encroaching army. "Fuck!" Without giving herself a moment to reconsider, she snapped the bolt's fletching off and yanked it the rest of the way through her body.

Her vision blurred, and she choked, but she dropped the bloody shaft and eyed her sword.

No way. There was no way she could carry or wield that now.

Struggling to catch her breath, she urged her legs into motion, leaving the weapon behind. Hot blood poured down her arm, but she ran. She ran and ran, and mercifully, no more bolts flew.

Blood thundered in her ears, turning into a rhythmic beat. A drum beat counting her heart's final moments.

Her sight darkened around the edges, but she couldn't let her feet stop. Couldn't let herself give up.

There was no way out.

But Ahria lived.

Amarie choked on another breath, which could have been a sob, as the drumming of her heart grew louder. Louder, and—higher.

No.

Frantic, she looked up.

Panic lanced through her at the winged beast in the sky. The *two* winged beasts flying straight for her.

Of course Uriel had other options to kill her. And she had no chance of outrunning a wyvern.

Amarie panted, but kept running. Maybe she'd get lucky, and the wyverns would—

No, that couldn't be a wyvern.

Her fear evolved into terrified awe as the beasts flew closer, and their size... They dwarfed the wyverns Feyor had used before. Because those weren't wyverns at all.

Dragons.

The nearest one, with scales like shining emeralds, bore a rider. She couldn't tell if the other did, as well, but it hardly mattered. One would be enough to wipe her *and* the entire army behind her off the face of the continent.

As it neared, closer and closer, Amarie's legs gave out. She fell, knees colliding with the hard ground in a shock that rippled through her bones. Hope disintegrated before her eyes as she looked back at the approaching army.

Eighty feet. Seventy. Fifty.

She tried to rise, but her muscles refused to move. Blood pooled beneath her hand, and she eyed the dragon coming for her. So close now that she could see its rider. Its—Her eyes widened.

Impossible.

Amarie sobbed, throwing her arms over her head as she ducked low. The dragon's maw opened wide and the scent of sulfur filled the air.

Shouts rose behind her, escalating into full blown screams as heat erupted directly above her.

The dragon's shadow blocked the sun for one... two... three seconds, the shrieks and wails behind her fading with the roar of flame.

The second dragon dipped low like the first, blasting its blazing breath over whatever remained from the first beast's pass.

Amarie looked to the green draconi, wondering if her eyes could have deceived her. Tricked her. But no...

Kinronsilis.

Kin sat just behind the dragon's head, face blood-splattered and snarling. Her gaze shot to the golden dragon.

Matthias.

Amarie tried again to rise, but her boot slipped on the bloodied ground and her shoulder jolted in pain as she braced herself. Breathing through her teeth, she looked behind her, but the army lay in ashes, charred and unmoving.

He'd come for her. On the back of a gods' damned dragon, Kin had come for her. It was all she needed to know.

Tears streamed down her face, body shaking at supporting her own weight.

Somewhere above, a dragon roared, and she smiled.

He'd come for her.

With a shaky breath, Amarie collapsed.

Chapter 45

As Zedren circled, Kin stared at Amarie's still form. "Get me down there." His chest felt heavy as he stared at the smear of red beneath her and still flowing from her shoulder.

Gods, if Matthias and I had been even a minute later...

He banished the thoughts of the army, now a black stain on the surface of Lungaz. He told himself they were Uriel's, not his own soldiers. And he couldn't feel guilt considering what they were attempting to do to Amarie.

He was glad he hadn't gotten off of Zedren after finding Ahria and Conrad. The moment his panicked daughter shouted at him that Amarie had stayed behind—stayed to possibly face Uriel, to give them the chance to escape—he'd urged the dragon back into the air and flown west.

Thankfully, it didn't take any more direction than words, and Zedren snorted in response as he banked, diving. There hadn't been any time for training when Dani and Liam agreed to stay behind on the Herald so Kin and Matthias could make a mad rush to Lungaz. Not that he needed training when Zedren could make all his own decisions. The dragon threw out his wings just as Kin wondered if they were going to splatter against the stone, his giant claws scraping against the ground.

Kin didn't wait for him to come to a complete stop before he detached the harness that secured him to the saddle on the dragon's neck. Zedren lowered his head, anticipating his hasty dismount, but his knees still barked as he hit the ground.

Rushing forward, he slid the final distance to Amarie. He fought the urge to pull her into him, eyeing her wounded shoulder. With the scent of her blood heavy on the air, he dug his dirtied hand into the satchel now always at his side.

He worked quickly to pull her shirt away from the wound, pressing clean gauze. He looked to Matthias as the king dismounted Zelbrali a few yards away. "She needs stitches. I could use your hands."

Watching Amarie's eyes for a flutter of her lashes, he wished she would wake, but the blood loss... He assured himself that she would. That when they got out of Lungaz, he could hold her.

This wouldn't be her death all over again. Last time, with Trist, he'd been too late. Last time, he'd failed her.

Not this time.

Matthias landed on his knees next to him, pulling supplies out of a pack as Kin held the gauze tight to her shoulder.

He eyed her left hand, wrapped in a blood-stained gossamer scarf, and then her face. Her lips were dry, nearly chapped. She probably hadn't drank anything in hours, at least, and had been running the whole time. They were miles from the Lungaz outpost.

Matthias tied a thin string to a curved needle, his hands steady as stone. "Move the gauze, but hold the wound together." When Kin did as instructed, the king inserted the needle, moving quickly through the stitches like he'd done it a hundred times before.

"I thought your wife was the healer," Kin muttered, trying to think of anything other than the warm blood soaking through the knees of his breeches.

Scoffing, Matthias inserted the needle again. "And she taught me well." He tied off the thread before checking her heartbeat at her neck, and lifted the injured hand. Glancing at Kin, he unwrapped her left hand and cringed. "Nymaera's breath."

Her hand... Black shards embedded in her flesh, some so deep he could barely see them. Some holes were vacant, as if the pieces had already been removed. It no longer bled much, but he could imagine the pain.

"Roll her over. We need to close the entry wound." Matthias wrapped fresh gauze around her hand while Kin rolled her onto her side.

Hoofs thundered across the rolling curved rock, a protesting whiny sounding as Ahria and Conrad neared the dragons.

Ahria leapt from the horse's back, and shrieked, "Mom!" She skidded through the pale dirt, eyes frantic. "Is she...?"

Matthias worked on stitching the entrance wound of what must have been an arrow or bolt that pierced her shoulder.

Kin shook his head. "She's alive." He breathed deeper, trying to let those words sink in for himself, too. "She's alive."

Ahria crouched near her mother's head, wiping dirt from her face as Conrad approached behind them.

Conrad looked across the field of charred and still smoldering bodies. "Any sign of Uriel?"

Matthias finished the second set of stitches, easing Amarie onto her back once more.

Amarie groaned, and Kin's heart jumped into his throat. Color had returned to her face, if only slightly. She tried to speak, but nothing came out.

Kin stroked his fingers over her cheek and through her hair. "You don't need to talk right now. You're safe. Ahria and I are here."

Ahria pulled a waterskin from her side, removing the cap. "Here, drink." She held it to her mother's mouth, pouring a little at a time for her to drink.

Amarie breathed easier, eyes fluttering open and focusing on Ahria and then Kin. "Uriel," she rasped. "Uriel was pushed out of his host. Alana..." She coughed, grimacing. "Alana destroyed his shard."

The loathing Kin had begun to feel quickly faded into confusion. Furrowing his brow, he wondered if the blood loss in Amarie was causing the delirium. "Alana?"

Ahria nodded, her throat bobbing. "Alana was my warden in Lungaz, but she took good care of me. She gave us information. And in the end..." Silver lined her eyes as her brow upturned in the middle. "She faced Uriel to let us get away."

Amarie managed a nod. "I saw her fight him." She paused, swallowing. "May Nymaera grant her peace."

A pang of grief stuck in Kin's heart. It seemed a wonder, considering all she had done to him. Yet, despite it all, the news made him ache.

Conrad moved closer to Ahria, brushing a hand over her back, though his face remained stoic. He met Kin's eyes for a moment before shifting his attention to Matthias. "Where to from here?"

Matthias wiped his bloodied hands, stashing the stitching supplies back into his pack before gesturing with his chin towards Kin. "We're going to Jaspa."

Chapter 46

"Bell." The heat in Damien's eyes doubled as he rushed down the curved dome of the arena to his son.

His dark brown hair, the same color as his mother's, sat messy on his head.

Is this real?

"I'm here," Bell murmured, glancing back at the rising water lapping up the curve of the dome. He climbed higher until his body collided with Damien's and he returned the shaky embrace. "I need to take you back."

Damien pulled away, gripping Bellamy's shoulders as he nodded. "How did you get here?"

"Ma sent for me weeks ago." The young man's eyes were somber, heavy with worry. "She feared I wouldn't make it in time."

A weight in Damien's chest lightened. While he'd heard Rae's voice, the last thing he'd seen was her being thrown into the Dul'Idur depths by Uriel.

But she's alive.

A million more questions bubbled into his thoughts. Had everyone else survived? Where was Uriel? But he buried them for now. The water caressed the stone at their feet.

"I haven't done this before." Uncertainty wavered his son's voice. "But we need to go right now."

Damien nodded, gripping Bellamy's biceps harder. "You know the lessons as well as I did my first time. Just remember—"

"Don't breathe in the water." Bellamy inclined his head, a quiver still in his jaw. "And follow the cord I laid on the way down."

Damien nodded again, lowering his hand to grip Bellamy's wrist as his son did the same. "And don't let go." He gave him a reassuring smile.

Determination spread over Bellamy's expression as he closed his eyes, tightening his grip.

As the young Rahn'ka focused, Damien's surroundings blurred. They whipped around him, becoming a torrent of wind and color, yanking his soul through the Inbetween. Cold enveloped him as they plunged upward, breaking into what felt like an endless ocean.

Pressure built on his chest, but Damien kept his eyes clamped closed. The water never felt so suffocating when he'd pulled others through, but now... Damien nearly gasped, but he managed to keep his mouth shut and his breath held until everything jolted to a jarring stop.

Darkness.

Nearly absolute darkness engulfed him, Bellamy's grip no longer on his wrist.

For a breath, all he could hear was his own heartbeat.

"Did it...?" Rae's whisper broke the silence. "Is he...?" A touch, so heart-breakingly soft, grazed over his arm. "Damien?"

His entire body throbbed as if even opening his eyes would be too much. Lashes stuck together, he blinked, realizing it was only his right eye that hummed with pain as light penetrated the thin slit he'd managed. His fingers twitched against rough fabric, solid metal beneath it.

"He's moving," Bellamy whispered.

As Damien choked on a breath, Rae spoke to someone else. "He's trying to breathe."

Movement shuffled around him, and a stranger murmured, "Hold on, let us take this out. Try to relax your throat."

Something shifted in his mouth before sliding out of his throat. He gagged, but the feeling passed quickly, and stale, damp air filled his lungs.

"Damien," Rae whispered. "Can you hear me? Can you open your eye?"

Sucking on his tongue to try to wet it, he fought a lingering nausea from whatever had been pulled from his throat. He blinked again, still only able to open his right eye before the blinding light encouraged it closed again.

Rae gripped his hand, squeezing, as her breath came in shallow, shaky inhales. "Please say something."

His tongue stuck to the top of his mouth, but he turned his hand over, entwining his fingers with hers. "I'm here." His voice hardly sounded like his own.

A choked sob erupted from Rae, and her weight suddenly landed on his chest. Her sweet scent overcame the strange sterile smell of the room as her hair tickled his neck.

Voices murmured between his son and the stranger before a door clicked closed.

"I thought I'd lost you," Rae mumbled against his skin, lips pressed to his neck as she held him. "Gods, Damien, I thought you were gone."

Despite the pain, he held her back. The warmth passing through each part of him helped him ignore it. He turned his head into her, deeply inhaling the scent of her hair as he placed a kiss against it. "I'm here." It was all he could say, voice still strange.

No matter how much he tried to blink, darkness prevailed over his left eye, along with a gentle pressure. Inspecting it with his hand, he furrowed his brow when his fingertips found hard leather over the socket.

Rae pressed a kiss to his neck, then his jaw, again and again, until she paused. Her hand closed over his, lowering it from his face. "They couldn't save your eye," she murmured gently, pulling his touch to her face. As his vision slowly focused on her, she smiled, eyes bloodshot with dark circles beneath them. "It doesn't matter." Her throat bobbed. "You're here, and that's all that does." Blotchy dampness marred her face, her bronze skin uncharacteristically pallid.

He brushed his fingers over her cheeks, blinking his single eye more open. The room beyond Rae came into dim focus, but so little of it made sense. Though he recognized the dense metal ceilings of the faction headquarters.

It wasn't completely destroyed.

The long hours alone in the Inbetween had led to endless possibilities plaguing Damien. He'd imagined each and every possible outcome, yet this one seemed so strange.

Why would Uriel leave this place intact?

Brushing a lock of Rae's unbraided hair from her face, his felt flush. Wetness gathered in his eye, blurring his vision. "I'm so grateful to see you."

Rae whimpered before her mouth collided with his in a desperate kiss. Warmth flared through him, only increasing as her hands explored over his neck, his chest, as if she didn't fully believe this wasn't a dream.

Despite the warmth flowing through him at her touch, his body thrummed. He couldn't hide the wince of pain as he tried to wrap his arms around her. The pain didn't make sense, either. With Bellamy bringing him back, the power of his son's ká would have worked to repair any injuries. Yet everything hurt.

Rae drew back, shaking her head at his attempted movement. "It's been a while, Lieutenant." Her voice held a gentle warning. "You'll have to ease back into things. Standing, walking. All of it." But through the dire words, she smiled.

Even after so many years, and the title long outdated, it still brought a smile to Damien's lips. The gravity of the situation eased it from his face as he nodded, taking her hand again. "How long?"

Rae's brow twitched upward in the middle as her chin betrayed her smile with a quiver. "About a month and a half."

Panic snuck in to double the ache in his body. Another wince fell across his face as his mind whirled to catch up to what all could have happened in that time. What all he'd possibly missed.

He tightened his grip on Rae. "Tell me what happened. What's been happening. Uriel..." The thought of the creature sent flashes of pain through his body. Memories of his strikes making his muscles burn.

Rae hesitated, rolling her lips together. "Uriel captured Ahria. The others went to retrieve her. Then Deylan sent word that Jarac was headed to Orvalinon, so they split up. Last I heard, Kin, Matthias, and Deylan killed Jarac and were flying to Lungaz to find Amarie, Ahria, and Conrad. But no messages have come through since. Deylan stayed behind on Andi's ship with injuries."

"But Uriel knows where the prison is? Jarac found it?"

Rae shook her head, easing his panic. "No. He'd sent his Shade there for something else. Some weapon. But it's all right. They failed and the prison location remains a secret." She paused, opening her mouth to speak before hesitating.

"What is it?" He studied her face, unable to help the worry swelling in his chest.

"I did a lot of reading while you were... stuck here." Rae smiled, seriousness lingering beneath. "I found the answers about Taeg'nok," she whispered. "I know how we all work together to imprison Uriel."

When Damien opened his mouth to ask for more information, Rae put two fingers over his mouth.

"More details can wait. Everyone should be on their way to rendezvous soon," she whispered. "I'll tell Bellamy he can come see you. I'll get you some water and food." She kissed his brow, then the bridge of his nose before resting her forehead against his. "And in case you didn't hear it all those times I've said it these past weeks... I love you."

Damien nodded, urging his body to relax back against the hard bed. "I heard you." He touched her hair again. "It's what kept me sane. Kept me here. I love you, too, Dice."

Two weeks later...

The click of the cane along the metal floor still grated on Damien's nerves. It was a significant improvement, but pain shocked through his lower back as he tried to hobble faster. It must have shown on his face.

"Don't push yourself so hard." Rae walked beside him at the embarrassingly slow pace he set. "You have time to recover. You're already ahead of what the nurses said." In a move he was familiar with by now, she reached to help him, but withdrew a second later. He'd asked her not to help him if he didn't truly need it.

Damien furrowed his brow, looking down the long underwater hallway. "There isn't time." He urged his steps back into a slow rhythm that didn't hurt nearly as much. "The faction has to be nearly done emptying this place out. We can't stay here. And there's too much going on out there." He jerked as he started to gesture above with the cane in his left hand, but remembered how poorly that'd gone last time he tried to stand without it. Groaning, he shuffled to a stop, glaring down at his feet and legs where the muscle still hadn't recovered from his coma.

"What's going on out there doesn't matter right now. We need to focus on getting your strength back." Rae touched his arm, guiding him to one of the few remaining benches lining the wide hallway so they could sit. "Deylan will tell us when it's time to leave."

Most of the rooms were empty of essentials, hauled away beneath the water by their alcan allies. To where, Damien had no idea, but he assumed that knowledge was highly confidential.

And Deylan hadn't offered to share it.

Not that I blame him.

Sighing, Damien leaned back against the cold wall, tilting his head up. The strap of his eyepatch tugged on his hair, and he rubbed at the spot on the back of his head. At least his arms had begun to regain their mass, mostly because Damien could work those while still in bed.

"Any word from Bell?" Damien leaned forward, rubbing his thighs.

Rae shook her head. "You would know better than me, but I'm assuming he hasn't reached Yondé's sanctum yet. It'll take him a couple more weeks to get there. I'm sure he's fine."

Bellamy had departed shortly after healing Damien. Keeping the only two Rahn'ka in the same place—a place known by Uriel—was just too great a risk.

And until Damien was able to connect with his son through his meditation, the anxiety would remain. He understood why Rae had sent for him and was grateful. But they had both worked hard not to rope their children into the war against the master of Shades.

Even though Bellamy would have been forced to take up my part if I'd died.

Meeting with Jalescé during Damien's nightly meditations had helped with the nightmares. The reptilian guardian aided him with wards against his own mind that dulled the effect Uriel's face still had on his psyche. But some dark imaginings still slipped through. And recently they had taken a turn, plaguing him with images of shadows destroying his son.

"I'm sure you're right." Damien reached blindly to Rae's lap, closing his hand over hers.

Footsteps encouraged his back away from the wall, and Damien had to turn his head more to the left than before to catch sight of Deylan.

Still getting used to no peripheral vision on top of everything.

The Sixth Eye's Locksmith slowed upon seeing them. Bandages still peeked out from beneath his collar, protecting the wicked burns inflicted by Jarac weeks ago. He surveyed Damien and Rae from head to toe. "How's the progress today?"

"It's good," Rae chirped before Damien could say otherwise. "He's come a long way."

Can't argue that.

Damien grumbled inwardly at remembering the first few attempts to walk. He'd relied almost completely on Rae to hold him upright, but his wife had never once made him feel lesser for it.

"How is the relocation going?" Rae squeezed Damien's forearm, as if she knew where his thoughts had gone.

Deylan gave a one-shouldered shrug. "A lot was destroyed in the attack, but we've almost finished salvaging what we can. The viewing chamber was left in ruins, but it looks like we may be able to rebuild it." The words themselves held hope, but the man's tone spoke his reluctance to believe it. His shoulders weighed with unspoken guilt. He'd been the one to bring them here, trailing Uriel. "We have two more days before everyone will depart. When we do, we will destroy the last lift to the bridge. So best be ready to come with us. When you reach the surface, we will have horses ready to take you wherever you're heading next."

What is *next?*

Damien and Rae had discussed their options, and nothing seemed like the right place to be. Home in Helgath would put everyone there at risk and possibly lead to Uriel discovering they were still alive.

"Oh," Deylan paused after taking one more step. "I almost forgot. I received word this morning from my contact in Jaspa that Feyor's artisans and scholars have confirmed Kinronsilis's lineage to the throne. And rumor is they're already moving to schedule a coronation. It's a positive step towards getting that country and its people out of ruin."

"And out of Uriel's control. He won't have any political pawns left."

Deylan nodded. "We still have no reported sightings of Uriel. He has a new face again, and the only two other Shades the Sixth Eye was aware of have vanished off the face of Pantracia. He could be anyone."

Rae's throat bobbed. "I don't know if I can think of a more unsettling notion," she muttered. "But at least Feyor can begin its recovery, too. We have to enjoy the small victories." She gave Damien a pointed look, and he could read the insinuation in her tone.

Damien frowned. He wanted to be happy for Kin. For Feyor. But the danger of not knowing where Uriel was left a nauseating knot in his stomach. He'd always had eyes on the creature. But now, it made everything feel so much more tenuous.

He's less powerful, though. We'll be able to smoke him out of hiding easier.

"Look, I know I've made it pretty clear that you won't be privileged to the location of our new headquarters," Deylan didn't bother trying to sound apologetic, "but I do think we need to be more open with each other about whatever is coming next." He drew a hand from his pocket, holding out one of the faction's communication devices to Rae. "At least with this, we can speak."

Damien lifted his eyebrow, meeting Deylan's gaze. "Vanguard know you're offering this?"

Rae took the round copper object, glancing at Damien.

Deylan huffed. "Actually, they do. But I sold it as more of a... keep tabs on what our reckless friends the Rahn'ka and Mira'wyld are up to... kind of deal. They were... rather unhappy with how my decision to bring you here turned out, but I think I won them back by keeping Sephysis safe." His jaw flexed. "Even if it isn't in the faction's hands anymore."

The Art-laden dagger that'd been sealed in an old Rahn'ka sanctum still baffled Damien. He, admittedly, hadn't visited the sanctum to meet the guardian yet, but with the connections between the sanctums... one of the others should have known of its presence. He'd been assured that the guardian of the sanctum where they built the prison hadn't expressed concern. But that had all been confirmed through Sindré.

And Sindré hasn't always been the most forthcoming.

"Thank you," Rae said to Deylan. "I'm sure it will come in handy."

Damien wrestled from his thoughts to nod his thanks to Deylan. "We'll keep you updated. It seems only fair, considering all the faction has done for us."

The Locksmith grunted. "Might help me earn back some favor, too." He gave a half-hearted smile. "But I'm quite relieved to see you recovering. We weren't so sure for a while there."

Damien remembered the look Deylan had given him upon his return to the bunker. The relief had been all over his face, even if Damien kept telling himself it was only because of their plans. But the truth stuck in his side like a thorn, a kernel of guilt that Deylan placed on himself for accidentally putting them in such a situation.

He never could have known.

With a slight smile, Damien nodded again. "Too bad you just missed meeting our son in person. You're still one of the few to even know about him."

Deylan dipped his chin. "And it will remain that way, my friend." He glanced down the hallway. "I'll come by with some whisky later. One less bottle will lighten the load, right?" He smirked, disappearing around a corner after their nods.

Rae fell silent, staring at the wall across from them as she dragged a thumb back and forth over her leathers.

He took her hand again, twisting on the seat to face her. Caressing her skin, the Rahn'ka summoned the Art within him, tangling a bit of his ká with Rae's as he always had. Hers surged in recognition and it made his throat tighten. "What is it, Dice?"

She looked at him, eyes weary and full of concern. "Just... Something doesn't make sense. It doesn't sit right."

There were plenty of things that felt the same to him, but she didn't need to hear that. He squeezed her hand tighter, sending another comforting pulse of ká. "What doesn't?"

Rae paused, a muscle in her cheek twitching. "Why would Uriel relocate Ahria from Jaspa to Lungaz? Where he can't even go freely?"

She shook her head. "I know they said he had a shard, but... He'd still be vulnerable. And they said when Amarie and Conrad arrived to break her free, there were no guards to stop them. It's... almost like Uriel wanted us to come get her. But why?"

Uncertainty coiled in his chest, but Damien held strong to her. "I think the theory was that Uriel wanted whoever came for Ahria to kill Alana for him. And it was important Alana not have access to the Art for that to happen."

Rae let out a deep breath. "Kill Alana, yes. But why hand over half of the Berylian Key? Why not make it a ruse, make us *think* Ahria was there? Why actually let us take her back?"

"He thinks we're dead. And without us, the plan to imprison him would be done anyway. Uriel plays long games... he probably thought he could risk losing Ahria for now."

"I don't know." Rae's voice became breathy. "I can't shake the feeling that we're missing something."

Not knowing what to say, Damien just pulled her hand up to his lips, kissing her knuckles. "Whatever it is, we'll figure it out. Like we always do."

Chapter 47

Three weeks later...

Kin stared at the mirror, hardly recognizing himself. He'd once worn fine clothes like this, but now they felt odd. And these were a step above what his mother and father had insisted he wear at the parties on the estate. He pulled on the bottom of the embroidered tunic, trying to grant his throat more room to breathe against the high collar.

The tailor fussed about behind him, working at the ostentatious dining table inside the king's personal chambers. Great pleats and layers of fabric spread out as they worked the hem of the royal cloak.

Kin frowned at the dire wolf fur decorating the shoulders and collar of it, knowing it was going to be far too warm despite the cooling season outside. He could see the distant birch trees turning golden through the full length windows beyond the tailor and her work.

"This really needs to be done now?" Kin longed to disappear back through the double doors behind him, where he could imagine Amarie still curled among their sheets and pillows, her body bare and inviting. One thing he certainly wouldn't complain about was the luxury of such a large bed.

"Yes, your highness." The tailor didn't look fully at him, but he swore he could still see the flush in her cheeks from knowing she'd interrupted something when knocking on his chamber door. "Your coronation is tomorrow."

Kin wrinkled his nose at the words. The title. The ceremony. But a necessary one for now, even if he intended to dismantle the entire monarchy. He had to be formally crowned to have the authority to do so. "So can't it wait until tomorrow?"

The tailor frowned as she tucked her needle between her lips and picked up the heavy cloak. She carried it over, stepping up on a stool behind him to drape it over his shoulders. "Almost done." She muttered around the steel.

The door to the bedroom clicked open, drawing Kin's gaze.

Amarie strode out, wrapped in a thin bed sheet that left very little to the imagination. She quirked a brow at him as she poured herself a glass of water, but didn't interrupt. She'd been supportive these past weeks, but a shadow always hovered behind her gaze when anything royal was involved.

Turning, she carried her glass of water in her bandaged hand back towards the bedroom. The sheet dipped so low on her bare back that Kin's mouth dried.

The fur on his shoulders suddenly felt so much heavier as the tailor reached around to secure the clasps. He searched for words, but his eyes distracted him by tracing each line of Amarie's body.

As she stepped inside the bedroom, she let the sheet fall, inadvertently—or not—granting Kin a glimpse of her backside before she shut the door.

Kin's body shuddered. "Are you finished yet?" He tried and failed to keep the growl from his voice. "I'm sorry." He swallowed, trying to ease his tone. "I don't mean to be rude, but..."

The tailor stepped off the stool, quickly removing the garments from his body. "I understand, your highness." The blush had returned to her cheeks. "I'll return tomorrow. I apologize for the inconvenience."

"No, it's all right. As you said, it needs to be done." Kin's eyes danced to the door, but he didn't lunge for it like he wanted to, to maintain at least some decorum. He refused to be anything like he was sure his brother had been.

As soon as the tailor left, the door to the hallway closing behind her, Kin tugged off the undershirt left behind after she'd taken the rest with her. He took another glance out the window that overlooked all of Jaspa, including the gentle flatlands beyond the city laced with autumn trees that led to the sea beyond. He looked down to the curving streets of the city, black and stained in the poor districts. Smoke rose from hundreds of chimneys, and the people walking along the street looked like insects.

It'd be too easy to start thinking about them like that from here.

Sucking in a deep breath, Kin felt the weight of that cloak like it still sat on his shoulders. Fear seeped into his veins. It'd be too easy to be like his brother.

Turning from the streets, he eyed the doors to the bedroom. To where Amarie waited for him to return. She was the one thing that would keep him from tumbling. She'd done it before. Shown him what he was capable of.

Crossing the lush carpet, Kin wadded the undershirt between his hands before passing through the doorway. The latch clicked quietly as he pushed it closed behind him, and he blinked in near darkness. Only patches of light seeped through the thick curtains covering the balcony doorway.

Amarie sat on the bed, still nude, braiding her hair along the side of her head. Her gaze flickered to him, warming. "How are you feeling?" She'd asked him that question so many times since they'd returned to Jaspa, and her care always eased his stress. Her left hand moved slowly in her hair, struggling with dexterity through the damage hidden by the bandages. Her other arm could hardly compensate, given the injury still healing within her shoulder. But she didn't complain, not once. He'd only wished calling for the best Artisan healer in Feyor had been an option, but the power she carried wouldn't have allowed the Art to mend her wounds.

"It's starting to feel more real." Kin settled onto the bed, crossing a leg beneath him to edge closer to her. "I think the cloak is a little much, though." He reached out to touch her bare skin, running his fingers over her spine. He avoided the diagonal line of bandages he'd helped change each day since Lungaz. "What about you?"

Tying off a small braid that ran the horizontal length above her ear, Amarie lowered her arms with a slight wince. "Still sore, but the healer said braiding would help me regain the strength in my hand." She flexed her fingers before eyeing him. "Ahria and Conrad will leave for Ziona after your coronation."

Ahria had agreed to let the public know about her identity as his daughter, giving Feyor the comfort of an heir. And subsequently, a connection to Ziona, who continued to provide aid more publicly, now. But she would return with the prince to his country, leaving an unspoken tension between Kin and Amarie. Through all their struggles and promises, they'd always said they'd stay together. But with their daughter leaving, and Kin's presence required in Feyor, Amarie had every right to want to be with the daughter she didn't get to raise.

But the thought of her leaving...

He honestly couldn't blame her, even if it was just to get away from all the politics. And the suspicious looks she already received in the hallways and dining halls. She and Kin hadn't hidden their relationship within the palace, but she hadn't attended a single public appearance, either. The monarchy had enough of a challenge adapting to a new king as it was.

I'd rather have a small cottage by a lake.

Kin ran his fingers down her spine again before scooting back towards the pillows. He leaned back, opening his arm towards her. "Lay with me?"

Amarie obliged, settling her head on his shoulder with her damaged hand carefully cradled in his lap. She breathed deep, the air wisping over his skin in a sensation he'd detest losing. "Do you have any more meetings today?"

"Just this afternoon." Kin wrapped his arm around her, his bare side tingling as she pressed against it. "But this morning I'll be right here." He tilted his chin, placing a kiss on the braid she'd finished.

She hummed, tracing patterns along his chest and stomach. "All morning, hmm?"

It was easy. So damned easy to get swept up in the passion and heat between them. But it also served another purpose, to distract them from talking about the future. But with his coronation only a day away, they were quickly running out of time for that conversation.

Kin nodded, kissing her again and urging himself to remain in control. To keep the thoughts that'd been running rampant in his mind straight. "I'm glad your body is feeling better, but what are you feeling here?" He reached up, touching her temple. "With everything... how are you doing?"

Amarie inclined her head, meeting his gaze. "It's not... exactly what I imagined for myself, but I'm making it work." Her brow twitched. "I, uh, I guess I feel a little...uncertain, perhaps. Unsure where we go from here, but after everything, it should hardly matter." She pinned her lower lip beneath a tooth, threatening his resolve.

"How you feel matters, my love." Kin touched beneath her chin, brushing his thumb against her lips. "It matters a great deal to me."

Her brow twitched again, but she gave him a slight smile. "I know. I just mean that there are bigger things to worry about than whatever future we may or may not have."

The thought of not having a future with her twisted his heart into a painful knot. Those thoughts had plagued him before, when he'd had to step away. But now he doubted he'd ever be able to do that again. But it felt so irrevocably selfish to insist she stay.

"You know I will always support whatever decisions you make. I may hope for something different, but I promise I will respect your choice." He brushed his hand over her hair. "It's the least I can do with all you've given me."

Amarie tilted her chin up, brushing his with the hint of a kiss. "And what is the decision you're dreading I make?"

Of course she'd see right through him.

His chest tightened, his grip around her doing the same. "To leave. I want you here. Even though our daughter is going back to Ziona. I want you to be at my side, here, in Feyor."

Her gaze met his again, her touch trailing up the side of his neck. "And be a king's secret mistress?" Shadowed amusement danced behind her eyes as she kissed his chin again.

I'd rather have a small cottage by a lake.

"No more secrets." Kin shifted, turning onto his side so he could look directly at her, his pulse hammering in his ears. "Our daughter is already set to become princess. And I want you to be my queen, Amarie. I want to marry you." The words came tumbling out, even though he loathed to put her in the position to make that choice. Loathed to know she wouldn't accept.

And he'd lose her.

Amarie's expression dimmed as she blinked at him, her breath catching. Her throat bobbed. "What?" Her gaze darted between his eyes, the lazy touch on his neck stilling.

"Marry me." He'd already said it. There was no backing from the words, even if he wanted to. But even then, he didn't want to. "Will you?"

She pinned that lip again, invisible thoughts flashing through her eyes that he wished he could be privy to. "I..." Taking a deep breath, she let it out slowly. "You're asking me to be exposed. In the public eye. Not even as just myself, but as a *queen*."

"You deserve to be seen, Amarie. You've hidden your entire life, but there's nothing to hide." He felt the uncertainty in him growing. The fear. But he let the things he'd been thinking come tumbling out. "*You* are the reason I want to be a good man. Be a good king. *You.* And with you at my side, I know we will finally give Feyor what it needs. Then we can go wherever you want. Be whoever you want to be. Yes, I am asking you to stand exposed, but maybe it's time."

Her hand resumed its caress, her fingers tangling into his short hair. Her mouth twitched in a brief smile. "I love you. And I have *always* loved you." She swallowed hard, rolling her lips together.

"And I would be... honored to be your wife." Her smile lasted longer, then. "Yes, I will marry you."

The tangle in him resolved suddenly, genuine surprise mingling with perfect joy. She laughed at whatever expression appeared on his face, smoothing a hand over his cheek. He blinked. "Say that again?" He couldn't help the crooked smile, tangling his legs with hers.

Chuckling, Amarie pulled him closer, pressing her chest to his. She kissed him, then broke the kiss long enough to murmur against his mouth, "I will marry you, Kinronsilis Lazorus."

He pressed into her again, eagerly claiming her lips. Running his hands along her naked body, his soul sang. Rolling her gently onto her back, Kin rose above her, snaking more kisses over her neck and shoulders. She arched gently against him, his tongue playing along her skin as the thrill continued through him. "You're perfect," he whispered against her. "And I'm the luckiest man alive."

"I have a condition, though." Amarie's words came out breathy and soft, a playful lightness to them.

Kin rubbed a thumb over her peaked breast, drawing a short gasp from her. "Just one?"

"Well... two, I suppose," she murmured, eyes fluttering closed as he continued kissing his way down her skin.

"Name them." He paused, looking up at her as he ran his hands over her hips and down the outside of her thighs.

"Small wedding." Amarie squirmed under him. "And Ahria has to be there."

He hummed as he pressed his mouth beneath her navel. "The second is easy." He trailed his thumb along the inside of her leg, his lips following the path as her legs parted for him. "The first might be more complicated, depending on how long we wait." He yearned to taste the warmth of her, but once he gave into that inclination, all hope for coherent conversation would be lost.

"Then let's not wait." Amarie propped herself up on her uninjured shoulder, looking at him with a fiery gaze that swirled with amethyst. "They're here. You're not king yet."

"I'm king tomorrow." Kin looked up, unable to resist edging closer. His lips nearly touched her.

Her hips rocked beneath him, and she smirked, breathing harder. "But it's not tomorrow yet."

He paused, then leaned in to press a gentle kiss upon the tender skin between her legs. "True." He couldn't resist the tease, flicking his tongue lightly along the swollen edge of her. "You'll marry me today, then?"

Amarie let out a quiet whine, her head falling back. "I'll marry you today."

The words sent a chill up his spine, coupled with the warm sensation of her against his mouth as he indulged in another taste, dragging his tongue up her center. He hummed again, working his tongue against that bundle of nerves.

She gasped, fisting a handful of bed sheets.

Running his hands up her abdomen, he explored her slowly. It took everything in him to pause, flicking her as he lifted his head slightly, a smile on his lips as he looked up at her. It would be an effort in itself to pry away from her at all that day. "Should I go and see to arranging things?" He dragged his nails down her.

Her gaze met his again, eyes vibrant with desire. "I think it can wait until this afternoon. I'm sure you can cancel that meeting of yours."

Kin smiled wider before lowering his head back to her. His tongue quickly found the bundle of nerves again, swirling around it. "Good idea." Diving back into her, he lived for each catch of her breath, every buck of her hips. He'd learned what she liked best over their recent months, and happily gave it to her now. The taste of her on his tongue only made him long to hear her cries of pleasure more. Only made him want her more.

He slid into the rhythm she craved, her thighs tightening around him as her body shook.

As he slipped a finger inside her, she moaned and clenched around him as release ruptured through her. He stayed with her through it, easing her down from the waves of bliss until she tugged on him. His mouth found her neck again, her legs wrapping around his.

"More," she whispered, voice rough and low. "I want you."

His body already screamed for it as he obeyed. The heat of her enveloped him as he slipped within her, sheathing himself to the hilt. A moan bubbled on his lips, buzzing against her skin as he rocked his hips back.

She met each thrust, driving him deeper.

All he could hear was the sound of their breathing, of their bodies joining, and the occasional thump of the headboard hitting the wall. Nothing existed beyond it, beyond their entwined limbs.

Amarie bit his shoulder, nails dragging along his back as his pace escalated. Need scorched through him. The need to have her, claim her, to keep her as *his* until the world fell to ash and shadow. And then beyond it.

Her body arched, and she cried out his name. His mouth collided with hers. Their tongues met in a flurry as everything in him rose in flames. He fought it, held it. Wanted more as he drove deeper into her, his hand slipping between them so his fingers could find that sweet bundle between her legs. Her body twitched as he circled it, a moan echoing from her mouth that he quieted with his own. Buzzing against his tongue.

Control waned as his skin tightened, heat building with intensity as he slammed deeper with his all-encompassing desire. He grunted, straining as his lips left hers to taste her neck. He nipped her, growling against her skin, and her body erupted again.

The sudden tautness shattered his restraint. Fire scorched through every inch of him as he thrust, heat spilling out of him in a soul-rending release. Gasping, he returned to Amarie's lips, desperately kissing her as his body twitched with the remnants of passion.

Her hands tangled in his hair as she kissed him back with equal fervor, breathing hard. She clenched around him, making his sweat-slick body convulse.

Grinning, Amarie looked at him, biting her lower lip likely just to further torment him. Her grin faded, replaced by longing. "I will always be by your side," she whispered. "Always."

Brushing his hand along the side of her face, he placed a tender kiss on her bottom lip. A strange sensation passed through him with her words, and he knew without doubt that he believed her. And that it was the only place he ever wanted to be, too. "I will marry you today and the whole of Pantracia will know I am your husband." He kissed her again, brushing along her jaw. "And that I belong beside you. The one I will love into the Afterlife."

Her smile reappeared, lighting her eyes. "Husband," she murmured. "I like the sound of that."

Chapter 48

This is so surreal.

Ahria squeezed Conrad's hand, a strange bloated joy in her throat that threatened to unravel her at any moment.

Kin stood at the front of the chapel, waiting.

Waiting, because Amarie wasn't here yet.

Her mother had found her that morning and explained with cautious excitement that she'd be marrying Kinronsilis later that day. A small ceremony, with the palace temple only hosting the three of them, plus Matthias, who was to perform the wedding.

Amarie had only needed a dress, so she and Ahria had spent a few hours that afternoon scrambling to find something suitable on such short notice.

Conrad squeezed Ahria's hand, catching her gaze. "Why are *you* nervous?"

"I'm not nervous." She shook her head, glancing at the entrance door again.

Her birth father stood remarkably still near Matthias, his face stoic, but tension lingered in his shoulders. His jaw knitted tight. He was probably nervous enough for the entire room. He kept glancing at Matthias, who whispered something with a smile on his lips. It seemed to ease Kin slightly as he smirked and nodded.

"I just hope she doesn't need help with her dress." Ahria let out a breath, swallowing. "Or her hair. Or jewelry. Or whatever." At the look Conrad gave her, she scowled. "Shut up. I'm allowed to be a little nervous, all right?"

Conrad placed his hand on Ahria's knee, scooting closer to her on the bench. He kissed the side of her head as he wrapped his arm around her. "Just as long as you remember to keep breathing," he teased. "I'm pretty sure you stopped a moment ago and I'd rather you not pass out."

Ahria scoffed, staring at the door. "If I start to feel lightheaded, I'll let you know."

As happy as the wedding made her, seeing her mother and father in love... the event held a subtle undercurrent of sorrow. Amarie would remain in Feyor with Kin. Ahria would return to Ziona with Conrad.

Parting from them, after having only known them for such a short time, made her chest ache. She wanted more. More time, more happy moments, just... more. But Conrad had assured her it wouldn't always be like this. He'd even suggested Ahria stay with them awhile longer, but after having been apart from him for so long, she couldn't bear the thought. But they'd visit every chance they got. Besides, their ongoing effort against Uriel suggested they'd need to be together soon. And, ultimately, when her father finished with his plan to restructure the country's monarchy into an elected republic parliament like Delkest and Olsa, her parents would be free to live wherever they pleased.

Her mother had assured her they'd settle close to wherever she and Conrad were.

The base of her hairline tingled, and she scratched at the itch.

Kin and Matthias chuckled again, and Ahria smiled at her birth father.

The soon-to-be King Lazorus wore a tunic of deep blue beneath a grey fitted vest. It lacked the embroidered embellishments that had been standard on most of the clothes he'd had to wear in the castle halls the past few weeks. The new dagger sheathed at his side stuck out against the blue, the red gem embedded in the black hilt gleaming in the sconce light of the chamber, the windows dark with night. She'd hardly believed the tale Kin told about it whipping around the ruins beneath the prison until he'd shown her Sephysis in action the day before.

The bloodstone blade seemed to wink at her before Kin's hand closed over the hilt to hide the jeweled eye. As if her father was responding to its awareness of Ahria looking.

It sent a shiver down her spine.

The doors to the chapel finally clicked open, drawing everyone's gaze to the guards who clasped their hands in front of them, holding the doors open with their backs as Amarie stepped forward.

Ahria grinned, tension finally leaving her stomach as she beheld the dress they'd settled on mere hours earlier.

A blue dress, tight at the bodice, flowed loosely from Amarie's hips, spread over the grey tulle petticoat beneath. Over the dress's chiffon fabric lay intricate grey lace appliqués. The lace continued above the dress's necklace, flowing all the way up to the base of Amarie's neck.

Someone had curled her hair, but left it down, and only a simple pair of dangling sapphire earrings adorned her ears. Rouge dusted her cheeks and lips, her lashes dark with kohl and shimmering silver that highlighted her bright blue eyes.

Gorgeous.

Ahria tore her eyes away from Amarie, wishing to see Kin's reaction as she scratched the back of her neck again.

Her father gaped, the tension in him easing completely. His now familiar smile broadened, still slightly crooked. He turned fully towards Amarie as she walked towards where he stood at the dais near the center of the temple, a basin of water held by miniature statues of the gods beneath it.

The Isalican king grinned, too, emotion shining in his eyes.

As Amarie stepped past Ahria and Conrad, giving them a broad smile, Ahria admired the back of her dress. The blue material cut low along her back, the semi-transparent lace covering up over her shoulders but leaving her arms bare.

Her mother took Kin's hand, and they faced each other in front of the Isalican king.

The doors to the temple clicked shut.

Kin looked down at their hands for a moment, but Ahria could see his eyes traveling the length of her body, then up to her face. "Definitely still the luckiest man alive."

Amarie's smile widened. "I love you."

"And I love you," he whispered. "Still crazy enough to marry me?"

She chuckled. "Definitely."

"Then let me begin." Matthias kept talking, and Ahria lost herself to the ceremony. She listened as they spoke their vows to each other, eyes blurring as her throat tightened. A symbolic ritual of a fine chain wrapping their touching wrists bound their souls.

When it came time for the rings, Matthias collected a dark wooden box from a table behind him. "Crafted from Feyor itself, forged with fire and water, these rings represent the piece of the other you will always hold with you. A testament to your vows, to your lives, now joined."

Amarie slid Kin's ring onto the middle finger of his free left hand, and Kin did the same onto Amarie's right.

In traditional Feyor custom, the rings were composed of a unique compound found only in the Feyorian forest to the east. A petrified dark wood, laced with a blue-hued metal that ran along the length like a river. The rings were beautiful, and boasted no stones, no other decoration than the material itself.

The chain slipped from their wrists, and Matthias smiled again. "Before the gods, between the elements, and beneath a sunless sky, you are forever entwined with each other as husband and wife."

Ahria and Conrad clapped, standing as Amarie and Kin kissed. Their hands entwined, the rings catching in the light as the kiss renewed.

Matthias laughed, joy rippling through the room.

Kin touched Amarie's cheek as they slowly broke apart. They turned together to step from the dais, looking at their daughter. His arm around his wife's waist loosened, already anticipating before Amarie moved to Ahria and took her into a warm hug.

"Nothing was more important than you being here for this," her mother murmured in her ear.

Ahria smiled as her eyes burned. "Nothing could have kept me away."

To be continued.

The story will conclude with...

OATH OF THE SIX

www.Pantracia.com

Six roles. Six fates. One chance.

While Kin adjusts to life as king, Amarie takes on a mission with their allies to find answers to their most pressing questions. The journey takes them to Aidensar, where Amarie faces painful memories of her past with the hope of finding a woman whose knowledge could change everything. But only if they find her before Uriel does.

When Eralas seeks aid from Helgath under vague circumstances, Rae sets off for the auer homeland, intent on learning more about the threat. But when calamity strikes, she makes a dangerous choice, putting her life at risk even if it means breaking a vow.

As chaos unfurls, victory is within reach. All the pieces of the puzzle are now together, and the final hour has come. Banishing Uriel from their realm is the most daunting task any of them have ever faced, but if they fail... Pantracia itself could shatter.

Oath of the Six is Part 3 of *The Vanguard Legacy* and Book 13 in the *Pantracia Chronicles*.